MW01032079

RATS OF
DWELTFORD

RAGE OF LIONS BOOK TWO

MATT BARRON

BLADE OF TRUTH PUBLISHING COMPANY

To the authors,
who pointed me to the ancient ruins and the cities of adventure;
who guided me through the dark shadows and the flash of steel;
and showed me how to find my way home again.
May the Lord bless you for the blessings you gave to me.

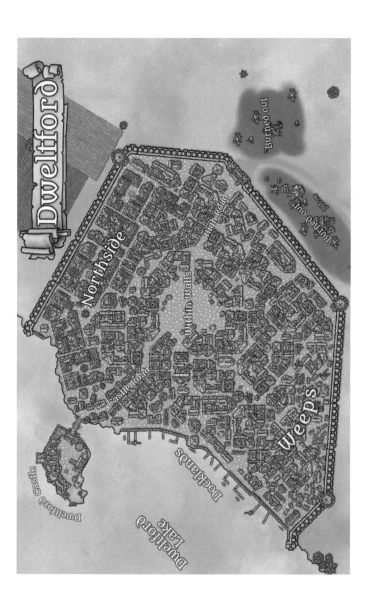

Dwelford

Northside

Burned out

Burning out

High Road

Within Walls

Castle Road

Weeps

Dwelford Castle

Docklands

Dwelford Lake

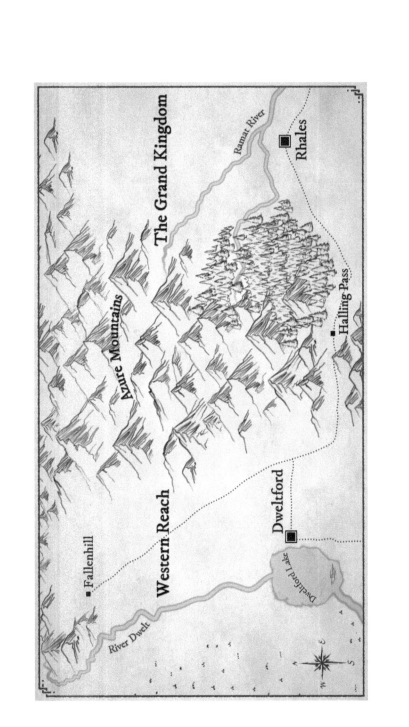

CHAPTER 1

P rentice stirred the coals of the last night's fire with a stick. A thin drizzle was falling out of the gray, pre-dawn sky, and the droplets hissed as they struck the coals. He blew hard to bring them back to flame before the rain put them out. Around him he could hear the sounds of the army rousing itself for a new day. Water was fetched from the lake, camp bread turned out of bowls and piled under coals to cook. After the swift march north and their victory over the invaders at the Battle of the Brook, Duchess Amelia's army had returned to encamp in the fields outside her provincial capital, Dweltford. Looming over the army, the crenulated edges of the town's mighty walls were slowly becoming visible against the lighter gray of the clouded, dawning sky.

Prentice scowled. It offended him to be on this side of the wall. They'd returned to find the gates closed to them. The duchess's own castellan, Sir Duggan, had shut them out. Rumor held that the old knight had hired mercenaries from the south to hold the town against them. While the duchess, her knights, her houseguards, and the rogues foot had marched north with Mercad, Prince of Rhales, to defend the province, Sir Duggan had simply remained behind and fortified Dweltford against its liege.

Prentice's indignant thoughts were disturbed by groans coming from the tent behind him. Looking over his shoulder, he saw the hulking figure of his best friend, Turley, stretching and yawning. The big man bent down and up again, then began to shuffle his feet until he suddenly burst into a prancing step, twirling in place.

"What the bloody hell are you doing?" asked Prentice.

"Enjoying the feeling of freedom," Turley replied.

For years he and Prentice had been convicts on chain gangs, their ankles shod with iron fetters night and day. He'd been imprisoned like that for over a decade. Mere days ago, the two had won their freedom by surviving the brutal battle against the raiders from the west. They had been rogues foot, convicts thrown into battle with little more than sharp sticks and never expected to survive the battle. Most had not. Those that did were rewarded with their freedom.

"A new morning and no shackles. Some of us are happy about that, is all," Turley said.

"I'm happy about it," Prentice retorted.

"You should tell your face," Turley taunted.

Prentice rolled his eyes and went back to stoking the fire. After a moment, Turley joined him, sitting on the damp ground and warming his hands by the sparse flames. He pulled a black bottle out from his shirt, and after a long swig, he offered it to Prentice. Prentice shook his head.

"Suit yourself, but it's down to the dregs." Turley finished it off.

The two sat in silence for a long moment.

"I haven't slept a night sober since the battle," Turley said at last. "I don't know how you do it."

"I don't sleep much."

"So why not take a drink? You barely touch the stuff."

"It's a hard habit to break, once it's started," said Prentice.

"Well, you're a harder man than me."

Prentice scoffed at that. He and Turley were both big men, over six feet and strong, but Turley was easily the taller of the two. That was the limit of their physical similarity, though.

Turley had dark curly hair and dark brown eyes that always seemed to see a joke wherever he was looking. Prentice was fairer, with skin that went brown under the sun and eyes of gray blue. Both men had their share of scars, but Prentice's back and torso were a mess of torture marks, souvenirs from his time in the care of the inquisition and his long years as a convict.

"When you were in that academy place, did they teach you anything about these nightmares?" Turley asked after another moment's silence. "Or don't knights get them? Is it only us lowborn folk who relive that hell in our sleep?"

Prentice knew what Turley was talking about. Battle was a horror, and men would often have brutal dreams after, reliving the terror and the rage in their sleep. He'd been through it himself often enough.

"Knights get them," he said.

"And what did they say to do about them? Or do I just drink myself to sleep for the rest of my life?"

"They said to pray."

"And does that work?"

"I have no idea."

The two men sat in silence for a time more, and while he was tending the growing fire, Prentice thought about Turley's question. Perhaps prayer wasn't a silly idea, even for an exiled heretic such as him. In the days leading up to the battle, he'd had visions, first seeing angelic creatures and then the Messiah himself—at least, that's who Prentice thought it was. Then at the brook, when the Grand Kingdom army was caught in the teeth of the enemy's trap, an angelic lion the size of a horse struck among the enemy like a bolt of lightning, and scattered their sorcerous beast-soldiers.

Many of the men on the battlefield had seen the angel, nobles and commoners both. It was the one thing that had saved the Kingdom army commanders from the trap that had been set to capture the prince and his closest courtiers. Even though Crown Prince Mercad had ultimately died in the battle, the holy lion's intervention had prevented a disaster on the field and allowed the army to rally and win the day. The prince's own chaplain, Porlain, insisted it was a miracle; he had already ridden east to tell the Church hierarchy about the mystical event. The self-important sacrist readily informed anyone who would listen that it was his squeaked, desperate prayer that had summoned the angel's visitation, and was eager to claim credit with his superiors.

For Prentice, that was too often the way of the Church of the Grand Kingdom—slow to act, eager to punish, and even more eager to claim the credit for good things in which they had so little part. Still, if he was going to be seeing visions and speaking with the Son of God, then maybe some prayer or counsel might be called for. He decided to seek out a friendly sacrist to ask what the visions might mean. A real one, a devout man, concerned with the true duties of heaven, not some soft pillow of a man, more interested in fine robes and rich dinners than the things of God.

Of course, the army first had to get back into Dweltford.

The morning quiet was disturbed by the tromp of swaggering boots, and a young squire approached them from the other side of the camp.

"Ho, convicts," the youth called. He was a skinny rake, with dark hair that swept into his eyes and pimples on his chin. "The duchess summons the one named Prentice."

Turley's eyes narrowed as he looked up at the messenger. "You must have a big arse."

"What'd you say to me?"

Turley sprang to his feet and stood over the squire, glowering down at him. "I said, 'I hope you have a big arse.' Otherwise, it's going to hurt when I knock you on it! That's what'll happen if you call him or me convict again."

The young man swallowed, seeming not frightened so much as shocked that the conversation had so quickly taken such a violent turn. "You can't hit me," he protested. "I'm a freeman!"

"So are we," said Prentice, in a cold tone that made it clear which side he would be on if it came to violence.

The squire looked from one to the other. "Well, however it is," he said, trying to gather some dignity about himself, despite the squeak in his voice, "the duchess has summoned you, and you have to go."

"He'll be along," said Turley.

The youth stood a moment, apparently thinking that he was supposed to escort the pair of them to the duchess directly, but neither man made any move to go. Instead, Prentice continued to work the fire, and Turley folded his arms in a belligerent gesture. He sneered at the squire and gave a dismissive nod.

"You can go now."

The intimidated squire turned and left.

When he was gone, Prentice gave his friend a wry smile. "You didn't have to threaten him. You'll never make chief steward, behaving like that."

"Oh, you can't blame me," Turley protested. He dropped to the ground and lay next to the fire, propped on one elbow. "It's not my fault the gosling was too stupid to know not to insult a man with a hangover. And don't you worry about my stewarding duties. I'll be chief before a year's passed, mark me."

"Graycen might have something to say about that," said Prentice, referring to the duchess's current chief steward and head of the household staff.

"Graycen's a thieving rat!" Turley responded.

"Is he, now?"

"I can smell it." Turley drained off his bottle and then absently shook the last drips at the fire. "I'll figure out where his little hidey-holes are and show him up for what he is."

"You've turned into quite the loyal man," said Prentice. He was surprised by the change in his friend's attitude. When they had both been convicts, Turley hated the nobility, just as all convicts tended to do. Now he was committed to ferreting out corruption in the duchess's household.

"The ladyship, Her Grace, she's done right by us," Turley explained. "She took us off the chain and seen us with proper jobs. She's given me a place in her staff, which is more than I ever had before they convicted me and transported me west. Her house is my house now, and I don't like rats in my house."

Prentice nodded. He had no idea how long his friend's newfound diligence would last, but he understood the sentiment. The duchess Amelia had been fair with her rewards after the battle—even generous, by the standards of Grand Kingdom nobles. Now that they were no longer convicts, they needed to start thinking and acting the way free and loyal men did.

"Graycen's not the only rat in the house," Prentice said, looking across at Dweltford's walls again. "Nor the biggest, it would seem."

"Sir Duggan," Turley agreed, shaking his head. "What's he playing at? Why take his liege's castle? He can't keep it, can he?"

"I don't know," Prentice said, though he had some ideas. "Time to go." He stood and clapped his hands together, shaking off the soot from the campfire.

"I suppose I better see to my duties as well," said Turley. He rose to his feet, and the two men looked down at the restored campfire. Now that they were going, it would have to be put out. They couldn't leave it unattended.

"Well, that's a bright little blaze you got going this fine, rainy morning."

The two men kicked dirt into the flames and stomped the campfire out.

CHAPTER 2

P rentice made his way through the camp, between tents and under guy lines. Things seemed so changed now; it was a completely different camp from what it had been only a week before. In the lead-up to the battle and in the first days after, it was an army encampment, overflowing with knights and their horses, their squires, and sworn men-at-arms. Most of those forces had turned back to the east at the crossroads, escorting the body of the fallen Crown Prince Mercad to his final rest in Rhales. Duchess Amelia turned westward with her own smaller group of men-at-arms, marching back to Dweltford, to find out what had happened to her castellan. What she found was her ducal capital in arms against her, and a crowd of refugees cowering in the fields beside the road not a half a league from the town.

When he closed Dweltford, Sir Duggan had ordered all buildings outside the walls and in front of the gates razed to the ground. It was a common strategy, meant to give an enemy nowhere to hide, no safety from arrows when they approached the walls. But it meant his men had burned thousands of people out of their homes. With the gates closed, those people were destitute and abandoned outside the walls to starve. Duchess Amelia couldn't help but feel responsible for them. Now her small rump of an army camp was swollen with a horde of refugees, hungry and unprepared for the coming winter.

The camp itself was split in two by the main road that ran straight out from Dweltford's gates and then turned south to follow the river, before turning east once more and heading back to the crossroads and the Azure Mountains. When Prentice reached that road, he could see all the way to Dweltford's heavy wooden gates, bound with iron. And in front of them, the scorched black earth. The sight reminded him of Fallenhill, the walled town to the north. The duchess's army had marched there expecting to find it under siege, but instead discovered the town conquered and the entire population chained together and burned alive in the town square.

He heard the sounds of horses' hooves beating the earth, and Prentice was forced to step back as a dozen riders came trotting down the road, heading south. They were knights, wearing plate and mail that was brightly polished but somehow seemed dull in the gray light of the overcast morning. Each man wore his family colors on their surcoats and tabards, but the pennants on their lances were cream and blue, Duchess Amelia's colors. At their head rode the duchess's knight captain, Sir Liam, recently raised to the rank of baronet after claiming credit for the victory at the Battle of the Brook. His surcoat was quartered red and sky blue, his personal colors, and he rode without a pennant. His dark hair and long mustache were combed and groomed. He wore a new helmet with no visor, and a pair of gold-chased antlers fitted on top. The tall, branching horns were a token of his "victory" at the Brook. As the distance closed between them, Liam's eyes met Prentice's. There was a flash of recognition, and Liam sneered. Then he turned away, fixing his eyes on the road ahead. He trotted past with his head high, as if Prentice did not exist.

Prentice smiled to himself.

He knew Liam hated him. On the march north, the nobleman had Prentice flogged almost to death, and it had taken the work of an expensive and powerful healer to get him walking again. Only the intervention of the prince's own knight commander, Sir Carron Ironworth, had put an end to Liam's vendetta.

Prentice kept out of the way and watched the mounted knights ride off. Then he quickly crossed into the other half of the camp and made his way to the duchess's tent. He was a free man now, but keeping her waiting too long would not be acceptable. Two houseguards stood sentry at the entrance to her tent, and one of them held the flap aside to let him enter, announcing him as Prentice Ash. A week ago, no one knew him from any other filthy convict. Now he was almost renowned, at least among the duchess's people.

Duchess Amelia was seated, and her maid, Teerah, was plaiting ribbons through her mistress's fair hair. The duchess wore an overdress of green velvet with an embroidered bodice. She was not a great beauty, though she was by no means ugly—"pleasantly plain" was the expression sometimes used to describe her. Her skin was fair, and her eyes were shrewd; it was a fool who mistook her intelligence. Though she had married into nobility, using her family's money to pay off the late duke's debts, she had the bearing of a duchess, and dignity befitting her rank.

Prentice went down on one knee and bowed his head, waiting for her to acknowledge him. The duchess dismissed her maid, and when the girl was gone, she told Prentice to rise.

"A nobleman newly raised in rank has the right to inspect his new lands and establish his lordship," she said coldly. "Did you know that?"

"I didn't, Your Grace," he answered her. "But I'm not surprised."

"Sir Liam..." The duchess paused with a scowl. "Baronet Liam," she said, correcting herself, "has left the army, along with a cadre of knights he calls his 'chosen men,' to inspect his new lands. Without so much as a 'by your leave.' He tells me"—she put furious emphasis on the word, making clear her offense—"that he will winter in the east and return in the spring, when he will be glad to lead my armies to take back my castle and town."

Prentice could think of nothing worth saying, nothing the duchess didn't already know. Because Liam had received his baronetcy from the dying prince, its duties and privileges could be said to be higher than his duties to Duchess Amelia. In truth, Baronet Liam was just getting petty revenge upon her for favoring Prentice, exploiting the fact that Amelia's power over her own duchy was still too weak to do anything about it. Doubtless, Liam thought a winter camped in a muddy field outside the walls of her own town and castle was an appropriate revenge upon the young merchant's daughter who had married above her station.

"He wants to catch up to the prince's body and join the cortege. As if a baronetcy was not honor enough, he wants to escort the fallen hero home and stay for the funeral." The duchess shook her head in disgust.

Prentice just nodded. He understood her frustration. "The king will come from Denay for the funeral," he said. "It's the best chance Liam will likely ever have to present himself as the conquering hero."

"Hero be damned; you did it, not him. Those horns belong to you!"

"I haven't got the helmet for it."

The duchess smiled at his jest. The gold-chased antlers on Baronet Liam's helmet had been cut from the head of the Horned Man, the leader of the invaders. The strange painted men from the far west used magic powers to merge men mortals and beasts together, and their huge general had sported those antlers. In the final melee, Prentice had confronted the Horned Man directly and cut his head from his shoulders. After the battle, however, it was considered impolitic to attribute the victory to a convict. Thus, the antlers had been awarded to Sir Liam, along with his new rank and title. The injustice of the situation didn't worry Prentice too much. He had his freedom, and that was enough for him.

"Do I really need him?" Amelia asked.

"He's your knight captain. You need someone to command your knights."

"And a siege, in winter? Is it really so difficult as they say?"

Prentice didn't bother to answer that.

The duchess sighed and stood up, straightening her skirts. "So, I am condemned to sit in the mud while my army goes cold and hungry waiting for spring, when my knight captain will deign to return and rescue me."

She turned and faced the direction of Dweltford, as if she could see the town through the cloth of the tent wall. "That is my town!" she said, her voice rising in anger. "That is my home. I shouldn't have to sit here and wait for someone to give it back to me!"

"Then don't," Prentice replied.

The duchess snorted, showing what she thought of this attempt at humor, then she looked at him. "What do you mean?"

"Take it back for yourself."

"How? You just agreed that a winter siege is too difficult. My knights, the ones loyal enough to stay, tell me it is nigh impossible, even for a seasoned commander. How do you propose I take it back for myself?"

"I think it can be done, with cunning," said Prentice.

The duchess stared at him for a long moment, and he met her gaze. "Cunning? You truly think it can be done?"

Prentice had a plan of sorts, and he opened his mouth to explain.

One of the sentries stepped through the curtain and bowed his head. "Your pardon, Your Grace, but there's a knight here, says he was sent for to see you."

Duchess Amelia nodded and the man withdrew, to be replaced by the figure of a hedge knight. He was tall and strong looking but lean, with a shock of red hair that was graying a little at the temples. He wore a mail hauberk, with sleeves and trews; it was an older style of armor, and it had obvious repairs in several places. He wore a longsword, a sure sign of his status as a knight, but his clothes and equipment were all old and worn, mended many times. Whatever color his tabard had originally been, it was now a washed-out gray, with no heraldry on the front or back. The bottom hem was ragged, and the garment seemed short, which made Prentice think that perhaps the man had cut the bottom away to form a makeshift bandage at some time. It was a common enough practice on the battlefield and, judging by the tabard's shortness, might well have happened to this knight more than once.

"Sir Gant," Duchess Amelia said, holding her hand out for the knight to kiss. He did so and stepped back to bow. The duchess continued, "This is my sworn man, Prentice, now called Ash. He is the one you asked to meet."

The knight turned and looked intently at Prentice. For his part, Prentice felt his mistrust for knights set his nerves on edge. Knights were men of war and privileged as members of the nobility, even when they were as poor as Sir Gant seemed to be. They tended to see violence as the solution to every problem, doubly so if it involved someone as lowly as a convict or a serf. Having been free for only a handful of days, Prentice tensed, anticipating danger. He could think of no other reason why a knight would seek him out.

He blinked in astonishment when the serious-faced Sir Gant suddenly went down on one knee before him.

"I owe you my life, Master Ash," the knight said formally, and he bowed his head. "I have come to offer my thanks, poor though it is."

Prentice blinked and glanced at the duchess. "I don't understand."

"Tell him, Sir Gant," said Amelia with a strange smile.

Sir Gant stood and looked at Prentice directly. "I was at the Brook. I fought in the line," he explained. "I and my squire beside me. The ambush was sprung, and all our forces were gathered together. We stood in the line, pressed right to the edge, where the ground dropped away to the stream. We were fighting and holding when the muddy edge gave way beneath us. We both fell. I saw Farrings, my squire, lying beside me in the shallow, and those wild bastards, they seized him. They dragged him by his feet into their midst and hacked him to pieces. I remember calling to him, but he was gone. Then I looked up, and the Horned Man was towering over me. He had that enormous black blade, and I was sure it was my doom. Then something, someone leaped over me and took the monster by the throat. I watched, inches away, as the Horned Man was wrestled and slain by one man with a dirk."

Sir Gant paused, staring into Prentice's eyes. "Master Ash, you took that monster's head, and I was awestruck. But for your intervention, I would be as dead as my devoted squire. I buried him on that field."

He paused again, seeming to feel the loss of his companion afresh. "Since then, I have been searching for you, to thank you. I tried to get close to Baronet Liam, hearing the praise being spoken of him. He wears the horns as a trophy, no doubt you have seen."

Prentice knew how to control his facial expressions; years as a convict, when any excuse might draw a flogging, did that to a man. He worked hard to never let his anger or contempt show at the mention of Liam, especially not in front of a man he'd just met. He was astonished when he saw the same emotions, the ones he felt but did not show, in Sir Gant's expression. The loathing was unmistakable.

"Where is the man's honor?" Sir Gant asked rhetorically, his lips twisted in a scowl. He turned to the duchess. "Forgive me, Your Grace. I know he is your knight captain, but the man is claiming honor and glory that do not belong to him.

He surrounds himself with sycophants who hang on him and demand the tale over and over. With each telling he becomes larger, the enemies he felled more numerous. Two nights past, he told a pair of men new to his retinue the tale of how he took the Horned Man's head. The cur had the audacity to draw his sword and reenact the final cut while the men at the table cheered."

Sir Gant looked down and made a noise like a growling animal. Then he spat on the ground in disgust. "Again, Your Grace, I ask your forgiveness," he said before turning to Prentice once more. "I nearly called him out right there, to settle the lies with steel, but it is not my honor he steals."

The duchess stepped closer to Prentice. "Sir Gant has asked to swear himself to my house."

Sir Gant nodded, and the duchess continued. "He has made it clear that he will never follow Baronet Liam as a knight captain, not until he apologizes to you and settles his debt of honor."

"Little chance of that," muttered Prentice. He knew he should have held his tongue, but Sir Gant's tale had stirred up his resentment for Liam. The duchess didn't seem to disapprove.

"I think you're right, Master Ash," Amelia said. "The new baronet is not a humble man by nature. That is why I wish to put Sir Gant under your command."

Prentice was stunned. "I'm a mere freeman, and I've only been that since the Brook—not even two weeks. I was a convict for more than ten years before that. I have no rank to command a knighted man."

He turned to look at Sir Gant. There was no way he could imagine even a hedge knight would accept such a demeaning position. It would be humiliating. A man-at-arms might consent to act under a freeman, but a knight had his own name and his own honor to look to. Sir Gant seemed to understand Prentice's thoughts.

"My horse was killed at the Battle of the Brook," he said. "I carried all my worldly possessions with me on my own back the whole way here. I couldn't even spare coppers to hire a man to carry for me. Last night I sold my saddle to pay my board. I have enough coin for another week if I am frugal. Besides that, I have my sword, my skill, and my name. If I am to pledge those for my meals, then I would rather pledge them to a man whose courage and honor I can trust. I would stand beside you, Master Ash, at least until I have returned the favor you paid me when you slew that fiend. And if you turn out to be unworthy of my loyalty, then I will quit your service and seek another. I have made my way in the world that way for some time."

"You ask to enter my service by telling me you will quit it?" Duchess Amelia asked. "Why should I accept your pledge if your first act is to set limits on my commands? Would you demand such things of another liege lord?"

"I would, and I have, Your Grace. I live by a simple code: loyalty above all else, except honor. If you and Master Ash are honorable, as I believe you are, then I will willingly give all service, even my life. But take your own man, Baronet Liam, as an example; not every lord is worthy of loyalty. I have my conscience."

"No wonder you're a hedge knight," Prentice said, and instantly regretted it. He bowed his head to Sir Gant. "I am sorry, sir. The bitterness of my years on the chain has taken hold of my tongue."

Sir Gant accepted the apology with a nod.

Prentice turned to the duchess. "Your Grace, Sir Gant has been forthright. He could have kept quiet and let Baronet Liam's story stand. He could have joined that new retinue and ridden east out of your camp this very morning. Instead, he has looked to a harder road because it leads to a more honorable destination. He knows the distinction between honor and glory and has sought the better goal. Your Grace, it would be a mistake to turn this man away. You need men like him."

Duchess Amelia nodded and then turned back toward her chair. She sat in it and straightened herself to a dignified posture. "I agree, Master Ash. Sir Gant, I accept your service and your terms. You will pledge your service to me, and I will serve as your liege with honor. That is my pledge to you."

Sir Gant went down on one knee again, this time facing Amelia. "My thanks, Your Grace."

Prentice looked on, remembering the night not so long ago when he had done exactly this, down on one knee, pledging himself to the young duchess.

"You have my thanks, sir," Amelia said. "I accept your pledge. Now rise and attend. Prentice was about to outline his plan to reclaim my town and my castle for me."

"It's more of an idea than a plan at the moment," Prentice explained. "But if it works, the town will be in your hands again before sundown tomorrow."

"And the castle?"

"Will be a more difficult prospect."

CHAPTER 3

T he next night, an hour after midnight, Prentice led a rough-hewn band of armed men along the lake's edge from the south to infiltrate Dweltford. The plan he outlined to the duchess was a simple one, but it required the help of a specific type of man he hoped to find among the refugees camping with the army.

"Gong farmers?" the duchess had asked when Prentice explained his intention.

"They clean the waste and leavings through the streets into the sewers, to be flushed away by the lake water."

"I know their task. How will they help you?"

"They will know where the outflow of the sewers is and the safe paths through them. With their help, we will be able to sneak right into the center of town, avoiding any patrols."

"And from the sewers you will go to the gates?"

Prentice nodded. "Take them from behind."

"If it is that simple, why shouldn't I send my whole force into the town this way?"

"Too much noise, Your Grace," Sir Gant said, even before Prentice had time to explain. "Men in armor are not quiet, and the larger the number of men, the louder the noise. If they were to catch men in the sewers, they could lock the gates and turn the tunnels into a prison—capture them or just leave them to starve."

"Or dump oil into the sewers and burn them alive," added Prentice.

The duchess nodded grimly. "So, a small force can take the town by stealth in the night."

"No, Your Grace. A small force can take the gate by stealth. Once we have that, your knights and men-at-arms will have to take the town, Castle Road, Within Walls, the docks, and all the other quarters. And they will have to do it quickly, or it will become a pitched battle in the streets, and your people will suffer."

The duchess had not been pleased by that notion, but she had consented to the plan. Prentice went searching among the refugees until he found two gong farmers who agreed to show him the way.

So it was, in the darkest hours of the night, a dozen men felt their way along the lake's shore to the sewer outflow. There was only a sliver of a moon in a sky half covered with clouds. The long ribbon of pale light that some called the rampart, which arced over the northern sky, was also in rare eclipse, so there was not enough light to see by. That was all to their advantage. They carried hooded lanterns, but these they kept fully shuttered until they were in the sewers themselves.

The gong farmers, two men named Dran and Calles, led the way. The two used to live with their families in homes outside the gates, but their little houses had been burned away by Sir Duggan's siege preparations. Both men were eager to get a measure of revenge and were more than happy to lead Prentice and his force through the sewers. The rest of the small company was made up of former rogues, freed convicts who were veterans of the Battle of the Brook. Of the hundreds of such men sent into the battle, fewer than fifty survived. And of those, most left the army when they gained their freedom. Prentice was able to find seven who were willing to join this desperate night raid, along with Turley and himself.

The last man was Sir Gant.

The whole company was armed, mostly with maces or picks, which would work well against armor or mail. Sir Gant carried his longsword, and Turley had found an axe for himself somewhere. None of them wore any armor for fear of the noise it would make, so any fight they got into would have to be an ambush. They would not last long in open combat against the well-equipped mercenaries Sir Duggan had hired.

At the south edge of town, the high defensive wall extended many yards past the water's edge, out into the lake. But now, at the end of the summer, the water there was not even ankle deep. It was little more than a thick layer of silty mud. Beyond the wall was a dense field of pointed stakes sunk into the lakebed, which protected the south edge of the dock. Between the stakes and the mud, it would be all but impossible for armored men to make their way around the walls here. Prentice's small force was dressed only in their trews and tunics, and they found the going brutally difficult. They were all barefoot because there was no point in wearing shoes or boots—the sucking mud would take them right off their feet.

As it was, they labored across the muck slowly, hands ahead of them in the darkness. No one spoke a word. Their bare feet ached with cold. Directly above them, the town wall ended in a watchtower, and when they looked up, they could see light from a watch fire that burned there. When they held still, they could hear the soldiers on duty around the fire. Sneaking through the wet shadows, every man held his tongue and groped through the darkness.

When he reached the corner of the wall, Prentice poked his head around and saw that the stone-built docks began only paces away. Everything was dark, but a foot patrol of three men with two reed torches was marching up and down along the waterfront. They were some distance away but were walking south toward him. Prentice pulled his head back and whispered to the men waiting in the darkness, pressed into the shadows at the base of the wall.

"One patrol," he told them. "They're heading this way now. We'll wait until they turn back, and then we go." He addressed the gong farmer nearest him, the one named Calles. "How far is it to the outflow?"

"Not twenty paces from here."

"And you're certain we can get in?"

"The pipe is low, but broader than three men across. In winter it's fully under the surface, but now it's knee height above water."

"And we can walk up to it? We won't have to swim?" Prentice asked.

"Normally it's dredged in late summer, to keep the flow fast, but what with the invasion and that bastard Duggan burning us gongers out of our homes, no one's done it. The bed's so muddy it's a wonder the sewers ain't backed up yet."

"One good rain and they will," hissed another voice in the dark, that of Dran, the other gong farmer.

"But we can duck under?" Prentice asked. "We can get in?"

"We got out this way," Calles assured him. "You'll get a face full, but you can get through. Once we're inside, there's a locked gate, but I have the key for that."

"Good man."

Prentice put his head around the corner once more and looked for the patrol. The three mercenaries had reached the south end of the dockside and were about to turn around to head back north. In the flickering light of their torches, Prentice thought he could just see the outflow, a low row of arches built into the base of the dock.

"Be ready to go," he told his men. "And whoever's got the lanterns, be prepared. You've got to keep them above the water level. Pass them through if you must."

He was about to order them to go when there came a loud splashing sound. He froze, and through the darkness he imagined he could feel the men around him tense as well. Whatever it was, the splashing persisted—a long, continuous noise. Above them the light of the watchfire flickered, and the entire group pushed themselves up against the wall to keep in the shadows as deeply as they could.

"Ho there," called a sentry from the watchtower. "Who goes?"

There was no answer, but the splashing started to dwindle.

"Who goes, I say," the sentry demanded again. "Name yourself!"

"Name your arse!" a voice from the dock retorted.

"What-ho?"

"Taking a slash," the dock voice called back, and it was immediately obvious what was happening. One of the patrols on the dock had just urinated into the water.

"Password?" the sentry shouted down, obviously maintaining a sense of duty and decorum his dockside comrades didn't feel. "What's the password?"

"Under your mother's poxy skirts," the voice on the dock replied.

"I know that's you, Makru. I can tell your voice."

"Then you don't need a sodding password, do you?"

Prentice held his breath until he was sure the conversation was over, and then ducked his head around the corner again. He could make out the silhouette of one of the patrol members racing to catch up with the other two as they carried their torches away to the north.

"We go now. Quick and quiet."

He slipped around the edge of the wall, resting one hand on the sandstone blocks to guide himself and keep steady. Even moving as fast as he could, it was desperately slow going. With every step, he sank up to his knees in deep mud and had to clamber out of it. Slipping and pulling, he fought to keep his weapon—a brass-ended, wooden cudgel—from falling from his grasp. If he dropped it, there would be no way to find it again in the dark. Finally, his wall-side hand touched the top of the outflow, and he used the stone arch like a ledge to pull himself up. As his men came behind him, he acted as a guide to push each one in turn through the low tunnel. Turley came last.

"What if I don't fit?" the big man whispered.

"Then go back. If you stay here, you'll just get found when the patrol returns."

"Sod that!" said Turley, and Prentice imagined the expression of disgust his friend must have had on his face. If there was one thing Turley would never accept, it was the thought of running back home while his friends shouldered danger. It just wasn't his way.

Once Turley had ducked his head, Prentice took a breath and then squatted down to crawl through the tunnel himself. Almost at once, he dipped his head too low in the dark and, exactly as Calles predicted, got a face full of the noisome water flowing out of the Dweltford sewers. His reflex was to pull back, but that just caused him to butt up against the pipe's roof. Cursing inwardly, he steeled himself against the rank stench and began to crawl forward, his one hand holding his cudgel above the water and his other hand clawing into the soft mud. His feet slipped behind him, and every push to go forward seemed to yield mere fractions of inches until he felt as though he was just stuck in place in the darkness, unable to go forward or back. Then, quite suddenly, lamplight shone in the end of the pipe. He was almost there. One more push, and then hands grabbed his leading arm. He was drawn forth and helped to his feet.

The two lanterns had made the trip safely, and now both were open and shedding their light. Prentice's men stood dripping mud and filthy water, like a crowd of ragged river wights, risen from their sunken rest. They spat and retched as they tried to clean the worst of the muck from their faces and hair. Their shadowed expressions were grim in the wan lamplight.

"Don't go soft on me now," he chided them quietly. "You've marched on chains and slain beast-men in bloody streams. We've all been through worse than this."

"Most of us have," said one of the ex-convicts, Pallrin by name. He cast a wary glance at Sir Gant.

The knight saw the gesture and snorted in derision. "This isn't the first time I've tasted ditchwater!" he declared.

"Ditchwater? Is that what the pretty folk call this?"

"The pretty folk, as you call them, don't have a name for anything like this. All the pretty folk I've ever met would faint at the thought of this." Sir Gant flicked dark water from his fingers, then hawked and spat. "Oh God, that tastes disgusting!"

"You'll be tasting that for weeks," said Pallrin smugly.

Prentice thought he would have to step in soon if Pallrin kept pushing his resentment.

Gant didn't rise to the ex-convict's hostility.

"As will you," was all he said back.

Pallrin opened his mouth for another snipe, then must have sucked something in with his breath because he suddenly bent over coughing. When he finally stopped, he hawked and spat as well. "You're right, that really does taste disgusting!"

They both chuckled, and the tension was dispelled.

Prentice hissed for quiet, then pointed to Calles the gong farmer. "Show us the gate."

Wading forward, the mud and water level quickly dropped to ankle height, and Calles led them to a set of iron bars at the end of a sewer tunnel. The bars were wall to wall and floor to ceiling, anchored into the stone. In one corner was a gate with a lock whose bolt was shot into the wall as well. If anyone tried to sneak into the town through here without the key, they would be forced to use hammers and picks to break the bars. They'd make so much noise they would be discovered for sure. Calles took the key from around his neck, where it hung by a leather thong.

The key turned well enough in the lock, but when the gong farmer leaned on the gate, the bars screeched against the stones. Every man tensed, straining their ears to hear if the patrol on the dock had noticed the noise. Prentice didn't wait to find out for sure, ducking through the gate and waving to the others to follow him. He grabbed Calles by the wrist and pointed down the passage. In short order, the company had left the entryway behind them.

At first the path seemed simple enough to follow, but the main tunnel they were walking along soon passed through several intersections. After Calles turned on the second and then again on the next, Prentice realized that without a guide, they would soon be lost.

"Do we know we can trust these two?" Turley whispered in Prentice's ear, doubtless feeling as lost as his friend.

"Why wouldn't we?" Prentice asked.

"If they were leading us into a trap, we'd be hard pressed getting out of here."

The other gong farmer, Dran, leaned in between them, holding his lantern up toward Turley's face. "The bastard Duggan is a rebel who's raised arms against our liege lady. He's seized her castle and her town and put my home to the torch. But any time you think we're down here to betray you all, then just look for one of these." He pointed to a section of the tunnel wall where two notches were carved in the stone. "Wherever these marks are, you turn right and you're facing downhill, back to the waterside. If you want, you can follow the marks and make your way out—all by yourself, if you think you can't trust us."

Turley nodded a grim apology. Dran went back down the line to hold the lantern for the rest of the men coming up.

"Good enough for you?" Prentice asked, a mocking edge in his voice.

"Shut up," Turley said, and they started off again, following the light ahead.

The journey seemed too long in the darkness, as if the tunnels stretched farther than was possible, but Prentice assumed that was a combination of their slow caution and the shut-out sky. With only blackness and arched stone above, no stars or moon to guide them, it was hard to measure time and distance. And there was a strange smell that teased at Prentice's memory. It felt odd to him that he should think to pick a memory out of the oppressive stench, but somehow it was there, a reminder of something he'd forgotten, something he'd long wanted to forget.

He pondered it for a moment, and the memory returned like a lash from a whip.

It was the smell of his cell under the academy, where the Inquisition had taken him and hung him by his wrists on the wall all those years ago. It was the smell of wet earth, stale air, and the dust from the stones, all mixed with the stench of filth as he'd soiled himself so many times, while the blood and sweat from the torture ran down his stripped body and pooled at his feet. Suddenly, in his mind, he was back in that cell, trapped like an animal and bitterly afraid. His breathing grew shallow, and he began to push his head up like a drowning man trying to reach the surface. Somewhere inside his thoughts, there was a calm part of him that knew his fear was irrational, that he was in the sewers in Dweltford and not in that cell under Ashfield again. But that calm part could not quite rule over the rest of his mind. Self-control was the core of Prentice's being, the pillar around which the rest of his psyche was built, and it only added to his fears when he felt that control eroded by this terror that he knew was false but could not ignore.

A hand touched his shoulder, and he gasped loudly.

"Shhh," whispered Calles. "We're almost right under Within Walls."

The Market Within Walls was Dweltford's central market square. Castle Road ran straight through the market, from the gates in the outer wall to the castle's drawbridge. They were almost where they wanted to be.

Prentice gulped fetid air and forced his fears back under control while he listened to Calles explain the last part of their underground journey.

"That direction will go back to the river eventually, but there's no way through up there. We take the middle path through this junction, and we come out in a dumping chamber. We can climb out there."

"Lead the way," Prentice managed to force out, hoping his voice sounded like a deliberate whisper and not the fragile croak it felt like in his own ears. Calles moved away, and Prentice compelled himself to follow.

As they entered the last chamber, a new level of stench rose up to greet them, accompanied by a swarm of flies that circled in the lantern light and batted against eyes and mouths and nostrils, making them spit and curse quietly. The source of this new disgust was a huge mound of animal and human dung that sat like a small hillock in the middle of a vast chamber.

"This is where we dump all the leavings from the market," Calles explained. "In winter, the water just washes it all down to the lake, but at the end of a dry summer, it's all piled up like this. Was coming time due for us to come down and shovel it out, like the river pipe."

"But Duggan burned you out?" Prentice said.

"But Duggan burned us out and took control of the town for himself. He'd have found out his mistake if an early autumn storm hit, though."

"How so?"

Calles pointed at the noisome mound. "This much wouldn't wash away before the sewer backed up. It'd flood the streets above, and the good folk would be up to their ankles in shit."

"Just like us?" asked Turley from the darkness.

"Oh, aye." Calles smiled. "It's only happened the once as I remember. The guild council pays us right and on time now."

"So how do we get out?" Prentice asked. Calles's words were helping him think about something other than fearful memories, but he still felt a strong need to return to the outside.

"We climb."

"Of course we do."

Prentice allowed the gong farmer to lead the way as the group began its last filthy climb to come out in the middle of the enemy-held town. They scrabbled up the mound of dung, feet plunging in and hands fumbling to grasp. Prentice controlled himself with the thought that every nauseating inch was one closer to the surface and the clean, open air.

When they reached the top of the mound, Calles slid across to a wall and drew the lamplight to reveal a wooden ladder hanging from iron hooks. It had flat wooden feet on one end and hooks of its own on the other. With a quiet grunt he maneuvered the ladder around until the wooden feet slapped against the revolting mound and the hooks caught on something above.

"It's set," said the gong farmer.

"You're sure?" asked Prentice.

"Of course. You can shine a light up to look, if you want..."

"But that'll be seen above us."

"That's right. Shall I go first?"

"No," said Prentice. "I'll go."

He put one hand to the ladder's rungs and pushed himself up before there could be any argument. He wanted desperately to get out of the sewers, but even without that pressing at him, it had to be him first. This was his plan, his responsibility.

He managed his cudgel as best he could as he climbed upward, wary that it might knock against the ladder or the sewer wall. At last he reached up with his free hand and touched one of the iron hooks on the end of the ladder. Running his fingers along, he found that it was hanging on a lipped ledge and there were steps cut into the stone. Finally, he felt the cold iron grate, and so close to the end, there was one last moment of remembering his imprisonment, as though the bars of the grate were the bars of a prison cell. Then a small gust of air washed through the bars. For a moment, the sewer's stink was driven away, and Prentice breathed a wholesome breath.

It was like a splash of cold water on the face of a sleeping man. He blinked and gulped in the air. For a long moment he paused, feeling almost hidden between the vicious memory below and the danger in the street above. The ladder creaked, and he realized that someone was coming up behind him. Taking another step up, he put his shoulder to the grate and pushed as gently as he could. The metal scraped against the stones, sending dust down into his eyes and face, but the heavy iron moved easily. Soon Prentice was able to put his head above the level of the street. The sky was still clouded and dark, and there were no open lights in the street. As he peered in one direction, he could see that the dark silhouettes of the houses that crowded out so much light opened up to form the edge of the Market Within Walls. Beyond that, over a farther ridge of dark rooflines, were the firelights of the watchmen on the walls.

"The way's clear," he whispered down the ladder. "We go now. Remember, not a sound."

Prentice slithered out of the opening in the street and held the grate so that it didn't fall back. In quick succession, the other men came up the ladder. The wooden rungs creaked with their rush, but there was nothing for it but to take the risk. Soon enough, all twelve men were out of the tunnels and clustered in the silent street. The lanterns were completely hooded once more. With the only light coming from the watchfires on the far walls, each of Prentice's men was nothing but a patch of darkness to his fellows. They stole toward the open square, and at its edge, Prentice reached out to touch each man's shoulder, picking the two gong farmers from the rest.

"You've done your duty," he whispered. "Go and find a safe place to lie low."

"Bugger that!" cursed Dran.

"We want to see this through, Master Ash," Calles said.

"They've been sound up till now," said Sir Gant. "Why not let them give the whole service."

"They got heart enough to go through that every bleeding day," hissed another of the men. "That's braver than I'd want to have to be for a crust. I nearly filled me trews down there."

"I thought you had," whispered another. "Smelled like it!"

"That was your own breath, you rotten turd."

Several of them chuckled softly.

"Shut it, you fools!" Turley said, stilling them. "You'll get us all caught and killed."

"All right," Prentice whispered when everyone was quiet again. "It's been an adventure so far, but now we get down to business. This is why we're here. We make for the gatehouse and we take it."

"For the duchess," Sir Gant added, and many of the men copied him.

"For the duchess and the Reach," Prentice finished, and he led them out of the side street and across the market to Castle Road and the gatehouse.

CHAPTER 4

The gatehouse in the Dweltford wall was much the same as any in any other fortified town in the Grand Kingdom. There were two thin towers with arrow loops that faced out onto the approaching road, with the gate itself between the towers. That was ironbound wood, over a handspan thick, with hinges mounted into the stones of the towers. Behind it was a portcullis that could be lowered if the gate were broken. In the space between the gate and the portcullis, the ceiling was pierced with murder holes. The room above the gate held the winch for the portcullis and more arrow loops looking over the approaching road. In the bottom of each tower were bunkrooms for guards to sleep. Like all well-made gatehouses, it was a small fortification in its own right, but with one essential flaw—it was built to defend only against attacks from outside the walls.

As Prentice and his comrades snuck along Castle Road toward the gate, they could see the door to the right-hand bunkroom was open and firelight was spilling out. In its glow, they made out the base of the stairs that curved up the tower to the next level, just to the left inside the door. Prentice waved his men down to crouch behind a horse trough and the front fence of a farrier's yard.

"That's our way in," he said, pointing to the open door. "Once we're there, go hard. Do not stop for anything. We must take the upper floor before they can lock us out and drop that portcullis. Then we lock the doors onto the outer walls to prevent any other watchmen getting in and we hold the gatehouse until the knights come through those gates. Then the town is Duchess Amelia's again."

"Too easy," said Turley.

"We can hope."

"If it's that easy, won't they just take it back from us?" asked Calles.

"It depends," Prentice said.

"On what?"

"On how hard you fight!"

"Don't fear," whispered Sir Gant. "We are loyal men; they are mercenaries. Loyalty trumps money in true men's hearts every time. We will fight harder than they."

Prentice was glad of the darkness, because he wasn't sure he could hide the doubt he felt from his face. Sir Gant's words were noble, but Prentice had seen the difference between professional warriors and simple stout men before. Training counted for a lot more than loyalty some days. He just hoped this wasn't one of those times. He led off, hefting his cudgel, ready for the fight. It was strange to him that now he felt calm. The terror from the sewers was forgotten, the memory of his interrogation and torture gone hazy again. In its place he felt a cold calm. He scanned the walls in case a patrolling guard might look down and spot them, even in the dark. Then he watched the open door and the similar door in the other tower that remained closed. He strained to hear any sound that might warn of an approaching enemy.

His silent steps brought him to the edge of the last house, and he only had to cross the cobbles to the door, no more than half a dozen paces. He had just started off when he heard a voice grumble something from inside, and a mercenary appeared in the doorway. The man was wearing a patched gambeson with ruffled sleeves, opened to the waist, over brightly striped

black-and-yellow breeks. He had no weapons, and he stretched
his arms wide as he yawned loudly, taking in the cool night air.
There was no chance to go back and hide now, so Prentice threw
himself forward.

"What-ho?" the mercenary managed to say just before
Prentice surged out of the night and crashed into him, leading
with the head of the cudgel, which he jabbed end-first into
the man's stomach. The mercenary crumpled backward, but
Prentice kept shoving him, using the cudgel two handed and
thrusting it like a ramrod, so that the man was pushed through
the door, down the short passage beside the stairs, and into the
barrack room proper. The mercenary tripped over something
on the floor and sprawled across a low table that was set between
the bunks that lined the walls and where a handful of others
were playing dice. The tinkling of scattered coins merged with
the crash of breaking furniture and shouts, as men recoiled from
the violent return of their comrade to the room.

Before the noise had even ended, Prentice was among them,
swinging his cudgel. The first sweep smashed one guard in the
face, and he fell unconscious. Prentice turned back to attack
to his other side, but Turley was already there, casting his
axe about side-to-side in the tight space. It was a desperate,
bloody business, but the element of surprise meant the fight was
doomed to be one sided. A third ex-convict crowded into the
bunkroom, stepping on the first fallen mercenary and delivering
a hefty kick to the man's face before jumping to the back of the
room and attacking a fourth mercenary as he tried to draw his
sword.

"The stairs!" Prentice shouted out the bunkroom door. "Up
the stairs. Quick now!"

There was no more point to stealth. They had to take the
gatehouse and hold it, or they would never get the gate open
before enemy reinforcements came from the castle. He looked
back into the bunkroom to see that Turley and his other man
had the swordsman pinned against the bunk. There were no

more doors or chambers. Prentice rushed back to the stairs and followed the men who were already fighting their way into the upper gate house. Looking over their shoulders, he could see that they were driving hard against the mercenaries that were there. He burst into the winch room.

"The other tower," he shouted and he pointed to the door on the opposite side of the room. From the outside there came a long horn blast, and all Prentice's men stopped for a moment to listen. Prentice listened too, and then he pinpointed the source of the sound.

"The roof!"

He dashed back out of the door and started racing up the next twist of the stairs. The spiral turned to the right, which meant that he had to change his cudgel to his left hand or risk it being caught on the central pillar when he tried to swing it. As he climbed, though, he met no more resistance, and he reached the level of the town's main wall rampart to find the door open. Looking along the battlements, he could see confused guards rushing toward the gatehouse, while some others ran in the other direction, to come down from the wall somewhere else, he supposed. His men had only moments before they would be attacked from behind. Above him, on the roof of the gatehouse, the alarm horn sounded again, the low note echoing over the roofs of the town.

Prentice pulled the door shut and shot the heavy wooden bolt hard. He hoped it would hold long enough. Then he threw himself up the last set of steps, emerging through the wooden floor of the tower's top. An iron brazier lit the open space, the flames whipping about as a breeze was picking up from the west and dancing over the battlements. Near the brazier was the mercenary with the horn. He was a young man, holding the horn in his left hand and the naked blade of a side sword in his right. They locked eyes as Prentice climbed out of the stairwell, but before he was fully clear, he heard the heavy twang of a bowstring and a crossbow quarrel bit into the stones only a hand's breadth from his head, spitting shards of rock at his face.

Prentice turned to see a second mercenary with a crossbow and a broad-brimmed helmet. The crossbowman already had his foot in the stirrup and was drawing the string back for a second shot. Prentice cast his eyes back to the man with the horn. Their eyes met, and the mercenary sneered at him as he put the horn to his lips for a third alarm call.

"Fool," Prentice said quietly and ran at the crossbowman. The man with the horn should have guarded his comrade first. The alarm would not save them quickly enough. With crossbow and long blade working together, the pair would almost certainly have been too much for one man. Prentice charged the crossbowman but as the man tried to back away, he immediately began to trip, with his foot still caught in the stirrup. Before he could fall, Prentice swung the cudgel in an upward arc and the brassbound end caught the man under the jaw. The blow knocked out teeth, and the crossbowman fell insensible. Prentice turned on the mercenary with the horn, who cut off his third blast half blown and raised his sword in guard.

"Should have watched your partner, lad," Prentice said as he stalked forward. There was a savage gleam in his eyes. He checked the sword's blade as the mercenary tried a thrust. The young man reset his stance and thrust again, trying a different angle, but Prentice checked him again. He was astonished when the mercenary took a half step back and raised his blade in a salute. What did the young fool think, that this was an honor duel?

The swordsman set his stance a third time, and Prentice lost his patience. When the thrust came, Prentice stepped in as well, using the cudgel to smash the blade aside and following that with an elbow to the face. The move caught the young man so unexpectedly that he staggered backward, falling against the crenulations. To his credit, he kept his blade raised and pushed back off the stone to keep up the fight, but he was too dazed. Prentice kicked his knee out from under him and brought the brass head of the cudgel down on his face as he fell. He was unconscious before he struck the floorboards. Prentice took the horn from his body and threw it over the walls.

There was a metallic rattle from beneath him, like the anchor chain of a ship running out and a heavy boom. He rushed to the town-ward side of the watchtower and looked down. In the dim torchlight on the street, he saw a mercenary bursting out at a run, heading for Castle Road. The man made it only a few steps before Sir Gant ran him down and caught him with a low slash that hamstrung him. The mercenary collapsed to the cobbles, grabbing at his thigh and crying in pain.

"The gate, Sir Gant," Prentice called down. "We must open the gate."

"The portcullis is down."

"How?"

"I don't know. I was clearing out the north tower," Sir Gant replied.

"Meet me in the gate room. The castle already knows we're here."

Prentice rushed back down the stairs. As he passed the battlement level, he heard the guards outside hammering on the door; it sounded solid enough so far. Down the next flight to the winch level, he ran into Turley and three of his men looking lost.

"The portcullis is down!" Prentice told them.

"We know," Turley answered and looked to the other end of the room.

As soon as he did, Prentice could see the problem. The winch room was divided by a wooden wall. In the rush of the assault and the dim torchlight, he hadn't noticed that the winch was on the other side of that wall, behind a locked door. He and his men had captured the murder holes, but the portcullis winch was still barred to them. Prentice cursed under his breath.

"There's at least one in there," Turley continued. "He's bolted the door."

"Give it the axe."

Turley shrugged and laid his heavy axe to the door. A few splinters flew from the first strike, but the door stayed sound.

"Keep at it," Prentice urged, then he turned to the other men. "Axes, picks, anything you can find." They hurried off to help.

Sir Gant rushed in from the other side of the room, coming up the north tower stairs. "The battlement's locked off, but they're trying the door with whatever they've got."

"Same on the south side," said Prentice.

Sir Gant looked at Turley as the big man swung the axe again, thudding into the planks of the door. "Winch is on the other side?"

"Aye," Turley replied.

"So, it's a race?"

"With a fourth team coming from the castle on horseback, no doubt," Prentice said.

One of the ex-convicts returned with a battle-axe and two warhammers. "S'all they've got," he said with an apologetic shrug.

Prentice snatched the battle-axe from his hand. "There's room for only two of us to take the door." He stepped around Turley to swing from the other side. "The rest of you, get down into the gatehouse. Soon as we lift the portcullis, you have to unbar the gate."

"If the portcullis doesn't rise, we'll be trapped there," came the protest. "And with more coming from the castle, they'll slaughter us."

"The only way it doesn't rise is if I'm already dead!"

Sir Gant nodded and tapped the man next to him on the shoulder, then rushed out of the gate room. Prentice turned to the door, and he and Turley began to swing their axes in turns. Turley gave him a look but neither spoke, not wanting to waste the effort. Sweat streaked down their faces, dribbling trails over their filthy skin. They strained for breath as, stroke after stroke, they hammered on the door. Prentice's axe was made for war, lighter than Turley's, with a back spike opposite the blade and another spike on the end for thrusting. It was not as suited to the task as Turley's simpler weapon, but he swung with all the force he could muster.

The door began to make loud cracks with every blow, and soon the wood was rattling free of the iron hinges. Still, the door was in place, and Prentice and Turley, impatient that the barrier did not fall, redoubled their efforts. Suddenly, Turley's axe head punched through the door and caught in the gap. He grunted as he wrenched it back, and the door split completely apart, with small pieces left hanging from the hinges and the lock bolt. Turley fell back with the effort of pulling the axe free, but Prentice jumped through the broken door, battle-axe in hand.

"Throw down your arms or die where you stand!" he bellowed. Like a demon spawned from hell, face and limbs covered in filth, he glared wild-eyed around the room. The only person in the winch room was an older man, maybe fifty years old. He crouched in a corner of the room, holding a dirk out in front of himself. Terrified, the man dropped his dagger on the floor. The fear in his eyes made Prentice feel vaguely ashamed.

"Get out if you want to live," he growled.

The man nodded and made a quick escape.

Turley came into the winch room. "Just him?"

Prentice only grunted in reply.

"Old bastard looked like he was going to soil himself."

"Help me with this!" Prentice hissed.

There was a large wooden capstan fixed to the tower wall, with a heavy chain hanging through a square hole in the stones of the floor.

"That looks heavy," said Turley.

"There's only space enough in here for two men to turn it, so we must be able to do it."

"Makes sense."

They each took up a position on either side of the capstan and began to pull on the hand bars. Surprisingly, the winch turned easily, a simple system of gears between the capstan and the winch chain creating a mechanical advantage.

"Well, that's not so hard," Turley observed.

Prentice nodded. The wheel turned so effortlessly that it was possible that one man on his own could raise the portcullis. Then Prentice realized that the innovation created a new problem. The same mechanical advantage that made the turns easier made the portcullis rise slowly, coming up barely an inch per turn.

"Faster," he urged his big friend.

The wheel creaked as they turned it, and over that sound, they heard another: the staccato noise of approaching hoofbeats.

"I hope that's ours getting here before theirs," Turley said.

"It won't matter which ones get here first if we don't get this thing up!"

They pulled on the handles with all their might, turning the wheel as fast as they could. The chain rattled through the hole in the floor, and the mechanism squealed as it was made to run faster than it likely ever had before. There were shouts coming from the gatehouse below, and the sound of approaching horses grew louder. Prentice's arms burned with fatigue, and the filthy sweat dripped into his eyes, but he pushed himself on, reaching for any extra bit of speed. No matter how fast the wheel turned, it seemed the chain stubbornly refused to rise at any but a sedate pace.

Then there was a loud clack, the sound of two heavy pieces of wood knocking together, and the wheel refused to turn any further. Prentice kept pushing at it until he realized it meant the portcullis was raised. He slumped against the wheel, and Turley leaned back and slid down to sit on the floorboards. Both men gasped for breath. From below they heard the gates opening, and Prentice prayed inwardly that they weren't too late. He bent down and picked up the battle-axe he'd dropped to turn the capstan. He also fetched the old man's dropped dagger, tucking the naked blade into his waistband. He put his hand out to help Turley to his feet.

"Come on," Prentice said. "We still have more to do this night."

Turley accepted his hand with a weary sigh. "Of course we do."

CHAPTER 5

P rentice and Turley emerged from the bunkroom door to find their little force standing to one side as the duchess's army, led by knights in plate and mail on horseback, charged in through the gate. A column of men-at-arms came with them, wearing mail under surcoats, as well as flat-brimmed steel helms. They had weapons and lit torches in hand.

"No convicts in this fight," said Turley, seeing the well-equipped footmen trot past.

"Except us," Prentice said.

"Speak for yourself. I'm a free man."

Prentice smirked at his friend. Sir Gant appeared at his side, a jug in hand. He offered it, and Prentice accepted, taking a swig. As he drank, though, he also took in all the muck and sweat from around his mouth. The mixture tasted foul, and he spat it out before he gagged.

"You might want to wipe yourself off and wash out your mouth first," said the knight.

Prentice nodded, smiling. As he looked at the men gathered around him, he realized how truly filthy and disgusting they all looked and smelled. Some were splashed with blood, and Prentice wondered about the number of injured.

"How many did we lose?" he asked.

"Just the gong farmer." Sir Gant gestured to the shadows next to the bunkroom door, where Dran's body lay flat on the stones. Calles knelt next to him, cradling his head.

Prentice approached and saw that Dran's chest was a puddle of blood, bubbling as air escaped through the wound. He was still alive, but his lung was pierced, and he was drowning in his own vital fluids. Prentice turned to a nearby youth. The youngest of the ex-convicts was barely a man, with close-cropped hair and a brand under his left eye that marked him as a killer who had murdered someone in a brawl.

"Go in there and get him a blanket or two," Prentice told the young man. "He shouldn't have to die cold on the stones like this."

The youth nodded and ran into the bunkroom. Prentice crouched next to Calles and looked down at Dran. He took the wounded man's hand and drew his attention.

"You've done well," Prentice told him. "I'll see that the duchess hears of your bravery and good service."

Dran tried to say something, but all that came out was a dribble of blood. The young man returned with blankets. Prentice folded one blanket and placed it under Dran's head, while they put the other over Dran's legs.

Prentice stood and put his hand on Calles's shoulder. "You stay here. Keep him company. The rest of us have to go."

Calles nodded and took his friend's hand.

Prentice turned to the young man standing beside him. "What's your name?"

"Cutter," the young man replied, managing to make the single word a belligerent challenge, despite his youthful voice.

Prentice pointed to the brawler's mark on his cheek. "Cutter, eh? You like a knife, do you? Is that why they call you Cutter? You know how to cut a man?"

The young man sneered defiantly and tossed his head.

"Then you should have this." Prentice pulled out the captured dirk and handed it to Cutter.

"What's this for?" he asked suspiciously, though he accepted the weapon.

"I want you to find any of the duchess's enemies that you can tonight, and I want you to stick that in the belly of each and every one of them."

"I can do that." Cutter smiled, eyes glittering in the firelight at the prospect of more violence.

Prentice turned back to the rest of his small command. "Right, you lot. You're free men and you've done what you pledged to me to do. So, if you want to sit here and take in the night air, I won't stop you. But I am sworn to the duchess Amelia, and I'm going to go show those preening popinjays on their pretty horses how a veteran of the Brook fights for his liege. You can stay here, come and watch, or get stuck in beside me. Your choice."

Without waiting for anyone to say anything else, he hefted the battle-axe, slung it on his shoulder, and began to march down Castle Road toward the sound of a growing fray. The first man beside him was Sir Gant, which didn't surprise him. The knight was scrubbing at the dirt on his longsword blade with a handful of straw he had souvenired from somewhere.

"When you call knights 'preening popinjays,' you know you're talking about me as well, don't you?" said Sir Gant.

"I most certainly am not, sir," Prentice replied with a roguish smile. "You are a filthy beggar-knight who just crawled through a sewer to take a gatehouse and a town from the hands of a rebel. And I would rather have you beside me, than any twenty of those popinjays." He put his hand on Sir Gant's shoulder and leaned in close. "The longsword is the right of your rank, but your honor is here." He poked a finger at Sir Gant's heart. "Right here."

Turley and the others caught up, and Prentice was pleased to see that not one of his men had chosen to remain behind except Calles, who stayed to nurse Dran. He turned on his heel and led them toward Within Walls, where it sounded as if a pitched battle had broken out. Indeed, when they reached it, Market Within Walls was a dark, seething mass of steel and flame, as lanterns and torches scattered dancing shadows across the walls and roofs. Shouts and cries writhed through the darkness, punctuated by the staccato clash of steel on steel. Prentice and his men held back at the edge of the square, trying to keep clear of the danger.

He slapped Turley on the shoulder. "Give me a boost."

With his friend's help, he clambered up onto a long roof gable jutting out from a house wall. From inside he heard a frightened cry that cut off suddenly, stifled. Likely all the homes around the square were filled with terrified citizens, hiding in their inner rooms and praying for the cacophony to end.

"What are you looking for?" called Turley.

Prentice scanned the square, not answering the question. The battle was doomed to be one sided; even with her reduced numbers, the duchess commanded too many knights and soldiers for Sir Duggan's small force to hold the town, now that they were inside the walls. The real problem was that the longer the battle took, the worse the damage to the town, with citizens in fear and at risk like the ones in the house beneath him. The duchess needed the capture to be swift, and the best chance of that was to take Duggan out of the fight. So, Prentice searched the firelit battle for any sign that the rebellious castellan was out of the castle and in the battle itself.

After a moment, he found it.

"There!" He pointed and shouted down to his comrades. He'd spotted a pair of pennants on lances at the back of the mercenary force, near the western opening of Castle Road. The other ex-convicts strained, but there was no way they could see that far over the affray.

Prentice dropped down to them. "Duggan's here, commanding his troops."

"You saw him?" asked Sir Gant.

"His pennants. It's hard to make out colors in this light, but I'm sure it's him."

Sir Gant appeared skeptical.

"What are we going to do?" Turley asked.

"We circle around through the alleys, or over the roofs if we have to," Prentice explained. "We get behind Duggan and cut off any chance to get back to the castle."

"Just us?" asked Sir Gant.

"If we take Duggan by surprise, we can grab him and force him to surrender."

The shadowed light did nothing to hide the doubt on Sir Gant's face, but the knight made no further objection. Prentice led off, dashing back down the road to work their way west behind the houses. They jumped fences and pushed through animal pens, tripping over water troughs and hay piles. The torchlight from the square was little use to them, with tiny, dim shards barely cutting into the dark of the back alleys. So, they stumbled and cursed, their only advantage the fact that the noise from the battle covered any that they themselves made.

"Next row over should be Castle Road," said Cutter, the youth poking a head around a corner to look between two houses.

Prentice looked as well. He could see two men on horseback, in the finest interlocking plate armor.

"We're right where we want to be," he said, but the gap between the houses was too narrow for them to fit. "We'll go over the roof."

Cutter didn't even wait for an order; with one foot on the top of a low wooden fence, the youth scrambled up onto the roof. Prentice was about to follow when the house's door burst open. A heavyset man stepped out with a pitchfork in his hands. Behind him a small woman cowered, holding a rushlight. Prentice and his men froze in the sudden light, dim though it was. The man grunted and stepped forward belligerently.

Cutter was almost directly above and Prentice reached out to hold him back, sensing the young killer tense for the attack.

"Duchess's men," said Turley, looking the townsman and his wife straight in the face.

The man grunted and then stepped back, putting his fork up. "Well, that's all right, then. Don't break my shingles is all."

"We won't."

The man and his wife went back into the house.

Prentice called his force on, and soon they were all on the rooftop, clambering up to the gable. They crouched behind the peak of the roof and looked down into the next street. The two knights Prentice had seen from a distance were there. They were dressed in the finest plate, sometimes called white steel because its surfaces were so well polished. Every piece was articulated to fit into the ones next to it, and the whole moved together so that almost no gaps showed for a blade to fit between. Even their helmets interlocked with the bevors that guarded their throats, which meant they could barely turn their heads. Both men had their visors open, or else they'd have been virtually blind in the shadows of the night battle. The two sat their horses with lances held high, like an honor guard, and each with a long dragon-tail pennant. Now that he was closer, Prentice could confirm the pennants' colors: gray and purple, Sir Duggan's personal livery. The usurper himself was not there.

"He's not here now, but he will be," Prentice whispered to the others.

"How do you know that?" asked Cutter.

"His honor guard."

Sir Gant snorted with derision. The others looked at him. "Honor guards are a thing for princes and knight marshals. He's even got them dressed for a joust."

"Be hard to get through them plates," said Turley. "Even with an axe."

"We can overwhelm them, but it will not be easy. Our advantage is that they can't see past their own helms. Even from the side, they won't see you coming."

At that moment, a third horseman disentangled himself from the battle and trotted back between the two honor guards who were waiting for him. This knight was dressed in much more common plate and mail, nowhere near as protective but much more functional for open battle where danger could come from any side at any moment. The knight pushed back his helmet's visor and revealed the face of their target, Sir Duggan. He had an arming sword in one hand and a shield on his other arm. Draped over the shield was a length of cloth, a pennant of the duchess's colors, cream and dark blue. Duggan threw the trophy pennant to one of his companions.

"Told you I'd take it," he said, raising his voice over the sounds of battle. "Serve that conceited pup right. Never knew how to show respect." He turned his horse around between his guards and surveyed the battle.

"Someone's pleased with himself," said Turley.

And why shouldn't he be? Prentice thought. Sir Duggan's mercenaries were fewer than the duchess's forces, but they had staked out a solid position for themselves at the Castle Road opening of the market and were maintaining a disciplined line of defense.

"He knows his business," Sir Gant said.

"Like the Brook," added Turley, and every man nodded, undoubtedly remembering the hard-fought battle they had won.

It was worse than that for the duchess this time though because her forces lacked the cohesiveness they had had at the Battle of the Brook. Back then, they had stood side by side, rallied by Prentice and the prince's knight commander, Sir Carron Ironworth. But for this battle, the duchess's knight captain, Baronet Liam, had ridden away, so her little army had no clear leader. Knights fought together and led their own men-at-arms, but they did so without natural coordination. That confusion made it possible that Sir Duggan's mercenaries might win the battle and throw the duchess back out of her town after all. That was not something Prentice would allow, not after what he'd already gone through this night.

"We take him now," he told his compatriots.

They began to carefully clamber over the gable, pressing their bodies close to the roof to keep out of the light. Turley and a couple of others lowered themselves down the side into a tiny, dark gap between this house and the next one over. Prentice and Cutter slithered on their bellies to the edge of the roof so that they were only two or three paces distant from the nearest guarding knight. The group was ready to spring.

Without warning, a duchy knight on an armored charger broke through the defenses just ahead of Duggan's honor party. The man waved a short-handled flail, the spiked ball at the end of the chain whirling a wild circle. Even as he surged forward, there were mercenaries behind him, trying to hack at his mount. Then several things happened at once. The knight nearest to Prentice and Cutter lowered his lance and charged the challenger. Duggan's own horse, blood still high, snorted and tried to rear while Duggan fought to regain control. When his mount twisted beneath him, Sir Duggan looked up and straight into Prentice's face. There was a moment of recognition, and then the usurper began to shout his warning. Even as he did so, Cutter launched from the roof. The young ex-convict's leap took him past Duggan and almost all the way across the street, to crash bodily into the other heavily armored knight. The force was not enough to knock the knight from his saddle, but Cutter scrambled like a monkey to clamp on to the knight from behind, wrapping legs and an arm around the armor and brutally stabbing the dirk Prentice gave him into the man's face.

Then Prentice and the rest of his men leaped from the shadows. Prentice threw himself for Sir Duggan's horse, but the experienced knight easily guided his mount out of the way, leaving Prentice to land exposed on the cobbles. Duggan raised his blade to strike Prentice down but found his attack intercepted by Sir Gant's longsword. By the time he recovered from the parry, the rest of the ex-convicts were surrounding him, grabbing and striking.

Prentice ducked aside as Duggan's horse turned again, its body shoving attackers aside like nine-pins. He swiped at the mount with his looted axe but missed. Duggan sliced with his blade, and a man fell away with a cry. Prentice struck again and was rewarded with a resounding strike against Duggan's leg armor. The blow would have done little damage, but it got the knight's attention.

"Filthy convict bastard," he said with a sneer.

Prentice dodged back as far as he could go as Duggan brought his mount up to rear downward. The horse's ironshod hoofs struck sparks on the stone. One hit from those would put a man down for good.

Duggan was still cursing as he lay about himself with his blade. "Scum! Filth! Dog shit!"

It was as if the knight had lost control of himself, cursing without thought and raging against the world. Seeing an opening, Prentice side-stepped a sweeping strike and lunged. The head of his weapon smacked not into Duggan's stomach, where Prentice aimed, but into the side of his mount's neck. The force of the misguided strike threw Prentice backward, almost making him drop his axe. The heavy blow stopped the horse dead for a moment and the suddenness of the halt created a moment of calm in the midst of the melee.

That instant's peace seemed to pierce Sir Duggan's battle rage, and Prentice could see the knight blink as he looked around himself at the chaos in the night. Cutter had taken his target from his horse finally, but had fallen pinned under the man's armor. The youth was struggling to get free and beat at the dying man, shrilly cursing the whole time. Something about Cutter's voice seemed to catch a moment in Prentice's mind, but he didn't have time to pay attention. The other honor guard who'd charged with his lance had beaten his target, running the other knight through the throat. But the duchess's men were pressing at the gap that had let the knight through in the first place, and the mercenary line looked like it would soon buckle.

"It's over, Sir Duggan," Prentice shouted. "Yield!"

"To you?" Duggan's face twisted in a hateful snarl. "Never. Never to you, dog!"

His sword came down again, but this time Prentice deflected it. His counterattack rang off Duggan's blade, but Sir Gant struck again with his longsword, a quick slash that took advantage of Duggan's focus on Prentice. Duggan's nerve broke.

"Withdraw to the castle!" he cried. "Withdraw!"

"No!" Prentice shouted. He tried to stop him but had to dodge the charging mass of Duggan's horse as the usurper spurred it into a retreat.

Sir Gant attempted to intercept the fleeing horse and rider, but more hoofbeats as the remaining honor guard also spurred for the castle. Prentice threw himself at Gant and pulled him aside before the second retreating knight rode him down.

"Damn! We'll never catch him," Sir Gant hollered at the retreating knights.

The two of them looked back to the battle and saw the effect of Sir Duggan's retreat on his hired men. It was like watching a dam slowly collapse. At first in ones and twos, then in a growing flood, the mercenaries began to break from their lines and the duchess's men started to push through.

"Get to safety," Prentice called, and he and Gant pulled Cutter from the path of the rout. The youth had begun looting the dead knight's body and shouted voice-cracking curses when dragged from the prize.

The three pressed back into the shadows as more and more mercenaries ran past. Then there were pursuing knights among them, laying about with their weapons, driving the rout and knocking fleeing men down indiscriminately. Soon the armed men were not mercenaries, but men on the duchy's side; their blood was up, and filthy armed men in the shadows were not readily trusted.

Prentice, Cutter, and Sir Gant held their weapons up to protect them against their own allies' fury. "Duchess' men! Duchess' men!" They shouted themselves hoarse for a long, desperate moment until the sound of the drawbridge being pulled drew everyone's attention.

"Well, he's safe now," said Sir Gant. "They'll never get him tonight."

"But they'll want to," Prentice said.

Duchess Amelia's forces had taken the town back, and they were in the grip of victorious bloodlust. Armies that took towns were not known to be gentle. Without Duggan and his last few men to vent their ire upon, the town was in real danger that the rescuers' rage would turn on the townsfolk.

"We need to move quickly," Prentice said.

He pushed out from the shadows and joined the ends of the crowd running up Castle Road. He looked over his shoulder only once, hoping to see his men following him, but he didn't have time to wait. Tired as he was, he pushed and ran and dodged through the armed men wherever he could until the castle came into view. The castle proper stood on an island in the middle of the lake, and the water between the edge of the town and the castle gatehouse was bridged by Castle Road, with a drawbridge at the castle end.

Dawn was close, and Prentice realized he could see the drawbridge pulled across the water. The rump of the bridge on the town side and the road leading up to it were crowded with knights on their horses and men-at-arms, pressed right up to the edge. Some on the bridge were shouting at the castle, and a flight of crossbow quarrels came from the walls and tore their way into the crowd. A knight fell from his horse, and the whole army growled like an angry beast. They wanted to attack the castle, but there was no way to do it. They were not ready for a siege. At any minute they would turn their frustrations to another target—possibly any target.

Prentice couldn't make it any farther through the thronged men, so he snatched a burning torch from one man and jumped up onto a fence, and from there onto an overhanging roof.

"Men of Dweltford," he shouted, straining his voice as loud as he could. "Men of the Reach. The duchess's town is freed." Some of those nearest turned toward him. He tried to raise his voice higher. "Your town is free. Your wives, your mothers, your children can be safe now. The usurper is beaten! His men are beaten. Let them surrender."

"Why?" called a voice from the crowd.

"Never," cried another.

"The duchess has offered them amnesty if they lay down their arms," Prentice lied, saying the first thing that came into his head. "Any man who harms them now will have violated high law."

There was a new grumble at that, and Prentice noticed that among the men-at-arms were mercenaries already captured and being held by the duchess's forces.

A knight pushed his horse through the crowd. "Who are you to give this order?" he demanded, his tone full of challenge.

"I am the duchess's man."

"Are you indeed? You look like a filthy beggar to me. Perhaps you are a brigand of the traitor, trying to save your own life."

Prentice's shoulders slumped, and he hung his head. The sky was brightening, and dawn would be up soon. He knew every man could see him, see his obscenely grimy state. He did look like a beggar, or worse. He'd been a freed man for little more than a week, and sworn to the duchess Amelia. Yet now, when it mattered most, he seemed like the basest convict. Duggan had called him scum, a dog. And he felt like it. He was tired and sore. His throat was raw from shouting. He wanted to lie down and sleep, but he steeled himself for the argument.

"He is indeed my man!" declared a woman's voice from the other end of the road.

Prentice turned. Duchess Amelia sat on her horse at the rear of the army with a guard of five mounted knights. She projected her voice through a leather speaking trumpet, her words carrying a long way in the still morning air. When they saw her, the men in the street went to their knees, many of them dragging prisoners down with them. Knights removed their helmets.

"He is my man, and he speaks with my voice." The duchess regarded them all like a mother proud of her children. "Well done, every man. Dweltford is ours again!"

The army stood and cheered her, but from the castle came mocking jeers. The duchess had her town, but not her home.

CHAPTER 6

"Being free with my largesse has become something of a habit with you, Master Ash," Duchess Amelia said.

Prentice nodded. In the days leading up to the Battle of the Brook, he had offered the duchess's amnesty to every convict who survived the battle—without first obtaining her consent. He'd been confident of her support in that case, because the duchess hated the practice of convicts being forced to fight. With Duggan's captured mercenaries, Prentice had just been trying to find a way to prevent a massacre.

"I still have knights coming in and insisting that I rescind my amnesty." She paused and looked Prentice in the eye. "Your amnesty, given in my name, in point of fact. They want to take prisoners and seek ransoms."

"They were mercenaries, Your Grace, and foreigners mostly," Prentice answered, meeting her gaze. "They have no more than the clothes on their bodies and the money in their purses. There are no ransoms going."

"My knights think otherwise."

"Your Grace may do as she wishes. But if the amnesty is withdrawn, then those men would become convicts and the responsibility of the crown, thus your responsibility. You would have to house and feed them."

"Not if the knights claim them," she said.

"The knights don't want convicts. They'll go through the lot hoping to find a name of status, and when they find none, they'll leave Your Grace and the duchy to feed them and pay the bill."

"I don't understand how Sir Duggan planned to pay the bill."

Duchess Amelia slumped down into her chair, and her eyes ranged over the wooden table in front of her, which was strewn with papers and parchment—letters and reports from factors, noblemen, merchants, and the guilds. After they had taken the town, the duchess's forces had marched the captured mercenaries to be held on river barges, ready to be shipped south into exile. The duchess herself had taken up residence in Dweltford's guild conclave house, sleeping in an upper room and spending her days holding court behind this table in the conclave's main chamber. She had been here eight days, and she looked wearier to Prentice's eye than she had on the march with the army.

Money was the cause of her exhaustion.

Last summer she had traveled south to pay off her husband's debts to merchants and trading houses in the Vec. Amelia's own family were merchants, and her fortune had been the reason the duke married her. Her fortune cancelled his debts. Then, while she was away, Duke Marne had died and as she returned north, the invaders had come from the west. She'd had no time to grieve, and still the demands of her new status seemed to grow and grow. And there was no money.

"How did he plan to pay?"

Prentice realized the duchess was asking him a direct question. "I have no idea."

"At least your generosity in victory hasn't cost me any money."

"How is th—" Prentice stopped the question on his lips, but it was too late.

The duchess looked up at him. "You have a question, Master Ash?"

He wanted to deny it but knew she would not let him. The duchess had appointed him as an advisor, and she expected him to fulfill the role. Generally, Prentice was wary of nobility who liked to think they had the common touch, speaking with familiarity to the lower orders. The familiarity was more one way than they liked to think, and he'd seen the common touch harden into violent contempt when a subordinate overstepped an unexpected boundary. He had to admit, though, that by and large, the duchess was cut from a different cloth. Being born a merchant's daughter and having skipped several ranks of nobility in her marriage, she was by no means a typical peer of the realm.

"Where is the money, Your Grace? That's all I meant to ask."

"What money? My money? Gone to pay my late husband's debts. You know this."

"And where did his money go?"

The duchess's eyes narrowed, and she sat back in her chair, holding her head up. She was not quite twenty years old, yet she understood dignity and could wield it like a weapon when she chose.

"What possible value do you think there is in reviewing the duke's spending? Do you imagine I would like you to pick over his expenditures to judge them for yourself? A duke is second only to a prince or a king, and owed the same fealty within his lands. It is his prerogative to spend his money as he sees fit, and certainly he should not have to fear having his legacy picked over by factors and reeves after he has passed into our Lord's care."

Prentice bowed his head apologetically. Whatever the financial basis of her marriage, the duchess held her husband in high regard and was fully committed to preserving his legacy. She once told Prentice that she had grown to love her husband wholeheartedly in the short time of their arranged marriage, and he believed it.

"I meant no disrespect to Duke Marne, Your Grace," he said. "But I cannot understand how he was ever in debt in the first place. The Western Reach is bountiful. More food than its people can eat, thriving livestock and farms. There's good timber in its woodlands, and silver and iron in the mountains north of Fallenhill."

He paused as the duchess flinched at the mention of the destroyed barony with its slaughtered population. Then he went on. "A goodly source of either one of those metals would be the making of any noble house in the inner kingdom, and the Reach has both. How can the Reach's lord be bankrupt? The duke should have been able to raise an army and keep it fed from his own purse alone."

"Marne didn't care about money," Amelia said, a fond but rueful smile on her lips. "He did not care about it, and so he didn't manage it well."

"But it must go somewhere, Your Grace. You know this. If he wasn't feasting two hundred guests every night, on ten courses each, with swans and peacocks imported from Masnia, then what was he spending the money on? And if he wasn't spending it, then back to my first question: where is it?"

Prentice watched as Amelia absorbed his words. He was certain that, with time to think and time to reflect, the duchess would have come to these questions on her own. But between her husband's death, the foreign invasion, and now Duggan's rebellion, she was running just to stand still. She had not had time to reflect.

"Duggan's mercenaries?" she said, and Prentice knew she was connecting the pieces together. "He's only a knight and a castellan. How did he plan to pay a force of mercenaries out of his own purse? Unless it wasn't out of his purse. Is he paying with my husband's money? With my money?"

Prentice could see her fury rising. "Who collects the taxes?" he asked.

"I always assumed it was handled by Bastian Fern, my seneschal."

"Not by himself, he wouldn't."

"No, he wouldn't," Amelia agreed. "He'd need guards, and they'd have to be provided from household men. Men under the command of…"

"Possibly the castellan, or the knight captain. Either might have the duty," Prentice said.

The duchess fell silent and looked down at the papers on the table again, this time with a more thoughtful eye. She began to sort them into piles, pushing some sheets aside to find specific documents.

"But how would Sir Duggan do it?" she said. "The seneschal would have to know, wouldn't he?"

"Perhaps. What measure of man is the seneschal?"

"Bastian?" Amelia paused to think. "Quiet. Advanced of years. No wife that I know of. I've always had the feeling he took vows at some time, that he was a monk or lay brother to one of the church orders. He's the sort of man who always seemed happy with his lot in life, content to serve."

Prentice was suddenly reminded of Turley's insistence that Graycen, the duchess's chief steward, was stealing, and his comment that every house has rats.

"The bigger the house, the bigger the rats," he mused.

"What was that?"

"Something Turley said."

Amelia nodded with a kindly smile. "He's a good man, Turley. I see him working well as steward. He seems very diligent, never shirks."

"You'd never catch him shirking if he was," Prentice assured her. She cocked an eyebrow. "He's too canny for that. But he's your man, that you can believe." He stepped back from the table. "In fact, Your Grace, with your permission, I'll take him with me if you don't mind."

"Take him where?"

"Have you seen your seneschal since we marched for Fallenhill?"

The duchess pursed her lips in thought. "Well, no. I suppose I always assumed he was in the castle."

"But he doesn't live in the castle?"

"He has a house in town. In Northside, I think."

Northside was the wealthiest district of Dweltford, so it made sense the duchy's financial master would live there.

"You need him found," Prentice said. "All these days after the town's recaptured and he hasn't been seen? That's too suspicious to ignore."

The duchess nodded, but there was a guarded expression in her eyes. "Suspicions or not, Prentice," she warned, "Bastian Fern has served the duchy a long time, and he must be treated with the proper respect. I'll not have him beaten for suspicions. Mark me on this."

"Understood, Your Grace."

"Then you have my leave to go. Find my seneschal. And find my money."

Prentice bowed and left.

Out the front of the conclave house, Sir Gant was waiting for him. The knight wore a homespun tunic and breeks under his faded gray surcoat, with simple leather shoes. If not for the sword belt buckled at his waist with the longsword hanging at his side, there would be no way to measure or know his status. For himself, Prentice had on a short brown doublet that was new, with dark breeks of heavy cotton and a pair of fine leather boots. After years of being barefoot with manacles on his ankles, the boots had been his highest priority. For his courage in battle, the prince's knight commander had awarded him a purse full of silver, and Prentice had spent over half of it just on the boots.

A short distance past Sir Gant, Cutter crouched and leaned against a wall, still dressed in a dirty shirt and ragged trews with no shoes, but hidden somewhere in the ragged folds was the dirk that Prentice had given him. Prentice couldn't see it, but he knew it was there. The other former convicts had melted into the Dweltford populace, seeking their own way in the world, but Cutter refused to go, seemingly disappointed to have no more enemies to fight for the moment.

"Have you seen Turley about?" Prentice asked Sir Gant.

"The steward? I saw him earlier, but I don't know where he is now."

"They're all out back of the Duke's Rest," said Cutter.

The Duke's Rest inn was one street south of the conclave house. The entire duchess's household had taken up residence there, including her lady's maids and their overseer, Matron Bettina. The matron had no time for Prentice or Turley, having met them both as mere convicts.

Cutter insisted on showing the way to the rear yard of the Duke's Rest, even though all three of them knew the way. Behind the inn they found the stewards heaving ironbound water barrels and heavy grain sacks about the yard. Turley was among them, running the show but carrying his fair share of the weight. He and all the other stewards were stripped to the waist and drenched in sweat.

"Busy, I see," Prentice said to him.

"Oh, aye. I told Graycen that we should have the grain sacks off the ground, or the mud and the wet would rot them out before winter's even half over." Turley dropped a water barrel next to two more to form a row, and then stepped back to let others lay planks across the top, making a shelf. "So, he told me to get them up off the ground."

"And you thought this was the best way to do it?"

"Oh, no, this was his idea. He made sure we filled the barrels at the well first." A general grumble among the stewards made it clear what they thought of that order.

"Seems a little petty." Sir Gant smiled as he twisted one end of his mustache.

"I'd have told him to stick his sacks up his bum," said Cutter.

Turley hefted another sack onto the makeshift shelf. "Sure you would, sure you would."

"I would." Cutter's jutting chin challenged Turley, but the big man ignored it.

"No one doubts your word, lad," said Sir Gant. "Or your courage. But as you get older, you'll learn that not every battle that can be won is worth the fight." He tousled the youth's raggedly clipped fair hair.

Cutter shrugged him off, glaring now at both of them, but Gant and Turley only chuckled. "I'm older than you think," he said in a sullen voice.

"We've got duchess work," Prentice told Turley.

His friend looked around him. "My big mouth brought this woe down on us. Can't just walk off and leave everyone else to it."

"Fair enough. We'll wait for you out front."

"You could always help, if you wanted."

"Wasn't my big mouth."

Prentice led Sir Gant and Cutter to the front of the inn, where the three sat on a low bench and watched the townsfolk passing on their daily business. Children played and ran in the streets while mothers cooked meals and hung their washing, fetched water, and swept their houses. Many of the men were still bound to the army, serving to keep up the siege of the castle, but there were many older men and craftsmen on the street, distinguished by their journeyman pins, the brass signets that they wore on their breast, declaring them members of one of the trade guilds. King Chrostmer and the nobility ruled the Grand Kingdom, east to west. "From the ocean to the Azure Mountains" was the old saying, though now it went west beyond the mountains to the river Dwelt and the grasslands beyond, as vast and endless as the eastern ocean. But as truly as the nobility ruled, it was the guilds that ran every town, east or west, north and south, on both sides of the mountains. Dweltford was no different. There would be no guildsmen in the army. They were exempt.

"Good to have a trade," muttered Sir Gant.

Prentice looked at him. "I was thinking something similar."

"Good if they'll let you," Cutter said, then spat.

"Someone keep you out, did they?"

"Been kept out of things since I was born."

"Is that why you fought with us?" Sir Gant asked. "Because you didn't want to be left out?"

"You could've left me out of the sewers," Cutter answered, and Prentice and Gant both chuckled.

"No, I don't think any of us want to do that again."

They were quiet together, each with their thoughts, until Cutter shrugged and said, "I ain't afraid of a fight. Never have been."

"That's for sure," said Prentice.

"What do you mean by that?"

Prentice shook his head, but he smiled. Everything was a provocation to this youth, a call to arms or a challenge to prove himself. Cutter was a well-balanced individual—there was a chip on each shoulder.

"I mean that the way you threw yourself at that knight, I thought you were going to break your neck."

Cutter gestured to Sir Gant. "He said to go for the face. How else was I going to do that?"

"He's got a point," said Sir Gant.

Cutter scowled and looked away. Gant shrugged, leaning his head back on the wall behind him and closing his eyes. Prentice looked from him to Cutter. The youth noticed Prentice's attention and turned away like a sulking child. Prentice stood and walked around Gant to squat beside Cutter. He put his hand on the youth's shoulder, and he could feel the bones under the skin. Damn but Cutter was thin, and long limbed. Being on a convict chain was a hungry life, but if Cutter didn't find a way to make an honest living soon, it'd be filching or fighting just to eat and then back on a chain again soon enough. Prentice tried to turn Cutter to face him, but the youth just shrugged him off.

"Don't sulk, lad," Prentice said, but gently. "A grown man doesn't sulk, and you aren't that far from grown."

Cutter turned around and looked Prentice in the face. They stared straight in each other's eyes, and Prentice was shocked as he realized what he was seeing. He took in all of Cutter's features at once—the narrow, bare face; the high cheekbones with their judicial scar; the hazel eyes that were sad, sullen, and defiant all at once; and the hair, savagely short, as if he cut it himself.

"How old are you?" he asked in a quiet voice.

Cutter's angry stare turned suddenly to terror. He was about to say something, but at that moment, Turley rounded the corner of the inn and stretched his arms with a loud groan. The interruption seemed too much for Cutter, and the youth jumped up and bolted down the street in the opposite direction.

"He was in a hurry," said Turley. "Something he ate?"

"I don't know." Prentice watched Cutter run until he lost sight in the crowd. If his suspicions about Cutter turned out to be true, then the sudden flight would make sense, but as it was, Prentice had no time to think about that now. He tapped Sir Gant on the knee and stood up. "We're going to Northside."

"Ooh, how la-di-da," said Turley. "Good thing I'm wearing my best shirt." His shirt was soaked with sweat and clinging to him.

Sir Gant rolled his eyes, and the three set off.

CHAPTER 7

As they made their way through town, Prentice informed them of the duchess's suspicions about her seneschal and the province's finances.

"You mean she's richer than she knows?" said Turley. "Sounds like a pleasant problem to have."

"You think?" Sir Gant countered. "Makes it harder to know when you're being robbed."

Turley chewed that over for a while. "Well, we can't have that," he declared at last.

"Glad you see it that way," said Prentice.

Once they had passed Within Walls and crossed Castle Road, they moved into streets where the close houses started to become interspersed with bigger manors, where fenced and walled areas encircled larger houses and finely tended gardens, separated from the street and the commonality of the town. At one corner, they met an aging widow sitting in the street and working at an ancient-looking butter churn. She turned out the contents and patted it to shape with a pair of wooden butter hands, as grooved and old as the skin of the woman who wielded them. They asked her directions to the seneschal's house, but it took some time to pick the meaning from her gummy, phlegmy speech.

"Thanks to you, grandma," Prentice said, and he pressed copper coins into her surprisingly soft hands. As he did so, she chuckled and gave him a quick kiss on the cheek. The three men all laughed as they walked off.

"She liked you," said Sir Gant.

"She has good taste," Prentice retorted, but Turley wasn't having it.

"You were the one that paid," he muttered.

"Enough."

They found the house of Bastian Fern, ducal seneschal, at the end of a long row of rich houses with stone footings. It was not as fine as the other buildings, being only wood and plaster, but it was two stories high, with glass windows and fenced yards in front and back. The three men stood at the front gate, looking the house over.

"Not the richest house on the street, but nothing to be ashamed of," Turley observed.

"Shame is a relative thing," countered Sir Gant.

Turley's grunt in reply made it clear he didn't understand the hedge knight's point. "Is anyone home, d'you think?"

Before anyone could answer the question, there was a heavy thud from inside the house, followed by a muffled cry of pain.

"Someone's in there," Prentice said. "I think we should take a closer look."

He opened the fence gate quietly and stalked to the front door. The other two came up behind him while he listened intently, before trying the latch. It was not locked, and the bolt moved smoothly. With a finger to his lips, Prentice led them inside.

The door opened onto a hallway that ran back through the house, with a staircase to the left and a front room through a door on the right. A second doorway came off the hall farther down, and then the passage ended in a third. The door at the end of the hallway was open, and it looked as though there was a kitchen back there. From above them came the sound of feet shuffling and voices cursing.

Prentice stole up the stairs just enough to look over the lip of the floor above, leaving the other two in the hall. The chamber above seemed to run the length of the house, with a table and a chair, a pair of long shelves, and at least one bed. That was all Prentice could see from where he was, because every piece of furniture was overturned, and three men were stalking among the wreckage. Two carried long daggers, with which they poked at the furnishings, apparently searching for something but with little enthusiasm. The third man sat on the upturned bed, reading from sheafs of parchment and paper that he moved back and forth between, searching the documents with the same impatience his companions had in ransacking the rest of the room. But that was where any similarity to his companions ended. Where they were lean and slender, he was a mountain of muscle. They were like ferrets; he was a bull. His face had the flattened, lumpy texture of a pugilist at the end of his career—too many heavy blows, too many broken noses. But on that battered nose sat a set of spectacles obviously built for the man. As Prentice watched, this bull threw away the papers he was holding.

"These aren't it either," he declared.

"Maybe he didn't write it down."

"He wrote everything down!"

"Ain't that the truth."

One of the ferrets lifted a pile of papers and let them cascade back to the floor.

"Damn you," said the bull. "I need to go through those."

"Well, they ain't in any worse mess than they already was."

"I should never have let you two search by yourselves."

The other ferret, a man with lank, greasy tresses that clung to the side of his head, took exception to the criticism. "You said they'd be hidden, so we searched for what was hidden. You said he might have a strongbox, so we looked for a strongbox. Maybe you should've let us question him."

The bull grunted in disdain.

"We can't have done a worse job than breaking his neck."

"Don't you blame the boss for that," said the first man, distinguishable in Prentice's eyes by a beak-like nose. "Old geezer had a neck like a bird's. Boss only slapped him once or twice. Wasn't even a good, solid hit."

"Well, he's probably starting to stink back there. We can't keep coming here. Someone's going to find him or figure us as wrong'uns, and then we'll be stuffed."

The boss sighed and took his spectacles from his nose. "I hate to say it, but you're right. Grab every bit of paper or parchment you can find—every book, tome, and scroll. We'll take them with us."

Prentice withdrew quickly back down the stairs. He planned to follow the men when they left and see where they went. From what he'd heard, Bastian Fern was dead, and the huge man upstairs had killed him, but Prentice wanted to know why and to find out what they were searching for, if he could. He gestured for Turley and Sir Gant to follow him down to the kitchen to hide there. They were not halfway down the hall when a man appeared in the kitchen doorway. He had the same savage look as the men upstairs, made worse by a long burn scar and half an ear missing on one side of his head.

"Oy, what are you about?" he shouted as he pulled a fighting dirk from his waist.

Prentice didn't hesitate, lifting his boot and planting a charging kick in the man's chest. The man staggered backward, but still had enough in him to swipe with the blade. Prentice jumped backward, slamming up against Turley. From upstairs there was a sound of panicked footsteps.

"Don't let them go," Prentice commanded over his shoulder, and he caught a glimpse as one of the ferrets was already whipping down the stairs and out the open door. Then he had to duck and dodge again to avoid the swings of the dirk. He felt Turley's bulk move from behind him and heard the scrape of Sir Gant's longsword leaving its scabbard. The burnt-headed man swung with wild abandon, and he ducked back again. Prentice had the man's measure when the blade came back for a reverse stroke, and instead of dodging, Prentice stepped in on the blade arm and checked it. He used his weight to drive the point of the blade into the plastered wall, where it stuck for a moment. Holding the man's arm locked, Prentice pushed hard, hoping to break his elbow. Instead, it was the blade that broke, the cheap metal snapping with a crack. Prentice lost his grip on the man's blade arm, and the thug scrambled back with a panicked look on his face. He threw the useless hilt of his broken blade at Prentice and then bolted out through the kitchen. Prentice followed as far as the kitchen door, watching the thug's retreating figure sprint down an alley and turn a near corner. He paused to get his breath and then went back into the house.

From the kitchen end of the hallway, he could see one of the ferrets lying dead in the front entrance. The long slash down his back made it clear that Sir Gant's blade had won the race for the door. There was no sign of Gant or Turley, and Prentice assumed they'd run off after the others. He passed the stairs and looked at the dead man.

Was there any way to identify the corpse?

A creak on the stairs made him realize that not all the thieves had fled yet. An avalanche of muscle fell on him as the thugs' bull-like boss charged down the stairs, flinging Prentice back against the opposite wall, next to the doorway to the front room. Prentice tried to get his feet back under him but was stopped by a low left punch that crashed into his belly. It was followed by a right hook that swiped the side of his face and threatened to dislocate his jaw. The boss might have looked like a bull, but he fought with the savagery of a devil.

Prentice covered up as best he could and took a series of blows on his arms as he tried to get his legs back underneath him. The thugs' leader gave him no breathing space, firing short, heavy jabs at any vulnerable point. A sharp strike to Prentice's kidney finally took the wind out of him as he managed to push back through the doorway into the front room. He staggered backward, gasping for air and playing for distance, but there was too little distance to gain. The massive thug paused at the doorway while Prentice leaned against a dining table in the middle of the room. He sucked his breath in painful, wheezing gasps and tried to clear his vision.

The boss smiled. "You picked the wrong house to thieve from."

"I was going... to say... same... to you," Prentice managed to get out before the agony of speaking made him suck in another breath.

"Do you know who I am, you little turd?"

Prentice shook his head and winced at the pain of the motion.

"I'm going to beat you to death with my bare hands," said the bull, holding both his monstrous fists in a boxer's guard. "Then I'm going to hunt your mates down, flay 'em, and tan their skins in my own vats. I'll wear them like doeskin, you hear me?"

Prentice didn't respond, just took up his own position as best as he could while his head swam with pain and he waited for the coming assault. The bull started to advance, and Prentice threw a right punch. It was weaker than it should have been, but at least it landed on the bull's leering mouth.

The advancing thug paused to lick his split lip. "Oh, now I'm going to take my time."

That suited Prentice fine. The longer he took, the more chance that Turley or Sir Gant would get back and kill the bastard. Prentice threw a combination, but the bull barely noticed, covering with good form. He threw another and got caught. He groaned in pain as the thug leader trapped his arm and punched him in the head again. Prentice tried to step back, but his foot gave out from under him. He slipped against the table and fell to one knee. He wanted to protect himself from the next blow he knew was coming, but his arms wouldn't respond. The massive thug leader towered over him, and all Prentice could do was wait for the impact.

It didn't come.

Instead, he heard an angry shout, and the thug stumbled for a moment. He turned around to look behind him, and as he did, Prentice could see Cutter, dagger in hand, challenging the bull. The thug said something Prentice couldn't hear, but its tone was disrespectful, and Cutter clearly didn't like it. The blade began to flash in a swift series of strikes. These weren't the wild cuts of an angry boy. They were fast and precise, and a detached part of Prentice's mind observed that whatever else there was to Cutter, the skill was impressive.

The bull seemed surprised by Cutter's assault as well, and he was forced back, covering his face with his arms. Cutter's dirk made dozens of cuts, but there was surprisingly little blood. Nevertheless, the pressure of the assault seemed to be more than the thug wanted to deal with. Letting out an angry bellow, he pushed Cutter aside, scattering the youth like a leaf on the breeze and fled the house out the front door. Prentice watched him go and then felt himself slumping all the way to the floor. His vision was darkening as Cutter's worried face rushed toward him.

"Hells, but he's done you good."

"He caught me by surprise," Prentice whispered, and his lips felt wet. "I got my licks in."

"Oh, sure you did."

CHAPTER 8

Duchess Amelia looked up from the papers to regard the young page who stood before her with cap in hand. The boy was barely ten, and he gasped and huffed as he tried to catch his breath and speak his message at the same time. She raised a long finger.

"Stop, child. Get your wind back." She waved to a steward who stood nearby. "Bring him a cup. Water."

The steward ran to fetch a cup of water and offered it to the page, who gulped it down. When the cup was drained, the boy handed it back to the steward and managed to take a deep, calming breath. With all that done, he took his cap in both hands, looking truly earnest.

"I have a message, Your Duchess," he said.

"Your Grace," the steward corrected in a mutter, but Duchess Amelia heard him clearly enough.

The boy nodded, accepting the correction and then, as if the one admonition reminded him of other mistakes, he dropped straight to one knee and bowed his head. "Sorry, Your Grace, ma'am."

"What's your message?" she asked.

"The prince and the knight captain."

"Knight Captain Liam?"

"Yes, ma'am, Your Grace."

"'Your Grace' will do." Amelia nodded and smiled encouragement. "What about Baronet Liam?" Using Liam's new title still galled her a little, and she realized that she was frowning as she did it.

"He's come and brought the prince, Your Grace."

The boy's words made no sense to Amelia. Mercad, the Prince of Rhales, had died on the field at the Brook, and the next day his knight commander and the main of the army's knights had begun the cortege procession back over the mountains so he could be buried in state. Baronet Liam had been incensed when she had not immediately released him to join them. How could Liam have brought the body back? That was impossible.

"I think you're missing the right of it, lad," she said gently. "Think again. What were you sent to say?"

"That the prince and the knight captain are both come, at the head of an army. That's the truth. I've run an hour down the road, just to get here ahead of them."

"The prince is dead, son—"

"Not him. Daven Marcus, Your Grace. The new Prince of the West. The Prince of Rhales. Glorious, he is. His armor shines like silver and gold, and his horse is a powerful charger. And Baronet Liam is at his side, and an army of knights in columns that go back on the road for leagues."

Duchess Amelia's mind rebelled at what the boy was saying, it seemed too fantastic to be believed. Daven Marcus was Mercad's nephew and heir, but last she had heard, the young prince was chasing Vec bandits in the south—and maidenheads as well, according to rumor. His taste for virginal bed companions was a reputation both well-deserved and cultivated for years, if the gossip of court ladies in Rhales was to be believed. How could he have traveled up from the south and crossed the mountains, then been named crown prince all in the short time since Mercad had died?

It would be impossible, wouldn't it?

"You have seen the prince?" she asked the page. The boy nodded. "And Baronet Liam and the army you speak of?"

"All of it, my word to God." The boy touched his chest over his heart and raised his hand.

"And where were they when you saw them?"

"Where the road turns by the river."

That was less than a league from Dweltford. Even if the boy had run flat-out the whole way, he wouldn't be more than half an hour ahead of the prince. Amelia dismissed the page and sent the steward to fetch Graycen, as well as every messenger he could find, her lady's maids, and Matron Bettina. As messengers arrived, she sent them out with swift orders. Graycen arrived from the Duke's Rest and looked like he was about to faint when she told him the crown prince would soon arrive. He was a short, dumpy man with a bowl haircut, who reminded her of a carnival dwarf, though she had no time for comic thoughts now. He stood stammering for a moment, and Amelia was forced to repeat her instructions twice before he finally nodded and left, tugging his forelock. By the time her maids arrived, Amelia had already left the conclave house and was heading to the town gate.

"Your Grace, please wait," Bettina called as she led her pair of lady's maids, who carried brushes, ribbons, jewelry boxes, and makeup.

Amelia waved at them to catch up but did not slow down. Two knights were marching by her side, and others were already approaching through the streets. By the time she had crossed the Market Within Walls, she was surrounded by a small crowd of retainers, knights, and servants, all trying to recover their dignity and coalesce into a respectable entourage for a duchess of the realm. Amelia strode down Castle Road as quickly as decorum allowed, and when she reached the gatehouse, she rushed up the stairs and came out on the wall. She looked south to the road and east over the meadows, and the sight that met her brought her up short.

A column was approaching along that road, but "column" was too mundane a word for it. At its head rode four or five men who flashed silver and gold in the sunlight; plainly, they were knights in highly polished armor, and their mounts were caparisoned in the brightest colors. Then came another rank, riding seven or eight abreast and equally brilliant. Behind them rode another rank, and beyond them another—and on and on until there was no point in counting. After the riders came folk on foot, and while the riders maintained their column, the crowd that followed spilled out from the road to occupy the meadows. They led wagons and mules, and they carried sacks and packs upon their shoulders.

"There must be five thousand, at least," the duchess whispered.

Bettina huffed her way out of the gatehouse onto the battlements. "Your Grace, Amelia, please," she managed to gasp as she struggled to regain her breath. She was not a woman built for rushing, but even out of breath she was making every effort to improve Amelia's appearance. With a spray of colored ribbons in one hand and a brush and hair pins in the other, she began to fuss and fawn.

Amelia shied from the distraction. "What are you doing?" she demanded.

"Your Grace is to receive royalty. You must be presentable."

Amelia grabbed her matron by the wrists and shook her gently. "For God's sake, Bettina, look!" With a sweep of her arm, she indicated the growing army that was marching up to their walls. "I do not have time for ribbons."

Bettina looked over the crenulations, and she uttered a small squeak. She turned back to her duchess and bobbed a little curtsy. "Please, Your Grace," she murmured. "A necklace and a ring."

Amelia sighed and nodded her permission. It occurred to her to wonder exactly what ornaments her matron had in mind. Almost all her jewelry had been stolen when her barge had been ambushed earlier in the summer. It was a sad memory, not for the loss of the jewelry but for the deaths of her companions and retainers. The memory was not as bitter as it had once been, softened even in the short time by events since, but that only caused her to marvel inwardly. Had everything really only happened in this last summer? Was it still just a year since she had married and become the Duchess of the Western Reach?

It seemed inconceivable.

The necklace Bettina chose was a simple one, though of fine craftsmanship, gold without gemstones. It sat well around Amelia's neck. The ring was similar, though it had a sapphire stone. It was a gift from her late husband; he had given it to her on their wedding night, and she was glad it had not been stolen. She took another moment to look out on the advancing army and wished she had had time to have her husband's signet ring resized for her own finger. She would have liked the reassurance of the reminder of her station.

A sudden thought burst in her mind.

"Bettina, send and have Meadow Dancer brought to me."

"Your horse?"

"Yes."

"Why?" Bettina asked.

Amelia moved back into the tower, heading for ground level. "Because I cannot receive the Prince of Rhales from the walls of my town, and I will not do it on foot."

Bettina nodded. She undoubtedly understood the importance of the instruction and hurried to obey.

"And somebody find me Prentice Ash!" Amelia commanded.

Even as she was rushing to reach her horse, she heard a blast of trumpets. The prince was at the gate. She realized she'd forgotten to send instructions to the houseguards, and she hoped they knew to let him in. She felt a wash of relief when she heard the sound of horses' hoofs striking the flagstones under the gatehouse, which meant they hadn't been held up by a foolish guard. Then a fresh panic struck her. That meant the prince was inside the town. She lifted her skirts and ran as best she could back to Within Walls.

The market was buzzing like a swarm of bees, with townsfolk of all stations rushing about in the excitement of the prince's arrival. Flower sellers and drapers suddenly did a riotous trade as women young and old sought some way to quickly put on a festive appearance, winding ribbons and dried blooms through their hair. Other merchants rushed to put away merchandise, fearful that the sudden chaos might give an opportunity for thieves to strike. Laborers and craftsmen stopped work and were pushing toward Castle Road to see the prince and his entourage approach. They pressed so close that Amelia had to stop running, and her guards had to shove and manhandle the crowd to let her through.

At least they'll slow the prince as well, she thought. She heard a cheer behind her and smiled to know that her people were welcoming him. Then she broke free of the crowd. Graycen stood with Meadow Dancer, holding the gelding by the bridle.

"I gave you instructions," she told him, surprised that he was wasting time with so menial a task.

"I've passed the word and everything is in order, Your Grace," he responded smarmily. "And, begging your pardon, but with a prince arriving, I couldn't trust this duty to some filthy stable boy."

Amelia noticed that he had made some effort to comb his hair, and there was a dried pink rose tucked into his jerkin. She put her foot in the stirrup and mounted up, thinking that, despite his unctuous manner, she could not really fault the man for wanting to be present for the prince's arrival.

As she settled herself to her saddle, she looked over the crowd. The prince's heralds were now doing for him what her guards had done for her, shoving the crowd aside and making a path into the center of the market. Amelia breathed a sigh of relief. She was on her horse, and though her castle was still in the hands of a usurper, her people had at least welcomed their prince in a fitting style. She looked about quickly for Prentice Ash, but he was nowhere to be seen. She thought to ask for him again but decided there wasn't time.

I have faced princes before. I've done it before alone, I can do it again.

An advisor was useful, but not always necessary.

She settled her face into what she hoped was a regal, welcoming expression and waited as the prince and his nearest men rode toward her. Daven Marcus was a gorgeous figure, wearing a suit of steel so polished that it reflected, like a mirror, all the bright colors of his panoply and companions. His horse was a perfect white charger, with a crimson caparison embroidered with gold thread. The prince was not wearing his helmet, but it sat on his saddle pommel as he rode. It was a bascinet with no plume, but it had a gold diadem set with diamonds on the brow. The prince's own head was bare, with a glorious cascade of soft brown curls; his face was high cheeked and his nose straight. Prince Daven Marcus was the picture of youthful vigor and glory.

He spurred his horse directly toward Amelia. The crowd hushed, watching expectantly. She waited a moment to see if one of his heralds would announce him by name and title, but when they did not, she took the lead to greet him directly. As a peer of the realm, even if only by marriage, protocol allowed her the familiarity.

"Greetings, and the warmest welcome of the Western Reach, my lord prince," she said.

The prince looked at her with an almost disdainful expression, as if he had only just noticed her and didn't like what he saw. He glanced away and cast his eyes over the crowd and the town.

"You waited this long to send greetings," he said loudly. His voice was smooth, but not especially deep. "We expected at least some word along the road."

"Please forgive me, Your Highness," Amelia responded. "We only received word of your coming this very hour."

The prince did not acknowledge Amelia's apology, but looked over his shoulder at his knights waiting nearby on their own horses. "It is as you say, Baron Liam. The province is in complete disarray."

One of the knights walked his mount forward, and Amelia was surprised to recognize him as her knight captain, Liam. He wasn't wearing his usual armor or surcoat, but he had on a full plate suit, similar to the prince's. It was equally polished but didn't look like it fit as well. He carried his distinctive horned helmet as he approached, and placed it on his saddle in the same fashion as the prince. The high antlers looked awkward, seeming to almost poke into his breastplate and face. He ignored them, though he did have a troubled expression. It matched Amelia's own feelings in a way. She was so surprised by his presence in the highest ranks of the prince's entourage, and by his rich new panoply, that it took a moment for the prince's words to fully sink in.

What had Liam been telling the prince about the Reach? That it was in disarray? What did that mean? As she thought about it, she was sure that Liam had been reporting about her to Daven Marcus, possibly undermining her even before she met the new Prince of Rhales. Then she had an even more worrying thought. Had the prince just called Liam a baron?

Daven Marcus continued before she could sort her thoughts into order. "Still, you told us the young duchess was cowering in a tent in a muddy field. Yet here she is, mistress in her own capital."

"I am as surprised as you, Highness," said Liam, and Amelia perceived the reason for his unhappy expression. If he had told the prince that she would still be camped with her army, waiting for winter to pass before attacking the town, then her having recaptured Dweltford would make him look quite foolish.

Finally, Daven Marcus deigned to look at Amelia again, and she wondered if she were covered in the same filth Prentice and his men had been at the end of their journey through the sewers. The prince's lip curled in a slight sneer as he examined her. Amelia was used to the contempt of those born and bred to the nobility, and she was careful to school her expression, to hide her anger.

"Duchess," he said at last. "Perhaps you could show us the way to the castle, and then I will receive your greeting there."

You will receive my greeting? As if I am visiting you in your castle? She was almost pleased when she had to explain her current position.

"I fear the castle is yet in the hands of a rebel, Your Highness," she said. "So, I must apologize that I am unable to offer you the hospitality of my home just yet. I do hope that soon—"

The prince raised a hand and cut her off. "It was too much to imagine a woman had accomplished the task in full. Especially a woman such as you. We will see the castle nonetheless. Doubtless, the proper application of rank will make the difference."

The prince geed his mount to walk past the duchess, who watched him and fumed within. How could this be the charming royal of courtly rumor, a seducer of maids? There was self-possession and authority in the prince, but not one ounce of charm. Amelia was tempted to let him find his own way, to see if he could pick the correct road out of the market to the castle by himself, but humiliating the crown prince of the kingdom would gain her nothing, and he could just as easily ask Liam for directions.

"I will gladly escort you, Highness," she said, wheeling Meadow Dancer in place and quickly catching up to ride beside him.

Her retainers and the crowd parted for them both, while behind, Liam and the others of the prince's closest retinue were forced to narrow their ranks to squeeze along the road.

As the short journey up Castle Road passed, Amelia made a number of polite attempts to meet the prince's eye, to smile and make herself seem amenable. Daven Marcus showed no interest in talking to her, however, and she was relieved when they approached the last straight length of street before the lake and the bridge. The final paces of the road were taken up with the business of siege. The folk who lived in the houses on either side of the road had been evicted, and archers were now stationed in their windows. The beginnings of the bridge, up to the point of the draw, were lined with pavises—heavy wooden shields on stands, large enough for an archer or crossbowman to hide behind.

"As you can see, Highness, we are preparing to fully siege the castle," Amelia began to explain. She was shocked when the prince began to ride out onto the bridge itself. "Your Highness, it's very dangerous."

Daven Marcus ignored her and stopped his horse a few mere paces from the end of the bridge. His eyes ranged over the castle, its gate, and its walls, as if he were a sightseer studying a curious piece of countryside. The moment stretched. What was he doing?

Then, quite suddenly, he raised his hand over his head. "Heralds!" he called.

From behind her, two of the prince's trumpeters pushed their horses forward. They moved out onto the bridge, their fine mounts as beautifully arrayed as the prince's. They placed their polished brass trumpets to their lips and, in perfect unison, blew a complex fanfare. The blasts echoed off the sandstone walls of the castle, startling birds, and when the clarion died, it seemed as if an unnatural calm had settled over the whole of the town, the castle, and the lake. The prince simply sat his horse and waited.

At last the silence was broken. A voice called from the castle walls, one that seemed all too mundane for the epic moment created by the trumpets' announcement. "What do you want?"

One of the heralds answered in a powerful voice. "Daven Marcus, Crown Prince of the Grand Kingdom, Prince of Rhales, and Prince of the West, has come on a crusade to rid the Western Reach of the threat of invasion from the Vec usurpers. Open your gate that he may receive you."

There was a pause before the voice on the walls responded, "I'll fetch Sir Duggan."

While they waited, Amelia wondered at the herald's words. What threat of invasion from the Vec? And who still called them usurpers? The Vec lands had been subjects of the Grand Kingdom once, but that had been centuries ago. At every turn, Prince Daven Marcus added to her confusion. She was still musing over all these things when Sir Duggan appeared at the crenulations above the gate.

"Who are you, claiming to be a prince?" he shouted down. "I am no feeble mind to be tricked by some—"

"Oh, do shut up, Duggan," the prince shouted. "Order the damned gate opened! I'm growing old on your doorstep."

Sir Duggan leaned down and squinted. "Daven Marcus?" His voice was suddenly tremulous, a weakened mixture of surprise and fear. "How can you be here?"

"I am here to put an end to the foolishness of this last summer. Foolishness that took my uncle's life and puts the full weight of the west upon my shoulders."

Sir Duggan gave orders to a mercenary at his side, and the man disappeared from view.

If they shoot, Amelia thought, the prince will be the first one struck. She had no idea if his armor could withstand a hard-driven crossbow bolt; with his visor raised to speak, a good shot could take him in the face. Then she realized that she was exposed as well, within range. Wondering if she should be ready to turn her horse about and retreat, should Duggan's mercenaries begin shooting, she was astonished when she heard the draw chain ratchet being released and the bridge beginning to descend. Amelia feared that perhaps Sir Duggan had ordered a sally, a swift raid to capture Daven Marcus and use him as a hostage, but the prince waited calmly, fearlessly. The draw bridge fell into place with a heavy thud that vibrated the rest of the bridge, and the prince's horse shied a step from the impact, but he kept a firm rein.

In the gateway beyond, there was only a handful of guards and no one ready to rush out. There was no sally. Not waiting for any invitation, Prince Daven Marcus geed his mount forward and entered the castle. Amelia sat her horse, shocked that her castle was now open to her forces with no more effort than a direct instruction from this young man. From behind her, Liam moved up on her right and paused next to her.

"That's what true nobility looks like, slattern's brood," he hissed at her, his voice so low that she was sure no one else heard him. "Breeding is in the blood; it cannot be bought."

Before she could respond, he twitched his heels and his horse obediently broke into a trot. He quickly caught up to the prince, who was already in the upper bailey. More horses began to cross the bridge, passing her by as they did so. One stopped near her again, in the space Baron Liam had vacated.

"What shall we do, Your Grace?" asked a voice.

Amelia was lost in thought. "He called my mother a..." she whispered in disbelief.

"Pardon, Your Grace?"

She turned and saw one of her knights, a thin-haired, earnest man named Sir Babbek, watching her. "What?" was all she could think to say.

"Shall we take the castle now?" Sir Babbek asked. "The gate is open, and it looks as if the mercenaries inside have no orders to hold it against us."

"The prince has already retaken the castle," she replied, and for some reason the words felt bitter on her tongue.

Sir Babbek sat patiently, awaiting her orders. For a long moment she wondered why he bothered. How could he not see that the prince had made her look a fool? What she could not accomplish with all her servants and knights, with battle in the streets and loyal folk slain, Daven Marcus had achieved with a single command. Then, in the midst of her embarrassment, Amelia remembered her husband—how she had loved him, and he had loved her. Duke Marne was not yet dead a year. She would not dishonor his memory; she would not let them dismiss her as a commoner. She would not let them say that he married beneath himself. Anger bloomed in the fertile soil of Baron Liam's insult and the prince's unveiled contempt.

"Send word to our knights," she instructed Sir Babbek, her voice taking on a steely edge. "Every man-at-arms will enter the castle immediately. Mercenaries will be disarmed and put in chains, ready to be exiled. And send to my stewards and maids. I want my household staff back inside the castle's walls within the hour. The Prince of the West has come to our home. We must prepare a welcome for him."

Sir Babbek accepted the orders and moved off, pointing to every Reacherman he passed and ordering them into the castle. Her men rushed across bridge, and Amelia noticed that they were crowded in with the rest of the prince's column, knight after knight—from all corners of the Grand Kingdom, it seemed. It would be impossible for all of them to be stabled in the castle. Many would only have to turn around and come back out again, but at least their presence would make any of Duggan's mercenaries think twice about trying to resist.

The duchess geed Meadow Dancer forward and returned to her home, determined that no one should ever take it from her again. By the time she had entered the gate, she was already planning everything she would need to do, lists of orders that would have to be given. Her household must be put in order, and she needed to be ready to host the prince. Most of all, she had to plan for the future, and for that she would require Prentice Ash.

Where was he?

CHAPTER 9

Prentice awoke in a bed, with a soft pillow under his head and a blanket pulled over his shoulders. The experience was so foreign that he started with surprise, and then immediately regretted it. Pain burst in his head like a thunderclap, and as he lay back down, his ribs and belly clenched in agony, driving an involuntary groan from his lips.

"Aye, aye! You awake, then?"

He turned his head gingerly to see Cutter sitting cross-legged on a small stack of books next to the bed he was in.

"It would seem so," Prentice muttered, and felt himself dribble as he did so. He touched his mouth, and it, too, was tender.

"Got yourself a real thick lip," said Cutter, smiling at Prentice's discomfort.

Prentice laid his head back and, looking up, saw that he was under a thatched roof. "Where am I?"

"Upstairs in that seneschal bloke's house. In his bed, looks like, since there was only one in the house."

Prentice struggled to recall what had happened and then remembered the beating he had taken. "Did you drag me up here by yourself?"

"Me?" Cutter scoffed. "Nohow. Your knight mate came back, and he put you up here."

"Where is he now?"

"Gone to tell the duchess."

"How long have I been here?" Prentice asked.

"Hard to say." Cutter shrugged. "Sun's just going down now, so maybe a few hours. It'll be dark soon, but there's candles around, here and there, so I can kindle them up if you need."

"And what about the bull that trampled me?"

"The what?" Cutter's brows furrowed for a moment. "Oh, him. I saw him off. Big bugger, and faster than he looked, but he didn't want too many tastes of the edge of a fang." The poniard appeared and danced between fingers, spinning and catching the golden rays of dusk that were coming in through a window.

"He was wearing mail under that coat," Prentice said, closing his eyes. "Otherwise, you'd have had his kidney with those thrusts."

"Got his hand a good cut, though."

"That's true. You were too fast for him. Three Streets Vipers style, wasn't it? He was too used to fighting big brutes like himself."

"You know Vipers?" Cutter's answer had a surprised tone to it.

"Never learned it, but I know it when I see it," Prentice replied.

"I thought Turley said you were some kind of gentleman before they stuck you on a chain."

"Something like that."

Cutter eyed him suspiciously. "So how do you know Three Streets Vipers? That ain't no gentleman's art."

"Seven Rings Cross. I studied when I was a child."

"That's even less of a gentleman's art. Those Rings Cross masters are hard bastards."

Prentice drew in a long breath. The past was painful territory for him, but there was no way for Cutter to know that. "My father is a patrician, a man with a profession."

"Ooh, very fancy."

"I suppose. But fancy is a relative measure." Prentice paused, remembering Sir Gant's similar comment about shame. Perhaps he and the hedge knight had more in common than he realized.

"What's that mean?"

"It means that even though my father had more status than most men, he dreamed of getting more still. My mother gave him three sons and two daughters. He obtained advantageous marriages for his daughters, strengthening his alliances around the city."

"The girls are always married off," Cutter said.

"My eldest brother was taken to my father's vocation, and for his next son, he obtained an apprenticeship to a goldsmith. Advantage and security all around."

Prentice stopped speaking for a moment. He didn't like to think about his family and hadn't spoken to any of them since his trial. His brothers and sisters probably had children of their own by now, nieces and nephews he would never meet. Would they even be told of him?

"So, what happened to you?" Cutter pressed. "Are you the black sheep? You get some girl pregnant?"

"No."

Prentice turned to Cutter again. The blade was still being juggled between fingers on each hand. Cutter was a bundle of nervous energy, and Prentice supposed curiosity was unavoidable to someone like that.

"I was sent to Ashfield," he told the youth.

"What's that, then?"

"It's a school for knights."

"I thought you had to be born a knight."

"You do, except for knights of the Church," Prentice explained. "They come from reputable families, but they don't have to be noble-born."

"I've seen them. They're the ones with the crosses on their chests."

"Yes. Ashfield trains knights by birth and accepts devout sons of freemen to be knights of the Church. Devotion is proved by appropriately large donations."

Cutter nodded and smiled slyly. Only the Grand Kingdom's most naïve citizens knew nothing of the corruptions in the higher echelons of the Church.

"My father saved and planned from the day I was born," Prentice continued. "I was to go to Ashfield and study among the nobility, learn to be a knight, and then serve the Church with honor. After twenty or so years of service, with the right connections and the right money, I could press for a writ of ennoblement. My family name would be on the chivalric lists."

"I thought Church knights was eunuchs, like monks."

"You mean celibates."

"Same thing."

Prentice didn't bother arguing. "You're right, sort of. A Church knight can't have a legitimate heir, but he could pass his ennoblement to a near relative, say a nephew."

"So, you had to have a nephew?"

"That was my brothers' duty. They had to sire sons. In the meantime, I had to study every free hour that God sent, to be the best student Ashfield ever had. I could read and write before I was eight years old. I studied history, divinity, and law. And I was sent to a master of the Seven Rings Cross school of fighting. The average knight's son received his first training blade by the age of five. My father couldn't have me learn the longsword. Even a patrician's son has no right to that, so he sent me to the best common man's fighting school he could find. By the time I got to Ashfield I was the equal of anyone there. Except on horseback. I was rubbish with a lance."

Cutter sniggered, to which Prentice replied with a cold glare.

"Hey, I've seen you fight," Cutter protested defensively, but still with a smile. "You're as dangerous as any knight or street-fighting man I've ever seen. The thought of you bumbling on a horse is funny, is all. I like the idea you aren't good at everything."

"There are a number of things I'm not good at."

"Well, make sure you point it out next time one of them comes up, 'cause there are days when you might as well walk on water."

"I'm not so good at picking my enemies, for one."

"Is that what got you kicked out of knight's school?" Cutter asked.

"Not quite, but..." Prentice thought about his answer. "I suppose you could say that. I beat the wrong person in a duel, and his brother had me accused of heresy."

"Nothing's worse than a sore loser! And what kind of idiot thought he was going to beat you, anyway? I'll bet you were a real terror before you got old."

"I'm not that old," Prentice spat back reflexively.

"Take the compliment, would ya."

Prentice smiled at Cutter's admiration and decided it was time to press some questions for himself. One question in particular. "So, tell me, Cutter. How long have you been hiding?"

"Hiding? From what?"

"Hiding the fact that you're a woman?"

The poniard stopped dancing, and the hilt dropped neatly into a fighting grip in Cutter's hand. All the nervous energy was gone, replaced by a tautness. The sunlight was fading outside, but even in the shadows, Prentice could see the cold expression on Cutter's face.

"Who told you that?" Cutter hissed.

"No one told me anything."

"Oh, this notion just dropped on you out of the sky, did it?"

Prentice sighed impatiently. "What difference does it make? It's the truth, isn't it?"

There was a long moment of silence, and Prentice felt himself tensing under the blanket. He couldn't tell how Cutter was going to react now that her secret was out. If she decided to, there was a good chance she could cut his throat while he lay there. He tried to surreptitiously feel the strength in his limbs, but all he could feel were aches and pains. He wanted to look for exits. If she attacked, his best first move would be to throw the blanket over her like a net and then make a dash for the stairs. He was in no state to go up against her knife-fighting skills.

"When I was transported, I was the only girl on a chain for a long part of the way," Cutter said quietly.

Prentice listened attentively, on the lookout for any sign of violence.

"We got stopped at a village somewhere for the night, and this local rowdy and some of his mates got it in their heads they was going to have me. I can't say why; I mean, I was filthy from the road and my hair was a nest o' fleas, but they took me off the chain. When they did, one of the other convicts got all honorable on them, swore he'd tell a magistrate what they done to me if they took me away. Stupid fool."

Cutter paused. She sniffed, and in the failing light, Prentice thought he saw a tear forming in her eye, but it was gone as she wiped at her nose and face. She sniffed once more before continuing her story.

"I mean, he didn't have to try and be so holy. We was all convicts; he had nothing to prove. And it wasn't the first time someone had tried it on with me. I mean... what did he expect? We was on a chain, hungry, and tired. And there was four of them. They took us both, dragged us into the back of a barn somewhere and got on with it. They had turns at me, and in between they beat him bloody. I fought some too, of course, just 'cause I wasn't going to make it easy for them. I got my share of the beating, but him they weren't ever going to let leave alive.

"I don't know how long they went at us, but when they were done, they just left us there. I didn't move for a long time. I could hear him, nearby, gurgling as he breathed his last breaths. There was a loud catch in his chest, like he was trying to cough something up, and then he just sighed, one long, last breath. I knew he was dead then.

"When I felt strong enough, I scurried over and found what they'd done to him. There were lanterns all around outside; they were scared some convict might slip the chain. They had watchdogs and everything, 'cause we hadn't crossed the mountains yet. I could see the light through the cracks in the barn wall, on his face, and he was just a piece of meat. I mean, I look and I can't see his eyes anymore. They're just like dark pits full of blood. And his nose had just been pushed in, like his face had collapsed. I looked away. I'm not a coward. I've seen the bad things of life, but this was too much. When I did, I saw a set of shears—sheep shears—just hanging on a nail on the barn wall. First thing I thought was that I'd take them shears and find the bastards that did this to both of us and gut them. 'Course, it took no time to think how stupid an idea that was.

"I don't know how long I sat there before I figured my plan. I knew the overseers would come in the morning and find one dead convict and one living. Both of us were skinny, 'cause there's no such thing as a fat convict, so except for clothes and hair, what was there to pick between us? I knew my face must look a treat too. So, I took his trousers and gave him my skirt. I wrapped my shawl around his head. The shears I used to cut my hair off. It was hard, being sore from the raping..."

Cutter paused one more time. It was the first time she had used the word "rape," and it made everything worse. Prentice waited quietly; he knew better than to press at a moment like this.

"Anyway," Cutter said, shrugging the bitterness of her memories away. "In the morning, the overseers come looking for us. They find a boy in a corner of the barn crying and saying that they killed her, over and over. Give her the once-over and sure enough, the convict in the skirt is dead. They dragged the boy out into the light and left the body for the local magistrate. Killing a convict's not much of a crime, even if it's a girl raped to death, but they didn't want to be around if someone made a fuss. They marched us day and night after that, to get us over the mountains. And then I was a lad on the chain in the Reach, and no one thought another thing about it."

"And that's when you became Cutter," said Prentice. "How'd you give yourself the brawler's mark?"

"Hey, no, old man!" She was suddenly indignant. "I earned them fair and square, the name and the mark!"

"How?"

"My husband."

"You're married?" Prentice could hardly believe it.

"I'm a widow." Cutter pouted and pretended to frown, but her eyes were bright with mischief. "Got married when I was sixteen. Even got to wear a white veil and nobody laughed. But my husband wanted a knife, not a wife." She laughed. "Get it? He knew I learned Three Streets Vipers. He wanted a knife, not a wife."

Prentice shook his head.

"He put me into pit fights."

"You?" Prentice couldn't quite wrap his mind around the idea. The mountain of muscle that had beaten him nearly to death that afternoon, he had been a pit fighter once, Prentice had no doubt. But a girl like Cutter would never have lasted long throwing fists in a pit, even if you put back the flesh that being a hungry convict took away.

Cutter smiled a wicked smile. "You never heard of the maiden fights? Two fillies stripped to the waist and going at each other with fists and cold steel? There's many a well-bred man who'll step down off his rank to enjoy a night wagering on wenches."

"I had no idea."

"Well, now you do. Cutter Sal, that's what I was called. And I was good. You see any cut scars on me face?"

"No."

"Seventeen fights, three to the death, and not a single cut to the face. 'Course, the same ain't true for the rest of me. I swear, those bastards that raped me left me some extra marks; if they'd let me off the chain with a blade in my hand, that night would have had a different story, I'll tell you that for nothing."

Prentice believed her. "Scars are nothing to be ashamed of," he said, smiling. "You've seen me with my shirt off, I'm sure."

Cutter chuckled and nodded. "Like a half-cured ham a dog's gotten at."

Now Prentice laughed, even though it hurt. "I'd never thought of it like that, but it's not a bad description. And you were convicted for brawling because of the pit fights?"

"Nah, magistrates were in the audience half the time. But my old man, he started to use me for other business, like an attack dog. A woman can bring a pair of knives into a place under her skirts, and if she knows how to use 'em or has a reputation for killing, well, she's frightening to a lot of men. Unless those men are too highborn to back down. That's how he got me into a big fight, in a tavern right on the docks in Denay. Spilled out into the street and everything. By the time it was over, there were seven men dead and the rest of us was all beat up pretty well. My fool of a husband bled to death right on the cobbles in front of the tavern. No one turned dog on anyone, so we all got done for fraying mischief."

"You mean mischief and affray," Prentice corrected.

"That's the one—causing death. The magistrate was 'specially concerned we knew it was for the deaths. If no one had died, we would only have been flogged and branded, he said. The transport was for the deaths."

The light was gone now, and the two of them could hardly make each other out in the darkness.

"I'll go light that candle." Cutter headed off somewhere.

Prentice closed his eyes. It was over a decade since he'd been transported. In that time, he'd heard and seen many things as brutal and sad as Cutter Sal's story, and his own circumstances were no less cruel. Nevertheless, something in her words touched him. He thought it might be the hiding, the having to pretend to be a man when she wasn't. Prentice had hidden his own identity, buried it deep under the scars, forgetting his ambition to be a knight of the Church, his family, even his faith in God. But he had never had to pretend he was something he wasn't; at least, he'd never felt he was pretending.

He heard Cutter coming back up the stairs and opened his eyes to the candlelight. She hadn't bothered with a candleholder, or else hadn't found one. She dripped some of the tallow onto the bedpost and then set the candle into it, keeping it in place.

"So now that you know my secret," she said, "what are you going to do?"

"What do you think I should do?"

Cutter thought for a moment. "I don't see as you have to do anything."

"Sounds good to me."

Her eyes narrowed; she hadn't expected that response it seemed. She looked closely at Prentice, as if she expected him to laugh or say he was joking. "Really? You won't turn me over to some sacrist court? Have me done for undermining public morals or whatever?"

"Public morals? Let every man prepare his own soul for God."

"But I'm not a man."

At that moment, the stairs creaked, and they turned. Sir Gant came up, followed by a scarecrow-thin sacrist with a wispy brown fringe growing around his tonsure. The man's robe was little more than carefully arranged rags, and he had a wooden cross hanging by a leather thong around his neck.

"Master Prentice," said Sir Gant. "This is Fostermae. He is a sacrist and has some physician training."

"Some training," Fostermae agreed. "But enough to treat most common ailments."

Sir Gant shrugged. "He was the best I could do, I'm afraid."

Fostermae shrugged as well, as if apologizing for his lack of education.

"Well, if I'm too far gone for your skill, Sacrist, at least you'll be on hand to give me the final rites," Prentice joked, though he didn't laugh. A sly smile didn't hurt his injured mouth too much.

The sacrist stopped short at the comment and then, seeing Prentice's expression, gave a guffaw that seemed too deep for his thin frame. "The patient's spirits are high. Healing is easier under these circumstances."

Fostermae shooed Cutter back from her position on the floor so that he could get closer to Prentice in the bed. He knelt and peered at Prentice with a frown. "Fetch me that candle closer," he instructed. "Or better yet, find some more candles. I'll need better light if I'm to examine him."

Sir Gant headed off, while Cutter used her blade to cut the candle on the bedpost away from its footing. She handed it to Fostermae, who held it close to Prentice's face.

"Oh ho," said the sacrist. "You were in a right dustup, weren't you? How many were you fighting?"

"Just one," said Prentice. "But he was a big one."

"Of course, of course." Fostermae gently poked Prentice's bruises and turned out his lip, likely looking for missing teeth. His hands worked their way down to Prentice's chest, checking ribs and pressing into the flesh of his stomach and sides, checking for internal injuries.

Prentice flinched but was otherwise silent.

"That's a good sign. No crying out or screaming," the sacrist said. "So, odds are that your kidneys and bladder are all right. Once helped treat a farrier who'd had a cart run right over his stomach. Nothing to see but a few bruises on the skin. But oh, how he screamed any time someone touched him. He died overnight, and the apothecary demanded we cut him open to see what could have killed him. Inside was all ruined, every organ black or burst. It was foul, like the rot of a corpse, as if he had died from the inside out."

"You cut him open?" Prentice asked, surprised. Autopsy was not an unheard-of occurrence, but it was not widely practiced or approved. "Didn't his family object?"

"He had none that we could find. And I didn't see the problem. If monks and sacrists can have their flesh stripped for an ossuary, then why can't a common man's flesh speak to us of his injuries so that we might better learn to care for them in life?"

"Some worry that a mutilated body will not be raised whole in the resurrection."

Fostermae snorted in derision. "You believe in a God who has the power to bring dead flesh to life, but who lacks the power to heal a wound made after that flesh has died? Better to worry about the disposition of your soul than to try to pick between the capacities and failings of the Almighty."

"I didn't say I believed it," Prentice replied with a smile. "Only that some do."

"Well, they're fools!"

"I like you, Sacrist Fostermae," Prentice said, and he laid his head back and closed his eyes for a moment.

The stair creaked again as Sir Gant returned with more candles, and the sacrist completed his investigation.

"As near as I can tell, you've come away surprisingly well," he announced at last. "No damaged organs in the belly. No broken bones, except maybe your nose, but that might just be swollen. Some cuts and bruises. You'll be sore for days. And that eye of yours has a shiner, no doubt. Judging from those scars I could feel under your shirt, you've survived worse than this before."

"That's the truth," said Cutter.

Prentice looked at her. The light was brighter in the room with the addition of three more candles, lit and placed by Sir Gant. He glanced at the hedge knight. "Where's Turley?"

"Gone to help the duchess' household move back into the castle."

"Back into the... how the bloody hell did they manage that?"

"The prince came today, at the head of an army," Sir Gant explained. "Hundreds of knights ahorse and thousands of men-at-arms, they say. He just ordered the castle opened, and Sir Duggan let him in."

Prentice felt like he must be losing his wits. Maybe the fight had damaged his mind and he was in a waking dream. "Mercad is dead," he said. "His body is going back to Rhales."

"Not Prince Mercad, Prince Daven Marcus, Mercad's nephew. The new Prince of Rhales."

"His uncle's not dead a month and the nephew's already taking the title and bringing an army to the Reach."

"Odds are, he came expecting to find the province still at war," said Sir Gant.

That made sense, but Prentice found the news of the new prince's presence in Dweltford troubling. When he had marched north with the dead Prince Mercad's army, he'd been flogged almost to death. On another occasion, he'd almost been executed for a crime he didn't commit, all to satisfy the whims of cruel noblemen who were being frustrated by a clever enemy. The idea that the new prince had brought another army west, one that was fresh and soon likely to be frustrated that the war they came to fight was over, did not bode well.

But that was a matter for later.

"What happened in the chase?" he asked Sir Gant. "Did you catch any of them?"

Gant lowered his head in shame. "I fear not."

"Not one?"

"The one in the doorway went down under my sword. He was done by the time I returned. The other runner was faster than Turley or myself. We lost him in the streets before we were halfway back to the market. That was when we encountered a steward running to fetch Turley and you, Master Ash. He told us of the prince's arrival. Turley left immediately to see to his duties, and I came back to find you insensible, with Cutter standing watch over your body. I'm sorry, but I never saw the man who attacked you."

"I slashed his hand," Cutter interjected. "I said we should try look for drips of blood."

"But I decided that you needed care first."

Sir Gant's cold look at Cutter made it clear the two had not come to an amicable agreement. Prentice didn't care. He groaned painfully and levered himself upright in the bed.

"Take caution," said Fostermae. "I haven't given you any treatment yet. You should have poultices, te bark, and rest."

"Make your poultice, Sacrist," Prentice said. "I'll put it to my pains, but I cannot lie about and rest. There's too much to be done."

"You're going to the duchess?" asked Sir Gant.

"Not yet. I want to know what those bastards were doing here. They weren't housebreakers, they were looking for something specific. I need to know what that is before I return to Her Grace."

CHAPTER 10

"You were in a fight?"

"Yes, Your Grace."

Duchess Amelia looked at Turley as he tugged his forelock, an earnest expression on his roguish face. "And this was at Seneschal Fern's house?" she asked.

"Indeed so, Your Grace."

"Was there no sign of the seneschal?"

"None," Turley replied.

"And where is Master Ash now?"

"I don't know, Your Grace. That knight fellow, Sir Gant, he went back to fetch him. They should be here by now."

Amelia snorted in annoyance. Around her, the business of preparing a meal for hundreds drove every servant, steward, and kitchen maid into a frenzy of activity—placing chairs and tables, setting plates, working the ovens and spits. At the same time, armed men marched captured mercenaries through corridors from wherever they had been hiding. A small knot of the usurper Duggan's men had locked themselves in a chamber at the base of one corner of the keep, and knights had taken to the door with axes to dig them out. The fray that finished the encounter had been brief but brutal, and none of the mercenaries had survived.

Amelia wanted a moment to think, to plan and understand the implications of the prince's arrival in the Reach, especially if Liam had his ear. Since returning to the castle, however, she'd had little time to even draw breath and had not seen the prince even once. More worrying still was the disposition of Sir Duggan. He had raised a banner against her rightful rule. He'd usurped her castle and her town and held them by force. He was a rebel and needed to be tried. For all she knew, he had simply walked out the gate in the current confusion. She sent word to her own knights and men to keep watch for him but had heard nothing since. She looked for a page to send for word and found her maid Teerah approaching from the keep's main stairwell.

"Your Grace," said the girl, her flawless curtsy ruined by the flustered expression on her face. "We have been commanded from your apartments."

"What do you mean?"

"Matron Bettina gave us instruction to prepare a gown and jewelry for you for this evening's welcome feast for the prince. And to make certain that nothing precious was removed in all the commotion." The maid looked askance at the staff bustling around her, as if any one of them might suddenly reveal themselves to be a sneak thief.

"And?" asked Amelia, already too frustrated and beset to show patience. "Who commanded you out again?"

"Baronet Liam, Your Grace. He said it was at the prince's instruction."

"The prince commanded you from my rooms? Why?"

"He's up there now."

Amelia looked about her at the organized chaos that reigned on the ground floor of the keep and decided that, at least for the moment, it could survive her absence. She waved for her handmaid to lead the way and headed up the stairs to find the prince. This morning she had been living homeless, sleeping in a cupboard bed provided by the town's conclave, with her castle in the possession of an enemy. But even then, she had felt more in control of her circumstances than she did now. She wanted to put such thoughts aside as she climbed to the gallery that led to her apartments, but as she pressed past her ladies-in-waiting, who stood together near her chamber door, she had a sudden feeling that she was even less in command of her own castle now than she had been in the morning.

Inside her main chamber, Amelia found a knight in finely polished plate-and-mail armor and a surcoat in the royal burgundy and gold heraldic colors. From her bed chamber, she heard the voices of two men. Before she could go there, Prince Daven Marcus and Baron Liam emerged, talking like old friends.

"This will probably suffice," said the prince. "After all, martial men such as ourselves have endured greater hardships, haven't we?"

"Your Highness," said Amelia, curtsying.

The prince turned from talking and regarded her with an expression of disdainful surprise. "Duchess Amelia? What are you doing here?"

"These are my chambers, Your Highness."

"Oh, indeed?"

"They were the duke's chambers, Highness," said Liam in a condescending tone. "In his life, Duke Marne never hesitated to offer them to visiting royalty. Prince Mercad took his rest here a number of times in his life." To Amelia he said, "You surely didn't expect His Highness to sleep in a muddy field while you lounged here in luxury?"

No more than you expected to find me stuck in that field when you returned, Amelia thought. Outwardly, she smiled.

"I would have expected my retainer to inform me of the prince's needs, that I might see to the room's appointment appropriately," she said, not bothering to moderate the archness of her tone. "Surely the prince wouldn't want to climb through a garderobe full of ladies' gowns to find his trews in the morning."

The two men shared a look that Amelia didn't understand.

"She has a fair point, Baron," said the prince. "Perhaps we should be about other business."

Amelia was surprised that the prince conceded her point so easily, but she had other issues she wanted to pursue. "Forgive me, Highness, but you named Liam a baron. Do you not mean baronet?"

"My uncle was an old man," the prince began to explain with a soft tone. His voice quickly hardened as he spoke, though. "In truth, he was a doddering old fool who should have yielded the title to me years ago. If I'd led your petty little campaign, he'd no doubt be at home now, wrapped in a blanket and drinking some warm milk before his afternoon nap."

Amelia was astonished to hear the prince speak so coldly of his recently dead forebear, and her expression showed it. She looked from the prince to Liam and saw her knight captain sneering at her.

"When I heard the tale of brave Sir Liam, who rallied the army my uncle all but threw away, and whose heroism turned a certain massacre into a victory, I knew my uncle's dotage had led him to fail again, even on the doorstep of the next life. A baronetcy was too little reward for such a single-handed triumph."

"Brave Sir Liam...?" Amelia heard herself repeat the prince's words as if she didn't fully understand them.

"You have a barony without a baron, do you not, Duchess?"

Amelia nodded in spite of herself. "Fallenhill?"

"There. I have struck twice with the one arrow." The prince seemed very pleased with himself.

"You have made Liam a baron?"

Liam's sneer grew into a full, self-satisfied smile.

"Yes, girl," the prince said. "You saw him wearing the suit of armor I gifted him as well, no doubt. I made Liam a baron and have sealed his ennoblement with my own ring. It was either that or listen to Ironworth bang on about bitter victory and tactics or something."

The prince smiled condescendingly, as if the words of Sir Carron Ironworth—the dead prince's knight commander and hero of the realm—were a joke, a thing of jests. Liam shared the smile. "Or worse yet," the prince continued, "that tiresome sacrist with his ridiculous tale of summoning an angel with his prayers."

He and Liam chuckled.

"There are many men who shared that vision, Highness," Amelia protested, but her voice felt weak in her mouth. The prince was rewriting the story of the battle right in front of her, and she struggled to conceive of a way to stop him.

"I knew a blind beggar once who swore he'd spent a night in the embrace of a forest dryad and that it was her beauty that had driven him blind," Daven Marcus retorted. "I hear stories of angels with the same ears I heard that fool's rambling. When he swore to his story and refused to recant his heresy, I had his tongue cut out. The stories of nights with spirits stopped after that. You might wish to share that with any of these 'men' who tell tales of angels on battlefields, girl. It will be better for them and for you!"

Daven Marcus was barely a year or two her senior, and it grated on her pride to hear him call her "girl."

The prince moved to step around her.

"You mean 'Your Grace,'" Amelia said quietly as he passed.

Daven Marcus stopped dead in his tracks and looked at her. Amelia lifted her eyes to meet his, refusing to flinch or even grant him the deference due to his title.

"What did you say?" he asked.

"I said, Highness, that when you called me 'girl,' what you must have meant to say was 'Your Grace,' since I am a peer of the realm."

Daven Marcus shook his head, blinking in disbelief. He leaned close to Amelia, and his eyes narrowed. "Peer? I'm not sure your milkmaid mother didn't keep the afterbirth and throw her baby away, you pretentious slut!"

"I am my husband's widow, Your Highness, and regardless of my birth, I guard his honor and the honor of his name."

"You couldn't guard the honor of your husband's last turd. Whatever leftover honor you have because my fool uncle put the dukedom of the Reach in your fool husband's hands will be gone the moment we get you married off, bitch."

Amelia felt suddenly calm, the way she had felt when she confronted Daven Marcus's uncle in the Forfeits Council during the campaign. He was reduced to calling her names because he had no other criticisms to bring. It offended his honor that she was not born to her rank, but legally there was nothing he could do about it.

"I will marry, of course, Your Highness," Amelia said, putting a hard edge of her own into her voice as she spoke. "And provide heirs to the Reach, as is my duty. But until then, the duchy rests on my shoulders, and I will do my duty by my people."

The prince looked at Baron Liam in disbelief. He fastidiously took his leather riding gloves from his belt and pulled them onto his hands. They were barely in place when he snapped his open right hand across Amelia's face. The slap cracked loudly about her chambers, echoing off the walls. She felt her eyes immediately tear up but was pleased that she didn't fall under the force of the blow, only turning her head away. As she looked back at him, she thought she saw a momentary flash of surprise in the prince's eyes. Perhaps he'd expected her to fall. Nonetheless, the transient emotion was replaced with fury.

He glared at her, pointing his finger. "They're not your people, bitch! They are my father's, and when he dies, they will be mine. They are not ever yours."

He ended his declaration with a punch that landed in Amelia's stomach. This time she did fall, gasping for the breath that the punch drove out of her.

The prince stepped away from her but stopped at the door. "In the meantime, you can have your trollops take your damned dresses away. But send one of the pretty maids back when they're done—I might want some help disrobing this evening."

He left, and Amelia clutched at her stomach while Liam and the other knight walked past her as they, too, left. She could imagine the contempt in Liam's face, and she could not bear to look up at that—not in pain on the floor, not like this. She heard someone talking beyond her chamber door, and soon her maids were around her, helping her to her feet and escorting her to her bed. She refused to sit or lie on it.

"The prince will be using my rooms," she explained to them, though it was difficult to speak because she was still winded. "We must take out my things and make space for him."

"But you are hurt, Your Grace," said Teerah. "Surely, the prince will allow you some time."

"I would not think so."

"How did you fall, Your Grace?"

Amelia looked at her. So that was what they'd been told—that she'd fallen.

"I fell…"

"But what caused it?"

"I mistook my place."

They tried to press her further, but she waved them away, insisting that they must make space for the prince immediately. For herself, Amelia wanted to be away from her chambers as soon as possible. She wondered if she would ever think of them as hers again.

CHAPTER 11

Prentice righted the upturned chair in the seneschal's upper room and put one of the lighted candles on it. The effort made him wince at the pain in his chest. The sacrist, Fostermae, gave him a worried look, but Prentice ignored it. In all, they had found a half a dozen candles and lit every one, but the long upper room was still a mass of shadows.

"We would do better to come back in the morning," said Sir Gant. "At least then we could read more easily."

"Some of us, maybe," Cutter said. She picked up an untidy sheaf of papers from the floor and waved them around. "There's pretty ones and some that have little chicken scratchings on them. After that I can't pick nothing between them."

She let the pages fall to the floor again. Sir Gant rolled his eyes, but Fostermae only shook his head and smiled.

"More important, we have the duchess' summons. It would not be right to tarry," Gant explained. He looked to Prentice, who was staring at the documents still scattered as if he expected them to suddenly arrange themselves in correct order. "Shall we go?"

"No," said Prentice, flatly. "Not yet."

"We cannot ignore her command."

"We won't, but Turley's gone back. If her need is urgent, she can send for us. I want to find what they were looking for."

"Why?" Gant asked.

"The duchess's seneschal is missing, and when we come to look for him, his house is being ransacked. They weren't here for loot; they had a purpose. Something they expected to be written down and perhaps even locked away."

"One of them mentioned a strongbox," Gant recalled.

"Strongbox, eh?" Cutter's tone made it clear that the prospect of a locked treasure chest caught her interest.

Prentice sank to the floor, wincing again. His head ached, and he was parched. He blinked as his vision blurred for a moment, then picked up the first papers he could see.

"You need rest, Master Prentice," said Fostermae. "A meal and rest."

"Water, and something to eat if you can find it. But rest will have to wait."

Sir Gant tapped Cutter on the shoulder. "Let's see what food is in the kitchen."

"And if there's a strongbox," Cutter said as she followed Sir Gant down the stairs. Fostermae went with them.

Prentice began to sort the papers, skimming passages of writing to get the gist. It felt like an impossible task, since he didn't even know what to look for, and even if he did, the house breakers themselves hadn't been able to find it.

What were they looking for?

From the floor below came the sounds of Cutter and Gant searching through the kitchen. Fostermae returned soon with a tin pitcher and cup. He poured water into the cup and handed it to Prentice, who drank it and nodded his thanks.

"Sir Gant says that the man who owns this house is dead," said the sacrist as he refilled the cup and gave it to Prentice again.

Prentice drained this one more slowly than the first and then returned it to be filled a third time. "It seems likely," he said, going back to sorting. "They spoke of trying to beat answers out of him and breaking his neck."

"They sound like brutal men."

Prentice shrugged. "It's a brutal world."

"Is it? Or is it the sin of mortals that makes it so?"

Prentice stopped sorting and looked up. "There is disease and starvation. Storms that tear away roofs and bring down houses. Children go hungry and people go homeless through no fault of their own."

"None of which is brutality," Fostermae said. Prentice raised an eyebrow, but the sacrist pressed on. "There is suffering, I don't deny it. And injustice. We live in a fallen world. But brutality seems to me to be very much a product of our actions, we men and women."

"I suppose." Prentice went back to looking through the papers.

"You were on the march? You fought at what they call the Battle of the Brook?"

"I was."

"Did you see the angel?"

Prentice stopped. This was a subject he didn't want to discuss with anyone.

"Many saw it," Fostermae urged. "I've had a number of men, freed convicts mostly, come to ask me about the visitation."

Prentice wondered what he could say. That he had seen what other men had seen, or that it was not the first vision he had seen on the march, but the fourth. That two of those had been visions of the Messiah himself. That he, Prentice, had spoken with the crucified and risen Lord. How would the sacrist believe him? Visitations were granted to saints and holy children, pure innocents untainted by the brutality of men. They didn't appear to violent and angry convicts on the march to do more violence.

"I saw it," Prentice admitted, and immediately wished he had not. Now there would be more questions.

"What did you see? A bright light? Did you hear thunder?"

"I saw..." He paused, wondering why he was talking, but the memories within him seemed to be pressing out into words, and trying to hold them back was like trying to catch water with his fingers. "I saw a lion—a powerful beast, larger than a pony. Its fur and mane were whiter than the high clouds. It was a terrible and beautiful creature."

And it wasn't the first time I'd seen it. He managed to keep himself from saying that thought aloud.

Fostermae nodded and smiled. "Yes, I have heard one other speak of a lion. Your words confirm his. He will be glad to hear it."

"Will he?" Prentice asked doubtfully. "Why?"

"Because he fears he went mad. He wonders if the terror of battle overcame him and his mind concocted the story out of the ravings of his fear."

"Really? He said 'concocted' and 'ravings'?"

"No, those are my words." Fostermae peered at Prentice in the candlelight. "You are uncomfortable speaking of this. Why? The story's told nightly in taverns; men are trading the tale for ale, as they say."

For a long moment, Prentice kept staring at the papers in front of him—not reading, just staring. In his mind's eye, he was seeing again the lion angel and hearing the words that he had heard during the vision. The angel had been a figure of rage and power, falling on the warped beast-men warriors of the invaders. The men from the far west had champions who could transform their bodies to beasts, monstrous wolves and hounds. The angelic lion had torn those fiendish creatures to pieces and struck thunder and lightning where it attacked, so that after the battle, not a single beast-man body had been found, only a number of skeletal forms consumed by fire and ripped apart by mighty jaws. In Prentice's mind, it was a day when mortal men fought amidst demons and angels, and the terror and the rage were still fresh in his memory. They haunted his dreams, as they did others who survived. Like Turley, who still needed strong drink to get to sleep most nights.

"They trade the tale because they need the drink," he muttered, and then he turned a cold glare on Fostermae. "When you read the scripture and hear of God's mighty power falling on the Egyptians or the Philistines, it sounds so glorious. But you don't hear about the screams as men die, seeing the fury and hate in their killer's eyes. They don't speak of the stench of blood and shit and piss. The shaking and the terror as you stand and wonder which direction the next attack will come from."

"You're angry at God?"

No, Prentice thought, and he remembered the rage of the lion as it had torn apart the enemies from the far west. That was righteous anger, pure and unrestrained, and in the face of that fury, his own feelings had seemed small and petty.

"Not angry," he said. "The invaders were evil, and what they did to the innocent, to women and children, meant they had to be stopped. I just... that was a vile day full of bitter business. The tale's worth more than a cup of rye."

Fostermae nodded and clapped his hand on Prentice's shoulder before moving away. "Worth more than boasting about prayed-for miracles too."

"You don't believe the prince's chaplain, then?"

"Porlain's a soft twit who'd lose a theological debate with his own dinner, after he'd eaten it."

Prentice chuckled. From below, Sir Gant called for them. Prentice turned and stood as he heard footsteps hammering up the hall. They clattered up the stairs, and Cutter poked her rough-mopped head up over the floorboards.

"We found something," she said happily. "That seneschal fella you were looking for. Skinny sod with dark hair?"

It occurred to Prentice that he actually had only the vaguest idea of what Bastian Fern looked like. "Sounds right," he said.

"Well, come and have a look."

Prentice and Fostermae followed Cutter as she led them through the darkened house to the kitchen, an unassuming room with whitewashed walls, a single table, and a hearth with a large copper cauldron. An oil lantern hung from a hook in the center of the ceiling, making the simple kitchen seem oddly bright after the shadows of the rest of the house. The room smelled of flour and drying herbs that hung on the walls. There was another odor as well, the thick tang of blood that brought bile into the throat. Standing by the kitchen's one cupboard, Sir Gant showed them its contents—two dead bodies. There was a woman shoved to the back and a man whose feet were inside the cupboard, but the rest of him had fallen out when the door was unlatched, like a broom not put away properly.

"My guess is that this is our missing seneschal," said Sir Gant.

The man was thin and had dark hair, just as Cutter had said. His face was purple with bruises and so swollen that his eyes were almost hidden, and his nose was hard to distinguish from the other lumps in the skin. The body's neck was so badly twisted that it was impossible to doubt he was dead.

"They said they beat him to death," said Prentice.

"Hell of a way to die," Cutter added.

"Who's the other one?"

Sir Gant shrugged. "His housekeeper, if I had to hazard a guess."

It made sense. The woman had been middle aged and plump, dressed in a homespun dress and bodice with a white cotton apron over the top. Her throat had been cut, but other than that, there were no signs of violence on her body. Seeing the slash in her neck, Prentice looked around the kitchen.

"They killed her in the cupboard," he said.

"How do you know that?" asked Cutter.

Sir Gant's mind was faster. "There's no blood out here." He waved his hand at the kitchen. "At least, not enough for a slit throat."

They looked in again. Because of her cramped position in the cupboard, the housekeeper's blood had drained away beneath her body. When they shifted her weight, the stench of the congealing blood suddenly wafted out in a dense wave. They all coughed and stood back a moment.

"Why put her into the cupboard and then kill her?" asked Fostermae.

"Easier than killing her and then having to stuff her in," said Cutter. "Less carrying."

"That is a cold calculation."

"They were cold men," said Prentice. "Brutal and sinful."

Fostermae looked close at him. "Are you mocking me?"

Prentice shrugged. He wasn't sure, one way or the other. He stared at the housekeeper's body. "It's possible they found her in there."

"You think she was hiding?" Sir Gant asked.

"Perhaps. Four armed men have come to confront her master, demanding something from him. They're aggressive, threatening violence. She decides to hide."

"Why hide, though? The back door is right there. Why not flee?"

"They had a man guarding that way when we arrived. Maybe he was there right from the start. Maybe they were ready for the seneschal to flee."

"They sound like a right crew of villains," said Cutter. "They're lucky not to be on a chain somewhere already."

Fostermae and Sir Gant nodded, but Prentice was thinking further, his mind picturing the scene. "If he came this way, with her..."

"It's the kitchen. Odds are that she would already have been here," said Sir Gant.

"Either way, they're here and they look out the back door and see one of the thugs in the back alley. Probably the one that came at us in the hall at the first. So, their escape is blocked, and the boss and his two footpads are banging on the front door. What do they do?"

"Try to hide in the cupboard?"

"Not both of them, just her."

"How can you know that?"

"None of the doors are forced," Prentice explained. "Someone had to let them in."

"So, he let them in while she was hiding? That takes some front," said Cutter.

Prentice nodded. "He couldn't get away, so he tried to bluff it out, but only after she was hidden."

"Chivalrous."

"And maybe more."

Prentice crouched down to examine the dead woman. He ran his arms along her limbs and under the body, feeling as he went. There was a tearing sound as he peeled the poor housekeeper's dress out of the dried pool of blood and searched behind her.

"Good Lord, man!" Sir Gant exclaimed as Prentice lifted her skirts and felt up her legs.

"I don't know what he's looking for, but if a matron's hiding it, it's up her skirts!" Cutter said, coming to her boss's defense.

Prentice reached the waistband of the dead woman's skirt, and his fingers brushed against what he hoped to find—an edge, as of a piece of paper or a document. He had to lean forward to grasp it better, which brought him face-to-face with the corpse.

"Your pardon, mistress," he said to her dead body. He meant it seriously, but Cutter snorted out a laugh, and Fostermae tutted his disapproval of the seeming gallows humor. Before the sacrist could say anything, Prentice pulled back and withdrew his hands, untangling a small paper packet from the housekeeper's skirts. It was folded neatly, and he brandished it as he stood up again.

"A letter?" asked Sir Gant.

"No, it has no seal," Prentice said. "I think it is what they were looking for. What they came to get from Seneschal Fern. He hid it with her and died to make sure they didn't get it."

Prentice unfolded the little packet to find that it was made of three sheets of paper. He spread them on the table in the candlelight to see them better.

"What is it?" Cutter asked as they all leaned over the table to look.

"They're lists."

"Lists of what?"

"I have no idea."

CHAPTER 12

Duchess Amelia felt exhausted, and as she looked about her, she was sure her stewards and staff felt the same. Preparations for the prince's feast had continued apace all afternoon, and her maids had spent the time moving her personal effects out of her chambers. She had a few locations in the castle to which she could move. For a moment she had contemplated keeping her place in the conclave house, but she dismissed that as pique. It might feel like a protest to her, implying that the prince had left her in no better position than Sir Duggan's rebellion, but she doubted the prince would notice—or if he did, that he would care.

In the end she chose a solar in the keep's west tower. It was meant as guest quarters, and it galled her to take the place of a guest in her own home, but there was enough space for her and her maids and meant she was still in the castle. When she climbed the stairs to change her gown for the feast, she was struck by the notion that she was becoming a damsel in a tower, and she chuckled at that idea.

How many fairy tale damsels locked themselves in a tower?

But even though she wanted to remain in the castle, she wanted to stay as far from Prince Daven Marcus as she could. Her stomach still hurt from where he had punched her. Her face hurt a little as well, but her maids assured her that there was no bruising, and she was pleased about that.

Now that she had changed her gown and her hair was freshly done, Amelia found herself standing at the entry to the great hall an hour after sundown, watching the stewards take in food. The feast had already begun, and the hall echoed with the sound of merriment—a hundred guests, at least, eating and drinking. She should have gone in already; she should have been present to welcome the prince. But the pains in her flesh were nothing compared to the bitter fury that burned in her heart. There was no way she could face the prince and not vent her anger at him. She struggled to get it under control, but every time she thought to enter the hall—her great hall—all she could imagine was denouncing him as a coward or throwing a drink at him or demanding he face her champion for satisfaction by combat.

Did she even have a champion? Her mind churned as she realized that there was probably not a single knight in the whole Reach who would dare to face the prince on her behalf.

Then she thought, Prentice would do it. He was no knight and could never act as her champion, but it comforted her to know that she could rely on him, even if he'd been a loss to her this past afternoon. Thinking of Prentice and standing just beyond the entry to the hall, Amelia suddenly remembered how she had returned from the south after her husband's death. Weary and filthy from her escape from the invaders, she had met Sir Duggan in the great hall, seated in her husband's chair at the high table. Thinking back, she realized that Duggan was plotting rebellion even then. He had been evasive, trying to seem loyal while avoiding her questions. And she had to drag the news from him that Prince Mercad had crossed the mountains and would be coming to the Reach's defense.

How many princes will visit our province this year?

Of course, Mercad had never reached Dweltford, nor been feasted in the castle. Amelia had rallied her province and marched with her forces to meet the old prince's army on the road before they turned north and confronted the enemy. Prince Mercad had been a pale, sickly man at the end of his days, hoping to claim one last glory. He was selfish and perhaps foolish, but he had not been unkind to Amelia. Compared with his heir, she remembered him quite fondly. And he had accepted her place as duchess.

"Sir Duggan has been found," said a voice beside her and Amelia turned to see a houseguard standing beside her.

"What did you say?" she asked, having to drag her mind from her bitter thoughts.

"The traitor has been found, Your Grace. You wanted to be told as soon as it was done."

"And he is being held?"

"Yes, Your Grace."

Amelia was struck with an idea and a sudden resolve. Prince Mercad had accepted her as Duchess of the Reach, and when he had tried to ignore her place and rank, she had reminded him of it, cleverly and effectively. She would give Daven Marcus the same treatment. Many men could beat her with a fist, especially in private, but woe to the man who thought he could outwit her or rob her of her rank or honor.

"Fetch three more houseguards," she told the armed man. "Go and have Sir Duggan brought to me, directly. Be quick."

The man bowed and withdrew.

It took several minutes for the guards to arrive. Amelia met them at the main entrance to the hall, the great double doors with their elaborately carved panels. The four men had Sir Duggan between them. His hair was wild, as though he had come straight from his sleep, but he was fully dressed. His mouth was gagged and his hands bound with rope in front of him. He stared at her with cold contempt in his eyes.

"Why is he gagged?" she asked.

The guards looked at each other, and one of them shrugged. "He was swearing and spitting insults, especially about you, Your Grace. We didn't think you'd want that, so we either had to smack him about or do this."

Their loyalty touched her and helped her steel herself for the next part of her plan. She turned to face the doors. With a glance over her shoulder, she gave the guards final orders.

"You, open the doors and announce me," she said to the guard who had brought her the message initially. "Battlefield voice, loud as you can. Then go ahead of me to the center of the hall, in front of the high table. The rest of you, follow and bring the prisoner with you."

Sir Duggan's eyes narrowed at her use of the word "prisoner," but she ignored him.

The guard stepped in front of her and put his pole axe in the crook of his arm before pressing both hands on the doors. All four guardsmen wore steel helmets and buff coats dyed with cream and blue squares—Reach colors. Amelia suddenly wished they were in heavier armor, like knightly plate or mail, since they would make a much more impressive noise as they marched down the hall, but it was too late.

"Her Grace, Duchess Amelia of the Western Reach," the guardsman bellowed as he entered the great hall and began to stride forward.

On either side of the hall, long tables filled with guests quieted their talk and turned to look. Amelia straightened her back. She was the duchess and not frightened of the looks of these people. She set off behind her man and heard the guards behind her forcing Sir Duggan to follow.

As she walked down the hall, she kept her eyes on the high table at the other end, but in the periphery of her vision, she tried to assess the crowd as she passed. The tables nearest the main doors seemed to have faces she recognized, Reach knights and worthies. She even noted one black-coated member of the guild conclave, though she did not look away to take the time to recognize him. Then she was walking between tables seated with strangers, people brightly garbed but foreign to her. These were knights and nobles who had ridden west with Daven Marcus—his courtiers.

There was a whisper of conversation as she passed, but Amelia ignored it. She was as unknown to them as they were to her. Let them gossip. Her entire attention was fixed ahead of her. There at the high table, with its captured banner trophy set in glass on top, sat the prince and his closest entourage. It did not surprise her to see him sitting in the honor seat at the center of the table, but it galled her. The chair had been her husband's, and after his passing, she had sat there. Of course, protocol demanded that the chair be offered to the prince, even if her beloved Marne were still alive, but she hated to see her husband's place occupied by a man she had so quickly come to despise.

The guard in front of her reached the center space before the high table and stepped aside. Amelia stopped beside him and looked up at those seated on the dais. Baron Liam was there, which didn't surprise her, but other than him and the prince, she did not recognize a single person seated at her table. Predominantly men, they were a martial group. Every single man was wearing a doublet in his family's colors and sewn with his heraldry. She saw rampant stags and leopards passant. There were serpents and bears and hounds, even dolphins and fish, all vivid in colors. She looked among them, recognizing not one family, not even one of the knights who had marched with Mercad. Only two women sat at the table, both in gowns of silk and fine linen, and adorned with more gold and trinkets than Amelia's meager jewelry. As she watched the folk at the table, she realized that they, too, all had their eyes on her, all except for the prince. Daven Marcus had his face half buried in the dark tresses of the woman on his left, whispering something into her ear. The woman was smiling, but even she was looking straight at Amelia, with her guards and prisoner.

Amelia smiled to herself. It was a silly game the prince was playing; it meant nothing to her. She waited a long moment, and the stillness of the room grew. Everyone in the entire great hall was staring. But now they were not looking only at Amelia, they were also watching the prince, waiting to see how he would respond to her presence. This was his intent, no doubt, but Amelia knew he was close to a mistake. Waiting to acknowledge her put the attention on him, but if he waited too long, he risked looking like he didn't know what was going on. In her heart, Amelia thought it was all a stupid game, but that did not mean she didn't know how to play. Prince Mercad had underestimated her in a similar situation during the march north and had come to regret it. Daven Marcus would as well.

The prince, at last, turned to look at her. "Duchess Amelia, I didn't see you there," he said blithely.

Amelia gave a deep curtsy. "I am sorry, Highness," she said as sweetly as she could, rising again. "My herald's voice seemed quite resonant to me. But then, my hair is tied back. There was no chance of maiden hair stopping my ear."

The prince looked puzzled by her words. He glanced down and saw that his collar had caught some of the hair of the woman to whom he had been whispering. It splayed around the side of his head, and when he looked to see it, the woman leaned in again, likely thinking he wished to whisper some new comment to her. That only made the problem worse. He pushed at the woman's shoulder roughly and waved away the caught strands of her hair. When he was finished, he peered down on Amelia with a cold expression of anger. She had made him look foolish in front of everyone.

Good.

"You're late, Duchess. The feast began an hour ago. But we kept your seat for you." The prince waved to the end of the high table.

There, furthest from the prince on the right hand, was a single empty seat. It looked lonely and shadowed. The corner seemed so dark that Amelia wondered if the prince had ordered torches or lanterns moved. Nevertheless, she smiled as she replied.

"Your Highness is too kind. As mistress of the feast and the Reach, I have been busy seeing to my guests. It would have been rude of me to sit before I had attended to my duties. As my departed, beloved Duke Marne..." She paused as the sadness for her husband, still not a year dead, threatened to overwhelm her. She swallowed her tears before they could come forth. "As Duke Marne was always diligent in his duty, so have we, his heirs and his people, learned diligence, guarding the Grand Kingdom's western flank."

"Not that well, it would seem, being caught unready for an invasion and losing your capital," Daven Marcus remarked airily, seeking to mock her, but he had misjudged his audience. The high table, being stacked with his cronies, all tittered at his jest, as did many at the tables directly around Amelia. But from the other end of the hall, where the Reachermen sat, there was no laughter. Only a discontented, offended muttering.

That was a mistake. You can't humble me on that count without shaming all of them as well. And they are fresh from victory; they will not have it! You can hear it.

It seemed the prince could hear it, because he looked up toward those tables with a cold expression. Then he softened to an unctuous smile. "Of course, one cannot fault his choice of men, and his wisdom must have been great to have picked a hero such as Baron Liam here as his knight captain."

The prince indicated Liam sitting at his right hand. Liam smiled at the recognition, and there was a scattered applause from many of the ladies at the near tables, but Amelia kept her eyes assiduously on the prince. One enemy at a time.

"No doubt the baron appreciates your praise," she said. "But I fear Your Highness has been misinformed. Sir Dav was my husband's knight captain. Liam has his appointment from my hand. And a brevet too. Perhaps, when you are done with him, you might give him leave to attend his unfinished business with the duchy."

Amelia thought she heard someone suck in a breath; apparently, it was not common for a favorite of the prince to be taken down a peg in public.

Too bad. He should have been more loyal.

"Please take your seat, Duchess," Daven Marcus said wearily and, Amelia thought, a touch frustrated. "You are disturbing my feast."

"I beg but a moment more of your time, Highness, and I come before you only because it is a matter of King's Law that remains unattended. As duchess, the duty would normally fall to me, but with your presence in the Reach, I must defer to you."

She waved for the guards to bring Sir Duggan forward. He struggled in their grip, but they did not release him. "This man is a knight of rank and sworn retainer who rebelled against me, the Reach, and the crown. What is your judgment, Highness?"

"Could not this wait, lady?" He drew out the last word as if he resented using it.

"As I said, Highness, we are loyal and dutiful servants here in the Reach. We would not delay King's justice, and we have no tolerance for treason."

There were sounds of approval from the Reachermen. Amelia wondered how many had been present on the campaign north when she had faced down a tent full of knights and nobles just for the chance to stand before the previous prince. Then, she had felt completely alone. Not so much now. Nevertheless, she knew she was playing a dangerous game. If she directly insulted the prince or offended him in front of everyone, he would have cause to dismiss her summarily, and then she would lose. The point was to show the prince that he could not treat her as a doxy to simply beat into submission in private however he wished. She was the Duchess of the Western Reach, a peer of the realm, and she would defend the dignity of her station—even if these men despised her personally.

The prince leaned over and spoke quietly with Liam. Whatever he asked, the baron had no answers, Amelia could see that from his expression.

The prince stroked his chin for a moment, thinking. Then he pointed to the guards. "Take off the gag."

Amelia was pleased to see the guard look to her for permission before carrying out the prince's order. She nodded, and the gag was removed.

"Highness, it is all lies," Sir Duggan gasped as soon as the gag was removed. He stepped up next to Amelia, pleading with the prince. "The stupid wench—she is lying."

Amelia bristled to be described as a stupid wench but knew that it actually played into her hands. Even the prince seemed offended by Duggan's flagrant disrespect, his lips twisting in contempt. It seemed it was one thing for the prince himself to ignore Amelia's rank, but something altogether different for someone lower ranked to do it.

"You were not in rebellion?" the prince asked Duggan skeptically.

The castellan raised himself up. "No. It is this girl. She doesn't understand war."

There was another low mutter from the far end of the hall, and Duggan looked over his shoulder for a moment, as if surprised his words might not meet with universal approval. Amelia wondered if there was something wrong with his mind. He looked rattled, unsettled in his thoughts, but she assumed that was the result of his arrest since the prince arrived. Maybe it was something more. Maybe his rebellion was the result of madness or some illness, not a mere product of disloyalty.

"What has this to do with war?" asked the prince.

"The Reach was invaded... is invaded." Duggan paused after correcting himself. "The town and the castle were closed against attack."

"Closed?"

"Yes."

"Against attack?" the prince said.

"Yes."

"And against its liege and her victorious forces, it would seem."

There was tittering for that. The prince was warming to the questioning, and his entourage approved.

Duggan appeared incensed. "Marne was my liege!" he declared, almost shouting. "I swore to him, not his last whore. She's nothing to me." There were audible gasps and more angry mutterings, but if he heard them, Duggan ignored them. "I never rebelled against the Kingdom, Your Highness. You can see that. The moment you arrived, I opened the bridge to you. I never denied your authority. I am Castellan of Dweltford, sworn to the Duke of the Reach, Marne. Marne is dead; his widow should be in mourning, not traipsing around after armies like a camp follower waiting to be serviced. She has never been invested with the Reach. She's a duchess by marriage only. She's no peer!"

Amelia hated to admit it, but Duggan's argument had actual merit, at least as far as King's Law was concerned. She was not noble-born. It was potentially within the prince's power to strip her of her title. That was her main hope in bringing Duggan to trial publicly. Her position as duchess was balanced on the single point of her marriage, but if the prince could be impressed by the Reach's loyalty to her, she would have a second pillar to support her claim: the devotion of the gentry and people. Duggan despised her; she had known that the moment she returned to find Dweltford's gates locked against her. But by hiding in the town and castle instead of marching with the rest of the army, Duggan had made himself a coward in the eyes of every man and woman of the Reach, noble and lowborn. With a choice between her and the castellan, Amelia was certain the Reach would choose her.

She watched the prince's face intently, trying to read his thinking.

"You say she has no right to the duchy?" Daven Marcus asked Duggan, and Amelia's heart sank. The prince cast a glance from Duggan to her, and she could see the contempt in his eyes. In a moment, she would lose her rank and be a landless free woman;

she could imagine what the prince might want to do to her then. She felt like she was walking on a frozen river and hearing the ice creak and crack beneath her feet.

Baron Liam leaned across and whispered something in the prince's ear. Whatever it was caught Daven Marcus by surprise. The prince turned and looked him in the eye. The two had a heated conference. No one could hear a word whispered between them, and when it ended, Liam looked apologetic and Daven Marcus scowled. Amelia wished she could know what they said. Had Liam spoken for her or against her? She knew Liam had little respect for her, but he had at least never openly rebelled. Was this his chance to get power over her?

"Sir Duggan, you were called by my predecessor, Crown Prince Mercad, Prince of the West," Daven Marcus began. "Every sworn sword in the Reach had a duty to raise his banner at the call of his prince."

"And I did. I raised a troop to hold the town she left undefended."

"A troop of mercenaries," the prince said, sneering. It was taken as a given among the noblemen of the Grand Kingdom that mercenaries and soldiers for hire were worse than useless. That was why they still depended upon convict foot soldiers in battle. If you were going to use worthless men, better to use ones for which you did not have to pay hard coin. "Was the town attacked?"

"Well, no, Highness," Duggan stammered. The prince's question seemed to catch him off guard. "But it could be yet!"

Amelia looked at Duggan in shock. Daven Marcus appeared astonished by this claim as well.

"Truly, sir?" asked the prince with an arch tone. "Was Prince Mercad unsuccessful?"

"Highness?"

"Did my uncle give his life to no avail? Was the enemy not routed?"

Amelia was pleased to see the prince turn his ire on Duggan.

"There could be others," the traitor offered weakly.

"Others?" asked the prince. "Another enemy out there about which we have no report? Where? Do they lurk beyond our sight? Do they march in silence so their passing is never heard?"

"I heard…" Duggan began, speaking hesitantly as if reaching for the right words to say. "In the west… I heard reports in the west, of… of other raiders. Not just the ones to the north."

"In the west? I take it you have sent scouts west to see?" Daven Marcus glared at Duggan and then hammered his goblet down on the table. "Well? Well?" he yelled, all semblance of courtly manners gone.

Duggan shook his head. "No, Highn—"

"No, you hid in your castle! Except not your castle—your liege's castle! You failed in your duty and preempted your rank." The prince sat back, disgusted, tossing his half-empty goblet on the table. "A common occurrence here in the west, it seems. Must be something in the water."

Amelia knew that these last words were a dig at her, but she kept her tongue. As long as the prince focused his rage primarily on Duggan, that was enough.

"You know, my uncle used to speak long about his old friend, Duke Marne of the Reach," said the prince, remaining slumped in his chair as if the entire conversation were exhausting to him.

For a moment Amelia was struck with a memory of the frail and aged Prince Mercad, who had been so close to his death and yet had insisted on marching to defend the west. Such a difference between the old prince and this self-important young man who had succeeded him.

Daven Marcus went on. "I thought surely the stories were exaggerated. That however loyal and stout a man Marne might have been, my uncle had been indulging in embellishment. But if Marne drove off the Vec invaders leading men like you, he must have been a hero of monumental proportions."

The prince cast his eyes to the back of the hall, surveying the tables of Reachermen. "I can only hope that you are a canker that can be cut free, and not typical of your folk."

Duggan straightened and tried to gather some dignity. "Highness, you cannot—"

"Oh, enough!" the prince said. "From this moment on, you have no rank; I strip it from you in the name of the throne, the Grand Kingdom, and the king. You are a coward and a rebel. You are judged, and I hand you over to your liege for whatever punishments she might devise."

Amelia blinked in surprise. The prince had given her the judgment and acknowledged her right to punish Duggan. The entire hall was hushed, and nobody moved.

Unsure what else to do, Amelia curtsied to the Prince. "Thanks to you, Highness—"

She was cut off by a snarl. Duggan lunged toward her, his still-bound hands reaching out for her throat like the claws of an enraged beast. She recoiled, but need not have worried, for her guards were diligent in their duty. They quickly intercepted him, one knocking his feet out from under him with the butt end of his polearm, while another held the prisoner in check with a dagger at the throat. The dagger's edge made Duggan wary enough to stop struggling, but he still cursed furiously. "Stupid, useless bitch," he spat. "You've no idea what is coming."

"Shut up," said Amelia, stepping forward and slapping him across the face. He only laughed at her. "You compound your crimes by attacking me in front of witnesses? Do you want to die?"

Duggan's answer was to spit in her face. She felt it strike her and heard gasps from ladies at tables near her. She nodded to the guard holding the dagger, and the gasps came again—and louder—as the guard pulled back Duggan's head and slit his throat, right there in front of the whole feast. Amelia ignored the spittle on her face and refused to step back as the dagger did its work. Blood sprayed across her dress, and drops of it wet her hands. The guards held Duggan on his knees as he gurgled his last breaths and Amelia watched. She did not take her eyes from his but set her face like stone. Every eye in the hall was on her and her dying retainer, she knew it. Even the prince, with his affected boredom and contempt, would be watching.

Let them see.

She was the Duchess of the Reach and its strength was her strength. Not one duty would she shy from. Let the prince absorb that lesson if he could.

CHAPTER 13

Prentice did his best not to limp as he tromped over the bridge and into the castle bailey. He ached all over from his beating, and Fostermae had tried to insist that he still needed bed rest, but he couldn't wait. He had to tell the duchess of Seneschal Fern's death and show her the documents the man had died to keep secret. Along Castle Road, he passed retainers and bannermen of dozens of nobles, as well as servants, squires, and knights, all the way from Within Walls to the castle. A stream of the duchess's own servants and stewards flowed among the diverse crowd, carrying barrels, bundles, and long poles hung with recently killed fowl and haunches of meat so fresh they still dripped blood. The welcoming feast demanded an enormous quantity of food. If the prince's army ate this way often, the town would run out of stores long before winter finished, especially given the disruption the invaders must have made to the harvest.

Thinking of the invaders soured Prentice's thoughts even more. The enemy army was only four weeks defeated, but it was well past time for someone to hunt out survivors, if there were any. And where had they come from? The west was supposed to be empty. Lost in these thoughts, Prentice ran into a man carrying a sack on his shoulder. The man dropped it and cursed, but Prentice didn't stop, pressing on through the crowds. He wondered at the mass of humanity just standing or milling about, as if they had all come for a festival, and when they found none, did not know what else to do.

He made it to the bridge to the castle gate and thought he would have to declare himself to the guards, when he heard someone called his name, and he turned to see a familiar face.

"Bellam!" he exclaimed with a smile. "How goes it?"

Bellam was a former convict like Prentice and Turley. He had been part of the small group that rescued the duchess earlier in the summer, but he'd been badly injured that same day and had not been able to march north. The duchess had given him a place in her kitchens. With an open face and an eager manner, the young man limped over the bridge to Prentice. He offered his hand, and Prentice shook it readily.

"Turley said you'd be around," said Bellam. "Said you're some important man in the duchess' service."

"We're all in her service now, aren't we? How's life in the kitchens?"

"Better than I expected. I sleep warm every night, and head o' kitchen reckons I've got the makings of a real baker."

"An honest trade. Best thing for reformed convicts like us. How's your leg? You're still limping."

Bellam slapped his injured leg. "Don't hurt no more, but I can't quite get it to walk straight."

"That's better than I expected. After Turley and I carried you on that run, I was sure you'd never walk without pain again."

"Don't say that," the young man protested. "If not for you two I'd have been food for them wolves. I'm just glad I'm even alive to have a limp."

"Good attitude."

The two stood for a moment with nothing to say, and Prentice was about to excuse himself.

Bellam gave him a sheepish look. "How... uh... how well are you, you know... how are you sleeping?"

"Not on the ground anymore," Prentice joked, but Bellam wanted something more earnest.

"I mean, in the night? Can you... can you sleep?"

"You have bad dreams?"

"Not really, not as I remember. Some of the others say I mutter in my sleep, but I don't remember what I say." He paused, seeming to consider how much was safe to tell, then decided that he could trust Prentice and went on. "I hear them at night. The villagers, you know?"

Prentice nodded. He, Turley, and Bellam had barricaded themselves in a church with the duchess and her few remaining bodyguards while an ambushing force of invaders had systematically slaughtered the entire village outside, impaling them one at a time until they all bled to death on stakes.

"I think their ghosts are still wailing in the night," Bellam said. "I wake up, and it's like I can hear them."

Prentice frowned. Bellam had been unconscious through that night.

"You were down like a sleeping dog," Prentice said. "There's no way you could have heard any of it."

"I know that. That's why I think they're haunting me. I think they resent me sleeping while they died. They hate me for surviving."

"I think if their spirits are restless, they're probably haunting the men who killed them. It was a bloody business, Bellam, and you were as much a victim of it as the folk of that village. They've gone to their rest now, and you have to keep on living. That's all." Prentice clapped Bellam on the shoulder. "Now, I've news for the duchess. I'll see you later."

He moved off, but Bellam called him back. "Wait. The duchess is in the feast."

Duchess Amelia sat in her seat at the end of the high table. A servant moved to place a torch in the sconce behind her, to give her the light the prince had tried to deny her, but she waved him away. She stared ahead, neither eating nor drinking. Every so often one of the prince's entourage would cast a glance at her, and she could read in their expression a sense of uncertain curiosity; they didn't know what to make of her. Even Liam couldn't keep himself from a surreptitious glance, but she made no effort to meet his eyes.

Only Daven Marcus refused to look in her direction.

In her mind she kept seeing Duggan's death, hearing him choke on his own blood and watching it spill upon the floor. When he was dead, her guards had dragged his body back down the hall, leaving trails of blood upon the flagstones. Most of the guests had simply watched them go, but as the guards passed the tables at the far end of the hall, many of the Reachermen made a point of spitting on the corpse, or on the ground in front. Others did not spit but took their cups and upended them, spilling wine on the table. It was an old gesture to show that one would not drink to the dead man's memory, not even by mistake.

Amelia recognized their contempt for the rebel, and some part of her was pleased about it. She knew it meant that they sided with her, if only in this. She also knew that should Liam speak against her, they might just as easily turn to him. Nobles spoke of loyalty, but they were fickle. Their first loyalty was always to their own honor and pride. Duggan's cowardice had made them shun him and approve her execution order. Liam's heroic reputation made him a different proposition, and in spite of the fact that he seemed to have helped her with the prince, Amelia still remembered how ready he had been to ride off and leave her in a tent in a cold field just to put her in her place. He was no ally of hers and never would be. Not truly.

She lifted her goblet but stopped before the cup touched her mouth. The cuff of her sleeve was sprayed with blood. She studied the little dots that were already turning a rusty brown color. Looking down at her dress, she realized just how much of

Duggan's blood had reached her. She was not soaked in it, not the way Prentice and her other soldiers had been when they had returned from the battle, but it was enough that no one could mistake it.

"This blood is not on your hands," whispered a voice.

Amelia blinked in surprise and looked around to see who was there. "What did you say?" she asked of a steward standing well back near the wall behind her.

"Your Grace?" the servant asked in return, clearly not understanding her question.

Amelia shook her head. He could not have whispered anything to her from that distance. Perhaps she was hearing things; likely it was her troubled mind stirring. She drank her cup dry and signaled to the steward to refill it. When he was done, he stepped away again, and she turned back to the table.

As she did, her eyes lighted on Duggan's blood on the flagstones. There was a kitchen maid bent over with a bucket, a scrubbing brush, and a rag. She was working heavily, with both hands on the woven straw brush, pushing back and forth against the floor. To Amelia's eyes, the floor was still darkly stained, as if it resisted cleaning, and the water in the bucket was almost red enough to be blood itself.

A strange thought rose in her mind. It is a bitter task to purge the blood of generations.

It was a thought in her head, but it was in a voice not her own. The kitchen maid turned, and Amelia saw she had the same face as her, as clear across the distance between them as if Amelia were looking into a mirror. She started and put a hand to her mouth to keep from crying out. The girl went back to her scrubbing, and Amelia swallowed. She put her goblet down on the table.

How much had she had to drink already?

Shaking her head, Amelia was certain she was not drunk. Her breathing was shallow, and she wondered if Duggan's execution had unhinged her mind.

Was she going mad?

The maid finished her cleaning and stood, carrying her bucket with her. As she passed Amelia's end of the table, the duchess looked closely at her. She still wore Amelia's face, as if she were a twin sister. When she noticed her mistress's gaze, the girl politely lowered her eyes and bobbed a little curtsy, then proceeded out of the hall. Amelia looked down at her hands in her lap, frightened that she might be losing her mind and not wanting anyone else in the hall to notice any sign of it in her eyes or her expression.

I will not be mad, she thought, hoping by sheer force of will to keep her composure.

She heard a throaty growl coming from amidst the diners at the feast, but she ignored it, keeping her eyes downcast. There was a second growl, but she ignored that as well. Then she started as the growling suddenly burst forth to a titanic roar, like a storm gathering with gentle-seeming winds and then announcing the coming tempest with a single thunderbolt straight overhead. She looked across to the blood stains and there, next to the wet stones, was a lion, with white fur and a lustrous mane. It was not large, not for a lion, being about the size of a hunting hound. Nevertheless, it was proud and beautiful. She caught her breath at the sight of it.

The animal began to pad its way across the hall, heedless of the blood on the stones. As it walked across the wetness, its paws became stained red. It had no collar and did not seem like a pet. Amelia looked about her, but no one else seemed to notice the lion. They were not ignoring it, though. How could they? They seemed truly oblivious to it presence. No one even glanced at it, but the rest of the hall's happy calm only served to unnerve her further. She clutched at the table as the proud creature stalked its way up the dais toward her. It huffed and growled as it came closer, and she gripped at the table edge, forcing herself to not flee in terror. It was just a waking dream, it had to be. Her eyes fixed on the space in front of her while the lion studied her. It sniffed her hands and then placed its paw on her lap. Amelia could feel its breath on her face, feel the warmth of its body.

No dream was ever this vivid.

In spite of herself, she cast a quick glance at the lion's face, and for that moment the creature's dark eyes flashed golden in the torchlight. Then it turned away from her and sat next to her chair, its forepaw again resting on her lap like an obedient pet. Amelia tried to get control of her breathing, but her chest only drew in the shallowest gasps of air, no matter how hard she tried. So focused was she on the effort that, at first, she did not realize how dark the hall had become. When at last she did notice, it was as if every lantern and torch and fireplace had a dark veil drawn across it so that there was barely a twilight in the hall. Watching, Amelia knew, as with the lion, that she was the only one who perceived the darkness; the feasting continued and the drinking, the conversations, and the laughter did not abate.

In the deepening shadows, the diners at the high table took on a fiendish appearance. Their faces became birdlike, with noses extended and hooked like birds' beaks. Their eyes blackened, and their clothes resembled feathers. They cawed and cackled so that their conversation sounded like the cacophony of a flock of birds, and over it all, the prince's voice cried—a shrill, laughing call of a bird of prey gone mad. Amelia wanted to put her hands to her ears to shut out the noise, but she could not move. As she watched, the bird-people at the table began to peck at each other, fighting and tearing at each other's feathers until they were bruised and bloody. But no matter how wounded they became, they still laughed and ate and drank.

Then, from among the shadows, a third type of beast emerged—a vast, slithering serpent with a body as thick across as the width of a table. Its scales were multicolored, but they had no vibrancy, as if the colors were merely painted on. It pressed its way through the hall, and where it passed, it crushed guests in its coils. Their blood smeared its scales as it wove its way to the high table, and there it raised its head, towering above the cackling

flock of worthies. As it reared, the serpent's head unfolded like
the hood of a cobra and several other heads emerged, each that
of a different predator. Amelia saw a wolf and a bull, but she
quailed when she saw that a third head was of a great stag, with
branching antlers like the ones on the Horned Man's head. The
Horned Man, the invader from the west. Seeing those horns on
one of the serpent's heads, Amelia knew the power of one was
the power of the other. Somehow this serpent was tied to the
Horned Man and his bloodthirsty army from the far west.

The serpent's heads hissed and spat venom at the high table.
Some of the bird-nobles wilted under the poison, their feathers
blackening and falling out, but those that remained leaped on
the reptile with a raging fury, pecking at the scales and at each
other so that the entire table dissolved into a merciless melee.
Prince Daven Marcus especially, more eagle than man now,
threw himself at the serpent, clawing and tearing. The two
locked in combat with a frightening savagery. They tore at each
other's flesh, screaming, hissing, and howling until the table
itself was overturned and all the other nobles there were slain.
The battle was too much for Amelia, and finding she was able to
move again, she pushed herself backward in her chair, holding
her hands defensively before her.

The motion drew the combatants' attention, and both
surged at her suddenly. But before they could reach her, the
white lion by her side leaped into the gap, bellowing out a roar
that echoed to the rafters of the hall. Glorious and fearsome,
the lion stood its ground and took the serpent by the throat,
its noble mane flaring as its teeth bit through scales and drew
blood. The eagle-prince fell upon them both, but before he
could do much damage, he was swept away by a wave of white
fur. From out of the shadows, rats, each pale like an albino,
leaped into the fray. As they did, they grew and transformed
until they were first lion cubs, then fully grown lions. Some had
manes, and others were clearly lionesses, but they were all as

white as the first one she had seen, and they fought alongside
it.

The table cracked under the force of the battle, and the
famous banner cased inside it was released into the fray. Claws
and fangs and beak tore the once-royal pennant to ribbons,
but as a fragment came to her hand, Amelia clutched it,
thinking to save it as the remnant of her husband's legacy. The
cloth wrapped around her hand, and she turned to flee. The
more she pulled, though, the more the fragment grew, until
she was pulling an entirely new banner with her. Wrapping
it around her, she retreated from the hall. The scale of the
conflict threatened to pull the very roof down upon her. In the
passageway outside the hall, she crouched in a corner, drawing
the banner around her shoulders like a cloak and pushing her
hands into her ears against the noise.

"Are you well, Your Grace?"

Amelia looked up to see a steward standing next to her, a huge
tureen of steaming soup in his hands. He had a look of hesitant
concern on his face; it seemed he wasn't sure of the protocol
of the situation. Amelia looked about, and as she did so, she
realized the sound of the bestial conflict was gone. Looking back
through the nearby doorway, she could see the guests in the hall
still laughing and drinking and looking unremarkably human.
About her shoulders was a tapestry that, in her confusion, she
had torn partly away from its hooks. It was old and threadbare,
and she had ripped it beyond repair. She looked back to the
servant standing by attentively, despite the obvious heat and
weight of his burden.

"I fell," she said mildly. She regained her feet and straightened
her dress. "No need to stop on my account. Continue your
service."

The steward nodded, keeping his eyes down, though Amelia
was sure he was trying to get a look at the bloodstains on
her gown. Then he moved off, and she took a deep breath.
Everything was so normal around her now. From the kitchen

she could hear the chefs ordering staff about, and the scents of the feast—roast meats and fresh breads—filled her nostrils. The laughter and conversation in the great hall had none of the crazed mania she had heard when she saw… the vision?

Was that what it was?

"I need to rest," she muttered, and turned down the passage away from the door. She had not gone two steps when she heard a voice from behind her.

"You really are a fool girl."

CHAPTER 14

A melia turned. Baron Liam stood in the exit from the hall. He had a goblet in hand, and he leaned against the wall, as if he were having trouble standing. His face was flushed as he smiled down the passageway at her.

"What did you say to me?" she asked, trying to put steel into her voice that she didn't feel inside.

Liam drained his cup and bent down to place it on the floor beside him. When he stood again, he had to brush hair away from his eyes as he walked slowly toward her. His smile took on a mocking cast as he neared her, and he leaned in. "I said, you are a fool."

Behind them came a rattling sound as a kitchen maid rushed into the passage carrying a silver tray laden with the stripped bones of a roasted shoulder and ribs. Liam looked behind him in surprise as the girl curtsied without losing step and nimbly managed to maneuver around the two nobles before hurrying onward to the kitchens. Amelia took the moment's interruption to turn her back on Liam and continue down the passage. She had no desire to weather any more of his arrogance.

The new baron did not take the hint. "Bad enough that you were so rude to His Highness this afternoon," he said in her ear, leaning over her as she tried to walk away. "But to interrupt his celebrations so you could play frontier noble was just so..." He paused as his drink-dulled mind seemed to reach for the right descriptive. "...so petty."

In spite of herself, Amelia whirled around to face him. "I was rude to him?" she said, her frayed emotions arranging themselves into sudden anger. "He struck me. In my home, in my very chambers! He struck me!"

"Something you've been in need of for a very long while."

"You forget yourself, Baron." Amelia put the full force of her contempt into her voice. "Take care that in your adoration for our prince, you do not lose all other favor."

Liam blinked at her words. The drink was making him slow witted. As she watched him, Amelia realized that that only made him more dangerous. She had seen him lose his temper with her once before, and it had only been Prentice's intervention that had saved her from violence. She didn't want to have to fear him, but she knew that if the prince had no fear in striking her, Liam would not likely hesitate to follow his example.

"The prince sees my worth," he said.

"Then go back to him."

She turned on her heel and strode away from him again. She managed to reach the stairs up to the gallery that ran to the west tower, but she had put only one foot on the step when Liam caught up to her once more, grabbing her by the arm.

"Mercad and Marne might have let you run off the leash," he hissed, his eyes narrow. His strong fingers dug into her flesh as he pulled her around. "But Daven will bring you to heel, bitch. He's quite fond of mongrels. Can't see the appeal myself, but I know they can be useful. He'll get you fettered right, and then you might be worthy of my kennel."

"Your kennel?" Amelia repeated. What was he saying?

"You won't run free much longer."

Turley appeared next to Liam at the foot of the stairs. He had a large ewer of water in his hands. "Do excuse me, Your Grace," he said formally, standing stiffly upright. "I was just bringing the water for your abdolutions." There was a glint of anger in his eyes as he looked down at Baron Liam's hand on her arm. "After a big meal, I knew you'd want to wash the muck off your fingers."

Liam withdrew his hand reflexively, though he sneered at Turley. The steward showed no expression other than polite concern for his mistress, but Amelia was sure she saw a tautness in him that could unleash itself in violence at any moment. She had a sudden image in her mind of the ewer in his hands being used as a weapon, and it reminded her of an earlier time when she had ordered him and Prentice washed and made presentable for her service. He had been cheeky then, though not to her, and the memory made her smile.

"Ablutions," she corrected him.

"Your Grace?"

"The word is ablutions, not abd—"

"Very sorry, Your Grace," he apologized. "I'll remember next time. If I might be so bold, the water won't be warm much longer. If Sir Liam is done with his conversation?"

"That's Baron Liam, cur," spat the drunken nobleman.

"Oh, I am very sorry, Baron," Turley said, and for just a moment there was a hard edge to his voice. "I mistook your rank by your courtesy. Us ex-convicts don't treat ladies like that, you see."

There was a moment's pause as Liam's mood was distracted by his hatred for Turley, and Amelia took advantage of it, quickly heading up the stairs. It embarrassed her to leave her steward there, holding the line for her while she retreated, but she felt her nerve slipping. She swallowed heavily and knew that if she had to face Liam for much longer, she would not be able to hold back tears, and she refused to cry in front of him. Behind her she heard heavy footsteps on the stairs, and she prayed they were Turley's and not Liam's. At the top of the staircase, she turned onto the gallery and walked as swiftly as decorum allowed, pressing through the tower door and straight up the next spiralling stair. When she reached the landing, a shadowy figure seemed to jump from the darkness into the lamplight around the bend. She started with fright before she realized it was Prentice, who had been sitting and waiting outside her chamber door, and now had leaped to his feet.

"Are you all right, Your Grace?" Turley called from below as he came rushing up the stairs. He must have heard her short cry.

"Quite well, steward," Amelia replied fondly. "Master Ash gave me a surprise."

Turley appeared on the stairs behind her.

Prentice eyed the blood on her dress and cast an angry glare at his friend. "What happened to the duchess?" he asked.

Amelia pushed past Prentice, desperate to gain the refuge of her chamber. Inside the door there was candlelight and the dull glow of a banked fire. She went straight to her chair and table and sat down, grabbing a goblet and pouring herself wine, not bothering to ask Turley to do it. There was a noise from the back of the chamber and Bettina appeared, adjusting her hair and linen hood. Amelia's lady's maids would be at the feast still. It was probable they would not even have seen her leave yet. Bettina never attended feasts unless explicitly instructed; she observed her rank and role with utmost seriousness and only ever ate with the servants. Amelia knew Bettina would have been waiting, dozing fully dressed in her own bed, ready to jump to her mistress's service the minute she returned from the feast.

"Your Grace," said Bettina, moving to the fire to stir the embers. She glanced at the two men who had followed the duchess into the room, regarding them both warily. "What's going on?"

Turley took the ewer of water to a sideboard, where a cloth and bowl had been placed. He put the ewer on the board and waited with the cloth in hand for Amelia's instruction.

Prentice stood in front of her, frowning as he looked down. "The duchess has been injured," he told the matron.

Bettina turned from lighting a candle and, grabbing the silver holder, rushed to Amelia's side. "What? Where?" When she saw the duchess's blood-stained dress, she gasped in horror. "What happened?"

"It's not mine, Bettina," Amelia protested. "It's not my blood." Now that she was in her rooms, she suddenly felt deeply weary. Only a few hours ago, this solar in the west tower had seemed like exile. Now it was a refuge, and she was glad of it.

"There's so much," the matron exclaimed, holding the candle close to examine the dress.

"Whose is it?" asked Prentice. He looked to his friend, but Turley only shrugged.

"I caught the new baron making fresh with Her Grace in the passage outside the hall, but it ain't his blood," Turley explained.

"Liam did this?" Prentice's growled.

His tone surprised Amelia. She was used to him being more reserved, his emotions kept in check. It was unexpected to hear him so angry. The sound of his voice reminded her of the lions of her vision for an instant, seemingly echoing the sounds of their roars.

"Liam did nothing," she said and drained her cup. She waved to Turley to bring her the water. "This is Duggan's blood."

"The traitor?"

"I had him executed, in the hall."

"How close were you to the act?" Prentice asked.

"When I condemned him, he tried to attack me. One of the houseguards slit his throat for that."

"Oh, how horrid," said Bettina. "But the right fate for a traitor!" She took the cloth from Turley's hand while he placed the bowl on the table next to Amelia and began to pour the water. The matron began to mop the duchess's face and neck while Amelia washed her own hands in the bowl. As the cloth came away, she saw little drops of blood that had been cleaned from her own face. She'd never even felt them strike her skin.

"You condemned him?" asked Prentice.

"I brought him to the prince and forced a trial." Amelia knew she was being obscure, but in her exhaustion, she had no desire to explain herself more than that.

"You had the prince try him in the midst of the welcoming feast?"

She nodded, not looking up at him.

"Clever move," Prentice approved after a moment's thought.

Then Amelia did look up at him. "Are you mocking me?"

"Not in the least. You were abandoned by Baronet Liam, supposedly your own knight captain, and left to take your town back for yourself. And you did. Now the prince arrives, with the baronet riding his coattails."

"Baron," Amelia corrected, then gestured for Turley to refill her goblet.

"Sorry, Your Grace?"

"He's been raised to baron by the new prince," Turley explained as he poured the wine. He nodded immediately in apology, realizing he had overstepped his bounds. "Begging your pardon, Your Grace."

Amelia smiled at him and waved him away, forgiving his lapse in manners.

"Well, he's coming up in the world," said Prentice. "But to complete my point, Your Grace, the prince could well have presented him as savior of the Reach, as if you had nothing to do with it. By trying Duggan immediately and rendering the judgment yourself, you assert your place as sovereign over your own demesne. There's nothing to mock in that."

Amelia did not want to admit it in her dark mood, but Prentice's praise pleased her. At first, she had wanted to impress the prince with her rank and place over her lands, making him see her power. She wanted to counteract the memory of being beaten on the ground in front of him. The image of it in her mind still galled her, made her want to spit and rant in fury. But as the trial had progressed, she felt the nobles of the Reach gathering behind her in spirit. That Prentice saw it as well confirmed her impression.

"I'm glad to see your assessment is in accord with mine," she said as she drained the cup again. "I would have liked access to your opinion earlier in the evening. Where have you been?"

"My apologies, Your Grace," Prentice said without hesitation. "I managed to find Seneschal Fern, but I was too late."

"Too late?"

"Bastian Fern is dead, Your Grace, as is his housekeeper."

"How?" Amelia tried to understand what Prentice was telling her, but it seemed to make no sense.

"Their throats were slit, Your Grace, and they were stuffed together in a cupboard."

"Why?" Amelia lowered her head and rubbed her temple with her free hand. It seemed the evening had no depths to which it would not plunge. "Why was this done, and by whom?"

"I don't know exactly who did it, Your Grace," Prentice said, and he reached into his belt to pull out a folded letter. "But I believe they were looking for this."

Prentice politely took the candle holder from Bettina's grasp and placed it on the table next to Amelia. Then he unfolded the letter, spreading the sheets out in the candlelight.

"What are these?" she asked.

"I haven't had a chance to determine that yet, Your Grace. I thought it best to bring them straight to you."

Amelia let out a heavy sigh. She'd had enough for the night. The news of Bastian Fern's death was the last straw. She looked at Prentice and was about to tell him to go and come back in the morning, but in the closer candlelight, she saw his face properly for the first time. One of his eyes was nearly swollen shut, and there were bruises and cuts wherever she looked. Even his knuckles had nicks and swellings.

"What in God's name happened to you?"

CHAPTER 15

Prentice blinked under the duchess's sudden scrutiny. "The murderers were still at the seneschal's home when we went there," he explained. "We drove them off, but it was not an easy fight."

He cast a quick glance at Turley, who was standing by with the wine jug in one hand and the water ewer in the other. He had expected his friend to already have informed the duchess about the fight. That was why he'd gone back to the castle in the afternoon. Turley gave him a confused look, and it took Prentice a moment to realize that his friend had not heard about the part of the fight that had laid him out unconscious. Prentice gave him the tiniest of nods but knew he couldn't explain it all to his friend in the duchess's presence. Turley would have to wait if he had any questions of his own.

"You fought the killers?" the duchess asked. "Turley said as much, but he didn't make it clear how brutal the fight must have been. Are they dead or in irons?"

"One is dead, Your Grace," Prentice replied. "I'm sorry to say the rest managed to flee. They bushwhacked us and fled in the confusion."

"So, there are murderers at large in my town? And that is on top of a retainer who thinks to wield the favor of the prince as a weapon against me. And the contempt of the prince himself, who has banished me to a tower like a fairy tale damsel. And a vast army sitting on my doorstep who expect to be fed. And I'm seeing..." The duchess's voice almost cracked as her words tumbled out, but she finally trailed off.

"Seeing, Your Grace?"

For a long moment, the duchess did not speak. Then she shook her head, as if resolving something in her thoughts. "Seeing my night never coming to an end," she said, but Prentice was sure that was not what she had meant to say.

"Clearly you are tired, my dear," said Bettina. "Let us send the men away and you can rest. These matters will keep for the morning."

The duchess shook her head again. "No, Bettina, that will not do. I am the Duchess of the Reach; it is not a privilege, it is a responsibility. If I want the Reach to stand behind my leadership, then I must be ready to shoulder the burden of leading."

Prentice smiled at her words in spite of himself. For all that she was a young woman, she had an admirable sense of her duty, and it made it easy to want to follow her.

She looked to the papers on the table. "What are these documents?"

"Lists of some kind, Your Grace," he explained while she scanned each page in turn. "Of what, I'm not sure. I can ask others of the household. They might know what the seneschal was doing, and that could shed light—"

The duchess held up her hand for silence. She read on for a moment more. "It's a compact," she said at last. "A written contract between merchants."

"I had no idea, Your Grace."

"Well, it's incomplete, but the essentials are all there." Amelia laid the three pages side by side on the table. "The first lists names and the second lists territories, and this third page shows the disbursements."

Prentice peered at each page in turn. The duchess's explanation made a certain degree of sense, especially given her childhood as a merchant's daughter, but somehow the explanation seemed incomplete.

"Surely three lists aren't enough to form a compact," he said. "Are they?"

The duchess shook her head. "No, they're not. The top and bottom of each page is missing." She pointed to the blank parts of each sheet. "In these spaces, a proper compact would have terms, commencements, and conclusions—all the details of a legal contract. Just a moment."

She took one of the pages and held it in front of the candle flame.

"Looking for invisible ink?" Prentice asked.

"You know of the technique?"

"Vinegar or lemon juice? Yes, Your Grace."

"My father swore it was a guild secret, known only to the most cunning," Amelia said, clearly disappointed that her father's secret was more widely known.

"Your father may have thought it was."

They watched the paper in front of the flame for a long moment, but no writing appeared. Amelia put the paper back down. "It seems the terms were to be filled in later, or else these are copies and the originals are elsewhere. And with Master Fern dead, we cannot ask him."

"Nor Sir Duggan," Prentice added.

"Why Sir Duggan?"

"The last name on the list." Prentice pointed to the paper. "It is signed, 'the Man in Purple and Gray.'"

"Sir Duggan's house colors? Why name himself that way?"

Prentice shrugged. "Some effort has been made to wrap this compact in secrecy, and at least once, some have killed for that secret. Perhaps Duggan wanted to conceal his involvement, though it's a poor disguise to name himself after his own house colors."

The duchess looked down at the dried blood on her dress. "He was nearly mad at the end. He might not have been thinking clearly for a long time. Do you recognize any of the other names on the list?"

"No. Sorry, Your Grace."

Amelia sighed and rested her head in her hand. Prentice turned when he heard Turley edging closer to look at the papers.

"What's disbursement?" Turley asked.

"Do not speak in the presence of your betters," Bettina rebuked.

Turley shrugged apologetically. Prentice smiled, and then Turley's question fired an idea in his mind. He seized the third sheet and read it quickly. When he reached the end of the list, he smiled and handed the page to the duchess. "Disbursements, Your Grace?"

She accepted the paper with a confused expression.

"Payments, Your Grace," Prentice explained. "And where they go. We won't need names if we have the money."

The duchess scanned the paper. "This place," she said, pointing to one of the listings. "And this one. I think all of them are here in Dweltford."

"All except the last one."

"The hunting exchequer? What is that?"

"I have no idea," Prentice conceded. "But the rest we can look to easily enough."

The duchess studied the list in her hand a moment longer. "How would you begin?" she asked at last.

"Start at the top," Prentice said flippantly. Amelia gave him a sour look, and he nodded an apology. "I would take a small group of armed, loyal men to the first address and see what and who are there. Based on what we find, we move on to the next and the next, as quickly as we can. If we could, I'd ideally do it all in one day."

"Why such rush?"

"Whatever this conspiracy was, the seneschal was at the heart of it," Prentice explained. "Now that he is dead, the other conspirators will be watchful. If they see one or two of their number arrested and put in chains, they will likely go to ground. I want to give them the least amount of time to do that."

"Then shouldn't we send men to all on the list at once?" asked the duchess.

Prentice shook his head. "A sound idea, Your Grace, but who would you trust? Your houseguards are barely enough to hold the castle; they haven't the numbers for so many actions at once. And knights? After Sir Duggan's betrayal..."

"I cannot trust any of them?"

"Doubtless you can trust most, but which ones did Duggan take into his confidence? It would take only one to warn the conspirators, and then the conspiracy escapes entirely."

"So, you will use what, your little group of cutthroats that opened the siege?"

"I know I can trust them," said Prentice. "Or at least I know which ones I can trust."

"You know, I have heard that some nobles call you rats, and laugh that the city was taken from the sewers." A strange expression crossed the duchess's face, as if she was remembering something or putting the pieces of a puzzle together.

"Do you laugh, Your Grace?" Prentice asked.

"No, Master Ash, I am not laughing. However it was done, you took my town back for me, which only doubly proves how easily Dweltford can be captured. Sir Duggan took it from me; you took it back. Who will come next and take it?"

"You're afraid of the enemy from beyond the western grasses?"

"Shouldn't I be? It is not even a season since that army was beaten. And Liam has come back with the prince, thinking to make me his bride, to wed the province out from under me."

Prentice and Turley exchanged a look of surprise, while Bettina snorted in derision.

"Impertinence!" she huffed quietly.

"And he is my knight captain, leader of my forces. He has the prince's ear, and he means to trade on that for my hand. The Reach is slipping from my grasp. My husband's legacy is being torn apart by serpents and rotting eagles. I need lions to defend me, and all I have is a pack of rats—with no disrespect to your achievements, Master Ash."

Prentice was shocked by the duchess's words. He immediately remembered the visions he had on the march and the day of the Battle the Brook. He had seen a multiheaded serpent with a rotting eagle being one of its heads, as well as a lion he believed to be an angel of God, or else the Messiah himself. He'd never discussed those visions with anyone except the sacrist Fostermae, yet the young duchess spoke the same imagery as if she herself had seen them.

Had she seen visions of her own? And if so, what did that mean?

"You are thoughtful, Prentice," he heard the duchess say. He realized there had been a long moment of silence, and she must have asked him some question.

"You need your own militia, Your Grace," he said without thinking, and he had a sudden image in his mind of men gathered under the duchy's white lion banner.

"I need more than a town guard," Amelia countered. "And without an enemy to march against, I have no right to levy men."

"No, Your Grace. Not town guard, and not levies. Sworn men. Footmen, trained and equipped and ready to fight for you, to keep your peace and defend it against threats."

He watched the duchess consider his idea and knew immediately the objections she would raise.

"I cannot afford to train and equip an army," she said. "Daven Marcus has brought an army to my doorstep, and they'll eat us all out of house and home in short order. Mark me, Prentice. If I don't find money and soon, we will all be going hungry this winter, and there'll be paupers' graves full of starvelings. When

I sent you this morning to find the seneschal, I hoped to have him brought to me with news of monies saved for a day like this. Now, as I go to bed, I have no monies, a dead seneschal, and a mass of feasting nobles in my house bent on devouring our winter stores in a night."

"Maybe a feast wasn't the best idea, then," Turley said, and all eyes turned on him.

"The duchess was honor bound to feast the prince and his retinue," Bettina scolded with a cold glare. "And you will mind your tongue, steward. You are out of your place, again."

"Sorry, Your Grace." Turley tugged his forelock to the duchess, but when she had looked away, he winked at Bettina. The matron scowled.

The duchess sighed, and her eyes fell back to the three lists.

"Do what you suggest, Master Ash," she said. "Go to these places and see if you can locate these conspirators. I want this compact broken. Arrest any you suspect and question them all. Whatever remains in the west to threaten the Reach, I will not face it with treachery weakening me from within."

"We'll go to it immediately, Your Grace." Prentice bowed, but as he started to withdraw, he nearly lost his balance as the sudden motion made his head pound. Reflexively, both Turley and the duchess reached out to catch him. Embarrassed, he accepted his friend's help but pointedly allowed the duchess to withdraw her hand untaken. He hoped she understood that he didn't want to do anything unseemly by not respecting her rank. Looking at her face, he couldn't read the emotion there and, once he was upright, nodded stiffly.

"Apologies, Your Grace."

"I suggest you have a night's rest, Master Ash," the duchess said with a tone of compassion. "My day has been so full of trials that it is easy for me to forget that yours has had its own challenges. This business can wait for morning."

"Sooner would be better, Your Grace."

"That may be, but not if you drop dead from exhaustion. You are no use to me in a grave. Take rest."

"If you insist, Your Grace."

"I do."

Prentice withdrew and Turley followed him, taking the ewer, the cleaning cloth, and the bowl full of bloody water with him.

CHAPTER 16

Prentice awoke to the warm smell of baking bread and an herbal poultice pressed to his eye. A hand shook him by the shoulder, and he rolled over to find himself lying on a pile of sacks full of flour and grains. His wounded body ached brutally, and he groaned from deep in his chest as he levered himself upright.

"Turley said not to wake you, but you're in the way."

He blinked to see Bellam leaning over him. "Where am I?" Prentice asked.

"Kitchen storeroom."

"How'd I get here?"

"Turley brought you in last night," Bellam explained. "He said you weren't going to make it to your own bed, and did I have a place he could leave you. Wherever the two of you had been, you must have really tied one on."

"I wasn't drunk."

"No, 'course not."

Prentice shook his head and then regretted it for the pain. He pulled a rag bandage from his face and saw that it was caked with dried herbs and te tree bark. Doubtless someone had given it to him before he went to sleep, but he couldn't remember who or how. He stood up gingerly. Yesterday's beating had fully caught up with him. He rolled his shoulders slowly and tried to stretch some of the ache from his limbs.

"That bastard knew his business," he mumbled, referring to the man who'd beaten him in the fight.

"What's that?" asked Bellam.

"Never mind. Do you have any water?"

"In the well. What you need is hair of the dog. Got small beer in the jug on the windowsill, left over from breakfast."

Prentice ran his fingers through his hair and shuffled out of the storeroom into the kitchen proper. The morning light coming in through the windows and the bustle of the cooks and kitchen hands made him pull up short for a moment. He blinked at the brightness before wending his way between tables to the outer door. It was even brighter outside, a rare autumn morning of sunshine, and he rushed straight to the well. Lowering the bucket, he hauled it up full, and after gulping a large drink straight from the bucket's rim, poured the rest over his head, soaking the collar of his doublet in the process. The cold shock helped him wake, but only made his headache sharper.

"Dammit," he cursed.

Looking back, he saw Bellam standing in the kitchen doorway, holding a broad clay cup, more like a bowl than a drinking vessel. Prentice waved him over and took the cup from his hand, then drank the flat lager in one go. The brew had grains floating in it, and he gratefully chewed them as well. He handed the empty cup back. "That'll have to do for breaking fast today."

"Told you it's better than water."

Prentice nodded his thanks and headed off across the upper bailey, leaving Bellam to return to the kitchens. As he marched slowly out the castle gate and down Castle Road, his pace picked up. Even with the bright sunshine, there was a cool breeze blowing, and his wet hair made him shiver. It would dry soon enough. The town was strangely subdued compared to the night before. Castle Road was clear again; the crowds from the night's feast had withdrawn to their tents and pavilions outside the town. All that remained were the locals, clearing away the evening's detritus from the streets. A cooper and two apprentices were trying to save the remnants of a keg that had split after being dropped, and farther down a group of women were haggling with a castle steward who was selling the half-eaten carcasses of roasted fowl for soup. Prentice wondered if Turley or even the chief steward Graycen knew about this man's side trade. Graycen was probably taking a share from whatever the man made, if Turley was right about his corruption.

Prentice found Sir Gant waiting for him in front of the conclave house, just as he had the day before. Cutter was with him. After his conversation with Cutter the previous night, Prentice was struck with how feminine she seemed to him. Little mannerisms and details that he had before attributed to youth now spoke of a strange, frustrated womanhood. Cutter was suddenly a young woman in his eyes, and he almost couldn't believe that he had ever seen her any other way.

"I knew you wouldn't sleep the morning," Sir Gant said at his approach.

"How's that?"

"A little page boy came to tell us you was asleep," Cutter explained. "Said Turley told 'em to let you rest, that you needed it. The knight here figured you wouldn't take to a sick bed. Not in your nature, he said."

"My sick bed was a sack of flour. I had to get up; I was in the baker's way."

Cutter guffawed, and Sir Gant smiled.

"Do we have duties today?" asked the knight. "Tell me we are hunting down the villains who killed the seneschal and his housekeep."

Prentice shook his head, glad that it didn't hurt quite so sharply this time. "Not today, though they are not to be forgotten. For now, I want to scare up as many of the rats that went through the sewer with us as I can, and then we have some businesses to look into."

"You calling me a rat?" Cutter demanded, taking umbrage. "I ain't never turned a friend in to any law, not even that dog of a husband of mine."

Sir Gant started at the mention of Cutter having a husband.

Prentice put a hand on her shoulder. "Not that kind of rat. The kind of savage little rat street fighters that can come up through sewers and take back a town."

"Oh, well, I'm one of them for sure."

Prentice turned and drew her away in search of the nearest tavern, to look for news of the other ex-convicts.

"Did you say husband?" Sir Gant asked, following behind. He had a puzzled look on his face.

"Aye, why? Am I not allowed a husband like any other girl?" Cutter replied.

"You're a maiden?" Gant's expression was a mix of confusion and surprise.

"Not since I married, and truthfully not since before that, but I was born a girl and had a husband once."

"But the..." Gant pointed to his cheek, indicating the spot on Cutter's own face where she was branded. "Brawling? A girl... brawling?"

"Well, that was how I lost my husband," she said as if that explained everything, and then she turned back to follow Prentice, who had stepped through a gate and into a tavern yard.

It took until noon to scare up five men who'd come through the sewers, along with Turley, again pulled away from his steward duties. Of the rest, they heard that one had been recently killed in a drunken fight in a tavern, and the gong farmer, Calles, was not at home.

"Six men," said Gant. "Hardly an army."

"We don't need an army," Prentice replied. "This will do just fine."

He made sure they were all carrying some kind of weapon—knives, for the most part, though there were some staves, and Turley had Prentice's brassbound cudgel. They marched through the streets like a gang of thugs, heading down to the dockside. It had only been a few weeks since they had waded through the lake's edge mud to get to the sewers, but already the rains farther north had increased the level of the water; barges were floating freely, lower than the street level but right up against the jetties.

The first location on the list was the stockyard of a merchant on the Conclave Council, a man named Folper. He hailed from the Vec originally and owned a series of river barges trading up and down the Dwelt. Folper's stockyard was right on the quayside, opposite a private jetty used by his barges. The yard was a large square with a high wooden fence on all sides and one gate, which faced the jetty. Inside were piles of lumber and barrels stacked three high. In the back corner of the yard was a single shed, where perishables were stored out of the weather and Folper could keep his books. Walking down the waterfront road, Prentice paused just before Folper's yard and turned to his small force.

"The man who owns this yard is named Folper," he explained. "The duchess thinks he was helping the traitor Duggan to steal taxes."

That was not strictly true. It was Prentice himself who suspected that the conspiracy's purpose was to embezzle taxes. It was the only thing that explained the dead duke's financial difficulties and Duggan's capacity to pay mercenaries. Duggan had to have been siphoning off tax revenues, probably for years.

"So somewhere in that yard is the duchess' money," he said. "We're going to go in and find it."

"They just going to let us?" the ex-convict Pallrin asked.

"I wouldn't think so," Prentice answered. "So, when we get in there, I want you to round up everyone you can find, and someone shut the gate behind us so no one runs off for help. Think you can do that?"

Filthy faces with gapped-tooth smiles nodded back at him. Did a gang of ex-convicts know how to behave like thugs and bandits? It was a foolish question, and Prentice found himself smiling back at them.

"Right. Scare them up soon as we go in, and herd them to the back of the yard. You don't have to be gentle, but you don't get free rein for murder and affray. Keep yourselves law abiding. Think you can manage that?"

"It's not as much fun that way," Cutter joked.

"I mean it!" Prentice warned.

Cutter lowered her head and nodded. Turning on his heel, Prentice led his gang through the gates of the yard. Once all were through, Turley tapped Pallrin's shoulder and the two closed the gate behind them, shooting the bolt into place.

Almost immediately, a dockworker put down a bundle he was carrying and crossed from the jetty to the gate to see what was happening. "What's this, then?" he demanded of Turley through the bars of the gate.

"Duchess' business," Turley answered curtly.

"Bollocks!"

Turley shrugged and Prentice nodded, approving his restraint. With the gate closed, let the man believe what he liked.

"You can't just shut us out," the dockworker persisted, "we work here!"

The man's protests drew some of his fellows. Soon enough, there were a half a dozen dockers glaring in through the closed gate.

"This isn't right. We'll send for the bailiffs," the man persisted.

"Do it and see what it gets you," Pallrin snapped back, but Turley simply turned his back on the gate, treating the men's complaints with disdain.

Inside the yard, the rest of Prentice's rats were chasing between the stacks of goods, and they quickly cornered the only two workers still there. One was an older man with thick arms and shoulders and a bushy gray mustache. The other was a younger man, thinner than his comrade, but wiry and strong for all that. Neither man looked like they'd fear a fight, but they had no weapons to hand, and faced with a gang of armed thugs, they let themselves be herded into the shed. Prentice's men pushed the two up against a wall inside as he looked around. The shed had bales of cotton and other dry stuffs all down one side, and a small table next to a shelf on a wall. There were two books and an oil lantern on the shelf.

These would be Folper's accounts.

"You two are merchant Folper's men?" he asked them while the others pointed blades and bludgeons at them. The men exchanged looks, and the older one nodded. "Where does he keep his strongbox?"

The two captives met eyes once more before the older straightened himself up and thrust out his chin. "At his house," he said. "He never keeps money here."

For a moment Prentice was taken aback. Of course Folper would keep his treasury at his home. It made sense that any stolen taxes would be there, except... except that the contract specified disbursement to this location. Maybe Folper brought the strongbox to the yard only when a payment was being made. But then why not simply put his house on the compact? The trade yard was no more secret than the house.

No, Prentice was sure the disbursements were stored here. "We're not here to rob your employer. We're sent from the Duchess Amelia."

"Oh, 'course you are! And I'm the prince's long-lost nephew."

Cutter brandished her dagger under the man's nose, but Prentice pulled her back by the shoulder.

"I am Prentice, called Ash. I'm the duchess' man, and I'm acting on her orders. I know Master Folper receives payments here, and I am sent to seize them. They belong to Her Grace. So, if Folper keeps a strongbox at home, where's the one he keeps here?"

"There isn't one!" the older man declared confidently again.

His assurance was undercut by a hesitant noise from the younger man. "There is—"

"There isn't anything!"

"He's the duchess' man," the younger said with a shrug. "He could have us in irons. And thieving from the duchess? That's a sin against God, that is!"

The older man glared for a moment and then turned his head away with a snort of disgust.

"Well?" Prentice asked.

"Under the wool bales in the corner." The young man nodded in that direction. "It only comes out twice a year, when a man comes from the north. Master Folper makes us hide it the rest of the time and never talk about it."

"You won't never work the docks again, you Judas," said the older docker.

"There's always work for honest men," the younger countered.

Prentice held up his hand for quiet and nodded to two of his own men, who quickly pulled the pile of wool bales apart to find a small ironbound chest in the middle of the stack. They took it by the handles and hefted it out.

"Take it outside," Prentice ordered.

The men grunted as they hauled the heavy strongbox between them and shuffled awkwardly out the door. Prentice followed with the other rats. The two carrying the strongbox dropped it onto the ground at their feet. Sir Gant circled round and kicked at a heavy brass padlock that kept the chest locked.

"I doubt they have the keys," the knight said.

"Master Folper keeps the key himself," said the young man, following them out into the light. The older man came behind and clipped him behind the ear. The younger man turned and gave him an angry shove in return.

"So, we'll need tools," said Gant.

Prentice shook his head. "We'll get it back to the castle first." He looked toward the gate. "Turley, open up and get us a handcart and a tarp."

"Righto," Turley called back. "Only, we've got some trouble here."

Prentice crossed to the gate to find a squad of dockers outside, many holding boat hooks and belaying pins. They stood shoulder to shoulder, blocking any exit from the yard.

"Oh, here's another one," said the docker who'd first noticed the gate closed, as Prentice approached. "Looking to leave, are you? Well, you can't. Not until the bailiffs get here."

"Good," Prentice said. "They can escort us to the castle. Tell them to bring a handcart and a tarp."

The dock men blinked at his commanding tone. From behind them there came shouted instructions to clear the way, and two heavyset, well-dressed men shouldered their way through the group. Each wore a silver pin high on his breast and carried an ironbound rod that was both weapon and symbol of a bailiff's authority.

"What is this fracas?" one demanded.

"Banditry," answered the leader of the dockers. "They've seized Master Folper's yard!"

"Is that right?" The bailiff peered through the gate's bars.

"I am Prentice Ash." He stepped up to the gate for the bailiff to see him clearly. "I attended the duchess when she was in the conclave house. Do you know me?"

"I heard your name," said the bailiff.

"I have been sent by Her Grace to take back tax monies stolen by the merchant Folper. I need you to fetch us a handcart and something to cover the box with so that we are not seen transporting it through the streets."

The bailiff narrowed his eyes.

Prentice had no time for the man's suspicions. "Bring the cart, and as soon as you do, we'll open the gates. You can escort us to the castle."

"To the castle?"

The bailiff thought for a moment more, then pushed back through the dock men and started calling for a handcart. The dockers were not convinced.

"This is bollocks!" their leader declared. "Master Folper's no cheat. He's an honest dealer and always has been."

"Then you can speak for him at his trial," said Prentice.

"He is a Veckander," one of the other dockers said quietly, sowing doubt.

"What's it matter where he's from?" The spokesman was having none of it. "Has he ever pressed a shaved coin on you or played you false?"

The doubter shrugged. Before any more discussion could be had, a handcart with solid wooden wheels rattled up and was driven to the gate.

The bailiff pushed himself up next to it. "I'm coming in to see that none's been injured."

"Of course, good man," said Prentice, and he nodded for Turley to pull back the bolt. Then he, Turley, and Pallrin all jumped back as the cart was pushed straight in and the dockers all crowded behind it.

The cart rolled to where the strongbox waited on the ground, with Prentice's rats all standing around it, armed and ready for a fight. The dockers rushed up, and for a moment there was a standoff. Any moment there could be bloodshed. Prentice looked over his crew and saw that none of them seemed afraid, holding their weapons ready. Sir Gant had his hand on his hilt, and Cutter was juggling her dagger with a gleam in her eye and a feral smile on her face. She was more than ready for a fight, but that was the last thing Prentice wanted.

"This is the box," he told the bailiffs. "It must go to the duchess immediately."

"Nothing's leaving this yard without Master Folper's say-so," insisted the dockers' leader, but not all of those with him seemed ready to shed blood to enforce that. Some were simply puzzled by the sight of the box.

"That ain't Folper's strongbox," said one. "His one is brassbound. We all seen it, every week when he brings the pay."

"What difference does that make? So, the man's got two strongboxes? He wouldn't be the first merchant was so rich he needed more than one!"

"But I ain't never seen that one. Maybe these folks are right in what they say. You want to interfere with an appointed man? Remember what happened when Golhaben punched that bailiff two harvests back? They cut his hand off!"

"That's right," the bailiff confirmed, obviously nervous at being in the middle of the confrontation. For a long moment the dockers and Prentice's rats watched each other over the handcart and the strongbox.

Finally, the docker leader sighed and his shoulders sagged. "All right, but I say we should follow 'em all the way up to the castle. They do what they say, or we lay 'em down! You all with me?"

The dockers nodded at that.

Prentice instructed his men to put the strongbox up on the cart, but there was no cloth to cover it with. The dockers on either side formed a hostile honor guard, and the bailiffs led the rats and the cart out of the yard and onto the lakeside road. Walking out front and waving their rods of authority, the bailiffs cleared the route ahead of them. Workers and river boat crews stopped to watch the strange crowd push the strongbox-laden cart through the town and onto Castle Road.

So much for quickly and quietly, thought Prentice as he followed the cart. At this rate Folper would hear of what had happened before they got to the castle, and if he had even half the brains of a dog, he would flee within the hour. They'd have no chance to arrest him now. If they still wanted to catch the others, they would have to be very fast or very lucky.

The dockers followed them all the way up to the castle, only losing their nerve when the cart hit the planks of the bridge.

They watched sullenly as it was pushed through the gate, finally forced to accept that the whole affair was under the duchess's authority. The bailiffs likewise watched, but turned away first, returning down Castle Road.

In the upper bailey, Prentice stopped the cart, and he had the chest taken off and hauled into the stables. He wanted it away from prying eyes while the lock was struck off. A man was sent for a hammer and chisel and when he returned, Prentice took them himself. As he hammered at the lock, he found himself sweating. He was still weak from his beating, but that was not the main cause. This moment was the test; they could open the strongbox and find business papers, or coins, or any of a hundred other items that an honest merchant might keep secure. And if that happened, then Prentice was guilty of theft. Likely the duchess would keep him from the magistrate, but she would have to dismiss him from service, and he'd be a pauper with a reputation for theft, almost as bad as being a convict again.

The chisel didn't break the lock, but the hammering tore the latch from the wood so that the lock hung loose. Prentice handed the tools off and paused to wipe his forehead. He put a hand to the lid of the strongbox, and all the rats crowded around to watch the opening. Cutter was at his left hand, pressing close, and even Sir Gant had foregone the dignity of his rank to lean forward. All of them wanted to see what they had recovered.

"Let's hope it's not a disappointment, eh, lads," he said, then added to Cutter, "and maids."

"Open it!" she said eagerly.

"This isn't treasure, Cutter. Whatever we find belongs to the duchess."

Cutter gave a sneer that melted into a pout, but her eagerness didn't diminish.

Prentice pushed the lid up. An oilcloth covered the contents. Pulling the cloth back revealed two leather coin purses, too large for wearing on a belt. Prentice hefted one out, and the contents jingled like coin. All those standing around laughed at the sound.

"Is that all coin?" asked one. "Is it gold?"

"When did you see taxes paid in gold?" chided another.

Prentice pulled the drawstring of the pouch and tipped some of the contents onto his hand. "Coin of the realm," he said, showing them the silver guilders in his hand.

"Two bags full? How much money is that?" one asked with a tone of wonder.

"More than you'll ever see again," another replied.

"You don't know that."

"Oh, you got a noble title you're hiding that we don't know about?" A finger was pointed at Sir Gant. "He's got a title, and I'll bet he's never seen that much silver."

Prentice wasn't listening to the men bickering. He poured the coins back and drew the string, then he handed first the one purse and then the other to Sir Gant. The knight held them both close to himself and had a look on his face that said he dared any of them to try to take so much as one silver piece. Under the coin sacks was a folded pouch of paper lying on top of something metallic. Prentice reached in and pulled out a heavy metal ingot about the size of his palm and heavy. As he turned it over in the dim light, he whistled.

"What's that?" asked Cutter.

"Silver."

"What, in a lump?"

"Ingot."

"How many of them are there?"

They all leaned in to look into the chest. The bottom was stacked three layers high with the silver blocks.

"God in heaven," one of them whispered.

Prentice did a quick count in his head. "You could buy this castle with that."

"Don't be daft," said Cutter. "No one sells a castle."

"No, they don't," Prentice agreed. "But you can hire mercenaries to take one for you."

He cast a glance at Sir Gant and then at Turley. Both men nodded that they understood. They had uncovered the source of the traitor's funds. And this was only one of the disbursements. Even if only every second name on the list held this much, the duchess's fears were over. She could hire a militia and feed her people for the next year out of this strongbox alone. He returned the ingot and took the coin bags back from Gant, putting them in the strongbox as well. He was closing the lid when he stopped and looked around at the faces full of wonder. They were loyal now, but who knew what this much temptation would do to that loyalty.

He made a decision. He reached his hand into one of the bags and pulled out a handful of coins.

"Put your right hands out," he said.

They looked at each other in surprise, memories of convict life undoubtedly making them suspicious of unexpected good fortune. They were the kind who would just as happily steal as take honest pay. Only Cutter refused to look a gift horse in the mouth. She held out her hand, and Prentice counted five guilders into it.

"You did your work, you get paid."

Once Cutter had hers, each man readily held out his hand, and Prentice counted him an amount. When they were all paid, he dismissed them all, except Turley, Gant, and Cutter.

"There'll be more work in coming days. Don't spend it all on drink," he told them.

Pallrin laughed. "Do you have any idea how much drink I can buy with this? I couldn't drink it all, even if I wanted."

"Not in one night, not with your little girl bladder!" said one of his comrades.

They all laughed and left, making plans to treat themselves in food, drink, and working girls. Prentice took some more coins

out of the bag and counted ten for Sir Gant, Turley, and himself.
He made Cutter's share up to ten and then added another ten.

"What's all this for?" she asked, eyes narrow in suspicion.

"Buy yourself some proper clothes."

She looked down at her ragged shirt and short trews, filthy
and worn. "What sort of proper clothes?"

"Something that'll keep the winter wind out at least."

"You want me in a dress, do you? Make a weak little girl out
of me again?"

"What are you talking about?" Prentice said.

"It would be more fitting for a young woman," offered Gant,
but Prentice gave a scowl to show that the knight should butt
out.

"You do want me in a dress!" Cutter cried.

"Wear what you want! Why should I care?" Prentice retorted.

"Oh, just not this?" She pulled at her shirt. "You think to buy
me with gifts? Like a doxy girl, is that it?"

"Just give me the bloody money back."

Cutter shook her head and dashed from the stables.

Prentice sighed. "What was that about?"

"For such a beaten-down thing, she has a great deal of pride,"
said Gant.

Prentice closed the strongbox and motioned for the other two
to take it up. Once they had it lifted between them, he led the
way out of the stables and across to the keep, to get the money
to the duchess as quickly as possible.

"Cutter's a lass, eh?" asked Turley of no one in particular.
"Makes sense, I guess."

Prentice cast a black look back at his friend, but the burly man
only shrugged with a smile and adjusted himself to the weight
of his burden.

CHAPTER 17

"O h my Lord." Amelia sighed as she looked down into the chest.

When Prentice had led his two men in with the strongbox between them, she wondered what it could contain, but she had not dared to hope for this. She had waited impatiently as he ordered the other two from the room and then asked her to dismiss her maids as well. As he opened the box at last and revealed its contents, she reached her hand down to feel the weight of the coin bags and was surprised when Prentice pulled the bags out to show the ingots underneath.

She looked up at him and smiled. "Silver?"

"Ninety ingots," he said.

Amelia peeked in again. Ninety ingots of silver? That was almost a quarter of what she had taken south last spring, to pay her husband's vast debts.

"And this was from only one of the locations on the list?"

"Just the first, Your Grace."

Amelia did the sums swiftly in her head. If each disbursement on the conspirators' lists was the same as this, then not only would she make back all the money she had paid to the Vec bankers, but she would have more than twice that amount.

"Is this all of it?" she asked, as a wild flight of fancy offered the possibility that there might be even more.

"All but about eighty or so coins, Your Grace," Prentice answered with a severe expression.

"What happened to those?"

"I paid my crew with them."

The duchess was surprised, and she took a step back. "Did you indeed? Pray tell what gave you the thought to do so?" She arched her brow coldly.

"I had a gang of ex-convicts with a chest full of silver to hand, Your Grace," he explained levelly. "The best way to convince them not to pilfer from it was to pay them a share."

"You couldn't trust them, so you paid them off?"

"Just so."

Amelia frowned, but as she thought about it, Prentice's reasoning struck her as sound. She hated the thought of mercenary behavior, of men who served for money over loyalty. But then loyalty had to be rewarded, or else that only invited betrayal.

"I concur with your reasoning," she said, nodding. "But I have no love for mercenaries, Master Ash."

"The workman is worthy of his wages."

"You think to quote scripture to me?"

"Forgive me, Your Grace, if I am too bold."

She smiled in spite of herself. "I cannot fault you for your boldness, Master Ash. It has served me too well in the past to criticize you for it."

He nodded. He was always so formal when they discussed matters of state, and as she noticed it, she realized that she valued it as well. By keeping formal, he kept her free to make her own decisions. At times she saw him as a wise uncle in whom she could confide, but it was good that he never saw their relationship that way. She was the duchess; she might need help to wear that title, but she could not lean too heavily on any one person, for the burden was hers.

"Did you make any arrests?" she asked, returning her mind to the silver.

"There was no one there worthy of arrest. Only two workmen, who told all they knew."

"Are you sure?"

"The owner of the yard was a merchant named Folper, of the conclave. Issue a warrant, and your bailiffs and houseguard can take him tonight, if he's still in town."

"It would have been better if you had taken him with the chest."

"A task too big for my little squadron." Prentice's head dipped slightly, and Amelia thought she read disappointment in his expression. He would rather Folper was arrested along with the money as well.

"Perhaps you need more men."

Prentice didn't even blink before saying, "As I've said, Your Grace, it is you who needs more men. Your own men."

She nodded again, then turned away from the strongbox and sat in her chair. Prentice stood by, waiting. It took her a while to sort all the issues in her head.

"Do you know if Folper has actually fled?" she asked.

"I do not."

"Then I'll have a scribe up here and have a warrant for his arrest to the bailiffs within the hour."

Prentice nodded.

She looked at the open chest. "That money will get the province through the winter, I hope. There's no telling yet what state the small folk are in after the invasion, but with the prince's five hundred knights and all their retainers on our doorstep, Dweltford will be shipping in food before the winter's out, I have no doubt. I suppose I'll need to appoint a new seneschal to my purse, just to count and keep all this wealth. It's a better problem to have than want of it."

She settled to silence again. Prentice's expression caught her attention. "Is there something else you want to say?" she asked.

"No, Your Grace."

"Are you sure? You seem uncomfortable."

Prentice touched his fingers to the bruises on his face. "I am not fully recovered, Your Grace."

Amelia frowned as she realized that it was not even a full season since the Battle at the Brook, where he had been brutally battered, and now he had received a second beating. In that light, it was impressive he was on his feet at all.

She stood and offered him her seat. "Here, sit."

"Your Grace, no—"

"Do as I instruct. I shall sit on the bed."

She moved and sat herself on the mattress. Still, he hesitated. She cocked an eyebrow and nodded at the chair. He sank heavily into it and seemed to stifle a groan.

"Do you need a drink?" she asked.

"You cannot serve me from your hand, Your Grace."

"It wouldn't be the first time. Besides, I am at home now. I can summon a steward to the task." Instead, she stood and fetched her jug and cup from the sideboard and poured him a draught. She held it out to him, but he almost seemed to flinch from it. "Oh, for God's sake, take it, man."

Prentice took the cup and sipped at the watered wine.

"There can be limits to formality, Prentice," she said.

"We're not on a march anymore, Your Grace," he replied with a pained look on his face. "There are many more prying eyes and listening ears in a castle. And familiarity breeds contempt."

"If you ever show me contempt, I'll offer you the back of my hand for it!" she declared and sat down on the bed.

Prentice looked at her, and as their eyes met, it was clear they were both sharing the image of her cuffing him like a cur. In her mind she saw her hand flailing like the wing of a chicken, and she imagined it bouncing off him as if she'd struck one of the castle's walls. The thought made her smile, and she saw her amusement reflected in his eyes. Then they both chuckled, and she was glad of it. Since the death of her husband, he was the closest she had to a friend.

"All right," she said. "I'll have one of my knights cuff you for me."

"Quite right, Your Grace," he agreed, but his somber mood had broken. They sat together in silence for a moment.

"What of this merchant, Folper?" she asked. "Will he take up the rebellion now that Duggan is dead?"

"I don't think so."

"Why not?"

"The ingots, Your Grace."

That answer puzzled Amelia. She waited for Prentice to explain, but he merely nodded at the strongbox. Standing again, she reached in and drew forth one of the metal oblongs. It was cool and hard in her hand. Turning it over she saw it was stamped with the ducal lion and another emblem. It took her a moment to realize that it was the seal of the Fallenhill mint. The mint was the receiving house for all the Reach's silver mines, or it had been until the invaders had sacked the town and slaughtered all the inhabitants.

"They're from the mint?"

"Yes, Your Grace. And they are stamped with your own coat of arms, which means they're tax bars. These are literally taxes to the dukedom that have been redirected into other hands. It took ducal authority to do that—Duggan's authority. Whatever the conspirators planned with this money, Duggan was the center of it. With him gone and with Fallenhill and the mint destroyed, the source of their wealth is gone too. There'll be no more disbursements now, I'll wager."

Amelia considered what he was saying. A thought struck her. "The mines? Who's in charge of them? What's happened to them and the miners since the invasion?"

"I've not heard," Prentice said. "But the miners have their own guild. Their guildmaster should know their fate unless he was in Fallenhill as well."

"Another duty. The conclave hasn't mentioned a word of any of this to me."

"I think, Your Grace, that you will have to treat the conclave as suspicious until you have rooted out the others like Folper. Most, if not all, of the conspirators probably sit on the council."

Amelia laughed bitterly. "The nobles are fickle, the gentles are a mass of traitors, and the lowborn will steal from me if I don't pay them off."

"It sounds as if you understand rulership quite well, Your Grace." Prentice drained his cup and poured himself a second.

"How long would it take you to raise a force of men for me?" Amelia asked. "A militia to keep the peace and defend the Reach from invaders?"

"With this money, I could have a mob for you by the end of a week, but you don't want that, Your Grace. You need a trained cadre, disciplined and equipped. That takes time."

"How long, Master Ash?"

"Recruit over the winter, get them marching in the spring, and by the end of next summer you'll have what you need."

"End of summer? We raised the army that saved the Reach in a mere month."

"They were knights, Your Grace, you know that. As well as the five hundred convicts, almost all of whom died in the battle. As I said, I can raise you a mob in a week."

Amelia turned away and watched the fire in the grate while she thought. Prentice's words made sense, but they left her in a precarious position. She'd only been moved to the tower a couple of days and already it felt like a self-imposed exile. More than that, nowhere in the castle would feel safe while Prince Daven Marcus was still there. Along with her personal misgivings, there was one fear underneath them all that needed her best attention.

"Armies don't march in winter, do they?" she asked, staring into the flames.

"It's not unknown, but generally not."

"Because of the weather."

"Mostly. Cold is hard to march through, and rains turn the roads to mud. Men who are wet and cold for too long get sick and weak. But if an army is well equipped and well fed, then it can be done."

She closed her eyes.

"What are you thinking?" Prentice asked her gently.

"That no matter how the battle ended, even if Prince Mercad had lived, the army wouldn't have marched west."

"It's only just autumn, Your Grace. It's cool, but not cold. There are months yet for campaigning if that's what the army desired. You wanted to go west?"

Amelia clenched her fist and looked straight at him. "We know nothing about them. Not a thing! Why did they come? And from where? They slaughtered everything, man, woman, and beast. They took no plunder and claimed no land. What was the point? Why?"

"Why do you think, Your Grace?"

The question hung between them in the dimming light. The maids she had sent away would return soon, to light the candles and stir the fire for the cool of the night.

"All I can think is that they were mad; crazed with bloodlust. All they did was kill."

"They were testing us, Your Grace."

Prentice's tone was so full of certainty that it surprised her. He'd been thinking about this as well. Did it trouble him as much as it did her?

"Why do you say that?" she asked.

"For the reasons you listed. They did nothing a conquering army would do; as you say, they took no prisoners, no ground, no plunder. The only thing left is the battle itself."

"So, they were just lost to bloodlust?"

"I don't think so. They were disciplined, controlled, and had... they had those magical beasts."

Amelia was taken aback. Prentice always seemed so pragmatic, so even-tempered. He was not the sort to tell tall tales. Of course, she had heard the stories. Her maids delighted in passing along the gossip that was going around. And there had been sacrist Porlain's claim that he'd summoned an angel by his prayers to win the battle. That made her sneer with derision when she'd heard the cleric's tale, before the man rushed away to report his "miracle" to Church authorities. But if Prentice confirmed the stories, then perhaps she had to give them more credence. So, what did that mean?

"Why would magic speak to testing us? I don't understand your reasoning," she said.

"It takes too much effort to raise and feed an army, especially a disciplined one, to throw it away on the joy of fighting. Men who love to fight can beat each other senseless in a ring any market day. Or if they are highborn like Prince Daven Marcus, they can ride from tourney to tourney, matching arms against their peers. Armies are expensive, complicated, and exhausting. And magic speaks of study and effort. It is never a thing easily achieved if it is real."

That all made sense to her. She worked to figure his reasoning for herself. "So, if someone went to all that effort, you say it must be for a reason?" she said, and he nodded. "And you don't count just fighting to be a good enough reason?"

"No."

He said nothing more. Amelia could barely see his face in the dimming light, but she was sure he was watching her, waiting to see if she could puzzle it all out for herself. She found that she wanted to do it, not only for herself, but to please him. For a moment she felt like an eager student with an exacting tutor.

"They went to the expense and effort of raising an army, and they came to fight us." She worked her way slowly through her thoughts, turning each piece of the puzzle over in her mind before placing it in the sequence. "They took no plunder and made no claim on the land, and thus you think they came to test us. That would explain their brutality! They were trying to provoke us, pushing us to take the field in force."

"That's what I believe."

"And they waited to ambush us. They wanted the fight... and we beat them. Crushed them, in fact; they've learned to fear us. We shouldn't have to worry."

Amelia felt a rush of relief, but her joy was short lived as she saw Prentice shaking his head. The shadows of his face, and its bruises, made him seem so grim that his simplest gestures felt like judgment.

"But we beat them," she said.

"We beat this force, yes."

"So, it shows the cost of fighting us. Why raise another army to face us if the last one was so easily dispatched?"

"Why assume that that was their whole army? And why come to test us now? Out of the blue? No warning, no preamble."

"We have no idea what's coming," Amelia whispered fearfully.

"I think we can guess—"

"No, it was something Duggan said, just before he died. He said we have no idea what is coming. Did he know, do you think? Did he understand the enemy like you do?"

"I don't know, Your Grace."

"Oh Lord, have I made a mistake, killing him?"

"Mistakes are made. Don't dwell on them. Learn from them."

Now he really was treating her like a student, but she didn't mind. This was no time for pride or defending the niceties of rank. And, dire as the situation was, in her heart she relished these moments, when she could use her mind and speak freely to another. It was something she lacked, even with Bettina and her maids. It was her great pleasure to read, to study, to think, and that pleasure helped carry her through the bitterness of the thoughts.

"I need men in the west," she declared. Prentice nodded, and while she was glad that he agreed with her, she was even more pleased to realize that she wasn't just seeking his approval anymore. She was making decisions that had to be made, fulfilling her duties to her people.

"I cannot wait for your militia for that. The Reach needs squires or rangers, riders of some sort, who can track the remains of the invader force, find where they came from if they can. And..." A new thought occurred to her as she spoke. "And to warn us if a new attack comes."

"Yes, Your Grace."

"You cannot do that for me, Master Ash."

That seemed to catch him by surprise. "No, Your Grace?"

"Riders, especially squires, tend to be men of birth, Prentice," she explained, pleased that she had seen something he had not. "Such men will not answer your call, even now that you are no longer a convict. They will only take instructions from rank."

"You are right, of course," he said.

"You must concentrate on raising me this militia." Amelia realized the tone of her voice had changed, shifting from speculation to command. "Do what you think is right, but do what you can to shorten the time. The sooner this force is ready to serve, the better. I will send for a clerk now and give you that warrant before dinner. The more embezzled taxes you root out for me, and the sooner, the more money you'll have to fund your work."

Prentice nodded and drained his goblet. He stood up, and though his face was still shadowed, Amelia thought he looked more resolved. Perhaps it was her own resolve she was perceiving.

CHAPTER 18

It was fully night when Prentice left the keep with the duchess's warrant in his belt. Iron braziers were burning in the bailey and in front of the gatehouse. A chill autumn wind whipped the flames about, while houseguards warmed themselves nearby. Looking up at the sky, he couldn't see any stars or the ribbon, though its glow still backlit the clouds some. A storm must be blowing in. He rubbed his arms to warm himself as he walked out on the bridge and thought about the merchant Folper fleeing the town. It would be bad weather for traveling.

Prentice stopped in his tracks.

How comfortable was Folper? The man had to know by now that Prentice had seized the silver. Was he canny enough to flee straight away, or would he be slow to move? An optimistic thought occurred to Prentice; Folper might still be in town. The main gate would be closed for the night too. There was a good chance he hadn't fled. Prentice patted the warrant. It was intended for the bailiffs, but he was the duchess's man as much as they were. With a quickened pace he strode down Castle Road, looking for Sir Gant.

He found the hedge knight in a tavern nursing a tankard. Gant never seemed to drink or eat much, a product of a hard life with little money, Prentice assumed, and so he was not drunk now. Prentice didn't hold out hope that any of the others weren't deep in their cups already.

"Have you seen Cutter or Turley?" he asked.

Sir Gant shook his head. "Cutter? Not since she ran off, and your man the steward is in the castle, going about his duties, I expect. Did you need them?"

Prentice nodded. "I have a further warrant from the duchess, to arrest Folper and hold him for trial."

"Bailiff's work?"

"I can give it to the bailiffs, but if he's still in town I want to take him now."

"You think he might be?" Gant asked.

"There's a chance, and the sooner we catch him, the sooner we can have him tell us who the others on the list are and what their role was."

"Assuming he knows."

Prentice paused at that. Gant's point was a sound one. The papers from the seneschal had been drawn up to bind the conspirators together, but there were clear attempts to conceal identities within the compact. Prentice shook his head at the almost childish naivety of it all, like Duggan calling himself "the Man in Purple and Gray." He wondered if the dead castellan had thought he was being clever, choosing that pseudonym and not realizing how obvious it was. It reminded Prentice of his time in the academy at Ashfield, when young students were first taught about ciphers. Suddenly, every student had overwhelmingly important secrets that had to be written down in cryptic codes. If ever the documents were uncovered, they were usually simple to decipher, and amounted to little more than clumsy love poems to secret affections or lists of grudges, enemies upon whom vengeance would later be taken.

"Folper might not know any of the others, but I think he might know some," he said. "This is a compact of amateurs not used to conspiracy."

"Knights of the Grand Kingdom are too accustomed to announcing their every deed, lest they miss out on some fragment of glory," Sir Gant observed. "Even in the king's court. It is not unknown for men of rank to announce their un-marital affairs publicly, naming both the goodwife they have taken to their bed and the husband they have cuckolded."

"Surely not." Prentice shook his head and chuckled in disbelief.

"It ebbs and flows in seasons, but it's more common than you'd think."

"Well, maybe Duggan announced more to his little cabal than he should have."

"You're optimistic," said Gant, but he followed as Prentice led the way.

Not optimistic, Prentice thought. Hopeful.

He just needed to make something useful out of this pig's breakfast. As he marched through the town, through streets almost empty except for late workmen rushing home to their wives and families, he turned the various facts over in his mind, centered on the one possibility. If the merchant Folper was still in town, then Prentice was going to catch him before he fled.

Folper's home was a two-story house with whitewashed walls, a central rose garden, and diamond-patterned panes of glass in the windows. It lay on a broad lane off the south side of Castle Road, on the edge of the town quarter called the Weeps. The building was not that different from the dead seneschal's house, except for where it was situated in the town. The Weeps was the southeasternmost section of Dweltford and was where the tanners and slaughterers were found. The noxious fumes of their trade filled the air continually, sometimes so thick it made the eyes water, hence the quarter's name. Only the workers in the trade lived in the quarter normally, or the desperately poor, but if the merchant Folper traded in leathers, hides, and furs, then it made sense that his home would be near the area. Of course, a truly wealthy merchant would have soon bought a house on the north side of town and left the Weeps to their misery. So this home spoke of wealth and success, but its location suggested an upper limit to that success.

Sir Gant summed the house up in a single phrase. "Fine, but not grand."

Prentice nodded. "Near his business," he said, and then he remembered what the man who had assaulted him had said, that he would tan Prentice's skin in his own vats and wear it. The attacker was another leather merchant, or at least owned a leatherworks. Was that business nearby? The thought made Prentice uneasy, and he looked about involuntarily, suddenly more alert.

"Trouble?" asked Gant, noticing Prentice's shift in mood.

"Just keeping watchful."

Realizing that he had only a vague idea of what he was looking for, Prentice gestured at Folper's house and led the way to the heavy wood door. He paused before reaching for the iron ring of the knocker.

"Straight in," he explained quietly. "Don't give them time to think. If someone's in there, we cow them and make them give up Folper."

"His men at the wharf today were pretty fierce in their loyalty," Gant objected. "If he's got some of them in there, they could make a fight of it, hold us up long enough to let him get away, at the least."

"You could go around the back, if you like."

"And leave you alone to make the assault? We're vulnerable enough, just the two of us, without splitting up."

That made Prentice look around again, and Gant did as well.

"Your choice," Prentice said.

Sir Gant grimaced and rolled his eyes but drew his sword. "Nothing ventured... I suppose," he muttered.

"No guts, no glory!" Prentice agreed.

He put his hand on the knocker and then thought again. He tried the latch, and it was not bolted. With a smile he nodded to Gant and then slowly opened the door. Inside they found a dark hall with several doorways leading back into the house. Everywhere was quiet, but there was light seeping under one of the doors, so they crept to that one. The two positioned themselves at either side of the door, and after a silent count of three, they burst through.

They found themselves confronting three men sitting quietly around a table. The men wore cotton jackets and trews of a foreign cut and had long, dark hair, pulled back in tight plaits. Two were about the same age as Prentice and Gant, but the third was clearly in later middle age, with crow's feet by his eyes and wisps of gray in his hair.

"Stand fast in the name of the duchess!" Prentice declared loudly. He was surprised when the elder man sighed with loud exasperation.

"It is about time," he said in a lilting accent. "We have been sitting here waiting for some time."

"Waiting?"

"Nearly one half hour of the clock."

Prentice and Sir Gant exchanged confused looks.

"Waiting for what?" Prentice asked.

"Merchant Folper said you would be coming. He left us here to meet you."

Prentice's ears pricked up at the mention of Folper. He was only half an hour ahead of them.

"Who are you?" Gant asked.

The elder man stood and bowed with a flourish of his right hand. "I present myself as Yentow Sent, master smith of Hobaren in Masnia."

"Masnia?" Prentice repeated, his mind still on Folper's escape. Masnia was a far country, south of the Vec princedoms. Hobaren was its capital, as far as Prentice knew. This man had come a long way. While he was trying to sort out what was happening, Prentice almost missed Yentow Sent introducing the other two men as bonded craftsmen, like guild journeymen but pledged specifically to Sent's service, apparently.

"They do not speak your language well," Yentow Sent apolog. The two men nodded when they were indicated but did not stand. Gant returned their nods but left his sword unsheathed.

Prentice waved away the introductions, trying to understand what was going on. "Master Sent, you say Folper told you to wait for us. Why?"

"Merchant Folper told us that you would be coming. That the man we were brought to serve has lost his position, and his replacement would come to introduce himself. He said that we would have to negotiate a new contract. I must object to this."

"Who was the man you were going to serve?"

"The older man in gray, the one from the castle," Sent explained. "We met him once, weeks ago, but your names are not easy for my tongue. I do not remember his."

"Duggan," muttered Gant.

Prentice nodded. "So, Duggan brought you here to work for him?"

"No, it was merchant Folper. He is from the Vec, and his family has people in Masnia. They hired me in Hobaren to come here. The gray man was to build an army, they said. I would make them weapons and armor."

Prentice was torn. He wanted to go after Folper straight away before the merchant was out of his reach. But Yentow Sent had been hired by the conspiracy. He was on the inside. How bad was he with Kingdom names? He could be faking his ignorance, but Prentice's instinct was that the man was sincere. He looked at the three men's arms and hands. Their jackets had short sleeves and the men's bare wrists were slender, but wiry. Their hands were covered in small scars and callouses. They were craftsmen for sure.

"You make weapons?" Prentice asked.

Yentow Sent moved to a sideboard and pulled back an oilcloth. Underneath was a collection of fine weapons forged in cold steel. There were daggers both ornate and practical, as well as a bearded axe with a brutal-looking back spike, the blade etched and inlaid with gold. There was no longsword, the weapon of a knight, but Prentice's eyes were drawn to another sword-like weapon. It was a bar of steel the length of an arming sword, a large man's finger-width thick, with a cross guard and hilt. The end had a blunt point, and the steel was twisted along its length so that it seemed made of complex sections, with hard edges and corners. A swordbreaker. It would be wielded similar to a club or baton, weighing about the same as a longsword, despite being shorter. Its great advantage was its power to damage a forged steel blade. The heavy bar could easily block and parry any sword, and its weight and jagged shape would damage edges and bend blades with ease. It would take a strong man to wield properly, but in the hands of an expert, it would be the bane of any knight on a battlefield.

"A swordbreaker?" Prentice asked Yentow Sent, taking up the weapon.

"Graphon Turn made that." The master pointed to one of his two craftsmen at the table. "Merchant Folper has us making weapons to show our skill for the duchess and her men. We are not allowed to make longswords until we have her warrant. Merchant Folper tells us this is the law of the Grand Kingdom."

Prentice nodded. It was true that knights' weapons, especially the longsword, could only be produced with warrants from ranking lords, barons and higher. Warrants were so coveted and closely held that only a few crafts families in the entire Grand Kingdom knew how to forge quality longswords. It was an ordinance laid down centuries before, to keep the best weapons out of the hands of the peasantry. Knights and other men of rank would travel far distances to have a longsword made because so few warrants were issued. If Yentow Sent and his two craftsmen knew the art, then odds were good that they could be the only ones in the entire Western Reach who did.

"A silly law," Yentow Sent added.

"A law, nonetheless," Sir Gant asserted, taking umbrage at this foreigner's disrespect for Grand Kingdom institutions.

"In Masnia a man of skill follows his ability to its completion. He does not let petty rules curb his destiny."

"In the Grand Kingdom a man who forges a longsword without the warrant to do so has both his hands cut off, which would bring him swiftly to the completion of his destiny, I would think."

Yentow Sent sniffed at Gant's words, but Prentice had no interest in refereeing a jingoistic debate between the two.

"Leave it, Sir Gant," he said. He took up the swordbreaker and struck a formal pose, like a guard at attention. "Master Yentow Sent, I give you the duchess' apologies at keeping you here waiting. I will take this fine weapon to show her, as well as one of these daggers." He took up a poniard with a long blade and a steel-and-brass crossguard. "These bear true witness of your skill—"

"I did not make these!" Sent scoffed. "This is make-work, beneath my skill."

Prentice didn't let Sent's objection slow him. "Then how much greater must your works be, if this is the quality your mere bondsmen can create? The duchess will hear that also in my report. She will contract you, I am certain. When she does, a warrant will be prepared, and I will send for you to have an audience with the duchess herself."

"And in the meantime? You expect us to continue waiting here?"

"Did you have another plan?"

Sent was clearly not interested in Prentice's flattering promises. "Merchant Folper and the gray man from the castle have held us waiting here many weeks already. I did not come north to sit and do nothing. It is undignified. I am a master; princes of the Vec have waited days to have a meeting with me."

Prentice's eyes narrowed, and he clenched his fist in frustration. Every moment Sent went on meant more chance for Folper to get away. "I understand, master," he said through gritted teeth. "I will speak to the duchess as soon as I can."

Yentow Sent folded his arms and rolled his eyes, but Prentice had had enough. He gave the three men a short bow and tapped Sir Gant on the shoulder. They both began to leave but stopped at the door as Prentice remembered something.

"Just one thing, master. Did the merchant tell you which way he was going? Was he heading to the lakeside?"

"He had a horse and several mules packed," said Sent. "They went to the gate, I think."

"Very helpful. Thank you."

The journeyman Yentow Sent had named said something to his master. He and Sent had a short conversation, and the master smith fetched something from the other side of the room. It was a leather belt with a half sheath for hanging the swordbreaker in. Like the weapons, the leather was not ornate, but the craftsmanship was top notch.

"Graphon Turn wants you to take this as well," Sent explained.

"You make belts and baldrics too?"

"I would not allow a weapon of mine to be disrespected by inferior tack. All my workshop's weapons come with their full kit. My apprentices learn the leather, to respect the craft, before they learn the steel."

"This is apprentice's work?" That surprised Prentice.

Sent nodded. "My apprentices have lodging near the... waterfront, do you call it?"

"You've brought your whole workshop north?"

"There was to be a war, I was told. You can see my impatience at having all my business sit idle, I hope."

Prentice nodded, and then he and Sir Gant left Folper's house, heading toward the town gate.

"What happened to cowing them? Guts and glory?" asked Gant.

"I didn't expect to find a master weaponsmith sitting waiting for us. Did you?"

"From Masnia no less. Don't think I've ever met a Masnian before."

"Now you've met three." Prentice paused a moment to fit the leather belt around his waist and to put the swordbreaker into the half sheath. The odd edges of the metal flashed in the light of a nearby lantern.

"At a distance it looks like just a rough-edged metal bar," Gant observed. "But I'd hate to lay it up against my blade. It'd bite like teeth into the edge."

"Ruin a sword in a single strike," Prentice agreed. "I learned to use swordbreakers under Seven Rings Cross, but those were never much more than brass batons. This is the best I've ever seen."

"And so you're taking it for yourself? And the dagger too?" Sir Gant cocked an eyebrow.

"Master Sent made these as exemplars, demonstrations of his craft to a new employer. I'll make sure the duchess sees them when she hires him."

"You're sure she'll hire Sent on? He came here to work for Duggan."

Prentice didn't answer, and when the two reached Castle Road, he turned them east toward the gate. A cold wind whistled around down the street, and a driven spray of rain started to rattle on the rooftops of the houses. By the time it reached the street, it was a thin drizzle that swiftly drenched their hair and faces.

"Folper's not getting far in this," Prentice declared. Things were going his way. He pressed on along the road, feet slipping on the slick cobbles.

"But why would the duchess hire the servant of her enemy?" Gant persisted. He wiped his face and flicked some of the water away with his hand, but it was a pointless gesture. He was dripping wet again in moments.

"Duggan brought a master smith north to make him weapons. Sent isn't a conspirator, he's just a hired man—and a skilled one. Folper's left him behind because he doesn't know anything, I'm sure of it. The duchess wants me to build her a militia. A master weaponsmith with bonded craftsmen, apprentices, and a full workshop will make that a hundred times easier."

"A man like that won't be cheap."

"The duchess can pay the same way Duggan planned to, with tax silver!"

They rushed across Within Walls and on toward the gate. The rain slowed to a mere mist, but the cold wind bit at them through the shadow-drenched streets. Between the night's overcast darkness and the wet roads, they stumbled and slipped their way forward. More than once they nearly fell, but Prentice would not slow his pace. He wanted to catch the renegade merchant while he was stuck at the gate.

CHAPTER 19

When they reached the gate, Folper was already gone. They rushed out of the dark, like on the night Prentice had led the raid to take the gatehouse. Now the men who kept watch were houseguards of the duchess, but aside from that, everything seemed much as it had that other night, with one exception. The gate was wide open.

"Prince's orders," one of the men on duty said with a shrug when Prentice asked. "He wants his people to be able to come and go as they like. We ain't been allowed to shut the gate at night since they all arrived."

There was no point being angry, but Prentice cursed inwardly. The gate hadn't held Folper up for a moment. He asked the gate guards if they had seen him.

"Fella with a horse and mules? Yeah, we seen him. He's in for a rough night on the road, I'd lay odds."

"How so?" asked Gant.

"Mules were braying like a pack of wild things. Overloaded them with those boxes and bundles, I reckon."

"And he was trying to go with no lantern," added a second guard. "That's all fine with the camp out there, but soon enough he'll be in the pitch dark and he won't pick the road from his own armpit!"

"The camp?" asked Gant.

"See for yourself."

Prentice and Gant went through the open gate. Just outside the barbican, another group of houseguards warmed themselves by an open brazier that blazed beside the road. Beyond them the fields were swamped with a sea of tents, lit with campfires, lanterns, and torches. Not so long before, the duchess and the little remains of her army had camped in the same spot, but this was many times more than that. It was impossible to see the limits in the darkness, but from where they stood, it was as if a town of canvas had sprung up outside Dweltford. Five hundred knights with their squires, footmen, pages, and whatever ladies had accompanied them, plus servants, courtiers, and any other officials the prince brought with him. Then there were the horses, carts, and pack animals.

Prentice did some quick arithmetic in his head. "There's got to be at least four thousand or more there, plus their animals."

"If Folper's in there, he'll be hard to find," Gant said.

Prentice shook his head. "He's running now, not hiding. He'll be on the road."

"I hope you're right."

They followed the road that ran under the wall of the town and then down the lakeside, with the camp on their left and the water's edge on the right. The lake was flush again, the muddy flats washed away under the rainwater of recent weeks and the flow from the north. This night's rain had stopped, but the wind still blew cold and the stars had not come out.

The road ahead was looking darker as they passed the main of the camp, but soon they were struck by a bittersweet stench coming in wafts between the gusts of the wind.

"Gah, that's like the damned sewer again," Sir Gant declared, spitting at the smell. "Worse, even."

"I know that smell," Prentice said quietly, shaking his head.

Just ahead of them, they came upon a shuffling crew of convicts, all linked to a chain, as they made their way across the road toward the lake. They were led by two overseers, both wearing rough woolen cloaks over shirts and trews, with long coiled whips in hand. Every pair of convicts carried a body between them, the naked forms hanging limp, their silhouetted limbs thin like wizened branches. Prentice knew immediately what was going on. These were convicts that had died, either of exhaustion, or the cold, or starvation, or simple execution. He did a quick tally. There were six dead; that was a lot for one day's loss.

"Ho there, declare yourself!" One of the two overseers had spotted Prentice and Gant by the light of their lantern.

"Prentice Ash, duchess man," Prentice answered the challenge. Inside himself he felt a strange pleasure at being able to declare that to an overseer, to know he was no longer a convict, off the chain and immune to the overseer's authority.

"Who's that with you?"

"Sir Gant of the Reach, knight in service to Her Grace," Prentice replied.

"Of the Reach?" Gant whispered.

"Are you hers, or aren't you?" Prentice whispered back. "If you've got another title, we can use that."

Sir Gant shrugged.

The two overseers made their way around the shuffling convicts, who stopped to let the conversation happen, almost certainly glad of the distraction, if not the rest. The life of a convict was miserably dull when it wasn't disgusting or terrifyingly brutal. With their ragged clothing, every one of them shivered in the cold.

"You've lost more than a few, overseer," said Prentice. "Six in a day?"

"You should have seen it when we crossed the passes," the overseer answered, a moldy smile revealing rotten teeth in the half light. "Lost nearly one out of six through the marching and the cold. Prince was in such a rush to get here. Didn't make no allowances."

"I thought my feet was nothing but blisters for a while there," said the other overseer.

Prentice wanted to punch the man, whining about blistered feet in the same breath as people dying of exhaustion, but that was the way of things in the Grand Kingdom. A convict was less than an animal to these men.

"The ones left should be strong, then," Prentice argued. "How do you lose six in a day?"

"Most of them would be strong, but there ain't enough food to feed them all. Not proper."

"And we ain't coddling them," added the blister complainer. "There just ain't enough food."

Convicts never ate well. It was a point of their punishment. They were to suffer for their entire term, their labor hard and bitter, to purge their guilty souls. On top of all that, every overseer gang skimmed off some of any coin made available to pay for convict food.

"Whatever the prince's orders," Prentice said, an iron tone in his voice, "the moment these men crossed the mountains, they became the duchess's. She will have them fed."

"That's all fine and good, but there isn't any food. You can see that lot." The overseer gestured toward the camp of knights and nobles. "Their horses alone take almost everything we might feed these ones; all the grain goes to the nobles' mounts. And we got over two thousand to find food for. They're on straw and sawdust bread already."

"How many?" Prentice wondered if he had misheard. He looked at Sir Gant; even in the poor light, the knight was obviously shocked.

"We marched with over two and a half thousand out of Rhales. Every convict in the whole of the west, so they said."

"The prince called for them all," said Blisters. "Not this prince, the last one. Mercad, God rest him."

"It took that long to get the lot of them together. Daven Marcus waited a week to make sure he got every last one."

"It seems the prince thought he would need them," mused Sir Gant. "But if that was so, why let them starve?"

The two overseers had no answer.

Prentice found his thoughts torn in two directions. He was almost desperate to chase down and capture Folper now that he had come so far, but at the same time he couldn't bear to let this mass of convicts simply starve through the indifference of the highborn of society. He'd marched with five hundred others in the summer, and less than one in ten had survived the battle that ended that march. Now these wouldn't last to face a battle, and what battle was there to face? Daven Marcus had led his coterie west too late, to find the war over. Unless he planned to go farther and find the source of the invasion. That was a worthy aim, but one best attempted after the winter; and the winter coming to the Reach would be one where they would struggle to feed all the nobles and soldiers waiting to march west in the spring. The convicts would be long dead by then.

"Every man on the chain is answerable to the duchess," Prentice said coldly, his tone so harsh that the two overseers seemed to flinch at its suddenness. "You'll send to the castle at dawn for her dispensation, and food'll be sent back with you."

"Like her ladyship cares a spit about these curs," the rotten-tooth one scoffed, but Prentice stepped close and caught the man by his shirt.

"You don't speak for her, not a single word. Her cares are as far above you as the songs of angels, do you hear me?"

The man nodded, the shadows on his face doing nothing to hide his obvious fear.

"So, what are you going to do?" Prentice said.

"Send to the castle in the morning."

"At dawn, I said!"

"At dawn. We'll send at dawn."

"Right!" Prentice released the man's shirt and shoved him backward. For a moment the man held his whip hand loose, as if he thought to wield it like a weapon, but Prentice only stared at him in the lamplight. He had no fear of whips anymore.

The overseer hawked loudly and spat on the ground, then he turned to the convict chain and cracked the whip over their heads. "Back to it, you lazy bastards."

The gang moved off again, their chains clinking and rattling.

"You're not dumping those bodies in the water, are you?" Sir Gant called.

"No, sirs," Blisters assured them. "There's a pit for them. Not far."

"We'd best go with you, to see it for ourselves," said Prentice. "The duchess'll want to know the whole situation."

The two overseers grimaced at each other.

"Not that way," one shouted, changing the coffle's direction. "Down the road, you stupid bastards."

Prentice and Sir Gant followed the lantern at some distance. The little light danced in the dark while the chains tinkled their bittersweet music.

"I was right about the water," Gant said quietly.

"Easier than this long walk to a charnel pit," Prentice agreed. "Probably why they're doing it this late at night. So no one would see them thrown into the lake."

"Until the light and some goodwife goes for fresh water."

"They'd hope the bodies were washed away by then."

"Fool bloody plan."

Prentice only shrugged. Overseers' work was poorly paid and lowly; the men who took it on were neither wise nor diligent.

After a short while, the wind gusts brought a new smell out of the dark, the stench of rot. The gang of convicts reached the edge of a pit cut into the earth not far from the side of the road. Soon enough the six dead bodies were tossed in. The overseers stood by, holding the lantern high.

"You wanted to see," one called to Prentice and Gant.

They came close and looked down into the pit. The lantern shone onto a mound of bodies. The overseer waved it back and forth so that the dim shafts played over the corpses. Prentice did a rough count while he watched. There were easily fifty, and depending on the depth, perhaps twice that number.

"D'you want to see anything else?"

Prentice shook his head. "Take them back."

The overseer huffed in annoyance, the most disrespect he likely dared, and then the two men ordered their fettered charges back along the road toward the camp.

"Pay for a master smith from Masnia, and food for two and a half thousand convicts," said Gant. "On top of that, the prince's army and all the other needs of a duchy. The Reach'll drain that silver from the duchess' strongbox faster than your rats can drink their five silvers each."

"That's why we need to catch Folper and all the others, and get back every silver bar we can," said Prentice. "But you're wrong about the burden. It was two and a half thousand when they left Rhales. One in six never made it over the mountains, remember. And it's half a dozen less each day."

Sir Gant said nothing more after that, and Prentice didn't blame him. What else was there to say. The two marched down the road, the only sound the thudding of their boots against the cold, wet earth.

CHAPTER 20

D uchess Amelia awoke in the pre-dawn hours. She still felt tired and her bed was warm, but she was unable to sleep. Unlike many high noblewomen, she did not share her bed with her handmaids, but two slept in a truckle bed pulled out from beneath hers. Her matron, Bettina, slept in her own bed. Slipping out from under the covers, Amelia did her best to slither out of her own bed without waking her maids. She pulled on a woolen overgown trimmed in rabbit fur, and bent down to stir the coals of the fire. Despite her attempts to be quiet, one of her maids lifted her head.

"Your Grace, I should do that," said the young girl, Kristen. She was nearly eighteen, with a fresh face and rich brown hair. It would be time for her to marry soon, and Amelia wondered sometimes if she should keep her in service or release her to her husband's household. The duchess had no idea which decision would be the more appropriate, but Bettina would likely have some sound advice on the subject.

"Stay abed, Kristen. I can stir the fire."

Her maid shook her head. "Matron will tan my hide if she finds out," the girl said, pushing herself out of the truckle and blinking to force herself to wake up. She padded across the floorboards in her linen shift and bare feet, then crouched down next to Amelia.

"Well, let's do it together and make sure Bettina never finds out," Amelia whispered.

The two of them silently stirred the coals to life and put new wood on to warm the room. As the flames began to jump around the cut logs, Amelia shared a smile with her maid and noticed her shivering.

"Put something warm on, silly."

Kristen nodded and went to the garderobe. Amelia sat on her chair by the table and sighed. She'd wanted to be alone for a moment, to order her thoughts for the day, but making the fire and Kristen's quiet company had been a pleasant diversion nonetheless. Amelia's gaze went to the bound chest full of silver, pushed up against a wall. That was the source of her disturbed thoughts, the reason she couldn't sleep. It was a strong-looking thing, but with its lock torn away, that strength seemed pointless. She was confident that none of her lady's maids would pilfer any of the coin, and in truth she had little to worry about from any of her servants. As she thought about it, she realized that most of her uncertainty came from the way she had been turned out of her own chamber. If she could be ordered about in her own home, what was to stop someone like the prince simply taking the strongbox and its contents for himself? Kristen came back into the main of the chamber, adroitly plaiting a pink ribbon through her hair.

"Wake the matron, if you would," Amelia told her in a strong voice that cracked the quiet air and caused the young woman to start. "I will spend some time this morning at the tomb of my late husband. I am a widow in mourning, after all."

Kristen curtsied and quickly went around the curtain to wake Bettina. Amelia smiled and formed her plan while her ladies woke and began the day. Soon enough, water was sent for and a steward brought bowls of pease pottage for them to break their fast. The duchess ate and then washed herself. They dressed her in a dun-colored gown, tied and sewn with black velvet ribbons. It was a suitably somber dress for a woman in mourning, finished with a black lace veil and no jewelry except for her husband's signet ring.

"I must have this resized," she said to herself as the signet twirled loosely on her finger.

"Shall I bring you a shawl, Your Grace?" asked Teerah, Amelia's other maid.

"It will be cold in that little chapel, so deep in the ground," chided Bettina.

"I think that's a good idea, Teerah," Amelia agreed. "I will have some other items brought down as well. Send for stewards. I will give them instructions."

"Yes, Your Grace."

When the stewards arrived, the duchess commanded them to have candles and a brazier set in the crypt chapel and lit for her arrival. Then she pointed to the chest.

"I will use that as a seat," she instructed them. "Set it before my husband's sepulchre and then cover it with that tapestry. Bettina, have cushions brought for sitting."

"Surely a chair could be brought from the solar," Bettina protested.

The duchess cocked an eyebrow. "Have I ever been in the solar, matron?" she asked with a cold tone of voice.

"Of course."

"And were the chairs there when I was there?"

"Yes." Bettina's brows knotted in confusion. The older woman clearly had no idea what the duchess was getting at.

"Am I blind?"

"I... um... pardon, Your Grace?"

"Am I blind, Matron Bettina?"

"No."

"So, it is fair to assume that I know that there are chairs in the solar, isn't it?"

"I... yes..."

Amelia was making a point of not looking at anyone in the room, and she knew that every servant would be making an equal point of not looking at her. It was what she wanted. There was no good reason to have the chest moved to the crypt, and Bettina was right. It made far more sense to have chairs brought from elsewhere in the castle. But because Bettina had corrected her in front of others, it gave Amelia a chance to have the perfect excuse; she was doing it to remind her uppity matron of her place. In the servants' eyes it would look like she was taking umbrage to being corrected by her lady in waiting and thus was sticking to her original idea. Amelia hated being so cruel to Bettina, but within an hour the servants would have shared the story of Bettina's dressing down, and everyone would know better than to talk about the duchess sitting on a chest in the crypt, lest they also incur her wrath.

"Have that taken to the chapel," she told the stewards. The two men hefted the heavy box between them. As they reached the doorway, Amelia called after them. "And if my matron needs a chair of her own, see that one is brought to her... from the solar."

Matron Bettina slunk back to the garderobe, while the handmaids busied themselves sorting ribbons more fastidiously than they ever had before. Amelia decided to follow the stewards down to the crypt, pulling her lace veil fully over her face. She would find a private moment later to explain her actions to Bettina, and she trusted that her matron would understand her mistress's motivations. Passing through the household in the morning, she was pleased that there were few people about and that the chest reached the crypt directly. Once it was in place, the two stewards begged her pardon and headed back to fetch the tapestry she wanted from her room. While they were gone, another servant brought in a brazier and wood and started a fire for her. They did not speak. When the stewards returned with the tapestry, she directed them to place it over the chest and made a fuss of leaving some in front so that she could use it to kneel in prayer in front of her husband's sepulchre. She went down on her knees, then got up and had them adjust it slightly. Then she sat on the covered strongbox and tested it as a seat. Finally, she nodded, trying her best to seem regal and inscrutable. The stewards bowed and headed out, but before they could go, she called them back one last time.

"I see there is a lock on the door there," she said, pointing to the chapel's entrance. "Who has a key?"

"I'm not sure, Your Grace," was the stammered reply. She'd obviously unnerved these two men with her stern performance. That was good.

"Send to the chief steward. Have him find every key and bring them to me here."

They bowed to her again and all but fled the crypt. When they were gone, she slumped down to sit upon the chest. Looking at the plain stone of her husband's resting place, she suddenly felt tears rising in her eyes.

She missed him.

He had loved her, for all the political convenience of their marriage, but he had died and left her in a viper's nest, with enemies on every side. Tears ran down her cheeks, and she found that her grief was mixed with a sense of resentment. If the late duke had been more diligent in running the Reach and less concerned with hunting and reliving his past glories, then maybe she would not have inherited a poverty-stricken estate harassed by enemies from within and without.

She shook her head. That was unworthy.

She sniffed and tried to blink the tears out of her eyes. It was self-pity to blame others for her problems, and no matter his failings, Marne had loved her and she him. If he were alive, she would not despise him for having imperfections, and she would help him to fight off any enemies who sought to prey on his failings. If she would have supported him in life, it was churlish to resent him in death. No, she wanted to protect his legacy, which was now her legacy, and the strongbox underneath her was an important part of that purpose. As she sat there staring at the sepulchre, she thought about her conversations with Prentice. Until she had soldiers of her own to command, her wealth and her power would never be secure. She should have been able to trust her knights and nobles, but their own ambitions made them an unsure bet—the newly elevated Baron Liam was proof of that. She also should have been able to trust her houseguards, as they depended on her for their status even more completely than sworn knights, but they had all been under the command of Sir Duggan at one time or another. He plotted first against her husband, and now her; she could hardly trust her houseguard either.

"Dearest husband," she said to the stone sepulchre, "you have left me a treasure of cheese and a house full of rats."

That made her think of Prentice's band of low thieves—the one pack of rats she could trust, it seemed, if only because they made no secret of their greed and criminality. They had stolen, raped, or murdered their way into convict transportation and might easily commit any or all such crimes again, given the chance. Yet they were a known commodity. She couldn't trust them far, but as far as she could, she knew she could trust them completely, because of the trust she had in Prentice Ash to lead them. And he was an ex-convict. The irony of the whole situation made her smile for a moment, and she almost laughed.

Then she heard someone coming down into the chapel. She turned to see Bettina creep through the door, with one of the two stewards coming behind her. Both had their heads down, like naughty children expecting punishment. Amelia sat upright, waiting for Bettina to speak.

"Please pardon the interruption, Your Grace. The steward insists that you sent him for these." The matron held out a pair of iron keys.

Amelia nodded. "I sent him to fetch them."

"Very good, Your Grace." Amelia could see Bettina was confused. Behind the matron, the steward timidly cleared his throat.

"You have something to say?" Amelia asked.

"Begging your pardon, Your Grace," the man stammered. "You commanded all the keys brought, but that's not all of them. That's just the chaplain's key and the chief steward's key. He had them both on account that the duke, your husband there..." He nodded at the sepulchre. "He never appointed a chaplain to the castle, so that key never went to anyone."

"What other keys are there?"

"Just the castellan's key. 'Castellan has one of every key in the whole castle, 'course. They're all kept on a ring in a chest in the apartments over the barbican. Sir Duggan, curse him for a cur, never used those keys, just let the steward's set do the job."

Amelia wanted to smile to hear Duggan's memory cursed and was glad she had the lace veil to hide her delight. She was supposed to be down here as a grief-stricken widow in mourning.

"Why didn't you fetch the castellan's key, then?" she asked, working to keep a somber tone. "If you knew where it was to be found?"

"Baron Liam has men in the apartment. Two sworn swords, day and night, like houseguards of his own."

"Why?"

"It's his rooms now, since the prince made him castellan."

"The prince?" Amelia stopped herself. Daven Marcus had made Liam castellan? Did those two never sleep? Did they just spend their hours looking for new ways to undermine and control her? She nodded to the steward. "Of course you could not force your way past Baron Liam's men. I will see to this. Thank you, you may go."

The steward tugged his forelock and bowed before turning and leaving, looking obviously relieved.

"Your Grace," Bettina began, "I wanted to apologize—"

Amelia cut her off with an imperious gesture. "I was rude to you earlier, Bettina," she said, softening her tone. "I apologize. I know you are diligent to serve me and guard my dignity and..."

She stopped, feeling emotion rise in her voice. Bettina was trustworthy and loyal but had no mind for conspiracy. The idea of men and women of any rank conspiring against their betters was so at odds with who the matron was as a person that it would simply confound her. Lower orders obeyed and kept to their place, in the matron's mind. They served loyally and without question, or they were punished until they learned their place.

"At times I have to do things that may seem heartless or even cruel. I hope you understand."

"There is no need to explain yourself to me, Your Grace," came Bettina's reflexive reply, and Amelia sighed inwardly. She couldn't even apologize because to Bettina's mind, a duchess would never need to apologize to one of her servants. A duchess did as she chose, and servants worked to anticipate her needs. "Please," "thank you," and "sorry" never entered into it.

She's like a whipped dog, Amelia thought, and immediately regretted the uncharitable notion.

But it was true. Bettina was a faithful servant, but she lacked so many of the traits Amelia needed in her servants. That was why she valued Prentice so much. He had been whipped, he knew his place, but he was unbroken. He still had the mongrel in him, the vicious iron-hearted part of him that would wade through a sewer with a pack of curs and then leap out and tear her town out of her enemies' hands, ripping out their throats as he did it.

"Bettina, had you heard anything about Baron Liam being made castellan?"

Bettina shook her head. "No, Your Grace."

"I suppose I should find out what other changes the prince has made to my household."

Amelia led Bettina from the chapel, locking the heavy door behind her. The portal's hard wooden boards had a reddish color, deeply polished, and were carved with a cross inlaid with silver. Looking at it for a moment, she recognized that it was a chapel and crypt that she was using to store money, mere silver. However much her duchy needed the wealth, it was not fitting to misuse her family chapel in this way.

"Forgive me," she whispered prayerfully. "I'll build a proper strong room once I have control of my castle again."

CHAPTER 21

Prentice and Sir Gant led the merchant Folper back into Dweltford, arms bound with the reins of his own horse. They'd caught him on the rise where the road left the river and turned eastward toward the center of the province. Folper had missed the turn in the dark, and his horse and mules had become entangled in brush. They found him whipping his mount and cursing while the mules stubbornly stood their ground, refusing to be disentangled. Folper's horse had a small chest tied to the back of its saddle, along with heavily stuffed saddlebags, and both his mules were packed with bundles so high that each was taller than the animal on which they sat.

"Hides and furs," Folper had explained between curses once they had overtaken him. The merchant hadn't even tried to resist as they forced him from his saddle. "You took all the silver. I'm a furrier. My wealth is in leather and furs."

"You don't have any coin left?" Prentice could hardly believe it.

"I have my own purse. But you and your men got all of Sir Duggan's wretched metal."

"All of it, or all of your share?" Prentice pressed. He needed to know how much there was to search for.

"All of my share."

The merchant sat down on the ground and hung his head in misery. The wind had finally cleared the clouds away, and a slender moon joined the ribbon to let down just enough light to see by. Folper was wet, with hair plastered damply to his face. His heavy coat was soaked through, and he shivered.

"Was the rain worse out here?" Sir Gant asked as he and Prentice worked to calm the animals and get them untangled.

"I fell in a puddle," Folper muttered.

Prentice and Gant laughed.

"I was lucky I didn't break my neck," Folper protested, but that just made them laugh again.

Once they had the horse free, Prentice bound Folper's wrists with the reins. "You don't expect me to ride like this, do you?" the merchant demanded.

"I don't expect you to ride at all. You'll walk back with us."

Folper cursed under his breath. Through the rest of the night, they marched Folper and his animals back to Dweltford, reaching the vast camp outside the town just after dawn.

"My God, it's huge," said the merchant. Riding past it in the dark, he had doubtless missed the full sense of its scale.

"So, what was your plan, furrier? Ride south to the Vec?" Prentice asked.

"It's my homeland. My family would not be impressed to hear I abandoned our holdings here in the north west, but they'd take me in, especially with this load to trade."

"Should have taken the river," said Sir Gant. "Faster. Harder to catch you."

"I knew you'd have men on the dockside watching for me. I thought I'd outwit you going by road. I should have known you'd watch the gate as well."

Prentice nearly laughed and wondered how his prisoner would react if he knew just how few loyal men the duchess had to work with. "You knew we were coming for you?"

"Of course I knew. When Malden told us how you'd attacked him and his men at the seneschal's house, I knew we were all in danger. Oh, he waited till you'd seized my share to give us all the news, but once he said it, I wasn't going to sit around and wait for you to come put me in chains. Why should I? My part was done with the silver!"

"What was your part?" Prentice asked.

"To hold it until Duggan called for it."

"And what did you get for that?"

Folper glared at Prentice with hateful eyes. He'd been talking willingly through the night, as though he found himself relieved to be caught. It made Prentice wonder if Duggan had forced his cooperation somehow, and if the other conspirators were similarly compelled.

Not that brute that beat me, he thought, and he involuntarily touched his fingers to his face. The swelling was receding, and the skin didn't feel so puffy to the touch. The sacrist's poultice had done its job, but Prentice was sure he still looked like he'd taken a beating.

No one compelled him to do this. He enjoyed it.

"Come on, master merchant," he said to Folper. "Why stop now? You know the duchess will have the truth from you one way or another. Tell us. What did you receive for your part in Duggan's treasonous conspiracy?"

At the mention of treason, Folper's head dropped, and he groaned from deep in his chest like a wounded animal. Then he lifted his head and sniffled. He didn't look like he was crying; Prentice wondered if the cold night's journey had given the man a chill. It would not surprise him if they all caught one. Time by a warm fire was called for.

"Every fourth bar," Folper said at last, and his chest heaved with a sigh, as if releasing this one fact had sucked air right out of his lungs.

"Every fourth bar?" repeated Sir Gant. "That'd make you a rich merchant indeed."

"If I ever got to spend it."

"What stopped you?" asked Prentice.

"You did. You and your duchess, who Duggan swore was going to die because of the 'impossibly large army' coming out of the west." Folper sneered with disgust, spitting on the ground.

"Is that what he said?" Prentice turned to face him. They were almost to the town gates and already the traffic in and out was starting to grow. Soon the streets would be crowded and difficult to pass, but he wanted to get an explanation from Folper as soon as he could. The question of what had motivated Duggan gnawed at his mind. What had made a respectable retainer and veteran of the crusade west abandon his principles and seize Dweltford out from under its liege?

"What did he actually say?" Prentice urged.

"That they would cover the land like a swarm of insects," Folper answered, looking Prentice straight in the face. His eyes were red-rimmed and filled with hate. "They would be so numerous and wild it would be impossible to count them. The only way to survive was to hire soldiers and pay the invaders off."

"Pay them off? He was a knight!" Sir Gant growled.

He had moved in closer to hear the conversation while woodcutters and herdsmen pushed past, weighed down with heavy bundles of firewood or driving milkers to the market as early as they could. Servants from the prince's army camp, better dressed than the Reachermen, were also moving through and heading to the market to buy food and other wares. Some tried to buy on the road, to save a trip inside the walls, but the Reachermen wouldn't sell. If the bailiffs caught them, they'd be up before a conclave court for dodging market dues.

"Why would Duggan believe all this?" Prentice hissed at Folper. The crowd was beginning to jostle the mules, and he wanted this information before the whole process got even more complicated. It would be difficult enough getting the animals through the gate and up to the castle as it was; soon it would be a major undertaking.

"A vision and a prophecy," said Folper, starting to look askance at the crowds, as if sizing up his chances of escape.

"What prophecy?"

"Some wise woman he met in the west."

"The west? Where the invaders came from?"

"Don't be daft," Folper said.

Prentice was getting angry. He tugged hard on the reins around Folper's wrists, causing the merchant to stumble and almost fall.

"Stop wasting my time," Prentice said. "You were caught with tax bars from Fallenhill Mint. That's treasonous theft. The only thing that's going to keep you from a slow strangling in a hangman's noose is the mercy of the duchess. How merciful do you think she'll feel if I tell her you jerked me about like a spindle on a thread?"

Folper swallowed and tried to maintain his belligerent air, but it was clear the man was bone weary and had no heart to resist. He was bitter and probably always would be, but any fight was gone from him.

"Sir Duggan went hunting in the west with Duke Marne, back when he was alive. Soon after the crusade, he said. They came upon some woman of the woods, living in a hut in a little forest, just like in the stories. Like a bloody fey tale. People would laugh the first time he told them, but only the first time. He was in earnest. He meant every word."

"What'd this woman do or say?"

"Oi, move yourselves, would you!" a voice called from behind the mules. A goatherd was driving his clutch of milkers all leashed together and didn't want the cords getting tangled under the mules' feet. "Some of us have to make a living, you know."

Sir Gant moved back to deal with the man. He pulled his sheathed sword from his belt and used it like a herdsman's stick to fend the goats away. "Go around."

The goatherd muttered to himself but managed to wrangle his little flock around the mules, with Gant's help.

"What did she say?" Prentice repeated, ignoring the bleating goats.

"The story Sir Duggan told was that the woman called out to them while they were grazing their horses near her little hut. 'Hail Duke Marne,' she cried. 'While ever there is a Reach, its lords will be your descendants, your spirit in their blood.'"

"Duke Marne took that as a prophecy?"

"Marne took her for a fool old woman, so Sir Duggan said. He had his squire give the woman a guilder and rode off looking for another stag to hunt. But Sir Duggan's stirrup got twisted, and he was a moment later in leaving. So, while it was just him and the old woman, that's when she told him about an impossible army, vast as a horde of locusts, coming out of the west."

"And he believed her?" Prentice asked.

"He said that as she spoke, he could see it in his mind, as if in a vision."

"A vast army? So why not tell Marne?"

"Because of the other things she said. She told him Marne would die and that he, Duggan, would be ruler of Dweltford Castle when the invaders came."

"Well, that part was true."

Folper nodded. "Turned out that way. That wasn't all she said, though. She told him he would need silver. That only king's silver from a town of the north would save the Reach. King's silver—taxation bars. That's why he took from the mint. He thought he was saving the money to buy a defense for the Reach."

"Why do it secretly? Why not persuade Marne to do it himself? The taxes were his, after all."

"The woman told Duke Marne that his descendants would rule the Reach to the day it falls. How do you marry that to the claim that Sir Duggan would rule Dweltford when the army came? Duggan nearly soiled himself when Duke Marne was killed, sending out riders and messenger birds, looking for any sign of the invaders. He was talking about having all the silver moved into the castle, ready to ransom the Reach."

"And he hired mercenaries from the Vec and sent for Yentow Sent to make their weapons."

"And armor. Sent's a genius."

Prentice shook his head as he tried to put everything together in his head. Duggan had been trying to save the Western Reach from the invaders in his own way, making sure to put himself in the ducal seat as he did so. No wonder he'd seemed so harried, nearly crazed. If he'd had a vision, as he claimed, then odds were that he was a little mad by the end. Prentice's own visions worried at the corners of his own mind.

"Why did he involve you at all?" asked Sir Gant. "Why give the money to merchants to hold?"

"He couldn't keep it himself," Folper said as if the answer was obvious. "What if someone found out?"

"And that's why he drew up the compact, is it?" Prentice said, more figuring it out for himself than asking Folper for an explanation. "He fully expected to be ruling the Reach, maybe even acclaimed as its savior, having paid off the enemy army. He'd have the law under his control and would be able to bind you by your contract."

Folper nodded.

"And you would get a quarter share just for acting as his bankers. But you couldn't spend any until the army came out of the west and Duggan had paid them off."

Another nod.

"That's why the others were becoming so impatient," Folper continued. "To have that much silver close to hand is a huge temptation. I had many nights where I imagined simply packing my strongbox onto a riverboat and dashing home to the Vec."

"Becoming impatient?" Prentice asked. Folper's words stirred through his mind, and he suddenly realized that he had missed a vital detail. "You said Marne was killed. You mean he was murdered?"

"Poison," said Folper, and the way he said it made clear that while embezzlement hadn't stuck on his conscience, he felt ashamed to have been involved in the murder of a duke. "From somewhere a long way away. Further than Masnia, they said."

"Duggan stooped to poison?" Sir Gant glowered. Poison was plainly a sin too far for his knightly sensibilities.

Folper shook his head. "No, Sir Duggan knew nothing about the poison."

"Then who?"

Folper's miserable expression twisted into a strange smile. "Sir Duggan established the compact, but the whole thing is driven by another man's plots. Vardian Malden, master merchant and conclave selectman. Second highest on the Conclave Council and the most dangerous man in Dweltford, even with the prince and every one of his knights here to stay. More dangerous than you, Master Ex-convict Prentice Ash. He got the better of you, didn't he?"

"The big bastard at the seneschal's house?"

"That's right. You know, in the light now, I can see the marks of his handiwork." Folper pointed his bound hands at Prentice's face. "He was a river boatman in his youth and made extra money in ring fights, both the feast day ones and the illegal ones. A monster, they say, who took on two and three men at a time. There's no thief, cutthroat, or river smuggler in Dweltford that doesn't answer to Malden in some way."

"And he poisoned the duke?" Prentice asked.

"He was done waiting, he said, just like that."

"And the seneschal knew about it?"

"Everyone but Sir Duggan. Malden told the seneschal so he could threaten him into silence. Anyone who could kill a duke and get away with it could end a reeve of the purse soon enough. A jumped-up factor, Malden called him, to his face."

"Is that why he killed him, and his housekeeper?"

"Seneschal Fern was even more skittish than me, as it turned out. He'd gotten greedy at the first and put himself into Sir Duggan's hands, but he had love for the old duke still, and it was more than he could bear to see him killed by Malden's treachery.

He was going to the duchess and had notes of evidence, proof of the conspiracy."

"We found those."

"That'll displease Malden. He's been telling everyone that the notes were a lie, that Bastian Fern took his secrets to the grave. Of course, I knew better once you seized my strongbox. I mean, how else could you have found it?"

Prentice shared a look with Sir Gant and could see that the knight had the same thoughts. The revelation that the conspiracy had been responsible for the duke's death meant there would be nowhere for the traitors to hide. The duchess would seize every one of their businesses, and they'd all dance at the end of a gibbet. There would be no stopping it. Including the bull-like monster who had beaten him, Malden. Prentice would be happy to see that execution especially.

"Right. Let's get you to the castle," Prentice said.

"And you'll tell the duchess I helped you?" Folper pleaded, his voice suddenly breaking into a whine. "She had Sir Duggan killed in the great hall, right in front of her. Everyone's heard the story. You'll tell her? You'll help me plead for mercy? You said you would. Promise me! You said you would!"

Prentice shook his head and didn't know whether he wanted to pity the man or slap him. "I'll do as I said," he promised. "But when she hears about her husband's death, I can't say what will happen next. And if she orders me to slit your throat like Duggan's, then you'll die at her feet just like he did."

Folper let out another bitter groan, and tears began to run down his face.

"Oh, shut up!" Prentice yanked on the reins and dragged the crying merchant and his unmounted horse through the crowds and into town. Sir Gant led the mules behind.

CHAPTER 22

D uchess Amelia found Baron Liam, newly made castellan of her castle, seated with the prince at the high table in the great hall. There were other men standing before the prince, but otherwise the hall was mostly empty, a striking contrast to the rowdy atmosphere of the feast the previous night. Most of the tables had been pushed back against the walls once more, and though an occasional servant crossed the space and pairs of houseguards stood at the entrances, the main floor was empty of people.

Amelia walked from the main doors up the long passage, just as she had when she brought Duggan for trial. The floor had been scrubbed since the feast, but she was sure she could make out the stain on the flagstones where he had died. The sight gave her a sour taste in her mouth, and she wasn't sure if she felt disgust or righteous satisfaction at the thought.

Probably both, she decided.

As she approached the dais of the high table, it was plain that the men standing before the prince were wealthy, though they were a strangely mixed and unmixed group otherwise. They wore long black coats with fur-trimmed cuffs and collars. They had elegant leather shoes with polished gold or silver buckles and wore fine woolen hose.

Knights and nobles belonged to houses with long lineages and martial histories. On a battlefield, bright colors helped to pick an enemy from a friend in the dust or mud or blood. Thus, the nobility most often wore their house colors, as vibrant as they could afford, so that no one forgot their heritage. The sumptuary laws of the Grand Kingdom protected their rights to do so.

Merchants were different. Merchants, guildsmen, and even master craftsmen all dressed in black because, of all the colors, black took the most dye to create. To blot out all other colors from a cloth meant a lot of dye, and a cheap black cloth faded to gray almost as soon as its first wash. To wear fadeless black was expensive, and money was the measure of a merchant, just as family honor was the measure of a noble. Despite any other variety between them, one glance across the gathered men in front of the prince and Amelia knew she was looking at a group of Dweltford's richest merchants. She mounted the dais and walked around the small crowd, assessing them as she moved to a seat beside Baron Liam.

Several of the merchants were heavyset men, with large bellies bulging over belts. She expected this; girth was another announcement of wealth, of a man who ate well and didn't have to work hard to make his living. Which was why two men in particular stood out from the others. One was tall and as slender as a rake. His long coat was wrapped close around him, no belly to show, and it hung all the way to the floor like a robe, hiding his feet. He had a drawn, pinched face and a small nose, with dark eyes under strangely heavy brows. He steepled his long fingers in front of him, like a man at prayer, but there was nothing patient or devout about his scowling expression.

The last man stood in the middle of the little clutch and dominated them all. Even before Amelia was close enough to hear them speak, she knew he was their leader. He was heavyset, which seemed typical from a distance, but there was strength to his body that the others lacked. His shoulders were broad, and he was barrel-chested. The other merchants around him would pay men to carry the least burden for them; this man looked like he could heft a hogshead by himself. He was also the richest man there, evidenced by his jewelry. Every merchant wore a chain of gold, some with jewels, as well as a ring or two, but this man had a ring on every finger. Sapphires and rubies glittered among so much metal that Amelia wondered if he could even close his hands. As she noticed the rings, she caught sight of something else—the condition of his knuckles. The other men had soft hands, though some had ink stains, which was to be expected. The thin merchant's fingers were pale, almost cadaverous. But their leader had monstrous, thick-fingered hands, covered with scars. His knuckles even seemed twisted in places. They appeared to Amelia to be almost arthritic, but the man's age and health made her think it couldn't be so. What kind of activity could so warp and scar a man's hands?

Thinking and watching all these things, she quietly approached her seat. Without preamble she pulled the chair out and moved to sit down.

"What are you doing here?" Liam hissed at her as she adjusted her overdress.

The merchants who had been speaking fell silent, and every eye turned to her. Taking her time, she lifted the black lace veil and folded it back on her hair neatly.

"Good morning, Your Highness," she said to the prince, pointedly ignoring Liam's question. Liam sneered and seemed about to say something more, but she didn't give him the chance. "Baron Liam, you may announce me."

Liam scowled, but when he looked to the prince, Daven Marcus only smiled with amusement. It seemed the prince was happy to enjoy all the discomfort of others, even of his supposed favorites. Amelia noted that in her thoughts, but she schooled her face to a neutral, serene expression. With the prince not objecting, Liam sighed heavily and turned to the gathered merchants.

"Gentlemen, this is the duchess Amelia, Duke Marne's widow." The words sounded like it hurt him to speak them.

"And liege of the Western Reach, peer of the realm," she added with a sweet smile and a cold voice.

The collected merchants all nodded to bow. Except, she noted, their powerfully built leader, who reflexively put his hand up to tug his forelock—a peasant's gesture. He caught himself doing it and wrenched his hand away to his side in a savage motion. He pushed his head down, bowing at last with the rest.

You weren't born to your station either, she thought, trying to study him without being too obvious.

As he straightened, she could see in his gaze an anger and a cold calculation. Their eyes met for a moment, and the hatred in them caught Amelia by surprise. Then his expression became suddenly neutral, controlled. The sight reminded her of Prentice Ash, his resentment at being an exiled convict held tight under iron hard self-discipline. Was this a man like Prentice, strong willed and hardened by life? If he was, then he was truly dangerous.

"Welcome, gentlemen," she said as sweetly as she could. "The good men of the Reach are always welcome in my home. So, what are we discussing?"

The merchants all exchanged nervous glances, except the leader, who looked directly to the prince.

Daven Marcus smiled. "You are welcome as always, Duchess," he said. "We are discussing a dire matter related to your late castellan and his wicked deeds."

"A discussion that does not require your presence," Liam added, but Amelia hardly heard him.

Merchants discussing things Duggan did? These were the conspirators, she was sure of it, and when she made that connection, she knew their leader must have been the man who attacked and beat Prentice in Seneschal Fern's home. That explained the condition of his hands. The man was a killer who beat men to death with his fists.

"None of you has been introduced," she said, swallowing to keep her voice steady. She turned to the bull-shouldered leader with the hands of a street fighter. "You, sir. Perhaps you would be first."

The man nodded. "Malden. Vardian Malden, Your Grace. Selectman of the Conclave Council." For all his brutality and menace, the man's manners were impeccable.

"A pleasure to meet you, Master Malden," she managed to force out. "The Conclave Council ever does such fine work for our town."

Malden bowed to accept the compliment, and there seemed to be a release of tension among the other merchants, as if they had all been waiting for Malden's lead to know which way to go. All except the thin one, who stood apart and seemed neither pleased nor concerned with the duchess's presence. He introduced himself last, as Master Caius Welburne, also a selectman of the council. His voice had an acid tone to it, and he bowed only enough to be polite, unlike the others who were all unctuous, seeking to ingratiate themselves.

"He doesn't like you very much, I think," observed Daven Marcus as Welburne straightened up. Baron Liam sniggered and some of the merchants smiled nervously, but the slender merchant was not perturbed.

"Far be it from me to contradict you, Your Highness, but it is not my place to like or dislike Her Grace. I am a merchant, and she is the duchess."

"Well spoken, master," said the prince. "If only everyone in the Reach knew how to keep their place like that."

"I'm sure these men all know their place quite well," Amelia said, ignoring the prince's obvious gibe at her heritage. "And I shall keep mine. I will sit here quietly and listen while you gentlemen continue your discussion."

She had planned to find out about Liam's appointment as castellan immediately, as well as take the last key to the chapel from him, but now she wanted to watch these men, who she was certain were the members of the conspiracy. They were six in all, and none of them was Folper, whose money she already had. That meant that two were missing.

"Resume your story, Master Malden," said the prince. "The little duchess will catch up. Or not."

"When Sir Duggan came to us," Malden said, with no preamble, "we each assumed he was engaging us in something legitimate."

A number of the other merchants nodded.

"After all, he was castellan and he met us with the duchy's seneschal. Why would we think otherwise?"

"So, what was it that you did think?" the prince asked.

"That Sir Duggan was making investments on behalf of the duke, at his behest."

It was a lie, Amelia was certain of it. "When did you know he wasn't?" she asked, ignoring her promise to keep quiet.

Malden didn't seem to care. "When some of the conditions of the contract were made clear to us," he said smoothly. "There were... irregularities. When some of my fellows and I questioned the seneschal, he sent us to Sir Duggan. The knight threatened us, saying that we were bound in a compact now and as guilty as he was. We were trapped and didn't know what to do."

"Why didn't you tell Duke Marne?" asked the prince. From his tone, Amelia didn't think Daven Marcus was believing Malden's story either, but she couldn't be sure.

"I tried, Your Highness. I sent two letters by two different messengers—good men of mine, reliable. One never returned, and the other was found facedown on the banks of the Dwelt, his throat slit from ear to ear. I was sure that Sir Duggan was behind it. And then when the duke died in so strange a fashion?"

"And you are sure it was poison?"

"So mighty a man, full of health and vigor? How could it not have been?"

That shocked Amelia. She had not considered that her husband had been poisoned. She chewed the bitter idea in her mind while the conversation continued. Had Sir Duggan really murdered her husband? Poisoned him to usurp his dukedom? And could he have really cowed all these men into participating in his conspiracy? Was it all down to him? No, she was sure there was more to it than Malden was saying, if only because Malden was clearly not the kind of man who would be easily cowed. And he certainly was not so honest that he would balk at an opportunity to get his hands on so much silver.

"So, we have brought the monies, Your Highness. King's taxes forced on us by a dead traitor. They are on the cart under your men's guard. And the papers are all there before you. Every guilder accounted for."

The prince idly lifted a paper from a scattering of documents on the table in front of him. Looking at it and the others, Amelia was sure they were copies of the compact, similar to the ones in her chamber.

"Why have you suddenly come forward now?" she asked.

"For God's sake, woman," Liam muttered under his breath. The prince didn't correct him, but seemed to agree with Amelia's question nonetheless. He looked at the merchants, from face to face. Some of them looked like they were in pain, wringing their hands and twisting their expressions. Only Malden and Welburne looked calm.

"We had to wait until Sir Duggan was dead," one of the soft, heavy men blurted out.

Everyone looked to him, though past him, Amelia saw the expression on Malden's bulldog face. It was a look of pure, murderous hatred.

"It's true," the merchant bleated pathetically.

"You waited?" the prince asked lightly but with unmistakable menace, as if a wrong answer to the question could lead to a grisly outcome. "Why?"

There was a long moment of silence. The conspirators squirmed as their fear built. Except, of course, for Master Malden and coolly detached Master Welburne. Malden had a plan, Amelia was sure of it. That's why he ran the conversation. Welburne seemed equally as self-possessed, but she had no sense of why.

"Your Highness," Malden began quietly, "I am ashamed to admit, we were all scared. We are all mere merchants, men of commerce; gentle of birth, but too lowly to understand the whims of the highest ranks of the kingdom. Even when we heard of the traitor's demise, we were not sure what was right to do. Of course, we would have brought the money straight to the duchess, to beg her mercy, but with your own arrival, there seemed no way to reach Her Grace."

"You blame me, my arrival, for your actions?" the prince said.

"Not in the least, Highness. In fact, your presence has given us the best hope we have had to escape this horrid entrapment."

"How is that?"

"We know we can trust you, Highness," Malden replied.

Daven Marcus cocked an eyebrow.

"You do not think you can trust the duchess?"

Malden took a long breath and bowed his head. Then he looked straight at Amelia. He met her eyes once more, and for a moment she saw the same hatred again, the hatred he had shown the weak merchant who had spoken out of turn. Then his expression changed again, like the work of a consummate actor, and he looked overwrought with emotion.

"Your Highness, I recoil from criticizing the duchess' household in her presence, but something happened recently that makes us think that her house is no safer with Sir Duggan dead than it was before. At least not for us small folk."

"What was that? What has happened?" The prince affected a breathless manner, like a courtier sharing a juicy rumor, and Amelia knew that he had not the slightest interest in justice. This audience was entertainment in his eyes, and he was looking for his advantage. Duggan's death and the embezzlement of funds were irrelevant to him.

"The duke's man, Seneschal Fern, has been murdered."

"Indeed?"

"Yes, Highness," Malden said.

"By whom?"

"At first, we thought it must have been one of us, so paranoid have we all grown. I went myself to the seneschal's house, to see if I could uncover some evidence, and was attacked by the murderer himself as he ransacked the house. A man of the duchess' household named Prentice Ash."

"That is a lie!" Amelia declared, unable to hold herself back.

Her protest was swallowed up as Baron Liam surged from his chair, shouting victoriously and slamming his hand upon the table. "I knew it!" The baron turned to the prince. "I know this cur, Prentice. Let me take some men, and I will give you his head before sundown!"

"You don't think we should try the man before we execute him, Baron?" the prince said.

Liam paused, caught between his elation and the prince's obvious logic.

"He is a brutal dog of a man," said Malden, speaking quietly with his head down. "I doubt if he will let himself be taken prisoner. I've known ex-convicts before; they would rather die than be purged on a chain a second time."

"Your Highness cannot believe these lies," Amelia said, trying to appeal to the prince, but as soon as she did, she knew it was a mistake.

Daven Marcus smiled at her words, a predatory smile full of malice. By her passionate tone, he knew that she would defend Prentice, and that made him a weapon to use against her. She could see it in the prince's eyes. Nonetheless, the prince seemed too intent on enjoying the current entertainment to the full.

"Why would this man turn murderer?" he asked Malden. "What could a man in the duchess' service hope to gain by killing her seneschal?"

"He wanted to take over the conspiracy himself, to establish himself in Sir Duggan's place," Malden replied, ready even for that question.

"Another lie!" Amelia said.

She peered across their faces. The soft merchants looked at her with mocking expressions, obviously hopeful that Malden's plan was succeeding, getting them out from under their crimes by feeding the prince an ex-convict scapegoat. They had nothing like the cunning or skill in deception that their leader possessed. Amelia was shocked and horrified by their lack of guile.

For his part, Malden did not look at her, keeping his face bowed, maintaining his act as the penitent victim of Duggan's evil. Liam made no effort to hide his thoughts, looking like an eager hunting dog just waiting to be let off his master's leash. He spared Amelia a momentary sneer of utter contempt, but otherwise waited on the prince. Only Master Welburne seemed calm, almost uninterested, in fact. Since the moment she had learned of her husband's death, Amelia had never felt so alone as she did in the presence of these predatory men, and she wondered if any of them were represented by the vile beasts she had seen fighting in her vision. Were these men the creatures the lions had come to protect her from?

"The duchess does not believe you, Master Malden," said the prince. "Can you convince her?"

"I have the plan from his own lips, my lord. He boasted to me as he tried to kill me."

"Truly? And how did you survive this encounter with so dangerous a fellow?"

"Only by the loyalty of my men, who fought to deliver me from the traitor's clutches. If not for their swift intervention, I would surely be dead in the Dwelt myself."

"Well," said the prince, sitting back in his chair, "this dreadful tale certainly must be investigated." He paused and cast his eyes around the entire gathering, like an orator waiting to make sure he had his entire audience's attention. "Baron Liam, go immediately with as many men as you deem necessary and capture this man Prentice. Bring him in irons for trial. I will judge him for myself."

Liam bowed so eagerly that he nearly knocked his chair over. "I go at once, Highness." He turned on his heel and paused only to sneer once more at Amelia as he pushed past her, then he rushed out the main doors of the hall, calling for his bannermen. Watching him go, Amelia was certain he would tear the whole of Dweltford apart if that's what it took to find Prentice.

The prince, however, was not finished. "As for this matter of the stolen taxes," he said. Every merchant in the room hung on his words, even the detached Master Welburne. "I shall have my factor review these documents and count the silver you have returned. If all is in order as you claim, then I will regard your case with mercy."

There was a collective sigh of relief, but still the prince went on. "If so much as a guilder is missing, if even one coin has been shaved, then you will all hang in crows' cages for the rest of your short lives. Go now, but do not leave the town. Your names will be given to the bailiffs. If they do not find you in your homes at every dusk and every dawn, that will be taken as an admission of guilt and you will be hunted down. Mark me, gentlemen. I am the Prince of Rhales, and my word is law in the west."

Most of them quailed at the prince's threat. Even Welburne seemed unsettled, his equanimity broken at last.

Malden showed no fear, though, bowing his head again. "You are wise, just, and merciful, great prince. We will obey your every command, and you will see that we are men of our word, aspiring to follow your superior example."

Amelia wondered if the prince could see that Malden was playing him, but realized almost immediately that it didn't matter to the prince. Whether Malden meant his words or not, Daven Marcus held all the cards, and the only thing the merchants could hope for was to keep him happy. For his part, Daven Marcus seemed to be deeply pleased, accepting the compliments without review. She was surprised when he turned to her.

"Does this suit you, Your Grace, or would you like to say more? Perhaps you would prefer a different course."

The prince had ordered her most loyal man arrested and tried for murder and treason, on the word of a man who was most certainly a murderer himself. Amelia wanted to slap him, or to run from the room and find Prentice, to warn him, but she refused to let the prince play her like Malden played him.

"I would not think to question king's justice, Your Highness," she said stiffly, keeping her voice calm with difficulty. "You are, as you have said, Prince of Rhales; the law of the Grand Kingdom is yours to execute faithfully. Who would doubt you in your duty?"

The prince nodded.

"I have just one minor question," she continued. "What of this money that so many men seem ready to lie, cheat, and kill for? Once you have judged the truth of these good men's claims?"

"It's tax, isn't it? I will take it for the crown. Who better than me to see it to the king's coffers?"

And there it was, the prince's advantage in the whole business. He'd be able to feed his ridiculously large entourage for a decade with chests full of silver. Never mind that only a share of that tax was owed to the crown, and Amelia was certain that King Chrostmer's coffers would never see a single one of those guilders. But how could she stop him? He was the Prince of Rhales. He answered to no one except his father. Amelia would have to appeal directly to the king. By the time any letter was received and looked at, the prince could have the money in any one of a hundred places, hidden beyond any tax collector or king's herald. Or he could simply deny her claim, say that the money he took was only the correct amount of royal tax and that she was lying. Amelia had never met even the lowliest official from the King's Court; who there would believe her word?

"If that is your plan, great prince, then it relieves me of having to worry about it," Amelia said and bowed her head. Lifting it again, she stood. "With your permission, I will withdraw."

"You have leave." Daven Marcus waved an imperious hand.

Amelia looked to the papers in front of him. "Shall I send a servant for those, or would you like me to take them myself?"

He cocked an eyebrow at that. "What would you do with them?"

"Keep them for the trial, of course, Highness. Important documents such as these must be kept safe. Or else give them to your factor."

"And you think I should let you keep them?"

"Only if you feel you can trust me," Amelia said.

Daven Marcus stared straight at her, and Amelia met his eyes for a moment, then lowered them, as protocol demanded. He was trying to figure her out, she could feel it. His gaze seemed to pierce her, as if trying to dig any secrets out of her. She refused to be intimidated. Let him unravel her secrets for himself—she would not help him.

"Can I trust you with something this important?" the prince asked.

"Where could I lose them?" she replied sweetly. Then she looked at the merchants. "And even if I were foolish enough to lose them, I'm sure these honest gentlemen have other copies. Isn't that right, Master Malden?"

Malden's eyes narrowed, then he nodded. "These are the originals, but we have a number of copies between us. Good merchants are men of record."

Amelia smiled. Daven Marcus had no good reason now to keep the documents from her, at least not without adding to gossip. Maybe he wouldn't care about that. Amelia wanted a chance to have the documents, to compare them with the ones in her chambers, and to figure out which members of the conspiracy, besides Folper, were not present.

"Very well, Lady Amelia," the prince said. "If you wish to do the work of a servant, feel free to collect these papers for the trial. Send them to my factor or take them yourself, whichever you think fits you best."

The prince was trying to needle her, even as he granted her request, but she didn't care. She was no petty noble, concerned with every little rise and fall of honor and respect. She was the Duchess of the Western Reach. Her people and their welfare were her concern. She gathered the papers neatly and, holding them to her chest, curtsied to the prince before leaving the hall by the kitchen corridor. Out from under the gaze of so many hostile and treacherous faces, she wanted to go straight to her chambers, to lay out these papers and what advantages she could glean from them, if any. But first she went to the kitchens and, asking the staff there, quickly tracked down Turley. She knew he would be able to find Prentice faster than anyone else, and Prentice had to be warned.

Baron Liam was hunting him, with murder in his heart.

CHAPTER 23

Prentice and Sir Gant had marched Folper and his animals into the castle's upper bailey, planning to leave the beasts there before taking the merchant inside. However, the heavy burdens on the mules had to be taken off so they could be rested, and there were no hands in the upper stables to help with that, so they escorted the bound Folper down to the lower bailey, which opened onto the kitchens, and then into the huge holding barn that was used for convicts when regular transportation only brought a hundred or two to the Reach. The stone building was vast, with iron rings embedded in its walls for shackling convict chain gangs to, but it could not possibly fit the two-thousand-plus horde Prince Daven Marcus had brought over the mountains. With no one to help with the mules, Prentice took Folper and his mounts into the barn through its huge southern doors.

"This is beneath me," the merchant protested for a moment, trying to reclaim his dignity in the face of imminent imprisonment.

"The castle has no dungeons," said Prentice. It was true as far as he knew, but he could be wrong. "You'll be staying here."

He removed the bridle and reins from Folper's horse and, using the tack as a rope, dragged the merchant to the nearest iron ring and tied him to it so that his arms were behind his back.

"This is for convicts! I'm no convict."

"Not yet," said Sir Gant.

"Besides, I bet you've been here before," Prentice added.

Folper nodded and looked away, as if ashamed. Every season, when convicts were transported and marched over the Azure Mountains to the Reach for their seven years of exile, they were first brought to this barn. Then merchants like Folper, along with village headmen and wealthy farmers, would come and buy their indenture from the duke. They would take the convicts away to serve as virtual slave labor. Prentice had no doubt that a rich trader like Folper would have made use of the institution in his time.

"Now you can see what it's like from the other side," Prentice said.

They left Folper by the wall and busied themselves unloading the mules. From just by the door came Cutter's voice. "That's what I like to see, men hard at honest work."

They both turned, and Prentice was shocked by what he saw. Cutter had put her money to good use. She had on a yellow blouse with white lace cuffs, under a brown leather bodice that had to be laced to its limit to fit her thin frame. These she wore above a pair of striped trousers dyed alternately pink and dark blue. They were tucked into soft leather boots that were tied with scarlet ribbons. She'd had someone do her hair as well, it seemed. Although it was too short to properly plait, she nonetheless had it tied back with another ribbon, giving her a tiny tail like the bobbed tail of a dressed pony. The bright colors almost certainly violated some sumptuary law.

"Well, that looks comfortable," Sir Gant said affably.

Cutter nodded at him but made her way over to stand in front of Prentice, like a servant presenting herself, though not with the same level of respect. "How's this, then?" she all but demanded.

"Gant said it all. It looks like you'll be much more comfortable in that than your old rags."

"You bet!" She twirled about. "Even got myself a pair of silk lady drawers, can you believe it? Like being caressed with every step. Very fancy."

"How did you afford all that on twenty guilders?" Prentice asked.

"The silk drawers weren't cheap, I'll give you that, but the rest I got for a song down at the docks."

"At the docks?"

Prentice and Gant exchanged a confused look. An unpleasant thought occurred to Prentice, and he scowled.

Cutter shook her head. "Not like that. I mean, I'm good, but I'm not that good. I got it from them mercenaries."

"What do you mean, from the mercenaries?"

"The mercenaries the traitor knight hired. They're all in a barge just out in the lake, chained up and waiting to be sent down to the Vec."

Prentice eyed her suspiciously. "They gave you their clothes?"

"Yes! It seems the Kingdom don't feed its prisoners fancy enough for their tastes. They've got dockers rowing out to them each morning, swapping food and drink for bits of clothing. I never knew mercenaries dressed so fancy. They'll give you just about anything for a loaf of bread, and if you show up with hard silver for them, like I did—well then, they practically fall over themselves to offer you things. Plus, there's charwomen on docks who are still working through the bits that were looted from their barracks. Lord knows how they got hold of it all."

"How'd you find a pair of boots and trousers to fit you among a company of men?"

"They're not all men, you know. None of them's girls like me. 'Course, if they were, I guess they wouldn't have admitted it. But they've got pages and young boys among them, messengers and the like, drummers too. Got these boots off a lad who swore he was a cousin to some prince or other. I think they're rather cute."

"They are indeed fine, Mistress Cutter," said Sir Gant. He sketched a bow, and Cutter returned it with a bow of her own.

"You've done well for yourself," said Prentice. "Now help us get these mules unloaded."

"Who's he?" she asked, casting an eye at Folper, who had sunk down to sit on his haunches with his back against the wall. When they told her, she was indignant. "You went after him without me?"

"We didn't have time to search you out," Prentice said. "He was in the wind, and I wanted him caught. I couldn't wait for you."

A chill breeze blew in through the open doors, and Cutter moved to close them off, rubbing her arms as she did. The smell of rain wafted in as she shut the door, and for a moment there was the sound of drops on the wet mud before the closed door muffled the outside noises.

"Winter'll be in soon," Cutter said to no one in particular.

"You going to help or what?"

"You didn't need my help to catch him, don't see why you need my help with this."

Prentice scowled over his shoulder as he and Gant wrestled a heavy bundle bound in oilcloth onto the ground. "If you want to get paid, you'll bloody come and help," Prentice told Cutter.

The other end of the barn was built into the slope of the rise that the keep stood on, so that the single door at that end was high above the barn floor and could be reached by a set of stone steps. From that end came a sharp whistle, and they turned to see Turley standing at the top of the steps.

He waved at them. "Hey up," he called. They waved back as he approached. "They said you'd ridden in with a train of pack mules."

"Two mules. Hardly a train," Sir Gant corrected.

"And none of us rode," Prentice said.

Turley nodded. "I forgot, you don't like horses."

"Horses are fine," Prentice muttered. "I just don't like riding them."

Turley shrugged and smiled. He examined the loads sitting on the ground next to the mules, one of which unceremoniously dropped a load of dung. He glanced at Folper. "Who's the miserable bugger on the wall?"

"Folper. One of Duggan's merchant cabal."

"They went and got him without me," Cutter chimed in, still standing by and not helping.

Turley gave her a long look, as though he had trouble recognizing her. "A bodice and a pair of trousers? Are you a girl or a boy? I forget."

"Take a handsomer man than you to find out for sure," Cutter retorted.

Turley chuckled at that, and Prentice could tell the two of them would be fast friends before the winter was out. They had the same sense of humor and roguish attitude to rules.

"The prince had a bunch of merchants in the great hall this morning," Turley said.

That caught Prentice's attention.

"Including our friend," Turley went on. "The big brute from the reeve's house."

"The one that gave him the beating?" asked Cutter. When Prentice and Sir Gant scowled at her, she shrugged unapologetically. "What? It's true."

Prentice gave Turley a nod. "The brute's name is Vardian Malden." He glanced at Folper. "According to our guest, he's a selectman on the council."

"Oh, and me thinking I had a clever secret to share," Turley mock-whined. "Just steal the wind from me sails, why don't you!"

"He's a bold bastard to show his face in the castle," Sir Gant said of Malden.

Prentice agreed. He paused to think, rubbing his unshaven chin. Suddenly, he felt a heavy fatigue. It occurred to him that missing a night's sleep and trudging through the mud and rain to catch Folper was probably not the best way to recover from his last encounter with the street-fighting merchant conspirator. What he needed was to crawl into a bed and rest for a few days, at a minimum. He wasn't going to get to, at least not yet.

"Who are these other merchants with him?" Prentice asked.

Turley shrugged.

"You don't think it could be Duggan's cabal, do you?" Sir Gant's question tracked Prentice's thoughts. The notion seemed incredible—a move either bold or foolhardy, and probably both.

"If you're with a bunch of thieves and you think you might get caught, what don't you want to be the one doing?" Prentice mused.

Sir Gant looked puzzled by the question, and Turley seemed thoughtful, but Cutter reached the answer first of all of them.

"Holding the bag."

"Exactly," Prentice said. "If they are Duggan's conspirators, then they've got his money and know we're looking for them. They know judgment is coming, and they want to get out from under it."

"So why go to the prince?" asked Turley.

"Because he outranks the duchess," Gant replied. "And he isn't the one they've been treasonous against. If they can put a good face on it, make themselves out as victims of Duggan's treachery, then the prince can pull them out of the fire, so to speak. Save them from the noose, at any rate."

"That's not a throw of the dice I'd like to lay money on," said Turley.

"Nor I, but if it's your only throw, might as well put all your money on it."

Prentice went silent again, trying to think but finding the fatigue of the last few days hanging heavier on him with each passing moment. It took a long time before he realized that they were all standing watching, waiting on him.

"I need to speak with the duchess," he said at last, not because he had a plan to follow but because he didn't know what else to do. If Malden was trying to outflank them by going to the prince, then he might also know of the conflict between the prince and Her Grace. Even if he didn't, that conflict would only help the conspirators' cause, in any case.

"I can find her, tell her you need to see her," offered Turley. Then he corrected himself. "Sorry. I will bring word to Her Grace and tell her you request an audience."

He bowed formally.

Cutter and Sir Gant smiled, but Prentice was too lost to his thoughts. "Good man. Do that, would you," he said.

Turley turned to leave, but as he did so, the far door of the barn opened once more. Graycen, the head steward, entered, dripping water from oilskin cloak and hat. "Turley, you skiver, I've been looking for you for half a candle!"

Graycen's voice carried all the way to the other end of the barn, surprisingly loud from his short frame.

"And I've been right here!" Turley bellowed back. Then he turned to his friends. "Not twenty paces from the kitchen door to here and he needed a hat and cloak for the journey."

Cutter laughed and Sir Gant hid a smile. Even distracted as he was, Prentice smiled as well and shook his head.

"You're going to get yourself in trouble someday," Prentice said.

"No, that's your job!"

Graycen was impatiently waving Turley over and he trotted off, the picture of a helpful retainer.

"How did that man ever end up on a chain?" asked Sir Gant. "He'd charm the legs off a team of plow horses."

"That's the problem," said Prentice. "Once you've charmed the legs off a horse, you can't ride it anywhere."

Sir Gant gave him a puzzled look.

"Makes it harder to get away when they come to arrest you."

Cutter laughed at the comment, but Gant just looked confused. Graycen marched Turley out of the barn, and Prentice turned back to the mules. With the last of the supplies removed, he told Gant to take the three beasts to the stables and get them rubbed down, watered, and fed.

"You're the one who knows horses the best of us," he explained to the knight, but Gant seemed to have no problem with the instruction. He left for a moment and returned presently with lead ropes from the stable, then he took the animals away.

"So now what's to do next?" asked Cutter.

"Next? You haven't done anything yet!" Prentice tried to look baleful, but he didn't have the energy for it. "Next, I'd like sleep."

"Well, I've no need for sleep, and you don't pay me well enough to join you for that."

"I wouldn't pay you anyway," Prentice muttered. From her expression he could see that Cutter took the comment awry, but he didn't have the energy to tell her he meant it as a compliment. He walked over to another section of the wall, away from where Folper was tied and, removing his belt, sank to the ground. With his head leaned back against the stones, he closed his eyes.

Just for a moment, he told himself.

CHAPTER 24

D uchess Amelia was pleased to see her head steward return so quickly with Turley. As soon as she had entered the kitchens, she'd set men searching for Prentice's old companion. She sat on a chair at one of the preparation tables, head on her hands, trying to control her fretful thoughts. She worried that it would take too long to find Turley or that he would not be found—or, if found, he would not know where Prentice was. She tried not to think about the idea that Baron Liam was already kicking in inn doors in the town, terrorizing her citizens. And worse, that he would find Prentice, with the authority of the prince behind him.

"He'll kill him," she had just said to herself when Graycen returned through the kitchen door with Turley on his heels.

They made an odd contrast. Graycen was a small man with a flat face and few, if any, distinctive features. His mud-brown, pudding bowl hair came out when he pulled off his oilskin hat. He shook the water from himself fastidiously. Behind him, Turley was a mop-haired giant, water droplets in his hair not yet heavy enough to weigh down the natural curls. And there was that reflexive smile, easy and sweet to see. Amelia had no doubt there were half a dozen kitchen maids who had their eyes on him; good luck to them.

"Here he is, Your Grace," Graycen said, making a point of coming formally in front of her and going down on one knee.

It was a show of loyalty not usually required from one of his rank, and Amelia found the gesture presumptuous, but there was no point in saying anything about it now. Behind him, Turley tugged his forelock as he presented himself. "Found him shirking in the convict barn."

"I wasn't shirking, Your Grace, I swear—"

"Never mind that," Amelia interrupted. "Steward Turley, I need to find Master Ash. Do you know where he is?"

Turley's eyes showed his surprise. "I was just with him, Your Grace. He was only now saying how he needed to speak to you as well. I'll go fetch him."

"I'll come with you. Take me to him."

She stood and pushed past Graycen, who tried to stand at her passing and nearly tripped over his own feet in the attempt. Amelia waved for Turley to follow her as she went straight back out into the rain, not waiting for a cloak for herself. Even before the kitchen door had closed behind them, Graycen left the kitchens by a different door, breaking into a shuffling run.

Outside, the cold rain had begun to waver so that it was little more than a falling mist in the air. Amelia shivered at its chill, then squared her shoulders and ignored it. It was a short walk to the barn, and once inside, she walked quickly down to where Prentice sat against the wall. The sight of him here, leaning against the walls, reminded her of how short a time it was since he was a convict and how much had been expected of him in that time. Next to him was a young man who saw her coming. The youth jumped up and Amelia saw that it was, in fact, a young woman, wearing trousers and with her hair cut short. She said something to Prentice and then kicked him, waking him up.

When he saw Amelia, Prentice jumped up as well, though with more effort. He tugged his forelock for a moment before converting it into a bow, just as Malden had earlier. The sameness of the gesture convinced her that Malden had been lowborn before rising to the level of selectman, just as Prentice had been low, being a convict for a decade. Such men who could rise so far by their own hands had a fearsome strength of will.

"Your Grace," Prentice said quickly. "I would have attended you at your pleasure. There is no need for you to come to me."

He cast a wary eye at the girl next to him. She was staring at Amelia, and there was something in her expression that Amelia liked. The girl was obviously fascinated by her first meeting with a duchess, and naturally curious.

"You curtsy, Cutter!" Prentice hissed, but Amelia shushed him with a hand.

"There's no time, Master Ash," she said. "You have to get away from the castle grounds, immediately."

"What? Why, Your Grace?"

"The prince has sent Liam to hunt you down. You're to be brought to trial for the murder of Bastian Fern. Liam's gone into the town right now, looking for you."

"The seneschal's murder?" Prentice said, as if the words didn't quite make sense. For a moment, Amelia wondered if he was fully awake, then he cracked a rueful smile.

"Clever. Bloody clever," he said, shaking his head.

"Prentice?"

"It was Malden, wasn't it? He told the prince he saw me kill Fern."

"He's trying to stick you with the bag," said the girl, Cutter.

"How did you know?" Amelia asked.

"He knows we're looking for Duggan's conspirators. He knows we took Folper's share already."

Prentice nodded to the forlorn man sitting on the ground, tied to the wall. As she looked, Amelia realized he was wearing a long, dark coat, like those worn by the merchants at the prince's audience; this had to be the merchant Folper. Prentice had begun to make good on his promise to root out Duggan's accomplices. But with the ruthlessly cunning Malden leading them, the conspirators were working to outwit him.

"What does he know? Has he talked?" she asked.

"Some, Your Grace. Enough to know that Malden is the heart of the matter. If he's telling the truth, Malden even had the better of Duggan, fashioning the conspiracy for him. He's a criminal who's made a respectable name for himself."

"Are there no honest men in my domain? Is every institution corrupt?" Amelia sighed in exasperated disgust.

"Sounds like most places to me," said Cutter. Amelia gave her a hard look, and Cutter shrugged. "I'm only saying."

Amelia turned away for a moment, wanting to think. Sifting her options, she made the best decision she could, given the circumstances. She turned back to Prentice. "Come with me, right now. I will present you to the prince, and he can put you under arrest. I will claim charge of you as my sworn man, and you can be placed in a room here in the castle, under my houseguards. Knowing the prince's preference for swift justice, I will press him for a trial immediately—tomorrow or the next day. The prince can hear Malden's evidence sworn to oath, and I will testify on your behalf that I sent you to find Bastian Fern and that you were attacked by Malden and his men. I am the duchess, no matter Liam's and Daven Marcus' attitudes. My testimony will outweigh Malden's, and then the merchant will face a trial of his own. I'll have them all arrested then. I do not like brazen cockerels strutting up and down on the law in my own hall. They'll pay for their brazenness and their treason with Duggan."

"And for the death of the duke," Prentice added.

"How so?" asked Amelia.

"According to Folper, Malden poisoned Duke Marne," Prentice explained. "He told us as we were marching him back last night. He tried to flee."

Malden poisoned my duke?

It made a kind of sense. For all his treason, Duggan was a knight, a man of rank, and would have bridled at using so base a tactic as poison. She would have Malden executed within days, she swore it to herself.

Sir Gant reentered the barn through the main doors and immediately bowed when he saw Amelia. She acknowledged him but had no time for courtesies. She had Prentice give instructions.

"I have to go with the duchess. Take Cutter and find new lodgings. Somewhere you haven't stayed before. Send to the council house each morning to see if you've been called for."

It was clear Sir Gant didn't understand the reason for the orders, but he didn't question them. Cutter was another matter completely.

"Why can't we come with you?" she demanded.

"Because I'm about to be brought before the prince, and while the duchess can be forgiving of little violations of protocol, the prince is just as likely to have you flogged or take a finger if you make one of your clever comments."

"I know how to keep my trap shut."

"Then do it now and obey me, will you."

Cutter narrowed her eyes at him. Prentice ignored her, and after fetching his weapon belt and carrying it in his hands, he followed as Amelia led the way back to the stone steps. Gant and Cutter walked a few paces behind them.

"I like her," the duchess said quietly, casting a quick glance over her shoulder. "Where'd you find her?"

"Convict chain. You freed her, Your Grace, with the amnesty after the battle."

"She was at the Battle of the Brook? How?"

"Pretending to be a boy, so as not to be raped."

Amelia was appalled. To hide for fear of being raped only to be thrown into that cauldron of blood and terror?

"No wonder she speaks out of turn. She must be fearless."

"She hasn't had an easy life," Prentice conceded. "She's been through some terrible things."

Knowing Prentice's own history, Amelia could only imagine what might be encompassed in the two words "terrible things."

They reached the top of the steps, and she waited while he held the door for her. Outside, the rain had completely stopped, but the muddy yard was full of puddles. Amelia decided that she wouldn't walk through the kitchens, and instead led the way across the yard and around the keep to the upper bailey. The other two behind them kept their distance, as though following despite Prentice's orders, but what else could they do? There was only one way out of the castle and into the town, and it was the main gate on the other side of the upper bailey.

All four of them rounded the corner of the keep and separated to cross the bailey—Amelia and Prentice to the great hall, Cutter and Sir Gant to the gatehouse.

At that moment, Graycen, still in his rain cloak, led Baron Liam back to the castle from that direction. They spotted Prentice at the same time that Amelia and Prentice saw them. Baron Liam drew his sword with a triumphant cry and began moving forward, ordering Graycen to fetch his men from the town.

"I'll have your balls for my dogs, you bastard," Liam shouted as Amelia rushed forward to interpose herself between him and Prentice.

"Baron Liam, Master Ash is in my custody," she began, but Liam's blood was up. He moved to push past her. She put her hand out, catching him on the upper arm, hoping to hold him back. He shrugged her off. She did it again, more firmly, indignant that he would be so recalcitrant. This time he twisted free of her arm with force, swiping at her with his sword hand so that the pommel struck her across the side of the face.

"Unhand me, trollop," he said, not even noticing as she fell, stunned, in the mud. "I have the prince's orders. Your little pet's about to get the kicking he deserves!"

CHAPTER 25

Prentice cursed inwardly when Liam came into sight, and as the duchess interposed herself, he half turned to the two behind him. He did not want Liam to know who they were or that they were connected with him, if it could be avoided.

"Go now. Don't let him see us together," he whispered just as Liam struck the duchess. She crumpled to the ground, and the fatigue washed out of Prentice like a sluice of iced water, waking him up and firing all his nerves at once. A furious growl sounded from deep in his chest, and his hands went to the hilt of his swordbreaker.

Liam smirked. "Ah, the mutt awakens."

The baron started forward, longsword in hand, while Prentice carefully worked his weapon free of its sheath. The uneven edges and planes of the 'breaker meant that it would not slide free cleanly like a sword or dagger, but Prentice never took his eyes off Liam, warily moving sideways to make sure they were both away from the fallen duchess. When the weapon at last came free, Prentice threw the belt to the ground.

Liam sneered at the twisted steel, as if barely recognizing the odd artifact as a tool of combat. "I'm going to take that stick and thrash you to death with it, convict!"

"You couldn't do it last time," Prentice said, referring to a flogging Liam had ordered before the Battle of the Brook. The whips had ripped Prentice's flesh to bits, but not beyond the work of a talented, and expensive, healer marching with the army. "Do you want to send for some overseers to help you again?"

Liam's sneer contorted into a snarl and he surged forward, sword held loosely, aiming to strike Prentice down with a single swipe. As he came on, some calm part of Prentice's mind had just enough time to wonder about his chances.

When was the last time you used a swordbreaker? Ten years at least, isn't it? You had better be up to this.

Then there was no more time to wonder, as the first strike came cutting down diagonally. Prentice deflected it and the next one, as Liam followed up with a reverse of the first cut. Liam kept up the pressure, and Prentice was forced backward, deflecting reflexively as old skills, trained into him years before, began to reawaken. The 'breaker was shorter than the baron's longsword but just as heavy, so that it easily countered attacks. Nonetheless, Prentice had to keep moving, to keep from being out-reached. It was a desperate affair, and more than once the keen edge of the blade flashed so close he was amazed he wasn't cut.

Liam's hatred drove him forward at the first, but the baron was a trained knight and veteran of the field. After a moment he stopped and held Prentice at sword point while he rethought his approach. Liam had probably never seen a swordbreaker before, let alone fought against one, Prentice could see as much in the baron's expression. It wasn't surprising—the 'breaker, sometimes called a steel whip, was a peasant's weapon, and there hadn't been a true peasant uprising in the Grand Kingdom for over a century. Liam had trained to face other knights. Peasants were for throwing at the enemy in ill-disciplined hordes, not facing in single combat.

The baron changed his grip and shifted his stance.

"Well, now we're getting serious," Prentice muttered, but if Liam heard him, he ignored it. Out of the corner of his eye, Prentice saw Sir Gant helping the duchess. He couldn't see

Cutter but hoped for once the girl had done as she was told. Then Liam was coming on again, this time with a series of tight cuts, much more controlled.

Prentice absorbed the strikes, having to use both hands on the swordbreaker to move it fast enough to match the concentrated assault. Liam pressed his advantage, and Prentice found himself pushed against the outside wall of the keep. With Liam's sudden feint and switch of footwork, the sword sprang forward in a thrust to Prentice's belly, and he knew his deflection came too late and at the wrong angle. Liam's triumphant smile died on his lips, though. If Prentice had had a longsword, the baron's blade would have slid past the ineffective check and the point would still have struck home, but the swordbreaker's uneven edges caught the sword blade and wrenched it sideways. The deadly thrust was driven aside, and the edge cut a shallow wound in Prentice's thigh before crashing into the stone wall behind him, striking sparks.

Prentice kicked Liam desperately, driving him back, and then dashed clear to get more space again. He put his hand down to feel the wound and how much blood was flowing. The cut hurt, like a stripe of fire across his leg, but there wasn't much blood, just a sticky smear.

"The first of the blood I'll take from you," Liam said when he saw the crimson on Prentice's hand.

"You can't be proud with that little nick," Prentice shot back. "I've lost more blood than this shaving."

"You'll never shave again once I've got your damn head!"

It was a poor rejoinder, and Prentice gave the baron a condescending smile.

Enraged, Liam charged again, giving vent to his fury once more but still using the close driving techniques that put Prentice on the back foot. As he retreated this time, Prentice waited for his opening. He knew that when the moment came, if his timing was out by even a whisker, he'd see his own guts in the mud of the bailey. For an instant, he remembered the bloody

filth at the Brook and the wild hacking attacks he'd used to slay
the Horned Man. But this wasn't battle, wild and unruly, for all
Liam's fury. This was a duel against an expert and determined
opponent. It took cunning and skill, as much as strength and
courage.

The moment came.

Liam thrust for the midsection again, and Prentice caught
the blade with a parry, whipping the heavy steel swordbreaker
like the flickering tongue of a serpent so that it twisted the
longsword completely away and down. Liam saw the move and
tried to retreat, but the blade caught again on the 'breaker's jags,
just for a fraction of a second. That made the opening, and the
steel whip leaped upward in Prentice's two hands, crashing into
the side of Liam's jaw. The bone broke with a savage crunch, and
his body went instantly limp, insensible. Prentice kept driving
forward, using his weight to push the falling knight flat on the
muddy ground. The longsword was knocked from his hand,
and it cartwheeled twice before clanging against the stones of
the bailey's wall.

Standing over him, Prentice had the 'breaker raised and ready
to strike again. He wanted to; he could feel the hate in himself.
A swift, precise stroke to the skull, and Baron Liam would be
gone from the world, his brutal arrogance and petty ambition
nothing but a bad memory. Prentice clenched hard around
the weapon in his hand until he could feel his fingers and
knuckles aching. Then he remembered the rage of the lion on
the battlefield, how he had heard a voice amidst the smoke
and chaos, a voice he was sure was the voice of God. He also
remembered the feeling of being at the mercy of merciless men
when he was a convict, of enduring beatings for the pleasure of
sadists. He stepped back, suddenly tired again. The unconscious
Liam moaned but did not stir, and Prentice spat on him in
contempt.

Then he turned to the duchess. She was still on the ground,
and Sir Gant was kneeling beside her, cradling her head.

"It's just a faint, I think," the knight said.

Prentice leaned his ear close to her face and listened for her breathing. It was strong, but before he could be relieved, Graycen the steward shouted in the keep doorway. Prentice looked up and straight into the man's eyes.

"He's killed the duchess!" yelled the chief steward. "He's killed her and attacked the baron. Baron Liam is downed!" He ran into the keep, shouting all the way.

Prentice made to go after him, but Sir Gant caught his arm.

"That bastard'll have the whole castle down on us!" Prentice growled venomously.

"She lives, but she's unconscious. Who's going to refute the steward's report? The duchess down and the baron with her? They'll tear us apart before they ask for the whole tale. A court that hears her testimony will acquit you, but you must live that long. Besides, the prince wants you for the seneschal's murder, remember?"

Prentice knew Sir Gant was right. He was loath to flee, to act like a criminal, but there seemed no other choice. He helped Gant lower the duchess's head to the ground, and the two of them dashed for the gatehouse. Behind them they heard shouts from the keep as Graycen stirred up the household.

A guard came out of the barrack room in the barbican as Prentice and Gant jogged past. "What's going on?"

"The duchess is hurt," said Prentice. "Go help her!"

"We're going for a chirurgeon," added Gant.

The guardsman rushed away into the bailey, while Prentice and Gant ran out onto the drawbridge. Their feet thumped heavily on the boards, but Prentice's head felt stuffed with cloth, making everything seem distant. They reached the far end, and Gant was pulling ahead. The knight looked tired, but he still seemed to have more strength for running than Prentice.

He's not the one who took a beating a few days ago, protested the quiet part of his mind. And he wasn't just in another fight. And your leg's hurt.

Prentice looked down and saw the thin cut trickling blood through the slash in his trousers. He blinked and realized he was sweating, in spite of the coolness of the morning.

"This way," said Gant, pointing down an alley off Castle Road.

"Where are we going?" Prentice could hear himself panting as he tried to speak.

"I know a place we can stay. A friendly house."

"Good," said Prentice.

Then he felt his foot snag on a raised cobblestone, and he was falling. He put his hands out to catch himself, and he heard the swordbreaker ring on the cobbles. Hadn't he even resheathed his weapon? That was a mistake. Lying on the ground, he tried to put the 'breaker away, but he realized he'd dropped the weapon belt and would have to go back for it. Except, he couldn't. He felt so tired, and lying down, even on the hard cobbles, was such a relief. He closed his eyes for a moment, just a moment.

CHAPTER 26

Prentice awoke in bed with an aching head and pains in his body. For a moment he thought he was back in the seneschal's house, waking up from the beating that Malden had given him. But that was wrong. He rolled over and saw his clothes and weapon belt hung on a nearby chair. He thought about getting out of bed and dressing, but his thigh was still sore from the wound and the bed felt comfortable. He fell back asleep, wondering how Malden had given him the cut on his leg.

A shout from outside a window woke him again later, and he realized by the light that it must be evening. A crier called out the hour, and what sounded like a child's voice mimicked him. With a groan Prentice sat up in bed, then fell back again. He tried to push the sheet away, but it felt too difficult. Looking down at himself and feeling with his hands, he could tell he had a bandage on his thigh, and from the smell, it had a poultice underneath as well. There was another bandage on his head, he realized.

Glancing around, he could see he was in a loft, under a thatched roof that seemed so close he could almost reach it from the bed. The chair was still there and his things with it. There was a tiny paneless window with a levered shutter that was open, but there was only shadowy lamplight coming through. The only other light in the room was from a tallow candle that burned next to his clothes on the chair. They would stink of rendered fat next time he put them on.

From the floor below he heard movement and looked up as a ladder creaked. A woman's head, with a face he didn't recognize, poked up through an opening in the floor. She was round faced and mature, with a dun-colored bonnet and dark wisps of hair that escaped from underneath.

"Thought I heard you moving about," she said. "You feeling any better? Hungry? Thirsty?"

He thought about it a moment. "Thirsty," he tried to say, but his voice came out as a croak.

"Water it is," said the woman, and she disappeared again.

Prentice lay back in the bed and tried to figure where he was. He couldn't recall coming here or climbing up to this bed. He remembered the fight with Liam and then fleeing the castle. Then his memory failed him.

Where was he?

The woman returned presently, carefully hauling a tray with a jug, a cup, and a bowl up into the loft. The whole procedure was complicated by the lack of space, as she had to reach the tray through the hatchway first, resting it on the floor, then climb the ladder and push the tray away to make space to get all the way up, and then pick up the tray and bring it to him. Whoever had managed to get his unconscious body up here must have had a devil of a time.

The woman was wearing a brown shift and faded red bodice with a simple apron. She sat on the floor next to the chair, probably to save moving the candle. Her tray also had another tallow candle, and she lit it from the first's wick before putting it on the bedpost.

"Don't kick or move too hastily," she instructed. "Otherwise, you'll set your covers on fire and that'll be the end of you. And my house too, like as not."

She handed him the cup and poured water into it. He drank it thankfully, even though it hurt him to swallow at first. When he finished, she took the cup back and picked up the bowl. It was filled with a pottage, thick with oats, parsnips, and sweet potatoes. It smelled savory, and his stomach grumbled loudly. She grabbed a spoon and held the bowl near his mouth, proposing to feed him. He didn't feel so weak that he needed to be fed, but he wasn't going to object. There were other things he needed to know first, though.

"The duchess?" he asked.

"What about her?"

"What word of her is there? Does she live?"

"As far as I know."

That wasn't a comforting answer. The woman put a spoonful into his mouth, and he chewed and swallowed. It was as tasty as it smelled.

"Good?" she asked. He nodded. "More?"

"Please."

She fed him slowly, a small spoonful at a time. About halfway through, he began to push for another answer.

"Who are you?"

The woman frowned, though he wasn't sure if she objected to the blunt question or was offended that he didn't know. "I'm the one Sir Gant paid to look after you," she said. "And even if he hadn't, I'm too Christian a woman to leave another body to suffer under my roof without some care."

That helped his fears somewhat. Wherever he was, Gant knew he was here.

"Thank you for your care, goodwife."

Another frown marred her expression. "I'm a widow nowadays."

"Oh, I'm sorry to hear that."

"It's not your…"

She stopped, and Prentice wondered why. There was a moment of awkward silence between them.

She looked down at the bowl and sighed. "Can you handle the rest of this by yourself? You seem strong enough for that."

He accepted the bowl from her, and she stood, making her way out again, stooping under the low roof. She was halfway down the ladder and about to disappear when she stopped and looked at him. "My name's Eleanour," she said. "Dran the gong farmer's wife. Now widow."

Then she was gone. Dran the gong farmer, who had helped them find their way through the sewers to take back the town and died on the cobbles with a bloody hole in his chest. That was why she couldn't tell him it wasn't his fault. He thought about that night as he chewed his way through a few more spoonsful but found his appetite soured. Prentice put the bowl and spoon on the floor, then rolled over in the covers. Sleep came mercifully quickly, and it was welcome when it did.

He awoke the next morning, judging by the light and the sounds from outside, feeling significantly better. Sitting up in bed, he felt ready to try getting dressed. Before he could, widow Eleanour was up the stairs with more food, this time cheese and meat, both very fresh. The cheese was from goat's milk and had probably only been made in the last day or two. The widow left it for him and took his bowl and spoon after pouring him another cup of water. When he drank it this time, he noticed a faint taste of vinegar in it. She didn't speak at all this time, and he wanted to find something to say, but nothing came to him.

After the meat and cheese, he tried to rest again, but only managed a nap. By midday he was bored enough to try getting dressed, but the effort was such a strain that he fell back on the bed again once he had his trousers on. He noticed his shirt stank of sweat, so he stripped it off, but felt too guilty about the widow's husband to ask her to wash it. He levered himself off the bed and hung the shirt on the window's edge so it would at least air. He heard voices downstairs and hoped it was Gant. Sitting up in bed, he was surprised when Cutter poked her head through the hatch.

"Oi, look who's awake," she said, and scrambled up the ladder. Sir Gant followed.

"What's he doing with his shirt off?" the hedge knight demanded. "He's had a fever."

"I took it off, Gant," Prentice said. "It stinks."

"Well, have it here and we'll get it washed."

Cutter pulled it from the window and tossed it to Gant, who took it back down the ladder.

"You don't look so bad," she said, plopping down on the edge of the bed. "Except for the old scars, of course."

"Like a half-cured ham a dog's gotten at?"

"Just like that."

He smiled. "Gant's right, though, if I've been sick. Pass me my doublet."

Cutter lifted the sleeveless garment and passed it to Prentice. "What do you mean, if you've been sick?" she asked. "Don't you remember?"

"No, not much."

Sir Gant returned. He stood, hunched over, at the end of the bed.

Prentice shrugged into his doublet and then met Gant's eyes. "Thank you."

"You're welcome."

"How long?"

"Five days. You were feverish for three. A night in the rain after taking a thrashing, I suppose."

Prentice nodded. "That'll do it. What of the duchess?"

"She lives."

"Then why am I still here? I must speak with her." Prentice started to get up, groaning with the effort in spite of himself. He needed to see Duchess Amelia.

Gant shook his head, and Cutter put a hand on his chest to stop him. "Not now. You can't," the knight said.

"Why not?" Prentice looked back and forth between them. "What's wrong?"

Sir Gant hung his head for a moment, appearing shamed, and that only made Prentice more nervous. What had happened to the duchess? Even Cutter, usually so eager, seemed hesitant to speak.

"The duchess has been put in seclusion by the chirurgeon, told to keep to her bed," Sir Gant explained. "The prince tried you in absentia. Only Baron Liam and that dog Graycen were witnesses, and they lied through their teeth. The prince sentenced you to death and has put you out of law. He's proclaimed a reward of a hundred guilders for your head."

"Cheapskate," Prentice said. The two of them blinked in surprise. Prentice smiled his wry smile. "According to Graycen, I put a baron down and then attacked my liege, the Duchess of the Reach. Surely that's worth more than a hundred."

Sir Gant shook his head, but Cutter chuckled.

"Liam gave evidence?" Prentice mused. "I guess it was too much to hope he'd die from one hit, or catch fever like me." He remembered the hit—a clean, solid blow—as well as standing over the felled baron. He wished he had killed him but was convinced that not delivering a final strike had been right. It had seemed too murderous to finish him as he lay on the ground. Mercy was what God desired, so the Church taught. Mercy and loving his enemies. Loving Liam was beyond Prentice at the moment; he hoped the Almighty would settle for the mercy of not killing the lying cur.

"He had to give his evidence by hand, though," Cutter was saying. Prentice furrowed his brow, not understanding what she meant. "He had to write it down, 'cause he can't speak. You cracked his jaw but good! The side of his face is dark and swollen up like an overripe plum, so they say. He couldn't leave his bed to go to court. They brought the letter to the prince."

"He'd never faced a swordbreaker before," Prentice said.

"I could see that," said Gant. "I wondered about it when you took that thing. It looked to me like nothing more than a heavy baton. Now that I've seen it, I wouldn't like to face it any more than Liam did."

"He almost caught me, twice." Prentice gently tapped his thigh where the bandage was. He was glad that he felt no pain there; the cut was healing well.

"That little thing?" said Cutter. "I lost more blood than that the last time a mosquito bit me."

Prentice took a moment to consider all the new information. The duchess was the only one in the whole Reach who could protect him, and he was unable to get to her. Even if he could, he wasn't sure she had the authority, under the King's Law, to pardon him. If she didn't, then there was nothing that could be done.

"Have you spoken to the duchess?" he asked.

"No," said Gant. "But your man Turley has twice brought me a letter."

"From her?"

Gant nodded. "So he says."

"And what's her word?"

"To keep you safe, hidden. She will send to the King's Court, plead the truth, and seek the king's grace for you."

"The king's grace?" Prentice could hardly believe it. There was no higher authority to appeal to, and Duchess Amelia would do that for him?

"Nice to have friends in high places, hey?" said Cutter, reading the expression from his face.

"I should send a message to her."

"Could be done, but carefully," Sir Gant cautioned. Something in his tone told Prentice there was more they hadn't told him.

"What else is there?" he asked.

"The merchant Malden has supplanted Baron Liam as the new toady. He's got a warrant from the royal hand, allowing him to form a company of men to hunt you out. He calls them his ratters."

"On account of us being the rats that saved the town," said Cutter.

"I understood," Prentice said. "So, they're hunting me and...?"

"And putting the bracelets on any of the rest of us. Giving us the twists to see if we know where you are."

"He's got the others?"

"The ex-convicts," said Gant with a nod. "He took Calles the other night, but the guilds all put up a stink and they let him go. It's an ugly business, but at least gong farmers get the respect they deserve in civic circles."

"The whole thing's turning into an ugly business." Prentice sucked his teeth and shook his head, thinking about the whole sorry affair. "Right, here's what we'll do." He paused. "That is, if you're still happy to follow my lead?"

"I'm still Her Grace's man," said Gant solemnly. "And so are you. I know the truth of what happened to her and Baron Liam. I'd have said so to the prince's face if they'd let me."

"So would I," Cutter chimed in.

Prentice smiled. "That might have done my case more harm than good."

Her eyes narrowed. "Oh, and why's that? You still giving me grief for my choice of clothes?"

He put up his hands. "Never again, I swear."

"See that you don't." She frowned. "But I'm on your side, like him. I ain't your 'man,' but I'm on your side."

"Glad to hear it," Prentice said. "I'll write you a letter, and you can see it to the duchess."

"What will you say?"

"That I'm getting better. That I'm ready to start putting a plan into place to give her a militia and get control of her Reach back."

"You're not that well. Not yet," Gant said.

"No, but by the time you get the letter to her and back, I'll have had enough rest. As much as I'm willing to take, at any rate."

Sir Gant nodded to show he accepted Prentice's instruction, but it was clear from his expression that he did not share Prentice's confidence. It was too bad. Things were moving quickly now. If the duchess did not have a force of her own soon, a new piece on the board, then the prince would take the whole province away from her. And Prentice would never allow that, not while he still drew breath.

CHAPTER 27

A melia lay in bed and it frustrated her to the core. She was well—certainly well enough to rise and dress herself, or to receive visitors. Yet the chirurgeon still insisted on seclusion and bed rest. It felt paranoid in her mind to say it, but she was sure that the old man was acting on orders from the prince. She had awakened in the evening of the same day Baron Liam had struck her and had proceeded to be violently ill into a chamber pot. For the next day, bed rest had been easy and welcome. Now six days had passed, and the lump on her head didn't even hurt anymore. Her strength had returned, and her stomach was long settled; she was restless with energy. Even reading, which she enjoyed more than any other activity, offered little distraction. Yet still the medical man muttered about striking sickness and confusions.

At least her maids were with her and still loyal. They had balked when she called for pen and paper, at least at first, but she was careful to work in small stints, to make a show of not exhausting herself. She also hid some of the papers under the covers when she slept. That was how she got her first letter to Prentice finished and handed to Turley without her maids even knowing. It wasn't that she didn't trust Bettina, Teerah, or Kristen. She didn't want them to know anything they could be forced to tell. After her encounter with the prince when he'd arrived, she had no doubt that he would hand any of her servants or companions over to one of his men and have them slapped into unconsciousness, if he thought they knew something he wanted to know. He might even do it himself. Better that they never even knew there was something to know than to make them vulnerable to such a fate.

There was the rattle of a tray outside her door and Amelia sat up, hoping to hear from Turley once again. It had become the practice for him to bring her food, and she was thinking of officially making him her steward of the chamber—an odd position for a woman to have in her service, but not unheard of. Her maid Kristen opened the door, and Amelia was disappointed to see Graycen standing and waiting in the doorway. He had the tray perched on his shoulder.

"Luncheon, Your Grace," he said politely, dipping his head as deeply as he could while holding the tray. Amelia wanted to ask where Turley was, but was careful not to tip her hand.

"You do not normally wait upon me yourself, Chief Steward," she said, trying to sound disinterested.

"You have been indisposed, Your Grace," he replied, placing the tray of fresh bread and hard cheese on the table. He turned and faced Amelia in bed, keeping his head bowed. "At such times, the chief steward must take care that the service you receive is of the highest standard."

He sounded smug to Amelia, like a bad liar pleased to have a lie that could not be disproved.

"And you took it upon yourself to care for my well-being?" Amelia let just a touch of steel into her tone of voice. "You saw fit to take the care of your liege in your own hands?"

Graycen looked up reflexively for a moment, and there was a look of fear in his eyes. "Not my decision, Your Grace," he said hastily, bowing his head once more. "I was instructed by the castellan. He has command of the castle."

"Baron Liam told you to serve me yourself?"

"Yes, Your Grace."

There it was. If Amelia tried to replace Graycen with Turley specifically, then Graycen would tell Baron Liam, and that would mark Turley as her messenger. Liam would have him seized, or worse, even—watched and followed. Liam was treacherous and self-serving, but he was no fool. She couldn't use Turley to contact Prentice, but even as she assumed that, another thought occurred to her.

She could be cunning as well.

"Matron Bettina," she called. "Were you not saying that the sideboard was too heavy to move this morning?"

Bettina looked up from where she was sewing by the north window. "Your Grace?" she asked, obviously puzzled by the question.

"I agree with you that some of the furniture should be rearranged, but it is no task for ladies-in-waiting. Chief Steward, send me that ox of a man in your staff. Turley is his name. He has served me well this past season."

"He is an impertinent oaf," said the matron, making no secret of her opinion of the duchess's choice.

"An oaf is a perfect choice for the task. Have him sent, Master Graycen."

"As you command, Your Grace," said Graycen sourly. He bowed and turned to leave.

"Chief Steward, a moment?" Amelia called when he was almost to the door. He stopped and faced her again, head down. "I was told it was you who called for help when I was struck down."

"It was."

"And you testified before the prince about the assault?"

"Yes, Your Grace. I spoke only what I saw."

"And what did you see?" she asked.

"I saw Your Grace on the ground and the ex-convict Prentice attacking the baron, who was coming to your defense."

"Coming to my defense?" Amelia repeated his words slowly. "How did you determine who attacked me if you only saw me on the ground, and not the assault itself?"

"The convict had a baton. Baron Liam had his sword. You were struck but not bleeding. It had to be the baton strike."

Graycen's words had the feel of a rehearsed story. Amelia suspected that he had been told by Liam, or others, what to say before the prince at the trial, and now to her face.

"And you did not trust Baron Liam to be able to defend me?" she asked.

"Your Grace, I only sought to help in your time of need."

"You seem to be presuming upon my needs often in recent days," said Amelia, and she let her full displeasure into her voice this time. "See that you don't rise too high above your station with your presumptions. It might be a long fall back down."

Graycen could serve Liam if he wished, if he thought that was how he would get ahead, but Amelia would be damned before she let him think he could fool her while he did it. When the chief steward was gone, Bettina told Teerah to fetch the duchess a slice of the bread and some cheese.

"I don't remember talking about the furniture this morning," the matron said as Amelia's maid served her food. "Forgive me."

"Perhaps I dreamed it, Bettina," Amelia said. "The chirurgeon says I am still recovering."

She picked at the bread and cheese and was not finished before Turley appeared in the doorway, tugging his forelock. "You asked to see me, Your Grace?"

Amelia smiled. She knew he was still the cheeky rogue she had met after the ambush on the way back from the Vec, but his manners were vastly improved. It was clear he was deliberately working to better himself, and she approved.

"We have furniture to be moved."

"Of course. Point it out and tell me where you want it. It's as good as done."

Bettina snorted quietly in derision, but assiduously did not look up from her needlework.

"We'll start with the sideboard," said Amelia, ignoring her matron. "Not far, just a few feet to the side. I think to move Bettina's bed away from the garderobe. It is a poor place for her to sleep."

"Very good, Your Grace." He positioned himself at one end of the sideboard and began looking for the best place to grasp it.

"How goes that other man, the injured one, who was with you when I met you in the summer?" Amelia asked.

"Bellam, Your Grace? He's doing well for himself. Almost fully healed and not too much of a limp. He's working in the kitchens, making himself into a baker. Odds are he made that bread you're eating."

"This bread? Why, it's excellent. Teerah, head down to the kitchens and send for Bellam the baker. I wish to congratulate him on this bread."

Teerah jumped up, putting her own lunch aside, and went quickly from the room. Amelia smiled inwardly. In a moment there'd be two servants in her chamber that she could pass notes by. Next, she'd come up with a reason to send Kristen to fetch someone. If they wanted to spy on her or follow her servants, she would give them so many servants to follow.

"Give me my quill and ink. I think I will write a letter to the houseguards who held Sir Duggan at his trial. They deserve my thanks."

CHAPTER 28

A new storm blew down from the north, bringing clouds heavy with rain. They burst over Dweltford in a deluge that hissed on the thatched roofs and hammered on the shutters of Prentice's little window. Just as the storm came over, there was a knock at the door downstairs. When Eleanour opened it, Prentice heard Turley's happy greeting. Soon enough, the big man was working his way, with some difficulty, through the hatchway and up next to Prentice's bed.

"Hello there," said Prentice, sitting up on the bed in just his trousers, with the chair drawn near to use as a writing desk.

"You look just like Her Grace," Turley said.

"Like this?"

"Well, she's not naked to the waist, of course, and if she were, I'm sure she'd look a darn sight finer than you. But she's sitting up in bed, writing letters and notes. Has been all the day."

He sat down on the floor, the roof too low for him to keep standing comfortably. Prentice nodded but wasn't truly listening as he finished off his own note with a scratch of the quill. He smiled at what he'd written.

"Good, is it?" asked Turley.

"I'm happy with it." Prentice looked up at his friend properly. "It's good you're here."

"Oh, I ain't here. I'm currently in the back room of the Docker's Tankard, enjoying a quiet pot with old comrades. At least that's what two of Malden's ratters think."

"Gave them the slip, did you?"

"Silly louts, strutting about like knights on prancers. They get the prince's warrant, and you'd think they owned the bloody town."

"Their boss thinks he does," Prentice said. "Selectman, and now with the prince backing him. He thinks he's made of brass."

"We'll take the shine off—off him and off his browbeaters."

"You're sure they didn't follow you?"

Turley held his hand to his chest in mock offense. "What do you take me for? I was a convict on a chain for years. You saw me sneaking about. How often did you ever see me get caught?"

"You got caught once, at least, to end up on a chain in the first place."

"Grievous misfortune that could never befall a man twice. Certainly, never one so righteous as me."

Prentice smiled, but Turley feigned earnestness. "I have risen. I am now Her Grace's steward of the chamber."

"How'd you manage that?"

"I moved some furniture."

This time Prentice did laugh and Turley chuckled with him. Turley reached under his leather jack and pulled forth a small wineskin. He took a swig and then offered it to Prentice, who drank a long gulp. It was rough but sweet, and he nodded his thanks as he wiped his mouth and handed the skin back.

"So, how long till you're back on your feet?"

Prentice rubbed his chin. He knew he wasn't yet back to full health, but he'd spent ten years on a convict chain, making do with whatever strength he woke up with—and that was usually less than his best. He didn't want to move, though, until he had a fully formed plan. Since the army had marched north in the summer, he had been running to catch up to his circumstances, reacting with little time to review or plan. Now the enforced rest was letting him gather his thoughts, and he knew he wanted to put some more pieces in place before he risked getting caught and killed.

"What I need," he said to Turley without preamble, "is a way to get two thousand convicts up north, without the prince or any of his people making anything of it."

"Just two thousand?"

"Every last one the prince brought west over the mountains."

"Well, His Royal Highness Daven Marcus will be leaving Dweltford very shortly. Word is, within days."

"Perfect," Prentice said. "He'll leave them when he marches, and I can take them then."

Turley shook his head. "It won't be that simple."

"Why not?"

"The prince isn't marching east or south or even north. He's taking to the water and crossing to the west."

"He's going to track down the invaders?" Prentice was surprised, even a little impressed. The prince proposed to do his duty to secure the frontier by finding the source of the invaders. But that raised another question. "Why's he going now? Winter's coming in hard. Why isn't he waiting until the spring?"

Turley shrugged. "You'd have to ask the prince, but a little bird told me that Malden has teased His Highness with talk of even more silver, squirreled away by the traitor Duggan. Something to do with a hunting lodge or some such."

Prentice thought for a moment, then remembered the last location on the disbursement list from the seneschal's compact. "The hunting exchequer?"

"That's the one, I think. Malden's told the prince that what he's got is half the stolen silver. The other half Duggan kept in the west, ready to buy off the invaders."

"How'd you hear all this?"

"Servants hear a great many things, and I tell you, it's shocking how they gossip." Turley flashed a grin and took another swig.

"Does Her Grace know?"

"Not yet. I got this juicy piece from a kitchen maid that is friendly but doesn't take well to being used by the prince's men. Unpleasant lot they are, it seems. Like master, like servant."

"You'll tell her when you get back."

Turley cocked an eyebrow. "Did you want to teach me how to suck eggs too?"

Prentice shook his head and apologized. Outside, the sound of the rain slackened off.

"Sounds like a good time to get going," he said, reaching for his doublet and pulling it on.

"You and me?" Turley was surprised. "Where are we going?"

"Down to the docks."

They made their way downstairs and out the door. Widow Eleanour watched them leave from beside her hearth. Prentice wanted to say something, but everything that came to mind seemed so inadequate. The woman's husband was dead, and all the thanks and praise weren't going to bring him back. He resolved to do something for her, to bring her plight to the duchess's attention, but even that desire felt hollow. He had to live long enough and get out from under a death sentence first.

The cold air whipped down the lane, and though the rain had stopped, the wind still caught up water from the rooftops that dripped from the eaves, driving it through the air.

"You don't want to be out long in this," said Turley, as Prentice hugged his bare arms to his body. "Not in your condition."

"Let's just get to the docks."

"Follow me. I know all the secret ways."

Prentice shook his head and the two headed off, barely more than feeling their way through the dark streets that were lit only by slivers of light from cracks in shutters and under doorways.

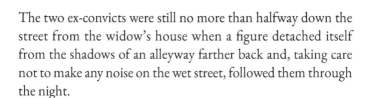

The two ex-convicts were still no more than halfway down the street from the widow's house when a figure detached itself from the shadows of an alleyway farther back and, taking care not to make any noise on the wet street, followed them through the night.

Dweltford's docks were built of cut stone and designed to service river barges and small fishing boats. Every inch seethed with activity, like a lamplit ant mound, because of the prince's intention to cross the Dwelt's lake with his entire army. Seemingly endless streams of dockers ran back and forth, adapting the jetties and piers to service the crossing and make the whole operation as swift as possible. While cold, the autumn rains were not enough to swell the lake or the river to its greatest height, so men labored on a heavy dredge, to deepen the draft of the waterway. Two enormous iron bucket spades, longer than the height of a man, were dropped straight down into the water, then teams of men heaved on thick cables to pull up the mud from the bottom. When the buckets reached the surface, the men on the ropes would rest their sweaty limbs while a second team maneuvered the bucket with pulleys, to dump the mud onto the land. Then they swung the empty spade out over the water and dropped it again.

"They should use draft animals for that," said Turley as they watched the men grunting and swearing in the dark. Then he smiled at the word play. "Draught animals."

Prentice took no notice of the joke. "With this uproar, there'd be too much chance one of the animals could panic, I would think," he responded. "Then it'd be a short drop into the water, and one panicked horse takes the whole team down with it."

"Ugly."

Along the rest of the dock, men hauled boats out of the water to make space, while barges were lashed together to form enormous rafts for transporting the prince's army. Huge vats of tar bubbled over fires, and young boys, stripped to the waist and smeared with the black muck, rushed around with buckets full. Every hull was being checked and recaulked; new ropes were being woven and tarred, and saplings were being cut to length as boat poles. The entire waterborne industry was being transformed. The prince's visit might leave Dweltford half stripped of food, but its river community would be revitalized.

For more than an hour, Prentice and Turley simply watched from the shadows. All the waterside taverns were closed, so the landward side of the dock afforded many dark crevices, but they had to keep watch for bailiffs who patrolled the docks and looked for workers shirking. The baton-armed lawmen kicked in the door of a tavern called the Reeds and Bank, not twenty paces from their hiding spot. There was the sound of shouting and complaints, and then three drunken rivermen were driven out and thrown into the murky water, made filthy with mud by the action of the dredge. When they were fished out, the drunks were cuffed around the ears and put back to work.

"Cutter said there were rag traders down here somewhere, going out to the mercenaries," said Prentice. "We need to find them."

"You think they're about in the midst of this?" asked Turley, and then he tutted at his own naivety. Chaos like this afforded too many opportunities for thieves, smugglers, and hucksters. Of course the raggedies would be at work. It was just a matter of tracking them down. "Should've got directions off Cutter."

"We'll do fine."

It took them nearly another hour, having to be discreet and asking directions, but at last they were face-to-face with an old woman sitting by a small pot of bubbling pitch. She looked like any of a dozen others engaged in the activity, but they watched her for over ten minutes and while the occasional person stopped to talk with her, no one was using her pitch. When they felt sure, they approached her. She had a face full of wrinkles, and when she smiled, her mouth was full with a set of wooden dentures and not a single live tooth.

"What can I do for you, gentlemen?" she asked. "Need a pot o' pitch for a skiff, do you?"

"You haven't got enough there for a whole skiff, Ragmother," said Turley, addressing her by the title Cutter had told them to use.

"What was that, dearie?"

"We need a boat," said Prentice.

The old woman cackled and slapped her thigh. "Take your pick, dear! 'Course, you'll have to pay the prince for the privilege."

Prentice shook his head. "We'd prefer to pay you. We need a special boat—one that goes out there." He looked over his shoulder and pointed out over the water in the direction of the barge that held the mercenary prisoners. It was lit by two iron lanterns at either end and was conspicuous as the only boat still out on the water not commandeered for the prince's crossing.

"Oooh, no one goes out there, not except the dockmaster," the old woman said in a low tone, as if she were telling a frightening tale to little children. "You don't want to do that."

Prentice fished a handful of guilders from his purse. "You said we'd pay for the privilege."

The woman studied the coins as they glittered in the firelight. Suddenly, the "senile crone" expression dropped from her face, and her eyes narrowed in shrewd calculation. "Even if there was such a boat around," she hissed in a savage whisper, "what's to stop its crew from taking your coin, slitting your throat, and flipping you over the gunwale? Many's a man lost in dark water where no one can see anything."

"Well, we can both swim, for a start. As for my throat, they'd best be fast and sure with their knives, because they'll get only the one chance."

The shrewd eyes studied Prentice's face for a moment and then she cackled again. The mad crone was back.

"All right, lovies, cross me palm with that round silver and I'll get you a little boat. For one trip, mind. And if you're caught, my boys'll be over the side and leave you to face the music."

Prentice gave her the stack of coins in his hand. "That's for the boat trip. And this"—he reached into the purse and pulled out another four—"is for forgetting you ever met us."

"A pleasure never doing business with you," said the woman, and she secreted the coins somewhere in her skirts. She waved over a young man who had been standing in nearby shadows, watching but not moving. "Tell Fulford that these two are going out to the Veckanders. And tell him to go now, while it's full dark."

"We make more when we have fresh morning bread to trade," said the youth.

"In this mess?" The woman waved at the chaos on the docks. "We wait to near dawn today and we'll be done for sure. 'Sides, them mercs is near tapped out, anyway. We'll make more rowing these two out than we would with bread. And a straight line, you hear me. Play this straight line. Fulford's to keep his bloody scaler in its sheath. He tries to whack these two, and I'll knacker him! Tell him I said so."

"Yes 'mother." The skinny lad jerked his head at Prentice and Turley. "Righto, then. Follow me, you two."

The confident young man led them through the crowd to where the dock ended and then onto a stone ledge that ran alongside the edge of the wall. The night they had snuck into the sewers, that ledge had been too high above them to reach. Now, with the rains, the water level was only a few handspans below the ledge's bottom. Once they reached the end of the wall, their guide hopped out into the dark, landing on a flat-topped buoy.

They followed after him while he skipped from that to another, and then another, and so on, like stepping-stones, until they reached the lake's edge. Despite the short distance, the area was fully in shadow from the dock lights, and in that darkness three men were crouched next to a small, flat-bottomed skiff that was pulled up under a weeping willow and hidden under a tarp. They were sitting, smoking pipes that glowed with little orange points in the night. The youth introduced one as Fulford, the leader of the crew, and then he gave the man the Ragmother's instructions.

Prentice looked back at the lights and the organized chaos of the docks, visible in the reflection of the water around the edge of the wall. He was glad to be away.

"Something worrying you?" asked Turley when he noticed.

"Just hoping we weren't spotted."

"In that mess? Not likely. And if we were, someone would've moved. Malden's got his ratters tooled up to kill on sight. They wouldn't have just watched."

Prentice nodded. "Fair enough."

He moved down to the water's edge to hop onto the skiff as Fulford's crew got it into the water.

"You know I can't actually swim," Turley whispered in his ear.

"Well, don't let this lot know that," Prentice whispered back, but he smiled. Then he and Turley were on the skiff, and the Ragmother's rivermen were poling them out to the prison barge.

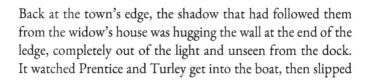

Back at the town's edge, the shadow that had followed them from the widow's house was hugging the wall at the end of the ledge, completely out of the light and unseen from the dock. It watched Prentice and Turley get into the boat, then slipped back to the docks and down into a narrow alley. Wherever they were going, there was no point waiting; there was no guarantee they would be coming back that way. The shadow had done its job this night, at any rate, and slipped away, happy with its success.

CHAPTER 29

A melia reread Prentice's note and frowned in thought. Turley had brought it to her with her breakfast, and at first she had been pleased simply to have word from Prentice. Now, after reading the letter three more times, she was more pensive, even though she was glad that Prentice hadn't run away. She had worried he might, having been made an outlaw by the prince and sentenced to death with a price on his head. She was satisfied to find that he was still in Dweltford somewhere, making plans on her behalf.

In Prentice's letter, his plan seemed to make sense, which made her think it could succeed. Nevertheless, she was troubled and wanted to take some time to put her own thoughts together before she responded. Her contemplation, however, was disrupted by a knock on the chamber door. Before she could send one of her maids to answer, a herald stepped through in royal burgundy-and-gold livery and announced the prince.

Amelia threw her coverlet off, but even as she managed to get her feet on the floor, Daven Marcus breezed into the room. Caught in mid-action, Amelia tried to curtsy while not yet out of bed and all but fell on the floor in front of him. She kept her head down, as from the corner of her eye she saw her handmaids do as well, and expected some arch comment from the prince about learning her place. Instead, Daven Marcus simply told her to rise and waited as she did so. She stood and awkwardly pushed her robe back into place.

"Forgive me, Your Highness. Had I known you were coming, I would have been more appropriately attired." She was wearing only a linen shift, and her fair hair was loose on her shoulders.

"You're cloistered for bed rest," the prince replied. "What attire did you think I would find more appropriate for that?"

It was an odd question, and Amelia wasn't sure if he expected an answer. She waited quietly.

"Get back in your bed, woman," he said at last. "And send your maids away. I will speak to you privately."

Amelia gave her ladies a nod to dismiss them. They moved swiftly out, followed by the prince's herald, who closed the door behind him. The prince surveyed the room while the duchess sat down on her bed, eyeing him warily. This was the first time she had been alone with him, and given his willingness to beat her in front of Liam, she had no idea what he might do in private. Nor did she know what, if anything, she could do to stop him. He moved to the sideboard and dramatically moved along to the specific drawer that held much of Amelia's correspondence, as well as the two books she had most recently read. He pulled it open with a flourish and dug out the papers. As he did, she carefully slid her morning letter from Prentice under her pillow. Daven Marcus clasped the pile of papers between his palms, not bothering to order them in any way, and threw them onto the table. When he seemed satisfied that he had completely cleared the drawer, he drew her chair to the table and sat down to read them. Amelia watched him, feeling like a mouse being toyed with by a cat. Page after page, the prince scanned her letters, throwing some back in the pile and letting others fall to the floor.

"I'm leaving in two days," he said without looking at her. "Did you know?"

"I did, Highness," Amelia answered, having learned that fact from Prentice's note. He had described the hectic activity at the docks and the rumors of the prince's plans.

"Good. Do you know where I'm going?"

"Taking your army west to hunt the invaders and punish them, I assume."

What Amelia didn't understand was why he was choosing to march now, with winter only days away. Why not wait until the spring? The military manuals and princely works she was studying all said a winter's march and camp was the hardest campaign that could fall on an army.

"Indeed. I've quite enjoyed the Reach's hospitality," Daven Marcus went on. "In spite of your efforts and the tedious local politics."

In spite of my efforts? Amelia wondered. I'd have welcomed you as a saving angel sent from heaven if you hadn't been such an insufferable degenerate.

She carefully schooled her face to keep her thoughts hidden. Daven Marcus was not a man to risk sneering at, not even in a passing moment.

"Ah, look at this." The prince held up the three papers from the dead reeve. He spread them out and peered from one to the other. "Exactly as Malden feared."

"Those papers are from my seneschal, Bastian Fern. Slain by the same merchant you speak of. They prove Malden's involvement in Sir Duggan's conspiracy."

"I'm sure they do," the prince said airily. "Malden confessed as much when he brought me the silver. All except the murder, of course, that he laid at your boy's feet."

"Malden is the murderer. Prentice Ash is innocent."

"And you have evidence, I take it? It's not just his word against the merchant's?"

Amelia looked down. Of course, she had no hard evidence to exonerate Prentice. She knew he was innocent, and her word should be enough. In most any proper trial in the Grand Kingdom, it would have been.

"No?" the prince prompted her. "Oh well. I probably would've taken your boy's word for it anyway. The word of a ducal retainer can't be questioned over that of a mere merchant, selectman or no. God, how he makes as much hay as he can out of that!" The prince sighed impatiently.

"You would take Prentice's word?" Amelia asked gently.

"I would have, but that was before his little indiscretion."

"Indiscretion? Liam struck me unconscious! Prentice was defending me."

"The baron was carrying out my orders." There was an acid look in the prince's eyes that made Amelia bite back her next response. He leaned toward her with a cold glare. "It's the same principle, you silly bitch. A merchant's word doesn't beat a ducal retainer's, and a ducal retainer doesn't lay a baron on his arse."

"Particularly not a baron with orders from a prince," she said.

"Precisely." He sat back and turned his eyes to her papers once more. "You needn't worry about Liam. Your boy put him down but good. The chirurgeon says that without alchemy to heal him, it'll be months before his jaw recovers, and it probably won't ever be straight again. He'll carry the memory of his defeat the rest of his life."

Amelia thought the prince seemed pleased by this fact, and it confused her. Had Liam fallen out of favor? How was that?

"Which brings us back neatly to the army marching. The baron will stay here—thankful, I should think, to have been made castellan. It's about what he can cope with."

"He would wish to march, Highness. Even injured—"

The prince waved her quiet. "Not on a winter march, I'm sure. You needn't worry, though; I won't be leaving you here in his clutches."

"Highness?"

The prince looked to her chamber's western window. "These aren't such bad rooms, wouldn't you agree? A duchess trapped in her tower. Doesn't have the same ring as a princess, does it?"

"I don't know, Highness." Amelia was lost. What had the prince meant about not being in Liam's clutches?

"Do you know that Malden tells me Duggan had as much silver waiting out there, hidden in a hunting lodge, as they brought in to me? As much again. More, probably, allowing for the amount Malden and his weasels would have purloined for themselves."

Amelia tried to speak, but again Daven Marcus hushed her. "I know they kept some back for themselves. Of course they did—they're merchants. Grasping little sods would eat dung to suck out a dropped copper."

That was an old saying about merchants in the Grand Kingdom, and Amelia had heard it before. The prince, like virtually all the nobility, had no idea the value of a copper to a truly poor man, nor how much money merchants wasted, spending to maintain their own conspicuous dignity.

"But think about all that silver," the prince continued. "All gathered by Duggan in less than ten years. Almost as much as all taxes the Western Court brought in over the same amount of time. I've said it before—Marne was a fool. You were married to a fool and are probably well rid of him."

From his cruel expression, she could see that he enjoyed trying to hurt her by mocking her dead husband. She refused to give him any satisfaction from his cruelty.

"I am his widow all the same, Highness, and I mourn his passing."

"You mourn Marne?" The prince chuckled at his own wordplay. "Naturally, you do. You're the dutiful widow and all the Reach loves you for it."

He looked down at the papers again. "You've been so busy, writing to everyone west of the mountains, and they've all come running. Ever since the word got out that we will be marching,

I've had Reacherman nobles beating a path to my door with two questions: Can they join my noble march? And how fairs the dear duchess? All your little letters have paid off."

Amelia was pleasantly surprised to hear the prince say that, in the main because she hadn't thought to write to any of the Reach's nobility. She'd just wanted to create a cloud of petty correspondence to hide her true missives from false.

"Every one of them," the prince went on, "down on their knees and pledging their swords, has made it clear how beloved you are to them. And Liam never shuts up about wanting to take you to wife. Of course, I didn't see the appeal for myself until I realized what kind of dowry you came with."

"Dowry, Highness?"

Was he talking about the money she had used to pay off Duke Marne's debts with the Vec banking houses? Or could he mean...?

"That's right, Duchess. If this much silver comes out of the Reach's mines—before we even count the iron, the produce, the herds, and the grain—then this is too rich a province to be a mere duchy. It's time it rose to a princedom."

"A princedom?"

"My father's always on at me about marriage. Might as well use the damned act to set myself up. And this silver is perfect."

"The damned act?" she repeated slowly. "Highness, are you proposing to me?"

"Princes don't propose, silly cow. They command."

"You are commanding me to marry you?"

"Yes, girl. Are you always this damnably slow?"

Amelia couldn't help herself; she stood in protest. Her face conveyed clearly how abhorrent she found the idea. "I am a widow in mourning! I cannot marry, Highness."

She remembered to address him correctly only at the end, as little more than an afterthought. The prince didn't notice.

"I know that. Indecent haste would be a step too far for Father, added on top of your birth. That's why you'll be coming west with us."

"Coming west?"

Every sentence out of the prince's mouth was like another surge of speed to a runaway horse. Amelia felt like all she could do was hang on until the wild thing wore itself out.

"Don't fear. You'll bring your maids with you, and there are many ladies with us. You'll have plenty of company to natter and giggle with. I'll lead us to victory in the west. The Vec will be driven off for good, and you will be smitten with me, seeing a prince who can ride to your defense and not get killed in the first minor fracas. Then, when we've waited a short space for decency, I'll get your vow, then get you with my heir. And the king can get off my back, old fool."

Amelia couldn't tell if the prince was composing a story he would tell to cover the indecency of wooing her so soon after her husband's death, or whether he actually believed what he was saying. Did he genuinely expect her to swoon and sigh on command? But for all that his manner repulsed her, there was one fact that stood out in his plan. If she married him, the Western Reach would be secured, and she would be the second most important woman in the Grand Kingdom; only the queen would have more influence.

Daven Marcus had not finished spinning his plans and fictions, however, and as she came out of her thoughts, Amelia found herself mentally running to catch up again.

"The court will gossip, no doubt, but if they make too much fuss, we can always invent some story about you having an ancestor of blood somewhere. A frontier baron of some sort. Didn't one of your baronies get wiped away in the summer? That family would make perfect candidates."

"Baron Stopher and his family were burned alive. Only his wife survived him." It hurt Amelia to say the words, and for a moment she remembered the ruin of Fallenhill—the ash, the smoke, and the bodies scorched by flame and twisted in agony. She felt tears welling in her eyes.

"And all the rest of them?" he asked.

"Highness?"

"Were all of them burned?"

She nodded. "As far as we know."

"Perfect, then. If they complain, we'll say you were a long-lost descendant of this Stolling's line."

"Stopher, Highness."

If the prince heard her correction, he took no notice. He slapped his gloved hand on the table and stood. "So, make yourself ready and order your chamber to the task. I hear you have a new steward. Strapping thing, if a little scruffy. Doubtless he can arrange your furniture for the journey. No more than one cart's worth, though. God knows we'll be slowed enough by the endless stream of hangers-on I can't seem to shake off. Try not to add to it."

He moved toward the door. He was reaching for the latch when Amelia's mind caught up with one of the prince's points that had slipped her before.

"The Vec, Highness?" she asked.

He turned to look at her. "What did you say?"

"The Vec, Your Highness?" she repeated in a stronger voice. "You said you would drive off the Vec for good. The invaders came from the west, not south. They weren't from the Vec."

Daven Marcus walked back over to where she was sitting and stood over her. He took her cheeks in his hand and squeezed, as though she were a cute but dull-witted child. "Of course they were from the Vec, silly cow. No one lives in the west; it's just grass. Everyone knows that."

"But they looked nothing like Veckan—"

The prince slapped her with his gloved hand. A soft strike, but insistent nonetheless. "They marched west and then north, twit," he scoffed. "They painted themselves up like barbarians and then came at you 'from the west.' An obvious trick, even if my dead uncle and his prissy knight commander fell for it. They were Veckanders; what else could they be?"

With that, he turned away and strode out the door, as if fleeing further questions. Amelia sat on the edge of her bed as her handmaids cautiously reentered her chambers, obviously concerned about what state they would find her in. She hardly noticed as they began to tidy the papers on the table. Then she realized something else.

"The seneschal's documents," she blurted out, leaping up so suddenly that Teerah and Kristen both started. Amelia rushed to the table. She scrabbled through the scattered pages, but she knew it was too late. Right in front of her, while she was distracted by his words and plans, the prince had folded the reeve's documents up and taken them away with him.

"Curse him," she swore, shocking her two maids. "Curse him to hell, and Malden go with him!"

The two women kept their faces down.

"Where's Bettina?" she asked them.

"In the kitchens, I think, Your Grace," said Teerah.

"Fetch her now!"

Teerah curtsied and rushed from the room, probably thankfully, Amelia thought. Kristen kept tidying.

"Just put them back in the drawer," Amelia told her. "We've got far too much to do." She looked back down at her bed and fished Prentice's letter out from under the pillow. "And I've had quite enough bed rest."

CHAPTER 30

"He called Carron Ironworth prissy?" Prentice said in disbelief. He had met Prince Mercad's knight commander at the Battle of the Brook. In his late forties, after a lifetime of service as a knight and a war leader, Sir Carron was a stern, confident man that Prentice would never have liked to face as an opponent. To call him "prissy" was like saying a warhorse was just a big mouse with a hairy tail.

"That's what catches your attention?" demanded Turley as he split an orange with his hands, biting the flesh and sucking the juice from his fingers. He'd brought a small bag full of oranges from the castle kitchen, and apart from the one he kept for himself, he'd given the whole thing to the widow Eleanour. He and Prentice sat on chairs in her ground floor, along with Sir Gant and Fostermae, the sacrist who had been treating Prentice's wounds. Eleanour stood aside in one corner, making boiled puddings with the oranges, her little son clinging to her skirts and sucking his thumb.

"I'd have thought the prince's plans for marriage was the big news," Turley finished off, and then bit into the orange's flesh.

"Princes are ever in need of money," said Gant with a shrug.

"Huge armies aren't cheap to feed or house," Prentice agreed. "Working for their wealth is beneath them, so they have to get it some way. He's marrying the Reach, not the duchess."

Turley snorted. "He's marrying the Reach? What, all of us? That's a lot of wedding rings."

Turley was making a joke, but Prentice's attention was caught by his description of the Reach as "us." His friend really was committing himself to the duchess and her land. It wasn't something Prentice would ever have predicted.

"She's going to the conclave house this afternoon?" he asked, returning to the main topic of the conversation.

"That's what she said she was doing."

"Well, that's where I'll have to be, then. There probably won't be another chance before she leaves, assuming the prince starts his people crossing the Dwelt tomorrow."

"And what of the ratters?" said Gant, voicing the main concern. "If the duchess leaves the castle, won't Malden's men think to follow her in the hope you'll show your face?"

No one said anything for a moment, mulling the question over. Eleanour's boy sat himself down in a corner and practiced throwing a little wooden ball against the wall. Prentice smiled as he watched and then felt a rush of guilt. The child would grow up without a father to teach him how to catch properly, or give him a trade, or any of the things a father did for a son. In his heart, he knew the responsibility for that loss was Duggan's, but still Prentice felt the guilt.

"I can get into the conclave house readily enough," he said. "I could find a hiding spot."

"In the day?" said Gant. "It's a busy place, a lot of traffic. Easy bet that Malden will have someone inside."

"He doesn't need anyone special; the council's all but in his pocket, anyway," Fostermae agreed. "Someone there'll give him the word as soon as they spot you."

"Then what do we do?" Prentice asked.

"You need a disguise."

"You could go hooded," Gant suggested. "A clerical robe? Could we dress him as a monk?"

Fostermae fidgeted, looking uncomfortable at the prospect. "Impersonating clergy is a sin. I couldn't help with that."

"Didn't David eat the temple bread intended only for the Levites, the priests?" Prentice contended. "Wouldn't that have been a sin, and yet God loved him and made him king over Israel?"

Fostermae stared at Prentice in wonderment. "You are an educated man. I suppose from that perspective, I could do something—"

Prentice clapped the sacrist on the shoulder. "You are a good man, in spite of your position. But I think I have a better plan—one that shouldn't stretch your conscience. Tell me, Fostermae, do you have any beggars in your parish?"

"Yes, there are several." The sacrist dipped his head, as if ashamed to admit the poverty of his little flock.

"Some injured that won't heal? Perhaps a few diseased or sick, not often seen in polite quarters of the city?"

"Yes, exactly so." Fostermae's eyes narrowed. He clearly did not like the heartlessness of the questions.

Prentice ignored the sacrist's displeasure and turned to Turley. "Tell the duchess to stop by the back of the conclave house after her meeting. There will be needy there, seeking her for alms. She should bring a purse and expect to find me there."

"That's a plan."

"You wish to use my people as a disguise?" said Fostermae, only slightly less distressed by this idea than by the notion of Prentice dressing as clergy.

"Yes, Rector," Prentice said, looking him straight in the eye. "It is distasteful and high-handed, but necessary. Your qualms speak to your love for your flock, and that is honorable, but I must ask you for this. And they will receive alms, real coin that can help them through the winter."

There was a bang at the door, and Cutter burst in, breathless and urgent. "Ratters!" she declared, half falling on the table in her rush. "Down at the corner and heading this way."

"Did they see you?" Prentice asked.

"I don't think so."

"We can't take the chance. Everyone out the back. Cutter, you stay here, in case they saw you come in."

She huffed. "Why should I stay?"

"If you disappear, that'll be suspicious. If they knock on the door and you're here, it'll be what they expect."

Cutter clearly didn't like that idea but didn't argue any further. To the others, Prentice gave quick orders. "Gant, you go with Turley. See that he makes it back to the castle safe. I'll go with the rector. Tell the duchess, and we'll meet you at the back of the conclave house this afternoon."

They clambered out through the rear window, since Eleanour's house had no back door. In the alleyway, they separated and rushed in different directions, although Prentice hid nearby, in case trouble broke out. He was sure Cutter would hold her own, but he couldn't in good conscience leave Eleanour and her boy to the ratter's mercy. He crept back to listen as Eleanour pulled her window shutter closed and a knock came on the door.

Two burly men wielding hardwood cudgels didn't wait for Eleanour to answer before pushing their way in and looking around suspiciously. They found her tending to her puddings as the strangely dressed woman with the short hair who they were following sat on the floor, playing ball with Eleanour's toddler. The men said nothing, but with a nod, one of them went up the narrow stairs to the first floor.

"Here, what's all this about?" demanded Eleanour.

"Shut it!" the man said, pointing the end of his cudgel at her. Her son began to cry, and Cutter gathered him into her arms. The thug with the cudgel spat in disgust. "Mewling little rat."

From upstairs there came a clattering ruckus as furniture was thrown about.

"Anything?" called the man on the ground floor.

"Nah, nothing," came the voice of the second. "Two beds and a cupboard. There's a man's doublet near the second bed."

"Man's coat?" the first thug said, looking at the two women with suspicion. "Your husband forget his clothes when he went to work?"

"My husband's dead," Eleanour said reflexively, then put a hand to her mouth.

"So, whose is the doublet?" The man advanced toward her. "And why are you so upset?"

"Her husband only died recent," said Cutter. "And the doublet's mine!"

He turned on her and sneered as he looked down at her trousers and man's boots. "Spinster," he said as if it were an insult, and spat on the floor a second time.

His partner came down the stairs. "Nothing."

"Fair enough." The first man turned to leave. "Widows and spinsters. Dried up and sad."

Then they were gone, and Eleanour suddenly burst out weeping. Cutter brought her little boy and the widow caught him up, comforting him while trying to dry her own tears.

Cutter sat down and picked up what was left of Turley's orange, taking a big bite. "No spinsters here. Just us widows!"

CHAPTER 31

D uchess Amelia left the castle shortly after noon. Seated on her roan, Meadow Dancer, she led her cortege of maids and guards across the drawbridge and down Castle Road to Within Walls. Her path through the crowds was cleared by a footman acting as herald, declaring her approach and wielding a long ash staff tied with cream and blue ribbons, her ducal colors. The colors of the Reach.

When she arrived in the market square, she turned to the conclave house, where a group of horsemen were waiting in their saddles. Many were knights, wearing surcoats with their own arms emblazoned front and back. Others were free men, who owned their horses but had no noble blood. In the east, over the mountains in the heart of the Grand Kingdom, no one without noble birth was permitted to sit a mount in the presence of anyone of knight rank or higher. Merchants or others rich enough to own a horse might ride their own beast on a road, but if even the poorest hedge knight approached, they had to move aside and dismount, or they would come to regret it. This was just another of the social niceties that was more relaxed in the wild frontier of the Western Reach. Amelia was glad of it.

When Daven Marcus had left her in the morning, the first notes she had written were to the boarding houses and livery stables, as well as lesser noblemen she knew by name—anywhere a man who could ride might be found. She'd written with haste and vehemence, until her hand cramped and her letters threatened to twist into an unintelligible scrawl. It pleased her to see nearly twenty men waiting for her. She walked Meadow Dancer across the front of their assembled group and waited. The rest of her small entourage gathered themselves behind her, and the herald stood in front. Turley, acting as footman, stayed at her left stirrup, in exactly the same place Prentice had on the march north.

"Do you see them?" she asked him, speaking as quietly as she could to still be heard over the hubbub of the market.

"Two over by that vintner," he said, not looking.

Amelia swept her head around, as if regally surveying the crowd, but taking special notice of the two men standing out front of a wine seller's wares. They looked like the rough and violent sort of men Malden would employ as his ratters. She wondered if either of them had been among the group who had murdered Bastian Fern and his housekeeper.

"Give ear to Her Grace, Duchess Amelia of the Western Reach!" the herald declared in a loud voice. It was a redundant instruction; every eye that mattered was already on her.

"Nobles, knights, loyal men of the Reach," she began, reciting the speech she had spent the rest of the morning composing and memorizing. "Soon, Crown Prince Daven Marcus, Prince of the West, the Prince of Rhales, will march west to bring the justice of the Grand Kingdom, to hunt out those foul and bestial men who laid waste to our lands and murdered our people. He means to find the source of the invasion and see that no further attack can ever rise against us again."

One of the knights present cried, "Huzzah!" and many of the others applauded by slapping their hands on their saddles.

Amelia smiled and sat a little straighter. "You do the Reach credit. Reachermen do not suffer insults and injuries like this!"

There were nods and more applause.

"I will ride with the prince, as I rode with Prince Mercad before him. In their hearts, every man, woman, and child of the Reach rides with him. I call on you now to come to my service for a particular purpose. I need men who know the Reach; swift, confident riders who can range away from the army. I need men who know the signs of an invader's passing. The prince rides to slay our enemies, and I mean to make sure that not one escapes his righteous wrath. And I need messengers to ride back and forth between us and here. What do you say to that? Can you be my eyes, ears, and voice across the far west?"

Already men were nodding, but their duchess hadn't finished.

"It will be hard. The army marches in winter, and wagons will struggle through mud, with no roads. But their hardship will be nothing compared to yours. I need men who do not fear to camp under trees and live by what they hunt alone. The prince's entourage will sleep under silk tents and fine blankets, attended by their retainers and surrounded by the army, as befits their status. My riders must be made from sterner stuff than that. No silk for them. The Western Reach requires men who can put aside their comfort and serve her in her time of need. What say you? Are you cut from that cloth?"

As she looked, she saw them smiling and nodding. Earlier in the year, when the war first came and she was alone as a young widow with no one she could trust, Prentice had advised her to educate herself about warfare, if only to know good advice from bad. With that counsel, Amelia had gathered every book her husband had on the subject. This morning, as she composed this speech, she consulted two of those books, which discussed how to recruit and inspire men. One had said that men will serve out of loyalty to either a great leader or a great cause. Amelia knew she was hardly a great war leader, but her execution of Duggan had earned her some credit with these men. Even if they hadn't been there that night, they would have heard the story. Partway to a great leader, she added a great cause, at least one she saw as great: punishing the invaders and protecting the Reach from further assault. These were Reachermen, so surely that was a great cause to them.

The other book had explained that a man will endure much if it is respected. Even the least man, said the author, would rather struggle and survive than sit in safety and know that other men proved themselves better than him. The thought amazed Amelia, and her maids had shaken their heads in disbelief when she read it aloud to them. Why would men prefer hardship? But taking the author's word, she crafted her speech to offer them difficulty, and it seemed to be working.

"Begging your pardon, Your Grace," asked a man in a yellow-and-black surcoat with a red tree upon it, "but will these riders of yours get to fight?"

Amelia hadn't anticipated this question, but she thought she understood its source. She nodded severely, no smile on her face.

"I expect when the time comes for the prince to give battle, every one of my men, and every Reacherman present, will stand in the ranks and fight. But hear me now: if any of my riders comes upon a man of the invaders, so much as one, I expect him to fight them and win. Ride them down and make them pay. This very moment, I declare a bounty of silver and honor on the head of every invader from the west. Any painted brute is an enemy of the Reach, and I expect you to teach our enemies to fear us!"

There were many more huzzahs at this, and Amelia knew she had them. They would be hers. She told each man to give his name to the herald and then to come to her when the prince's march made its crossing. Each would then be given her warrant and her welcome. With that, she turned away and rode toward the side of the conclave house. Her maids followed her, along with Turley.

"Steward, I will give alms now," she said loudly. "Have arrangements been made?"

"They have, Your Grace," he replied.

"Then show the way."

Turley took Meadow Dancer's bridle. The normally placid roan tossed its head a moment at the unfamiliar handling, but Amelia calmed the gelding by stroking its neck, and it soon settled to the lead. Turley turned down the side of the conclave house, through a short lane, and came out behind the grand building where a wide street ran from Castle Road down to the dockside. Behind the conclave house was a large dung cart, served by a pair of gong farmers, who were shoveling the cart's load into an opening to the sewers. The two men were filthy, dressed in ragged trousers, sleeveless jacks, and open leather hoods that left their faces clear but hung down their backs to keep filth from their hair. Every bit of their uncovered flesh was smeared and stained, and their faces were so dirty that they almost seemed the same color as the leather of their clothes. Amelia noted them a moment before the stench hit her nostrils, and when it did, she was thankful there were such men to take care of tasks like this.

To one side of the dung cart was a ragged crowd, every bit as heartbreaking to the duchess as the gong farmers were disgusting. They were beggars, poor widows wrapped in threadbare shawls, with scarecrow children clinging to their skirts. One or two were cripples of either sex. One was a legless man with hands wrapped in rags and half his nose rotted away. Tending to this unfortunate flock was a tonsured sacrist who seemed as poor as his charges.

When the horses drew close in the street, the sacrist quickly arranged the beggars into order. The women drew up their shawls over their heads and bowed down. The children likewise stood with their heads bowed low, and the man with no legs knuckled his forehead with his ragged hands. Amelia wondered if he still had any fingers left under the filthy wrappings. She quickly dismounted and waved to her maids to follow her.

"Your Grace does us honor," said the sacrist. The thin hair around his tonsure waved in the chill air as he bowed his head.

"It has been a bitter year for the whole Reach," Amelia answered. "But in such times, it is important we work to be thankful and remember those less fortunate than ourselves. The Lord himself commanded us to care for widows and orphans."

"Indeed he did, Your Grace."

Amelia felt like a fraud, and the words were bitter to her as she said them. In fact, she had given almost no thought to widows and orphans since the invasion. Her husband had died, and then she had been attacked when she came home to mourn; she had marched with the army and been shut out of Dweltford while it was in Duggan's hands. Then Daven Marcus had arrived, and she had been scrambling to preserve her power against his petty games. In all of that, these beggars would have been scratching at the world just to find crumbs to eat each day. Their condition put her own struggles into a different perspective. Even worse, she was not truly here on their behalf, even now. This whole event was a ruse to allow Prentice to contact her covertly. She scanned the bowed heads, all covered with hoods and shawls, ostensibly in a show of respect, and wondered which one he was.

"Your name is Fostermae, is it not?" she asked the sacrist.

"Yes, Your Grace."

"I commend you on your service to God and to our poorest. I will have legs of pork and mutton sent to your parish this evening. You'll see them roasted and shared among these good folk."

"You are too kind, Duchess."

"It is only a little, but children should not face winter without at least one good meal to line their bones."

Amelia reached behind her to where her maid Teerah stood waiting with a purse in her hand. She took the purse and opening it, began to walk among the bowed beggars, handing each one a silver guilder. It seemed so little to give, and yet each time she dipped into the purse, she felt like her limited resources were bleeding away. She needed the silver to secure the whole Reach, but she reminded herself that each coin was even more precious to the hands into which she placed it. The thanks of each beggar at receiving a single silver coin shamed her, and she felt like she wanted to cry.

"Watch out," Turley hissed behind her, and she looked up to see Malden's two men swaggering along the road. The ratters stood for a moment, taking in the whole scene. Amelia gave another coin, and the old woman who received it took her hand and blessed her. Suddenly, Malden's men were at the back of the crowd, meaty hands yanking away hoods and shawls. Amelia was appalled at their brazenness and frightened that they would spy Prentice out.

Would he fight them again?

She'd seen him face worse odds than two to one, but that would ruin everything. He'd be running for his life again, and she'd never get a chance to speak with him before she left with the prince. Many of the children started crying as the brutes shoved them aside, searching out the identity of the adults.

"What is the meaning of this?" she demanded of them, hoping to head off violence and because her heart broke to see these lowly folk so poorly treated.

One of the belligerent men stopped and looked at her, while his companion kept about the process of unmasking the beggars. "Prince's warranted business," he said with a sneer, showing her no respect at all. "You can't stop it."

"I can have you punished for your insolence." She glanced over her shoulder at Turley.

To her surprise, the ratter only smiled and patted a short sword hanging in a sheath at his side. "You try," he said, "and it'll get bloody. Your boy there might not live through it."

"I don't have to punish you now; I can send for you to be flogged whenever I wish."

"Oh yeah? What's my name? Who are you going to send for?"

"I'll send for your master. I know his name!" she said.

"Well, you do that, then!"

Amelia was trembling, and her fists were clenched. Not since long before she was married had a lowborn man showed her such disrespect, and she wanted to slap the smile off his face. The thug took a step toward her, and while she was offended by the man's arrogance, she was surprised when Turley grasped her by the shoulder and pushed himself in between her and the arrogant ratter. She staggered back while he confronted the man.

"Now come on. No one thinks that prince's warrant gives you the right to be rude to the duchess. You know it doesn't," Turley said.

"Don't worry. Turley knows how to handle situations like this," a voice whispered from behind her. Amelia turned and stared wide eyed into the face of one of the gong farmers. The filthy visage gave her Prentice's wry smile for a moment, and suddenly she knew who he was. "Say nothing. Just let Turley cool their ardor and then we can talk."

She turned back to see Turley with his hands raised placatingly. It looked like the sneering ratter might still make a fight, but his friend hissed at him, and he turned around to see that all the beggars were unmasked. Prentice was not among them.

Behind her, Amelia heard the sound of a shovel digging into the filth and chucking it down the sewer. The smell of it filled her nostrils, and though it was disgusting, the foulness made her smile, knowing it hid her man. The ratter cast a sharp glance at her, and she stopped smiling. Then the two men turned and left, taking care to shove peasants aside churlishly.

"That went well," Prentice said behind her. "Fan yourself as if near to fainting and hand the purse to your maid. Let her finish the almsgiving."

Amelia did as instructed and waved Teerah over. "You finish for me, Teerah. And see to a coin for everyone, even the children."

Teerah curtsied and took the purse to finish the task. Amelia feigned weakness, leaning against the filthy cart wheel and knowing she was ruining her dress doing it.

"You have a cunning mind, Master Ash," she said quietly, without turning to look at him.

"Years on a convict chain, Your Grace. Strong and cunning, or you die. The weak and stupid die quickly."

CHAPTER 32

P rentice scrubbed hard with a bundle of rope, using it like a
rough sponge, while the water in the tub he was standing
in turned the color of mud and stank like an unmucked stable.
A lump of harsh white soap sat on a nearby stool, and his
filthy disguise was discarded on the muddy ground. He had no
intention of ever wearing any part of it again.

"What do you think?" he asked Gant. "Will Eleanour let me
back in her house now?"

"I wouldn't think so," said the knight. He was sitting on a
bench, watching and wrinkling his nose in disgust. The pair of
them were in a back-alley yard with a well. Prentice had come
straight here after his meeting with the duchess. Gant had been
waiting with the tub and soap ready.

"Fetch more water, will you," Prentice said.

Gant stood and went to the well. He brought the full pail
toward the tub, but Prentice took it from his hands and then
poured the cold water directly over himself, sluicing away the
remaining soap suds and shivering with the cold of it. He
stepped out and flicked away the excess water, then pulled on
his shirt when Gant handed it to him.

"You'll go from one fever to another if you're not careful,"
Gant admonished.

Prentice smiled at him. "Ten years as a convict and hardly a
sniffle or a cough. It's all this soft living since I got freed."

"Oh, doubtless."

Gant stood watch as Prentice got dressed. Two children regarded them from around a corner, but soon got bored and ran off. Odds were many of the surrounding families used this well for wash water. A man naked in a tub was probably not that unusual. With his shirt and trousers on, Prentice sat to pull up his boots. He reached into the right one and plucked out a golden ring with a large boss. He looked at it a moment and then slid it onto one of his fingers.

"I can hardly believe she trusted you with that," said Gant, peering at the ring. "The ducal seal?"

"I'll need it to wield her authority, especially while she's in the west with the prince."

"You're a wanted man, but with the full authority of the duchy. A magistrate would have kittens before he sorted that mess out."

"Malden's men are never going to bring me to law, you know that."

Gant nodded. "But you have her authority and I'm sworn to her, so now I am to you. My oath binds me."

"I never needed your oath before, sir," said Prentice. "I trust you as well as any man I know."

"Even your friend Turley?"

"More."

"More?" Gant asked. "Why more? He is your friend, isn't he?"

"He is, but you've never seen him play dice," Prentice said. "When there's money on the line, he's canny as the son of a rat and a snake, who married a fox for a wife." He finished dressing and stood up. "The word from Cutter is that we need to be moving before dawn tomorrow. All the boats are ready at the docks."

"I hope she hasn't been seen."

"She's Turley's equal in cunning, I'd wager. She'll be all right."

"They found her this morning, don't forget," Gant objected.

"Fair enough, but now that they've been to the widow's house, we should be safe. At least for the twelve hours until dawn."

Gant nodded, though he had a troubled expression. Prentice smiled but understood the knight's misgivings. It had been a close thing when the ratters had come knocking on Eleanour's door that morning. There were plenty of places he could hide for the evening, and then after that it wouldn't matter. The prince would be across the river, and Prentice's and the duchess's plan would be in motion. Still, had the ratters known to knock on the widow's door, or had they been following Cutter? The worst possibility was that there was someone telling Malden's men where they were.

Prentice and Gant followed back alleys across the neighborhood to Fostermae's little chapel. There was a smell of roasting, and they found the church stoop crowded with the poor and destitute, watching legs of meat turning on spits over hot coals. Fat dripped from the cooking into the fire, spitting and hissing. Everyone there had a plate or bowl in hand, even the children, waiting to receive a share of the duchess's charity.

Fostermae watched over it all and welcomed newcomers from the chapel door as the smell wafted through the alleys. "Soon, brethren," he said loudly. "Let us thank our Lord for this unexpected bounty."

He bowed his head and the crowd joined him, as did Sir Gant. Since his transportation, prayer had not featured much in Prentice's life, but he lowered his head with those around him, and he felt glad to do it. When the grace was said, he lifted his gaze to see Turley making his way through the crowd.

"Duchess sent me to oversee this," he said by way of explanation. "Canny thinking on her part. Gives me a good reason to leave the castle in the evening." He looked west to where the setting sun was finally running away. The area was warmed by the cooking fires, but soon the night's chill would quench even that.

"Is everything ready?" Prentice asked him.

"Near as we can make it. I still don't think you should be at the castle, though."

"I concur," rumbled Sir Gant.

Prentice stepped aside as a woman ushered two children with little clay plates clutched to their chests toward the fire. The men tending the meat had already begun to cut slices, and Fostermae was calling for the children first.

"It'll be a tough job to do quickly," Prentice said, watching the fires and the food being distributed. "We need as many strong hands as we can trust."

"Are you up to that?" asked Turley. "I mean, you was just half-dead with fever not a week ago. Are you sure you aren't too sickly?"

Prentice gave him a cold look, but Turley smiled, enjoying teasing. "Time we went."

They wended their way through the small crowd, stopping on the way to take a slice of greasy meat in their fingers and thanking the men cutting it. Then they pushed back out gently, and Prentice nodded to Fostermae before they left the celebration.

"God bless you," the sacrist said.

"You too, Rector," Prentice answered automatically, hoping he wasn't being a hypocrite. "If we succeed, then we won't see you for some time."

"And if you don't?"

"Then we likely won't ever see you again."

"Then I shall pray to see you again, but not for some time."

"A goodly prayer," Prentice said.

They headed back out to the nearest street, where Turley had parked a cart from the castle in the hands of another steward. He left Prentice and Gant behind in the shadows of the alley and approached the waiting servant. Taking the reins, he dismissed the steward and flipped him some coppers, telling him to have a pot in his favorite watering hole.

"I'll take the cart back," Turley said lightly. "If anyone asks, I'll say you stayed on to pray."

The steward accepted his good fortune, jumped down, and went in search of a tavern. When he was well gone, Prentice and Gant emerged from the shadows. They hopped on the back, and Turley geed the two mules, turning them away to fetch supplies for the castle kitchen. It took the three of them a short while to get the barrels and sacks loaded, and then they headed back. Sir Gant and Turley rode up in the front, while Prentice lay down on the backboards, in a small pocket formed by the careful placement of sacks and barrels. He listened quietly while his two comrades drove through the night.

"What happened to that merchant we tied up in the castle?" Gant asked Turley, holding a bullseye lantern focused ahead for them to see by.

"They found him the next day, yelling and whining about being left to starve."

"Did they free him?"

"Indeed not," said Turley. "Malden saw to that. Folper's goose was cooked long before the meal was served. He was brought to the prince, told he was guilty of theft and treason, and that was that. He tried to beg for mercy, but the prince wanted none of it. Folper was branded and sent out to the chain. He's a convict now." Turley's tone suggested he felt no sympathy for the man.

"And you think Malden had a hand in that?" Gant asked.

"None of the cabal that he brought to the prince has paid a copper shaving in compensation, nor been charged or tried for anything. Folper went it alone, and I say Malden wanted him punished for the impudence."

"Impudence?"

"Malden's the kind of man that enforces obedience and loyalty with his fists if an iron rod isn't handy. He would have taken it bad that Folper didn't follow his plans. He's like a nobleman that way."

"Noblemen aren't like that," Sir Gant protested reflexively, but shook his head when Turley cocked an eyebrow. "Well, not all of them."

"Enough of them."

The heavily loaded cart rumbled over the 'bridge, and a guardsman stepped out in front, stopping them in the barbican. "You back? What's all this?"

"Flour and grain for the kitchens," he told the guard who, even in the darkness, looked more bored than attentive. "They'll be cooking all night for the prince and the duchess for when everyone makes the crossing over the Dwelt."

The guard nodded. "Into the west, huh? Wonder what they'll find."

"Grass, from what I hear. Just grass. You coming?" Turley asked.

The guard shook his head. "Not me, mate. I'm to keep the castle safe in Her Grace's absence. There's enough men-at-arms in the prince's army already. Apparently, they don't need a man like me."

"Well, better luck to you," Turley sympathized. "Least you'll be tucked up warm while we're out camping in winter paddocks."

The guard laughed with him. "Better you than me, mate. On you go."

Turley clicked, and the horses walked on. They crossed down to the lower bailey and the kitchen door. Everything was dark, save for tiny pools of firelight from torches, guttering and hissing in the cold night breeze. Prentice waited until they pulled the sacks off him, then suddenly sneezed from the grain dust as he hopped down. Turley and Gant looked around, but there was no one to see. Wherever Malden's ratters were, they weren't here.

"Quick as we can," Prentice said to them, and Turley opened the kitchen door. To Sir Gant he said, "You know your part?"

Gant nodded. "And if the keys aren't there?"

"We do something else."

Gant headed out into the night as Bellam hobbled through the kitchen door to help with the unloading.

This was the most dangerous part of the plan; if Prentice were to be seen and recognized, he would be seized for sure. They didn't know how many men Malden had floating around in corners only servants went, and on top of that, the prince was still in the duchess's quarters, probably enjoying his last night in a soft bed before he led his forces west. That meant men-at-arms loyal to him would be floating around as well. Baron Liam and any of his sworn men were also somewhere in the castle. A single alarm, and Prentice would be a convict again in a flash, assuming he wasn't just strung up in a crow's cage or killed where he stood. The entire castle was a viper's nest, and he was the mouse in their midst.

No, not a mouse, he reminded himself. A rat.

And rats were cunning.

CHAPTER 33

Amelia stood on a wooden gallery, peering through the only window of the keep that looked down on the kitchen door. The bailey was dark, even with the lit torches and braziers, but she could just make out the cart and horses and shadowy figures moving back and forth unloading. She couldn't pick out Prentice, if he was even among them. If his plan was running as it should, he would have already slipped through the kitchen and down into the chapel sepulchre, where the strongbox full of silver was hidden. A part of her wanted to be down there with them, to reassure herself that everything went according to the plan, but she knew that was a lie of sorts. She did want to be down there, and she did want reassurance, but she was almost certain she wanted Prentice's reassurance. She had come to depend on him so much.

Was it too much?

A sudden, terrible thought occurred to her. She had never acquired Liam's chapel key. She had meant to take it from him the day Malden and his conspirators came to the castle, but Liam had charged off before she could. Then the chaos of trying to deliver Prentice from Liam's wrath and her injury had stolen the key from her mind. She realized that she hadn't even had a chance to check on the strongbox. For all she knew, Liam had already found it and taken it. If that was the case, Prentice was risking himself for nothing.

As these thoughts churned in her mind, it took all her will not to rush straight to the chapel and confirm the safety of the strongbox for herself. She clasped her hands in tight fists and clenched her teeth.

Despite her fears, Amelia knew that her part of the plan involved her being somewhere else, and soon. She had spent the early evening writing notes and preparing herself. Prentice and the men he picked would unload the kitchen supplies and then reload the cart with things she would be taking with her on the march: tents, clothes, and furnishings. She had sent her clothes down with Bettina already. Her matron had almost balked when she learned that Prentice would be among the men loading the cart. However close Amelia and Prentice had grown as friends, Bettina saw him only as an upstart convict upon whom the duchess lavished too much care and respect. Moreover, he was now a wanted criminal. Amelia had been on the verge of losing her temper with the older woman but won her over when she explained that Liam might take the silver while she was away. Whatever misgivings Bettina had about Prentice, they paled next to her contempt for Liam, which had grown ever since Amelia explained his role in her injury.

With a sigh, the duchess turned from the window and made her way along the gallery, accompanied only by her maid Kristen, who carried a small candelabra to light their passage. They left the gallery through a door that led, via a short connecting passage, to the castellan's apartments above the barbican, where she was to meet with the injured Liam. In the hall outside, two knights in surcoats lounged on chairs. These were Liam's men, not hers, guarding his door and attending to him. Though she could not name either of them, she knew they were among those who had ridden away with him during the siege, leaving her in a field. Whatever else they were, they were her enemies, and would continue to be as long as they remained loyal to her treacherous retainer. When they saw her, they jumped to their feet.

"Your Grace? You were not expected. The baron is resting."

"I'm quite sure," she replied. "I will not take much of his time."

One of the knights opened the door and went inside. Amelia heard him announce her but did not hear Liam's response. She steeled herself inwardly while she waited. Prentice had asked her to find something to do while he and the others smuggled the recovered tax silver out of the castle—something away from the kitchens and the chapel, but where she would be seen so that no one would connect her to what they were doing. This had been the best thing she could think of, and while she had no desire to ever speak to Liam again, she knew she would not be able to avoid it forever, so sooner was as good a time as later. The knight re-emerged and bowed, inviting her to enter Liam's new quarters in her castle.

The whole space was lit only by the fireplace, where the fire had already been banked for the night. There was a small amount of furniture and a rug of some kind on the floor, but in the dim light, it was difficult to make out any pattern. Kristen's candelabra did little to improve the situation as she followed Amelia in. Across the room was an ornate bed, carved of a dark hardwood and enameled in red and pale blue, Liam's heraldic colors. It looked expensive and was large enough for two to sleep side by side easily. Amelia wondered if Liam had intended it as his marital bed, and if he had planned, when he had it made, to have her in it one day.

Liam was in the bed now, wearing a linen shirt and sitting back with his head against a mound of pillows. As the candlelight drew close, she could see the brutal results of his defeat at Prentice's hand. The left side of his face was still dark with bruises, and his jaw was yet swollen three or four times its normal size. Behind her, Kristen gasped at the ugliness of his injuries. He didn't bother trying to stand or even nod at her approach, and while she did not blame him, it felt like there was something deliberate and venomous in the breach of manners.

"Come to gloat?" he mumbled in a slur that was difficult to decipher.

You knocked me unconscious, Amelia thought. You got what you deserved.

"I have come to give you your final instructions before I go west with the prince," she said. "You've heard he is leaving, no doubt?"

Liam turned away, and in profile he looked almost like his old self. He had been handsome, but if his jaw healed wrong, he never would be again.

"The prince has made you castellan without consulting me," she continued. "It is not an honor I would bestow upon you, but it would be impolitic to reverse His Highness' decisions. Certainly not while he is yet a guest of the duchy."

Amelia had carefully composed this speech, just as she had the one to the riders during the day, but she had no expectation of winning Liam over. He was her enemy now—his ambition had raised him high, but his arrogance had poisoned his rise.

"As castellan, however, you will not be coming west with us," she said.

"Taking your mutt with you, are you?" he asked churlishly, still looking away.

"If you mean Master Ash, you know I cannot do that. Thanks to your false testimony—a sin for which God will make you answer, I do not doubt—he is an outlaw and under penalty of death."

"Some good comes to me, then."

"This is your doing!" she hissed at him, losing her temper but not wanting his men outside the door to hear her. "You brought this on yourself."

Liam gave a derisive sniff, reminding her of a petulant child.

"In spite of your lies," she said, "I have confidence I will be able to reverse the prince's decision."

"Some chance," he muttered.

"You may think so, but it appears that I have caught the prince's eye. He has asked my permission to woo me, and when my mourning period is finished, he means to ask me to marry."

Amelia felt like a fraud phrasing the prince's plan in such romantic terms. Daven Marcus's blunt self-interest had made any thought of romance between them a ridiculous notion, but Liam hadn't been in the room when the prince had "proposed," so how would he know the difference? This was the knife she had, and she wanted to twist it in the wound. Liam had once aspired to her hand, but as no more than a rung on his ladder of ambition. Now she put that ambition to death. He had risen as high as he ever would, and as the prince's wife she would be able to dismiss Liam as castellan and have him stripped of rank.

She saw all these things in his dark eyes as he turned to look at her; shock, disbelief, and horror blended one into the next in his expression. Then it all fell, and his injured face became a mask of contempt. He turned away again. "I wish you a raping on your wedding night and a lifetime of barrenness."

Kristen gasped again, but Amelia smiled. He was beaten, and she could see it. His bitterness was all he had left. For so long she had coddled his pride because she needed him to help her rally her own nobles and knights, but that was done now. She turned and waved for Kristen to follow her. Outside, she bid the waiting knights to shut the door.

"He needs to be alone," she said.

As Amelia headed back through the way she had come, she stopped once again at the gallery window and looked down at the cart. The process of loading was proceeding apace. The cart was already covered with furniture and cloths, and as she watched, a chair was tied into place. At the other end of the gallery, a figure emerged from a twisting stair. It was Graycen. He stopped and looked at her in surprise.

"You are abroad late, Your Grace," he said, bowing his head.

"You think to comment on my movements now?" she replied coldly. "I think the prince's visit has addled your sense of your place, Chief Steward."

"Of course, Your Grace. How thoughtless of me. Forgive me, I was surprised to find someone here. I only came because I noted the draft downstairs from the window and thought to close the shutter. If you are taking the air, I will return later."

"I am not taking the air, Graycen." Amelia could hear the impatience in her own voice. "I was returning from giving Baron Liam his final instructions as castellan before we go west. I will now retire until the early morning. Feel free to close the shutter."

Graycen bowed and Amelia passed him, leading Kristen back to her rooms. When she was gone, the chief steward moved to the window and reached out for the shutter. As he did so, he looked down at the bailey and saw the activity around the cart. For a moment, he stood watching. The cart began to move away, with two men on seat.

Suddenly, like a man awaking from a bad dream, Graycen started and, shaking his head, he rushed back down the stairs and out into the bailey. The shutter banged back against the wall in the wind.

CHAPTER 34

P rentice shivered as he crouched down on the backboards of the wagon. Despite the cold, he was wet with sweat from the effort of unloading the cart as quickly as possible and reloading it with the duchess's clothes and goods, as well as rushing to fetch the silver and hide it among the furniture. On the way into the castle, he had lain flat. Now he was squeezed and cramped between boxes and chests, covered with the tapestry from the chapel. Trapped in his little hidey-hole, he pulled his doublet collar higher on his neck and rubbed at his arms, trying to keep from getting chilled.

Don't worry about the ratter's clubs and knives. I can just stay here and catch another fever, then die from the weather.

The wagon rocked under him as Turley climbed into the driver's seat. A moment later they started off. Not long now. The wheels creaked with the weight as they crawled toward the upper bailey. Prentice heard the guard call a comment at them as they passed.

"Second time tonight," answered Turley. "And probably won't be the last. The duchess has retired, but her maids are still packing, from what I can see. I'll leave this at the dock and come back. What do you want to bet there'll be another load for me?"

The guard laughed, and Prentice held his breath as he waited to hear the man wave them through.

"Hold that wagon!" someone cried.

Graycen's voice.

Prentice leaned his head over to one side, peering out through a tiny gap between the packed goods. All he could make out was a patch of firelit wall on the side of the barbican. He heard Graycen approach, his feet grinding on the flagstones of the gatehouse, but the steward never came into sight.

"What's on this cart?" Graycen asked.

"What's it look like?" demanded Turley.

"Don't give me your lip. Duchess' favor or no, you still work for me."

"And who do you work for?"

There was a pause where Prentice figured Graycen was looking the cart over.

"Who's that up there with you?" the chief steward demanded, meaning the cowled figure sitting next to Turley. "You there, take your hood off."

"It's just me," Prentice heard Bellam say.

"The baker's boy? The one with the limp?"

Doubtless Graycen expected to find Sir Gant, or even Prentice himself, hiding under the hood. We're not that stupid, Prentice thought.

"What are you doing up there?" Graycen asked.

"Baker said I could take the run down to the docks and see the boats while the dough proves for the morning," Bellam answered. "And I ain't a boy; I'm an apprentice."

"Well, apprentice, the baker was wrong. Get down and back to the kitchens!"

"Here, what's all this about?" asked the guard.

"This one's an ex-convict, like that criminal the prince is trying to find—the one who attacked the duchess and thieved a chest of silver. I don't trust him."

So, that was how things had played out. Folper must have told the prince of his own seized share of Duggan's stolen taxes, and either Daven Marcus or Malden would have assumed that

Prentice had it somewhere. It hadn't occurred to them that it was already in the duchess's hands.

"I'm pardoned," Turley declared. "I'm not a convict anymore, and if anyone around here's a thief, it's you, you dog in a manger!"

"What did you say?"

"You heard."

"This cart needs to be searched immediately," Graycen insisted.

He must have said it to the guard because he was the one who answered, "Help yourself."

The wagon rocked, and Prentice was sure that Graycen had climbed up on the back step. Prentice clenched his fist and tried to work himself into a better position to move if exposed. He'd clout Graycen and make a dash for the bridge. If the guard got in the way, he planned to double back and try to lose himself in the shadows in the lower bailey. The wagon swayed and creaked as Graycen clambered around on it.

"What's that?" the chief steward asked.

"It's a bag, by the look of it," Turley answered. Prentice had almost limitless respect for his friend's capacity to lie, but it sounded to him as if there was a rising tension in Turley's voice. He wondered if Graycen could hear it as well.

"And that?" There was more rocking. "That's a strongbox!"

"So it is."

Prentice tensed. Graycen was close. His right hand went involuntarily to the steel dirk at his belt, the one Yentow Sent's journeyman had made.

"What's in it?" Graycen asked.

"Duchess' smallclothes and makeup, I think," Turley replied.

"In a strongbox?" The chief steward's voice was full of contempt.

"S'got a broken lock, so it's not so strong no more." Turley was working to sound casual.

"Open it!"

"Her Grace's smallclothes? On display in the castle yard? You open it."

Prentice swallowed at Turley's boldness. He risked provoking a full-blown argument with Graycen, which could ruin their whole endeavor.

"All right!" said Graycen, and Prentice heard the strongbox lid flung back. The wagon rocked more wildly still and the steward swore under his breath. The soft sound of cloth being cast aside could be heard. "What's this? Where is it?"

"Where's what?"

"The silver, you prat! This is just clothes!"

"I told you that," Turley said. "And I'll be making sure the duchess learns it was you who ruined her maids' fine folding and packing."

"Damn you!" The wagon rocked violently, and there was a loud thump as Graycen jumped to the ground. "We have to search the whole thing. Get your men out here."

"Bugger that!" said the guard. "This daftness's gone on long enough as it is."

"The man's a thief."

"So you say, but all I've seen is a steward who's been doing his lady's duty all night, while you've been making up stories. Stop wasting my time on such a miserable night. Now, drive on," he said, undoubtedly speaking to Turley. "Out of my barbican, the lot of you!"

The wagon walked on, and Prentice heard the guard add, "Dog in a manger is right."

The mules' hoofs clopped onto the drawbridge, and Prentice began to relax. He shifted his weight to sit down more comfortably, his backside chilled by the cold, hard surfaces of the silver ingots stacked underneath him and covered with only a thin cloth.

———◆○◆———

Hidden from Prentice's view, Graycen stood in the barbican and watched the cart reach the other side of the drawbridge and roll on down Castle Road. He was scowling as a cold wind whipped around him. The guard had gone inside to warm his hands by the fire. Graycen shivered, hands clenched in fury.

"They've already got the silver, you know," said a figure as it emerged from shadows on the other side of the barbican.

Graycen flinched with surprise, then peered into the dark. "Who...? You? What do you know about it?"

"I know where it is and where they're taking it."

"How?"

"I helped them bring it in, didn't I?" The figure stepped up close to him.

"And what, you want to gloat?"

"I want a better share," said the figure, flashing a feminine smile. "I mean, look at how they've got me dressed."

Graycen looked down at the figure's trousered legs and soft leather boots. "Not that bad," he said, sneering.

"For a boy, maybe."

Graycen snorted with contempt but didn't argue the point beyond that. "All right, then. Tell me where they've taken it, and I'll see you're sorted out."

The figure shook a finger at him. "It don't work like that. You'd take the word to Malden, and he'd take his ratters to seize them and the silver all at once. Then I'll be forgotten or, knowing Malden, given a cold baptism down the docks with a slit throat. Malden doesn't share unless he's forced to."

Graycen glared for a long moment. "What do you want, then?"

"You take me to Malden, he gathers his ratters, and I lead 'em to where they need to go. Agreed?"

A hand reached out from the shadows. Graycen hesitated a moment and then took it. When they had shaken, he refused to let go. Instead, he leaned closer. "I'm the duchess' man," he hissed. "More than that bastard everyone's hunting ever was! Play me false, and wrath'll fall on your head."

"Fair enough. Now get yourself a cloak. It's a cold night, and we need to hurry."

CHAPTER 35

T he wagon rolled through the streets toward the dockside.
Despite the late hour, by the time they reached the water,
every lane and roadway teemed with life. The rivermen who
were preparing for the prince's crossing were now joined by a
host of servants and retainers. Whole sides of the roads were
walled off by stacks of supplies: barrels, boxes, and sacks in every
possible variation. The wagon full of the duchess's goods was
only one of a crowd of similarly laden carts, each driven by
crews certain that theirs was the most important cargo for the
westward march. Interspersed among the harried workers were
occasional groups of petty nobles, motivated either by duty or
eagerness to be across the water before the rest of the army
began.

Rumors abounded as to when the prince would make the
crossing and whether the duchess would cross with him or by
herself. Some said at dawn, though most scoffed at that, either
because it seemed an unprincely hour or because they couldn't
imagine this chaos cleared enough for the prince to get through
by then. Others picked their own hours, with noon the most
popular guess, though in truth that was mostly because it was
a round number, and no one had any other reason better than
that.

Turley pulled the wagon up next to an inn yard, one street
back from the docks themselves, and waved the traffic behind

him to go around. He clambered over the cargo to the back of the wagon's load and began shifting pieces around carefully. After a moment, Prentice poked his head through and looked around. When he was sure they weren't being watched, he put his hand up and Turley lifted him out of his hidey-hole. They both sat down on the duchess's goods and watched the crowd pass by.

"I thought Graycen was going to find me for a moment there," Prentice said.

"Nah, he was never near you. I had my eye on him."

In spite of his friend's carefree demeanor, Prentice knew they had been close to discovery. "Thank you. You did well." He offered Turley his hand.

"Haven't let you down yet."

"Is that right?"

"That you can prove." Turley gave him a wink.

They sat together a moment.

"No sign of Gant?" Prentice asked.

"Not yet. Give him time."

Prentice had full confidence that Gant would fulfill his part of the plan. So long as Malden's men never found him.

"Any sign of the ratters?"

Turley shrugged. "Maybe one or two, but it's hard to tell in this mess."

"There was them two heavies by that tavern in the market," said Bellam from the front seat. Prentice looked to Turley for confirmation. While he had been laid up with fever, Turley had made an effort to learn the faces of all of Malden's men—at least the ones that swaggered around making a show of searching for Prentice in the prince's name. He was the closest thing to an expert they had, although Cutter could pick a lot of them on sight as well. It was a convict's instinct to watch for low men with authority behind them. Bailiffs and convict overseers were often little more than criminals themselves, just with the power of a warrant behind them.

"Wouldn't matter if there was a pair on every corner," Turley continued. "They'd never get to us through this crowd, unless they were already here."

He paused with a look of mock horror. He glanced around dramatically, as if he expected nearby members of the crowd to throw off their disguises and reveal themselves as ratters. "Oh, thank God; for a minute there I thought we were in trouble."

From down the road came the sound of a man shouting for way and mutterings from the crowd as they were forced aside.

"Make way, damn it!" Sir Gant demanded, wielding his sheathed longsword like a herald's staff. With his free hand he led the merchant Folper's two mules in train. Some folk were clearly angered by his push, but the sight of the longsword soon persuaded them to move; a longsword meant a knight, and only a more senior noble would hold ground against a knight.

Behind the mules came Folper's horse, carrying the master smith Yentow Sent. His journeymen trailed him, each one bent under a pack larger than himself. Gant caught sight of Turley and Prentice on the cart and pushed the last few paces to come even with the duchess's wagon.

"You didn't want to ride too?" Prentice asked the knight.

"Master Sent insisted that he have the privilege of the mount. He seemed to think it fit his station."

"Smiths are different in Masnia, I guess."

"It would seem so," said Gant, but he smiled as he said it.

Prentice hailed Yentow Sent over the noise of the crowd. The master smith nodded in return and walked his horse to the back of the wagon.

"A letter came to me, after the middle of day, brought by a most impertinent messenger," the master smith said. "It tells that the duchess will hire me and that I am to go with who she sends."

Sitting on the luggage, Prentice was at an equal height to Sent as they spoke.

"Then this red-haired man came—the man who was with you before—telling me to pack my men and equipment, to send for my entire workshop and bring it back to the boats. He takes boxes from merchant Folper's house and brings us all here. He insists! I am suspicious, but he says everything will be explained." Sent's eyes narrowed, and he peered directly at Prentice. "Are you packing us on a boat to send us back south?"

Prentice smiled and reached inside his jacket. He pulled out a folded document, closed with the duchess's own seal and addressed to Sent in her own hand. She'd brought it, along with several others, to him while she was giving alms behind the conclave house.

"This is your warrant," he told Sent as he handed the paper to him, leaning out over the back of the wagon. The smith stood in the stirrups and took the document. "The duchess is contracting you to make weapons for her, just as I said she would." Then he leaned back and grabbed two ingots he had kept apart from the rest hidden in the cargo. "And this is your down payment."

Sent took the two silver bars and looked at them for a moment. Even though it was night, there was enough light to make the metal shine, if only dimly. With a swift motion, Yentow Sent reached behind his neck and untied his own neckerchief, one-handed. Then he wrapped the ingots in the cloth and turned to his own saddlebags to put them away.

Prentice clambered over to the side of the wagon to speak with Gant. "Did you get them?"

Gant removed a ring of keys from his belt and held them up.

Prentice took them from his hand. "And the strongboxes?"

"On the mule."

Gant pulled back a heavy cloth to reveal two strongboxes, each similar to the one that had held Folper's share of the silver, but smaller. Prentice jumped down, and he and Gant untied first one and then the other, hefting them around the mules and up onto the backboard of the wagon. Prentice unlocked them both. They contained papers—trade contracts mainly, but also deeds—as well as two bags of coin. One bag was filled with guilders, the other with coppers of various kinds and also hacksilver—lumps and strips and shavings of the precious metal that also served as currency, measured by weight.

"He was a rich man, Folper," Prentice said as he threw all the papers onto the cart.

"And you're happy to rob him of it all?" asked Gant, looking uncomfortable.

"Everything he owned was forfeited to the duchess when he was put on a chain," Prentice responded. He felt no guilt for Folper's downfall and was not afraid to show it. "We'll keep the documents in case he's got any relatives that want to make a claim. The money's ours now."

Gant nodded, but he didn't look like his conscience was placated. "How did you know he'd have strongboxes at his home?" he asked, changing the topic.

"His men told us. At his yard, remember?"

"But why did he leave them behind? He was running away. Did he really think he'd be coming back for them?"

Prentice shrugged. "I don't know. Perhaps he thought to send for them. He took the keys and trade goods."

"There's a good chance he couldn't get them packed on a mule by himself," offered Turley. "He wouldn't want to ask for help from his own workers; too many awkward questions about where he was going with all his money, which was their wages."

Prentice finished putting the papers aside and then reorganized the space in the two boxes, to make sure he could fill them again quickly. Clambering back on the wagon, he nodded to Gant and to Turley, and they turned to keep watch. As swiftly and quietly as he could, he began to haul the silver ingots out of their hiding place among the duchess's luggage and into the two strongboxes. He worked quickly, because even if no one watching could recognize the silver for what it was in the dim light, he still looked like a retainer brazenly robbing his master's goods in the middle of transit. He didn't want anyone asking awkward questions any more than Folper would have when he tried to flee. Soon enough he was finished, though the tension made the short while feel like an hour. He closed the strongboxes and jumped down. They carried them back to the mules and lashed them into place again.

"Bet Graycen would love to catch us now," said Bellam, watching from his perch.

"Graycen, Malden, Liam, and the prince too," said Prentice. That quick list of their enemies sobered their moods.

"What next?" asked Turley.

"You wait here. The next part's down to Sir Gant and me."

"And your smith friend?"

Prentice turned to Yentow Sent. "Master Sent, I ask that you wait here with steward Turley."

Sent gave Turley a stern glance. Turley smiled and waved at the smith, who did not wave back.

"Sir Gant and I must arrange passage on the boats, as well as see to some other business," Prentice explained.

Sent nodded and said something to his journeymen, who sighed exhaustedly and shrugged out of their burdens, letting the heavy packs sink to the ground. Then they lay down at the side of the busy street, using the packs as pillows. One put his head down and looked to go to sleep, while the other pulled out a pipe and began to pack the bowl. It seemed that working for Sent made them accustomed to hard travel and odd arrangements.

"They're comfortable enough, I guess," said Turley. He exchanged a glance with Prentice and Sir Gant. Despite the differences in their birth, education, and rank, all three men knew what it was like to sleep on the ground by the side of a road.

Prentice waved to Bellam as he and Gant led the mules out into the crowd. "Next time I see you, I want to hear that you've made an honest woman out of one of those kitchen maids, you hear me?"

"Who's got time for all that?" Bellam answered. "I'm cooking from before dawn every day."

"Make time, lad," Gant added. "A good man needs a wife."

"You two ain't got wives."

"Proving the point!"

"And don't be too fussy," Turley said as he hopped over the load and back onto the seat beside Bellam. "Cooks' and bakers' wives all end up fat and jolly."

"What's wrong with fat and jolly?" Bellam asked.

Turley clapped him on the shoulder. "Good man."

CHAPTER 36

The Ragmother laughed at Prentice when he asked if she had received the duchess's letter.

"Oh, the invite to the bawrll, dahling," she said, affecting what she must have thought was a highborn accent. "How la-di-da. Tell Her Highness that I'd love to come and dance the night away with all her many noble friends."

"Her Grace," said Gant flatly.

"What?"

"She's a duchess, not a princess. She's called Her Grace."

"Ooh, I'll be sure to remember that."

Prentice sighed and put a hand on Gant's shoulder. "We're not here for etiquette lessons." He turned back to the Ragmother. "We need your man Fulford and a crew large enough to pole that barge full of prisoners."

The old crone looked at him suspiciously. "Planning a prison break?"

"The duchess wants those men moved," he explained.

"To where?"

"That's her business."

The Ragmother nodded. She smacked her lips while she thought a moment, making a sucking sound around her wooden dentures. Prentice was sure she was trying to calculate what he could and would pay for her help.

"Why don't you go to the dockmaster?" she asked.

"Because all his people are busy with the prince's crossing."

"Well, there you go. All the rivermen are taken by the dockmaster and the prince. What makes you think Fulford can scare up enough of a crew to move that bitch of a scow?"

"Because I'm paying better than either the dockmaster or the prince." Prentice tossed Folper's bag of copper and hacksilver into her lap. She scooped the bag up and tipped a handful of the contents out into her palm, holding them up to the meager lamplight.

"Coppers," she sneered.

"And silver. That bag's more than two guilders per man worth, I'd say. Enough to hire them and cover your cost as well."

She was trying to figure all the angles of the deal, Prentice could see it in her expression. The woman's eyes flicked back and forth between him and Gant, then down to the money. She kept sucking on her gums noisily while she thought.

"I hear stories about you, dearie," she said quietly in her colder business tone. "I know you're the duchess' man, but they say there's a price on your head. Talk is that she likes you, but the prince wants you. And that selectman's got his boys running all over town, looking for you. Ratters is what they're calling them. What happens if I take your money and then give your head to them?"

Sir Gant growled, his hand on the hilt of his sword, but Prentice smiled.

"What happens?" he said. "Maybe you get some of the prince's money and the prince leaves Dweltford happy. Of course, Malden and his ratters are still in town, and they think the prince's money belongs to them. Plus, the duchess will have men down here, tearing everything apart, looking for you, Fulford, your family, your friends, even your neighbors. And you all end on a gibbet if she's feeling kindly. She can be a deadly harridan when she's roused. You heard what happened to the traitor Duggan."

The Ragmother nodded with an expression of respect. "Everyone's heard about it. Is it true she cut the man's throat herself, right in front of the prince and all his pretties?"

Prentice hadn't heard that rumor, but he wasn't about to squash it. "Then she sat down to dinner with the blood still wet on her."

The Ragmother nodded again, a look of satisfaction on her face as she peered at them with cold, dark eyes. "That's how a woman rules in the Reach," she said, and they knew she was talking about herself as much as Duchess Amelia. "Down the end of the dock, wait there. I'll have Fulford and some men for you. And if you make it past the prince and Malden and all his ratters, tell Her Grace I hope she marries again soon and spawns a long line of daughters."

"Thank you, grandmother," said Prentice.

"Don't thank me, dearie. I'm only doing what you paid me to." Her eyes glittered like dark glass in the dim lamplight.

They waited at the water's edge while Fulford's crew gathered and pulled their skiff up from its hiding spot. The water traffic was chaotic in the dark, and one more rivercraft made no impression. Prentice looked around him as the boat drew near, and thought about how many other illegal activities were going on while the prince's army was shuttled across the lake. How many did the dockmaster have his hand in? Odds were that the Ragmother would have to pay a share of her bag of copper and silver to the dockmaster as well. Graft was just a part of life.

When the boat drew close, there were three times the number of men in it as last time. What kind of manpower could the Ragmother command, exactly? The men in the boat mostly sat, with only two at the rear and one at the prow poling the water. The rest had their long poles, as well as a half a dozen oars, all shipped in the middle between them so that the ends stuck out over the gunwales. No sooner were they aboard than the pole men pushed off again. Gant sat down awkwardly, forcing a space between the others, his sheathed sword off his belt and held vertically in front of him. Prentice took a spot next to Fulford, sitting on the gunwales and trying not to worry about falling overboard.

"You need all this crew for the one boat?" Prentice asked.

Fulford turned to him, eyes hidden in dark pits of shadow, then turned back without saying anything. The rest of the journey happened without a word spoken, the noise from the docks dimming as they poled out into the blackness. They were aimed at a pair of running lanterns, posted bow and stern, on the prison lighter. Little more than a flat-bottomed box, the lighter was ideally suited for its purpose. It had a solid roof and sides, pierced with barred windows and grates to let in air. Its bow was a ramp that was pulled up on the water but could be lowered when the craft was run up on the shore, to allow rapid loading or unloading. There were similar craft all over the lake and the river Dwelt, but few, if any, had a roof and high sidewalls. With these, prisoners could be locked in and left. A guard or two would pace the roof as an upper deck. There was a mast that could hang a sail if the lighter had to go a long distance up or downriver, but the mast had been taken down while the lighter stayed anchored near Dweltford.

"What-ho?" called a voice through the dark as Fulford's boat drew near.

"Duchess' man, come for your cargo," Fulford called back.

"Is that right? Let's see."

Fulford turned to Prentice and motioned that he should go forward. From on the lighter there came the flash of sparks striking, and a new lamp was lit from a linen tinder. The lamp was held up by a tan-skinned riverman missing half his teeth. He was bare chested, with a rough woolen blanket wrapped around his shoulders. Prentice made his way off the skiff onto the lighter's running board, reaching out to keep his balance.

The man with the lamp looked him up and down. "You the duchess' man?" he asked skeptically.

"I am." Prentice reached into his belt and pulled out another warrant the duchess had signed for him. He held it out, but the riverman ignored it.

"Why ain't the dockmaster with you?" He looked past Prentice to Fulford. Rivermen trusted their own, it seemed.

Fulford shrugged. "In this mess, what time's he got for this?"

The two men looked back out over the lake, the distant shouts of dozens upon dozens of boat crews and dockworkers echoing softly over the water. Dweltford's waterside was a mass of warm yellow lights, like a swarm of fireflies clustered together. The lighter guard looked back at Prentice, and it took a moment before he realized what the man wanted. Prentice reached into his purse and pulled out some guilders.

"The duchess wanted me to make sure you received her thanks for your service," he said, and handed the silver coins over.

The riverman took them and squirreled them away somewhere. "She's all yours, then," he said with a shrug, then clambered up off the running board. He hung the lamp on an iron hook on the rump of the mast.

Before Prentice could issue an order, Fulford whistled to his men and they rushed off their skiff, hauling the oars and poles with them. One of the men paused to secure the little boat, holding it steady for Gant to step off as well.

"Weigh up," came a call, and an anchor stone was hauled from the riverbed.

"Where to?" asked Fulford.

"Follow the shore," Prentice said, pointing south through the dark. "Down to where the road turns away to go west."

Fulford looked disgusted. "That's not even an hour away. Then where?"

"Then bring us up on the shore, and we'll wait there."

"For what?"

"For me to give you your next instructions," Prentice said.

Fulford sneered but called out orders to his crew, and the poles went into the water. With an almost painful slowness, the lighter turned in place and began to head south. They were traveling downstream, but in the open water of the lake, the rate of flow was so slight that the heavy, flat-bottomed boat would hardly move by itself. The rivermen grunted and strained as they got the lighter started, but soon they had a natural movement going and settled into a smooth rhythm.

"We'll be there well before dawn," said Gant, joining Prentice on the upper deck.

"As long as we get away with no one noticing, it won't matter."

"You're worried?"

Prentice sighed and shrugged. "Every step needs to go right. One thing out of place, and it all falls over like a game of skittles."

"It would be better to not have to trust the likes of these." Gant looked around at the rivermen. "How many do you think would—"

"All of them," Prentice interrupted, not even letting him finish the question. "If they thought they could get away with the whole reward for themselves."

"So, it's like your rats with Folper's chest; pay them and hope the easy money slakes their thirst for silver before they get the courage up to betray you."

"It's a desperate world we live in, my friend," said Prentice, and he smiled.

Gant nodded, then bowed his head. Even in the dark, the heaviness in his limbs and the dark circles under his eyes were evident. "I'm not as young as I used to be."

"How old are you?" It occurred to Prentice that he knew next to nothing about his new ally and wondered if asking Gant's age was the best first detail to gather.

Gant just laughed. "Not quite forty summers. Not that old, but since Farrings died, I don't know."

He seemed to want to say more but was silent for a time. Prentice waited, turning to look forward and watch the lighter's path into the darkness. Now that the lights of Dweltford were receding, he wondered how the rivermen would find the right part of the shore, or even if they could. There was not even a quarter of a waxing moon in the sky. Even the rampart was in partial occlusion. It was nowhere near enough light to make out the shore by.

"The thing of it is," said Gant suddenly, taking up his thoughts again, "I never minded the life of a hedge knight. Does that make sense? I was a third son. My father saw that I was raised truly and given the training my rank required, but he had no land for me or my brother Ranon. He was second born. Only my eldest brother, Horrocks, will inherit anything. And I never had any problem with that."

He turned to Prentice, slapping his hand on the folded mast spar next to him as he did so. "I mean, that's the way of the world. I took to the road happily; it was an adventure. I was squired to a fine knight—stern, upright, a good instructor. The kind of man you could respect. Then I won my spurs and my saddle, and I took my sword to the road to find my fortune. I never minded sleeping by a brookside or in a hayloft. Call me a hedge knight? I took it as a badge of honor. Of course, I was looking for a land to make my own, a battle to win, and a glory to pin to my name. And I've tried to pass on what I was taught. Farrings was..."

He paused again and glanced away, as if the mention of his dead squire's name filled him with shame. He looked forward for a moment. "He was my second squire. The first was a lad named Serrin. Admirable youth, tall and strong with a noble heart. His father had even less for him to inherit than mine had for me and my brothers. I liked Serrin. Never ran from a fight, and put himself into every task with his whole heart. But he was no swordsman. He just never had the feel for it, do you understand?"

Prentice nodded.

Many men learned to wield a weapon, to hold it right and strengthen themselves to the physical demands of combat. But there was also an instinct, a way of thinking, that separated the true warriors from the merely trained. And it wasn't by birth or rank. As he thought about it, Prentice trusted that he and Sir Gant were of that type, but so was Turley. And from the way Malden had attacked, Prentice was willing to wager he was the same. Some women even could be to, he thought, if Cutter was anything to go by. Whether it was a wild, hot rage that turned the vision to blood, or the cold calmness that Prentice himself felt when fighting—where his emotions seemed to flee to a far corner of his mind, leaving only his skills in control—there was an inner part to combat, where rage and will were as important as strength and skill.

"He lost three fingers on his hand in a tourney melee," Gant continued. "He took it like a man, and the wound healed readily enough, but he'd never hold a sword again. Truth was, I think both he and I were relieved. He went back to his father and became a farmer. Wrote me a letter to say he'd married a sweet village girl. They were happy, and I was happy for him. I took on Farrings a year later, and he's been with me three years." He sighed heavily. "Had been with me. He'd have won his spurs, I don't doubt. But when I sleep at night, just before I fall away, I see him again, being dragged beneath those spears and hacked to pieces. He didn't deserve that."

There was another long silence between them.

"I only asked how old you were," Prentice said at last.

Sir Gant glared at him and then smiled when he realized he was joking, and the two of them chuckled. "Someday you can tell me about your experiences on a convict chain, and I promise I'll make just as light of them for you."

"Just pick a time and place. But make sure we've got something to drink. These aren't stories to tell sober."

"True words are those."

The lighter's movement had changed, and Fulford swore at the rivermen, telling them to correct the drift. They rushed about the sideboards, swapping places deftly on the narrow spaces, heedless of the fall and the icy black water all around them.

CHAPTER 37

P rince Daven Marcus waited on his horse in the castle bailey as trumpeters rode across the drawbridge and began their first fanfare. While two stopped at the head of the 'bridge, the other two traveled down the road to the subsequent station, ready to give the next blast. The four men would overlap each other with a series of fanfares announcing the prince's movement all the way to the dock, where the boats that would take him across the lake were waiting. The prince put his heels to his mount, and he led his entourage at a walk out onto the drawbridge.

"He likes to take the time to let the people see him," Amelia said to herself, though not so quietly that her maid seated next to her did not hear.

"He's so fine," said Kristen. "A true prince of the realm."

Her tone made her admiration unmistakable. Ever since she heard of the prince's "proposal," she had been sighing and smiling, taken with the romance of a royal wedding. Amelia was already finding it wearisome but had refused to take Teerah or Bettina with her on this journey. Bettina was too old for living in tents, and Teerah had suffered the horrors of the summer's march north against the invaders. Amelia could not subject her to another such experience, not so soon. Kristen had been elated with the favor of being chosen, but Teerah had only seemed relieved, and the duchess was glad to give the girl that rest.

Amelia shook her head at her own thoughts. Teerah and Kristen were both seventeen and quite ready to marry, but she thought of them as mere girls. Marriage, widowhood, rulership, and war had aged her inside. She still seemed fresh faced to her own eye when she looked in a mirror, and as the prince had so bluntly pointed out, she now came with an impressive dowry. She was Duchess of the Western Reach, regardless of her age or birth.

She looked over her shoulder at the two lines of mounted men, knights of the Reach every one, arrayed in their own parade armours and she smiled. They were not so finely attired as the prince and his honor guard, but they were proud, with ribbons and flowers entwined around their lances. Behind them were the other riders, the ones she had rallied yesterday. Less fine again, but to her eyes so much more respectable, because these were the ones she trusted, the ones who wanted to serve her out of loyalty alone. She turned back and Kristen met her eye. The young maid beamed, her shoulders set back, and her golden hair woven in perfect plaits, under a snood of blue wool.

A chill breeze blew through the gate for a moment and Amelia shivered. The sky was clear, and the sun was high, but it shed a thin, watery light that did little to warm the land. The winter storms would come soon. It was a poor season to be marching into unknown territory. Ahead, the last of the prince's entourage walked out of the bailey and Amelia straightened herself in the saddle. It was time to go. She geed her horse into motion and led her own parade through the barbican.

Another blast of trumpets sounded the prince's passing farther down Castle Road. The sound of cheering could be heard, and as she crossed the bridge, new cheers arose. The sides of the street were crowded with onlookers. So many were dressed in bright colors or had ribbons of their own. The roadway was already strewn with flowers, thrown for the prince's passing, and now more were thrown in front of her own horse. Some came so close that Meadow Dancer tossed his head once, but the duchess comforted him. Being late autumn, the blooms were mostly limp and with fewer varieties of color, not like the wildflowers of spring and summer. It seemed a fitting display to Amelia, a withered beauty for a heartless quest. That was how she felt, and as she noted it in herself, she was reminded again of the horror of her vision in the great hall the night of Duggan's death—the prince and his closest attendants like decayed birds of prey, fighting a serpent, horrific and wild.

Was that what they would find in the west?

The serpent had five heads—or was it six? One of them was like the Horned Man who had led the invasion. Were the other heads leaders as well? Were they waiting in the west? And if they were, then where were the lions? Where were the pure white rats that would be transformed into noble creatures, to stand by her side and fight wildly to defend her?

"Are you unhappy, Your Grace?" asked Kristen.

"Just thoughtful," Amelia replied. "Wondering at how these ventures begin in flowers and cheering, and end in blood and tears."

"The blood and tears of our enemies," her maid said primly.

"What do you know about it?"

Amelia's blunt question seemed to catch the younger woman by surprise, her proud smile twisting to a hurt frown. Amelia knew it was a harsh thing to say, but she found no pity in herself. The silly girl would likely soon see the horror she was delightedly riding toward, and then she would see her own foolishness.

The duchess put her heels to her mount and moved forward a length, to ride by herself for a while. The folk lining the street threw their flowers and cheered, and Amelia forced herself to smile and wave. They must have denuded the local fields for miles to collect these flowers. It was a show of love and hope, of how they looked to her to protect them from enemies and to punish invaders. They needed to see her confident and happy.

By the time the dock drew near, Amelia was glad to think the whole sorry parade would soon be over.

"Fair, beautiful, and strong. Your Grace is the model every highborn lady would aspire to."

The strongly voiced compliment cut through Amelia's reverie. She turned to her left, surprised to see Turley standing on the backboard of a wagon, calling over the heads of people in the road.

"You are bold for a mere steward," she called back with a grin. She stopped Meadow Dancer, and behind her the entire march halted. She walked her mount over and smiled to the crowd nearby. They reached out to touch her hand, and she let them as she spoke with Turley. "Should you not be with my chattels across the river, steward of my chamber?"

"Everything's well watched, I promise. Just one or two bits of business on this side of the river before I cross."

"I trust everything is well?"

For a moment his charming smile slipped. He had a serious look in his eyes, and it reminded her of Prentice, his strength of will.

No wonder they are such friends.

He nodded solemnly, and then the roguish mask was back in place. "All is well, now that I've seen Your Grace and His Highness the prince. I can hie to my last chores for the day. I'll see Your Grace tonight at the camp across the river."

With that he tugged his forelock, leaped down from the cart, and rushed away through the crowd. Amelia blinked, realizing that many of the folk in front of her horse were still pressing at her hands and offering blessings for the prince's campaign. The goodwill almost undid her, and she had to swallow hard to keep tears from her eyes. She forced herself to smile and thanked the people. Then she turned Meadow Dancer away, and the parade started off again behind her.

As the dock neared, the road was lined by members of the prince's own houseguard—men in coats of plates, wearing mail coifs and surcoats of royal red. They held the crowds back with long staves. The prince's entourage had stopped at the water's edge, leaving a pathway between them, an aisle which Amelia rode up alone. At the end, Daven Marcus sat his saddle, waiting for her. As she made her way through the crowd of nobles, she forced herself to smile at them and meet their eyes. These were her peers, the society with which she was marching west. She would live among them for the next months, through a winter march and a campaign to avenge her people.

Were they all loyal to the prince? Were all sycophants, like his closest companions seemed to be? Like Liam? Or were some of them more honorable? Could she even win some of them over? Were they all crazed vultures, gleefully rotting as they went to make war with a many-headed serpent, or were some of them rats that would transform into white lions that would fight to protect her? She watched them as she rode past, but try as she might, she could not pick friend from foe. Time would tell.

When she reached the prince, he smiled at her with such genuine warmth that she was taken aback for a moment, as though her whole impression of him might have been wrong. Then she remembered that he was on display, that the whole of his army and Dweltford's society were watching for signs of the rumor of romance that would certainly be circulating. He was performing "admiration" for her, much as he performed everything. Life was an entertainment to him, and he liked to play a role. When she reached him, his words confirmed her suspicions.

"Keeping me waiting, are you?" he asked with a cold tone, though his smile never wavered. "Take care. Whatever you do in public, you'll pay for in private. Courtships do not last forever, and I have a long memory."

"I am sorry to be late, Your Highness," she said. "I was delayed by last-minute business."

He made no reply to that but turned his horse to look out over the water. They were stopped at the dock's edge, and in front of them was an open-topped lighter, with a ramp lowered for them to ride directly upon. The boat was strung with flowers and ribbons, and a canopy had been erected at one end with chairs and cushions. She and the prince would dismount and ride the short distance across the lake in comfort. Others would follow behind on similar boats. Dozens were already shuttling back and forth across the water, and when she looked, Amelia could just see across to the far shore, where a makeshift encampment was already in place. It would take the army the whole day to cross, and once on the other side, they would not march more than a league before they made camp for the night.

It seemed ridiculously slow.

As her eyes tracked the water traffic, she caught sight of two boats of similar size to the one in front of her, tied side by side. A vast metal object was secured across both of them. Astonished, she tried to make it out, but it seemed simply like a block the size of a cart, and though it was carved, she could not see its shape exactly.

"You like that?" Daven Marcus asked as he noticed where she was looking. "One of my Bronze Dragons. I brought five from father's troop."

Bronze Dragons? She had read about these in her husband's books. They were cannon, each a tube of bronze the height of a man and four times as long. They were said to be able to batter a castle's walls to rubble in mere days. The rebel city of Aubrey, on the Vec border, surrendered upon merely hearing the news that the king had deployed his Bronze Dragons. They hadn't had to fire a single shot. Looking behind her, Amelia wondered how long her castle or town would last if these were turned upon them.

She shivered. "I thought cannons were for sieges, Highness."

The prince turned to her and favored her with a condescending expression. "We're tracking the path of an invading army to find its origin. Do you not think they will have a castle or keep there?" The prince didn't pause to listen for any answer. "And how do we conquer castles? With a siege, obviously."

"I hadn't realized, Highness. I merely thought—"

"Well, stop."

As the parade of nobles and worthies drew itself fully onto the docks, the townsfolk crowded up behind, eager to watch the proceedings. The prince waved to them, and they cheered him.

"You're a woman, damn it," he said to her. "Nothing more than a milkmaid's get, from what I hear. Stop imagining you have any place to go thinking. Just ooh and aah appreciatively and be glad you get to sit among your betters while everyone pretends you belong here. War is the province of men, and great armies are led by great men. Be thankful you get to watch from such a privileged vantage point."

He turned to look at her then, and Amelia was struck how clear his intent was. He wanted to offend her. He wanted her to lose her temper and do something inappropriate, in front of everyone. It was so obvious that she wanted to laugh.

Did he think she was that inept? She was fighting him for control of her province at every step. He clearly had no respect for her, but did he really think so little of her?

She smiled sweetly and waved as well. "I am sure the Bronze Dragons will be as decisive as they have ever been," she said simply. "Thank you, Highness, for bringing them to the defense of the Reach."

His eyes narrowed, and she was pleased to see his façade drop for that moment. Then he smiled and, turning away from her, nodded to a sacrist who stood nearby. The cleric stepped forward and began a blessing upon the army and the campaign, calling it a holy crusade. The prince sat his horse for a moment, listening to the benediction, but as it went on, he appeared to become bored. Without any explanation, he suddenly geed his horse onto the waiting lighter. The sacrist was forced to jump back out of the way, and any protest he might have made was drowned out by the clatter of the prince's mount's hoofs on the boards.

Amelia gave the man an apologetic smile, then she followed and was soon dismounted, being taken across the river into the unknown west, seated next to a man she considered as vile an enemy as the ones they were going to fight.

And he planned to marry her.

CHAPTER 38

The rivermen found a spot to bring the prison lighter ashore before dawn. Since Prentice had not told them to rush, he got the impression they took their time and made life easy on themselves. The boxy craft ran aground on mud a half dozen paces from the shoreline. No sooner had it hit the bottom than the prisoners on the craft began to awaken and ask what was happening. As the cold dawn broke over the river, an increasingly aggressive conversation was spitting back and forth between the rivermen and the imprisoned mercenaries. The rivermen had nothing to do but sit on the edge of the boat and wait, while the prisoners wanted to know what was going on.

"Will that turn into a problem?" Prentice asked Fulford, after one of the mercenaries spat out through a barred window and one of the rivermen beat back on the bars with an oar.

"Not much either lot can do until you open this up, if that's your intent," said Fulford. "Unless we can just off you two. We could take you both and pole these out to the middle, hole the hull, and drown the lot."

Prentice cocked an eyebrow. From his expression, it seemed Fulford was deadly serious. He looked past him to the surface of the lake, where a soft mist moved over the black water, slowly being driven back by the coming sunlight.

"Your boys could probably take us both in the end," Prentice said, keeping his voice calm. "But I swear you'd have my dagger buried in your eye before they took me down!"

Fulford met his gaze, and both men judged the other's will. The moment seemed to hang in the air between them, as if time had stopped. A small bird flapped out from the bank, swooping and hunting water bugs. There was a splash as it caught one and flew back to the bank.

"It was only a thought," said Fulford at last, with a shrug.

"Think of something else and keep your men on a tight leash. You'll be packed off soon enough."

Fulford led the rivermen off the lighter, and they built themselves a fire on the bank. From among them, they produced skins of drink and hunks of bread and cheese, none of which they offered to share with Prentice, Gant, or the prisoners, though they let the two lighter crew join them. The cold morning wore on.

"How long do we wait?" asked Sir Gant as midday approached. The prisoners had lapsed to a sullen silence, only whispering among themselves. There was nothing else they could do. The rivermen lazed on the shore, walking about sometimes in boredom. "I doubt those men there will stay patient much longer."

"We have to wait until we hear word from town," Prentice replied.

"Which will be when?"

"When the prince leaves. Until then, we wait."

Prentice looked across at Gant. With the toe of his boot, the knight was worrying at a knot hole in a plank of the boat. He was chewing the inside of his lip as he did so. The man could not have seemed more tense if he had been a twisting rope, tightening under strain.

"If this is how you handle waiting, what are you like on a battlefield?" Prentice asked. "You must go mad standing fast for the call to charge."

"On the field, I can see the enemy. Here I'm just waiting. It's not the same thing."

Gant managed to control his tension until Turley arrived a short while after midday, driving a huge wagon with a team of four bullocks. Yentow Sent rode beside him on Folper's horse, while all his apprentices and journeymen, a crowd of over a dozen, rode on top of the wagon's load. Prentice jumped off the lighter and waded ashore to greet him. The wagon stopped just beside the rivermen still clustered around their fire. Not one of them moved for the horses.

"They're a sour lot," Turley said to Prentice quietly, once he'd hopped down.

"They're bored and can't figure out why they haven't just slit our throats and been done with it."

"Oh, that old dilemma?"

Prentice walked the short distance to where Fulford sat smoking a pipe. "You can go now."

"That's it?"

"It is for you."

Fulford shrugged and stood up. His men stood as well, and they whistled for the others who were wandering nearby. Without another word, the rivermen waded back to the lighter, shipped their oars and poles on their little skiff, and hopped aboard. They cast off and were gone in a short space.

"Do we worry they'll talk?" asked Gant when Prentice made his way back out to the lighter.

"Did they seem the talkative sort?"

Gant snorted a quiet laugh. "What now?"

"Now we hire some mercenaries."

They made their way along until they were standing over a grate in the upper deck. "Sergeant Ranold!" Prentice called.

There was a stir among the prisoners, and a heavyset man with a bald pate and a long, drooping mustache appeared under the grate. This was Sergeant Ranold, the current leader of the mercenaries in the lighter. There had been a captain, but he'd been slain during the battle to retake Dweltford. One of the duchess's knights had run him through with a lance. Prentice had met Ranold the night he had rowed out to the lighter with Turley.

"Time for a new contract, Sergeant," Prentice said. "Your men ready to hire out again?"

"I don't like negotiating through prison bars."

"You can stay there if you want."

"Bugger that!" declared another mercenary, and several of his comrades muttered their agreement.

"All right, so what's the contract?" Ranold asked.

"First today, you'll do escort duty on a crowd of convicts," Prentice instructed. "Then, you'll be training those same convicts to be soldiers. For that you'll get paid and the duchess will pardon you all. After the next year, you'll be free to seek other contracts anywhere you like."

"What's to stop us just making for the nearest border?"

"You'd be under sentence of death. You raised arms against the rightful ruler of the Western Reach. If the duchess wasn't busy with her own problems, she would've had you all exiled already by now. You leave before your contract's up and every rover, ranger, and boy with a bow will be hunting for the bounty on your head. You might see the Vec again, but I wouldn't bet on it. You'd die hunted and hungry."

Ranold grimaced and spat, but he didn't seem to have any doubt that Prentice spoke the truth. He looked about at his men. "All right, we're for hire. Open up."

"One thing first."

Prentice waved to Turley and had quill and ink brought. Then he sat down and had Ranold list every man in his company by name. Each name went onto the parchment, to be bound in the contract. When that was done, he had every man stand and swear an oath, to obey the duchess and the law, to protect the Reach for the term of their service, and to not turn their weapons on its citizens. It was a typical mercenary oath, though

Prentice deliberately had them swear to the duchess, not to the Grand Kingdom or the throne. He wanted men the prince could not command out from under her. As they recited the oath, he wrote it down. Once that was all finished, he climbed down to the bow and, with Turley's help, lowered the prow ramp. It fell into the water with a heavy splash. Prentice jumped onto it and waved the ring of keys Turley had brought with him from the castle.

"Right. Who's ready to get their manacles off?"

It was one part of the day that went quickly, as every man cooperated to get free of their chains. As the manacles fell, most simply rushed out onto the ramp and then waded to the shore. Some didn't hesitate to strip their clothes and throw themselves into the bitter water, washing their bodies that hadn't been clean since the breaking of the siege. Others fell on the ground and lay stretched out on the grass, laughing and smiling, ignoring the cold. Prentice understood their joy. Weeks of incarceration gave one an appreciation of the outside. Ranold stood by him until the last man was out of the lighter. Then they walked onto the ramp.

"If I never see another boat, it'll be too soon," the sergeant said.

"I've got some bad news for you," said Prentice. When Ranold gave him a cold look, he smiled. "Don't worry. On these ones you'll be the guards, not the prisoners."

"The convicts you want us to guard?"

Prentice nodded.

"And what are we to guard them with? Stern looks and harsh words?"

"That's been taken care of."

The wagon was loaded with staves, like those the prince's men used in the town, which Prentice showed to Ranold and told him to distribute to his men. Along with them were sacks of brown bread and wheels of cheese, which the hungry mercenaries tore into readily.

"All we need now is a lamb leg and a pot of ale, and it'll be a feast," said one happily, his chest bare and his hair dripping from a dip in the lake.

"That we haven't got for you," said Sir Gant as he helped hand out the food.

The man didn't look especially disappointed. As the mercenaries ate their fill, Prentice looked them over. They were thinner and paler from being locked up, but they didn't look weak. There were almost thirty of them, far too small to be a useful company on a battlefield, but as officers and instructors, they were just the right tool to turn convicts into a militia. They were mercenaries, and mercenaries were only loyal to the money. Good thing was that Prentice had money—enough to buy their loyalty for now at least.

"What next?" asked Turley.

"Have you seen Cutter?" Prentice said.

"No. When was the last time you talked to her?"

"Too long. I'll have to go looking. You know what to do when you get back to Dweltford?"

"I'll have the boats waiting for you."

"Good man."

Turley headed off, stopping only to grab Folper's horse from Yentow Sent. The smith shouted after him, but Turley clambered up and bounced away awkwardly, ignoring the protests.

"He's the worst rider I've ever seen," Sir Gant opined, watching Turley ride away.

"You haven't seen me yet," Prentice said.

Yentow Sent strode up to them frowning sternly and eyes slitted in anger. "Your man has taken my horse!" he declared in his lilting accent. "You drag my workshop out from the town with no explanation. Now he tells me we will be going straight back. And then he takes the horse. It is insulting."

"I apologize for your insult, master," Prentice replied. "Please bear with us. It is a chaotic day. Soon it will all be over, and we will be on our way to our final destination."

"Which is where?"

"North."

Sent scowled but raised no further objections.

Prentice handed Sir Gant another warrant from the duchess. "Time to collect the convicts. The overseers might insist on seeing them onto the boats with you; let them. No matter what you hear or what else happens in the streets, get the convicts on the boats."

"You think the prince has left men behind to watch?"

"Not the prince perhaps, but Malden's ratters are still there," Prentice said. "If they get wind of what's happening, they might make trouble. Don't let them. With the prince out of the town, the duchess is the highest authority again, and we are her men. We've got her signet and her warrants for proof. We answer to her and no one else."

"What about you?" Gant asked.

"Cutter's not sent word. I have to go into town to find her."

"You don't think she's in the back of some tavern, do you?"

"Have you ever seen her take a drink?"

The question plainly set Sir Gant thinking. Cutter never drank—not that either of them had seen.

"You happy with this number?" Prentice asked.

"I'll have no trouble. Will you?"

Prentice didn't answer him but told Ranold to rally his men, and he handed the command over to Sir Gant. "He'll give you your orders for the next hours, and you'll need to put a man on that wagon to drive it."

"I'll do that," said Ranold. "Who are the southerners up on the back already?"

"A smith and his men, from Masnia. They're a prickly lot, so don't let them get under your skin."

The sergeant smiled. "I think I can manage. What'll you be doing?"

"I've got to head back to the town. I'll catch you up at the docks."

"Why didn't you go back with that fella on the horse? It could have carried you both, at least that far."

Prentice looked north where Turley had already gone so far that he was out of sight. "I wish I'd thought of that."

With the warrant from the duchess in his hand, Sir Gant led the mercenaries inland to take command of the convicts on the chain and march them into town and onto boats. It would be what everyone expected. The prince's army was to be followed by the convicts, who would be thrown into battle as fodder for the enemy. Except Prentice's conspiracy would turn the riverboats and barges north, upriver as far as they could go, and then make them trek farther north to the ruins of the town of Fallenhill, where they would camp for the winter and be trained into a militia.

Assuming the next few hours went right and that he could find Cutter.

CHAPTER 39

The churchyard was empty, but the charcoal smell from the last night's feast still lingered in the air, along with the oily aroma of the roasted meat fat. Little more than a patch of mud in front of the chapel entrance, "churchyard" seemed too grand a title for it, even with its rough little paling fence separating it from the back-alley yards of the nearby houses. It was only midafternoon, but the sky was so heavy with clouds that an early twilight had fallen on Dweltford.

Prentice sat alone on the stoop of Fostermae's humble chapel. He had his doublet laced all the way to his throat against the cold, but the chill still numbed his toes in his boots, and he rubbed at his hands to keep his fingers warm. He ached in his bones, and he knew that it wasn't just the cold. He was not fully recovered. If he spent too much more time out in the elements, he'd probably sicken again, and that he could not afford. He reached down and picked up the long yew quarterstaff he'd grabbed up on the way into town. He twisted his hands around it, working his strength as another way to keep warm.

This wasn't the plan.

Cutter was supposed to meet them down on the edge of the river, along with the mercenaries. It was only if she couldn't make that rendezvous that they were to catch up to her here, at the church. But the hour was getting late, and Prentice was starting to think he would have to go to the boats without her. He did not like that notion. He stood up and was about to push on the door of the chapel behind him when he heard people coming through the alleyways to the churchyard. Even in the dimness, the richly dressed bulk of Malden—merchant, selectman of the Conclave Council, head ratter, and cunning leader of the remnant of Duggan's conspiracy—was unmistakable. He wore a fur-lined coat, and his hands were so heavy with rings that they seemingly glittered, even in the dim light. He came at the head of a line of harsh-faced men, who followed him out of the alley in growing numbers, until it looked like he had brought every one of his ratters, the full company. Most were dressed in rough clothes, made of simple homespun wool, worn and faded and patched in places. Each carried some kind of weapon, a club or a long fighting knife, and had the same symbol pinned to his chest—a small silver rat.

Prentice smiled at the sight of that. The tale told was that Malden had the pins made and paid for out of his own pocket, like the pins that guildsmen wore. Prentice didn't doubt there were layers of meaning to Malden's choice. The pins marked ratters out from mere thugs, giving them a legitimacy, like a reminder of the prince's order to capture Prentice and all the ex-convicts who had won their freedom in the summer campaign.

But there was another level.

The little rats were made of silver, and Prentice suspected that they were probably made of some of the actual silver embezzled by Duggan. It was the kind of thing a man like Malden would do, a small reminder of what he had gotten away with, continually on display and subtly mocking the power that sought to contain him. He had risen from a street-fighting dockworker to become a selectman of Dweltford and, if the rumors were true, one of the most influential bosses among the Reach's criminal fraternity. He was the kind of man who could give the likes of the Ragmother pause.

Prentice knew the depth of ambition and hubris that such a rise required.

As they approached, the crowd of thugs filed out around Malden, closing off the churchyard and leaving no possible escape. Standing right in the center of the line, at the opening in the yard fence, Malden looked over his shoulder and waved someone forward from behind him.

It was Cutter.

She stepped up next to Malden, and Prentice could make out a heavy bruise around one of her eyes.

"You've made some new friends, Cutter," Prentice said. "They play rough, do they?"

Cutter made to answer, but Malden spoke over her. "She came to me with an offer, but she forgot what she owed me for the first time we met. Little bitch cut me; I couldn't let that slide."

"So, you hit her." As he said it, Prentice realized that the glitter on Malden's fingers wasn't rings, but brass knuckles that were polished like precious metal. If he'd hit Cutter with those, it was a wonder he hadn't cracked her skull.

"It's done now," said Cutter.

Malden smiled at that. "See, now we're all friends."

"I was waiting for you by the river," Prentice said to Cutter, doing his best to ignore Malden. He wanted to smash the man in the mouth for what he'd done, and he needed to keep that thought under control. Now was not the time to give in to his temper.

"I had to make my own plans," she said.

Prentice looked at her and tried to fathom the expression in her eyes. All he could see was the injury, making her unreadable to him. He drew in a deep breath, steadying himself, then turned to Malden. "You've come for me?"

"That's right, convict. There's a bounty on your head. I brought all my boys because the treacherous little trollop made me think you wouldn't be so stupid as to be out and about alone. Shows what you get for trusting a woman."

"If you can call her that," muttered one of the ratters. Prentice recognized him as one of the men Malden had at the seneschal's house—the ferret with the beaked nose, the only other one to get away. "She's skinnier and flatter than a boy without a whatsit. I reckon she's one of them castrated boy singers."

Cutter flashed the man a look of pure venom, and Prentice felt the tension rapidly rising. These men had probably come to capture him, but odds were that they wouldn't settle for anything less than blood. It all depended on whether Malden wanted him alive or dead, and how much control he really had over his ratters.

"That bounty you want is from the prince," Prentice said. "I suppose you've heard he's wooing the duchess for her hand?"

Malden affected a look of mock confusion. "We came looking for a manslayer, lads, and all we get is a castle gossip, like an old washerwoman. What a disappointment, eh?"

Several of the ratters chuckled, but Prentice ignored them. "I'm the duchess' man. You know that, Malden. How long do you think it will take her to get the prince to revoke the warrant?"

"Longer than it'll take us to have your head."

There was no point trying to negotiate with Malden. He had the upper hand; he had the men and the backing of the prince's warrant.

Prentice cast a glance across the ratters. "What about the rest of you? You don't have to do this. Any man here afraid of the duchess' wrath?"

They laughed, and the beak-nosed ferret sneered. "If she's got problems, tell her to come see me. I'll sort her out."

"Oh God, this is getting boring," said Malden. "The rat's trapped. Grab him and let's be done with it."

"You know what the problem with rats is, Malden?" Prentice said loudly as two of the ratters moved into the churchyard.

"Even when you catch one, you never know how many are still hiding in the walls." Then he banged the end of his staff on the church door behind him.

It burst open, and men and women began to pour out, along with light from a suddenly uncovered lantern. Others came from the side alleys and closed houses. Mostly they were Prentice's rats, released from imprisonment by the duchess' last orders, but there were also friends and relatives, and even a volunteer or two, who were just sick of Malden's rats and their abuses. They carried shovels, picks, and hammers, along with meat cleavers and kitchen knives.

Malden let out a contemptuous guffaw. "You think this lot'll protect you? They're not even rats! They're little mice, and they should have stayed in their holes." He settled into a fighting stance, fists raised. The lamplight glinted off the edges of his knuckledusters.

"I wasn't talking about them," said Prentice, and he nodded to Cutter.

Malden turned, but it was too late. From somewhere hidden on her person, Cutter drew a short fighting knife and, crouching low, rammed it behind Malden's right knee, pulling it forth again with a spray of blood. His huge body dropped on the injured leg, and he waved his hands desperately as he fell. Cutter didn't wait to see the outcome of her attack, but while Malden's men were still surprised, she threw herself at the ferret, leaping and landing on his chest with her full weight. Her blade was tearing at his face and throat even while his body was still falling.

Cutter's strike was the signal to attack. The rats and their allies shouted with rage and charged at the ratters. Prentice drove forward at the two men who had stepped up to take him, on Malden's order. The men both carried simple cudgels, not even metalbound. Prentice's staff gave him the advantage of reach on them, and while the first dodged back from a lunging attack, the other was not ready for the flickering speed of a simple pole and took a crack to the face that drove him backward as well. The sudden gap between the two was all Prentice needed, and he dashed past, leaving the rats behind him to engage them.

He wanted Malden.

The leader of the ratters was struggling to get back to his feet. Grimacing, he had just managed to stand on his injured leg when Prentice reached him. Prentice had to respect the man's fortitude; it would take an ironhard will to stand with that injury.

"You're a treacherous piece of shit," Malden cursed. "Honorless, gutless, yellow bellied—"

"Honor's for knights and duels, not rats and street fights," Prentice said. "You should know that, Malden. I didn't come for a fair fight. I'm here on the duchess' orders."

He swung his staff up over his head and brought it down in a heavy, vertical strike. His brutish target lifted both his arms up, crossing them to take the blow. He grunted from the force, but Prentice was almost certain he was wearing mail sleeves under his coat, so the hit did nothing like the bone-breaking damage it might have.

Rather than step back from Malden's interception, Prentice whipped the staff end in a circle, over and under, to come up like an uppercut. The swing crashed into Malden's jaw, underneath his raised arms. Even as Malden staggered back from that strike, Prentice followed it up with a series of swift hits to his legs and body. None were significant blows, and they did no real damage, but they were intended to keep Malden off balance. Soon enough, the chief ratter fell back again, arms flailing.

As he tumbled, Prentice thrust the quarterstaff down into his meaty stomach, leaning with all his weight and strength to drive through the hidden mail armor. Then he clouted Malden solidly across the temple. The blow made a wooden cracking sound that echoed around the little back alley, even over the din of the other fighting.

Prentice turned and looked around. The melee was savage, but it would soon be over. Fighter for fighter, Malden's ratters were bigger and stronger, but Prentice's force had the numbers and a rage born of anger and fear. They were done being abused. Several of the ratters were already down and at least one had fled. Prentice dropped his staff and pulled out his dagger. Crouching next to Malden, he grabbed the dazed crime lord by the collar and dragged him to his knees. Blood poured down his face from a split in his forehead where the quarterstaff had struck him. Prentice held him by the arm, with his dagger point at his throat.

"Selectman Malden," he shouted so loudly that the few combatants still fighting glanced over, and several of them simply stopped to watch. "You betrayed your position as a conclave member. You stole from the king's taxes and from the Duchess of the Western Reach."

"I was pardoned," Malden said, spitting blood as he spoke. "You can't hold me."

"Not for the murder of Bastian Fern you weren't. Her Grace knows the truth. Liam might have had his false trial with the prince, but she had her own trial. You were found guilty."

Prentice paused. Malden grunted and shifted, trying to break Prentice's grip.

"More than all of these crimes," Prentice continued, leaning in close, "you poisoned Duke Marne, rightful liege of the Western Reach and the duchess's husband. For that, she has sentenced you to death."

"Go to hell, convict," Malden growled through gritted teeth.

Prentice said nothing more but shoved his dagger straight into Malden's throat and tore it free again. Then he released him. The bull-shouldered man fell, gasping and choking on blood. For a long moment he clutched at his own throat, as if he could somehow stop the rush of blood. Then with a horrid, gurgling groan, he stopped struggling and died.

As Prentice had hoped, once Malden was dead, the fight went out of his ratters. Another one of them tried to flee, but he was quickly run down, battered with rakes and shovels until he cried out for mercy. The others threw down their weapons and surrendered. Prentice made his way through the suddenly calm crowd, to where Cutter was sitting atop the ferret. The man was dead, slashed to ribbons by her fury. As Prentice reached her, he held out his hand and helped her to her feet. He frowned, looking at the swelling and bruising around her eye.

"It probably looks worse than it is," she said, turning away from his gaze. He put his hand out to turn her chin, but she pushed him away. "Leave off!"

Prentice refused to be deterred and grasped her more forcefully. "Let me look at it!" he commanded.

Cutter stopped resisting and stood in place while Prentice examined the side of her face. His finger gently traced the outline of the injury, careful not to press too firmly, but testing the bruising and the bone. "There's a little split," he said, "but I don't think it'll scar. Looks like your record's still intact."

"Oh, that's good," she murmured, looking up at him.

"I'm sorry it happened."

She blinked, saying nothing.

He looked down at the man she'd just killed. "That seemed personal."

"You were right when you said they'd want to search me before they believed my story," Cutter explained. "This one took that as free rein to touch me up in any way he pleased. I was so angry, I forgot to worry about how they could've found my little knife. Bastard deserves everything he got." She spat on the corpse.

"Enough of that. We've still to make our way to the docks."

"No ratters waiting, though. Not anymore."

Sacrist Fostermae came from out of the church and frowned at the dead body on the ground. He gave Prentice and Cutter a pained look.

"You don't approve?" Prentice asked.

"I had hoped there would be less bloodshed."

"Malden was always going to die. I told you that."

Fostermae nodded. "I was hoping he would have a chance to repent first, to call upon God's mercy."

"You think he deserved it?" asked Cutter, putting her hands on her hips and thrusting out her chin.

"No one deserves mercy," the sacrist responded, unruffled by Cutter's aggressive posture. "That's what makes it mercy. If you deserve it, then it's justice, whether it's good or bad."

"I'm sorry, Sacrist," Prentice said in a conciliatory tone. "We barely had the strength to oppose these men. The longer the fight went on, the more people would have been hurt. Stopping Malden was the only choice."

"I don't doubt that. And I don't regret giving you my assistance. I only hoped for a better outcome. Even if it would be a miracle, isn't it better to hope for a miracle than to simply embrace the worst possibilities up front?"

"You're a good man, Sacrist."

Fostermae nodded but didn't smile. He moved on, looking for wounded and seeking to treat them.

"He's being a grim bugger," said Cutter. "We won, didn't we?"

"But he's not wrong," Prentice answered her.

He didn't want to talk about it anymore. He quickly maneuvered around the captured ratters, the would-be enforcers now made prisoners. He removed their silver rat pins and wrapped them all together in a kerchief that he took from one of the slain, then made his way back to Fostermae.

The sacrist was assessing the leg of a man who had fought. From the look of it, the leg was broken. The sacrist finished his examination, then stood at Prentice's prompting. Prentice handed the rat pins to Fostermae.

"Malden meant these as a sign of his power," he explained. "That power's broken now. He was an enemy of the duchess, and she doesn't forget the debts she owes. Make sure one of these goes to the rats who came with me through the sewer to free the town, or to their widows or children. Then make a list of everyone who fought today. When I get back, I'll make sure there's a silver rat for each one, man or woman. Anyone who brings one of these to the castle, to any part of the duchess' household, will have food and a place to sleep the night—any night, for as long as the duchess has a household. I will see to it. Every servant and house guard will know to respect this symbol. The rats of the Reach will never be despised."

Fostermae blinked in surprise, then nodded and accepted the little bundle of silver jewelry.

"Let's go," Prentice said to Cutter. He turned away, but before she followed, Cutter stepped closer to Fostermae for a moment.

"Make sure Eleanour and her boy are on that list," she said.

"Of course," said Fostermae.

Prentice, hearing Cutter's words, stopped and looked over his shoulder. He nodded as well.

"Eleanour especially," he added.

CHAPTER 40

P rentice and Cutter found the convict coffles marching into the dockside in a long column, four to six abreast, that stretched all the way back down the road to just before Within Walls. The mercenary guards and the whip-wielding overseers seemed a paltry number next to the huge contingent of prisoners, and they ranged up and down, trying to keep the whole body in order. This was the time of greatest fear for an overseer, to have a large group of convicts in a chaotic place like this. If one could escape the chain, they would be able to hide and slip away unseen with relative ease. Not that the people around them would help the convicts. The crowds that had cheered the prince and duchess had thinned, but those who remained hissed and spat at the convicts' passing. That was the other half of the fear; if a convict took insult at the hate around them, they might fight back and then, fetter chains or not, that could turn into a brawl or even a riot. All the overseers wanted was to get through the town and on the boats as fast as possible.

Anything else meant trouble.

Ducking through back ways, Prentice and Cutter pressed on to the waterfront and then moved up to where the first chains were being marshaled onto barges and lighters. The entire dockside was filled with boats of all sizes held side by side, waiting to be loaded with convicts. The boatmen all stood by their craft, and to a man they had hard faces with sour looks. They had been paid well to ferry the prince's army and his entourage; the dockside would be funded for the rest of the winter. No matter the shortages that might be caused by the invasion, disruptions to harvest and loss of livestock, the docksiders would not be the ones to suffer. Their future looked bright. But first they had one last onerous task to perform, and all they wanted was to get it over with.

At the head of the column, standing right at the water's edge not twenty paces from the sewer entrance Prentice and his rats had used to retake the town, Turley waited with the dockmaster, a barrel-chested man in a leather jack, missing his right arm. The jacket's sleeve was pinned across his chest with a guildsman's pin that Prentice couldn't distinguish. Regardless of the symbol's obscure design, the man stood with unmistakable authority, and around him the dockers and riverboat men looked on, waiting for his word. Turley pointed Prentice out to the dockmaster as he pushed his way up the crowded dockside.

"Here he is," Turley announced when they were finally together.

The dockmaster cocked an eyebrow at Prentice. "All day we've been shipping folk and chattels across the water to that camp," he said without preamble. "We've been planning and ready to get these maggots and their chains across as the last task. Now, suddenly, this man here arrives, tells me he's the duchess' chamber man and that she wants the whole lot shipped up north."

"To Croft's Landing," Prentice agreed. "It's a stone pier just upriver from the lake."

"I know where Croft's Landing is," the dockmaster retorted. "I was born to this water and have worked on it every waking day since I was eight years old."

"Then you'll know it's not much more of a journey than a straight crossing. It won't take too long."

"T'ain't the time I'm thinking of, thank you very much. It's the command itself. This whole undertaking is to serve the prince now, and it's all been done at his order. I can't pack honest rivermen off up to Croft's Landing on the say-so of a couple of ruffians that look more like ratters than upright men."

"There are no more ratters," said Cutter vehemently.

The dockmaster gave her a suspicious look, then turned back to Prentice. Reaching into his belt, Prentice pulled out his last warrant and handed it over. The dockmaster reached into his own jacket and drew forth a reading glass, fitted to a carved wooden frame with a handle and hung around his neck on a leather string. He passed the glass carefully over each word. At the end, he lingered over the seal, impressed in red wax, before giving Prentice a raised eyebrow.

"Well, that's the seal of the duchy," he said with a sigh. Prentice imagined that the dockmaster was probably the only one on the dock, besides himself and maybe Turley, who could have said that with any certainty.

"Right. It's a change of tutherbank," the man shouted to the listening boatmen. "All them convicts is to go up to Croft's Landing."

There was some mumbling among the rivermen who heard the order.

"Don't be like that," the dockmaster chided. "You get going now and you'll be back before the small hours. Ain't like you lot ain't worked a night before. Remember the prince's silver. Now pass the word."

With unhappy glances at Prentice and Turley, the rivermen began to go to their boats and oversee the loading of convicts. Despite the dockmaster's encouragement, it would be at least an hour before all the boats were loaded and away.

"They're only shipping them, you know," the dockmaster said. "Once they reach the Landing, they'll just toss 'em off and then they're your problem."

Prentice nodded. Seeming happy he'd said his piece, the dockmaster turned away to help direct the flow of convict chains across his dock. Dweltford held more prisoners of the King's Law now than had passed through it in the last few years combined. In that context, Prentice could hardly fault the man's officious manner.

"Where's Gant, do you know?" he asked Turley.

"Back of the line, keeping an eye on stragglers."

"Like Tuke."

Turley laughed and Cutter frowned.

"Who's Tuke?" she asked.

"He was head overseer on the march north in the summer," Turley explained. "Fat, mean little bastard."

Cutter nodded, seeming to recognize the man by his description. "What happened to him? Did the invaders get him? I always wished they did."

"No. Prentice here laid him out flat on the day of the battle."

"You're joshing me!" Despite her words, Cutter's eyes glittered at the thought of an overseer being beaten.

Turley shook his head. "My hand to God. Didn't you see? One to the gut and then an uppercut. Put him out like a snuffed candle."

"I had my head down, much as I could," she said, looking at Prentice. "I might need to grow a new respect for you, boss man."

Prentice scowled. "I'm sorry I brought it up." He turned to Turley. "Is Master Sent aboard?"

"He is indeed, supervising the exact placement of every little piece of baggage and arguing with the boatmen over something called the trim."

"Good."

"He wasn't too happy about being taken out of town on a wagon only to be brought back and put on a boat. I told him I didn't make the plans, just carried them out."

"I didn't want Malden's men to find them," Prentice said. "We didn't know what Folper had said before they convicted him. Besides, if the ratters found us at the prison lighter before the prince crossed the river, I wanted to be able to hand Sent's sample weapons to the mercenaries, give us a fighting chance."

"You don't have to explain it to me," said Turley with a shrug. "How did we do on the Malden score, just quietly?"

Cutter beamed. "Rats over ratters, with a couple of executions for good measure."

"They got a hit on you, though," he said, noting her bruised eye.

"And came to regret it."

"No doubt."

Prentice was glad to see them enjoying their triumph. His plan was in its final phase, and he was becoming confident that it would succeed. He felt like a man crossing a swift river over a set of slick stepping-stones; he had only one step left, and then he would be on the other bank.

Just a few more tasks.

"And do you have a boat ready for yourself?" he asked Turley.

His friend nodded. "Oh, aye. With an extra passenger, no less."

"Passenger?"

"Come see."

Turley led them to a small skiff with a cloth awning hung on a wooden frame. A poleman stood by, leaning on his pole that towered over him out of the water, obviously waiting for the order to cast off.

"Your man in there is in a hurry, isn't he?" he said as Turley approached. "He's tried ordering me to go about five or six times now."

Turley ducked his head under the awning. From in the skiff came Graycen's voice.

"About time you returned," said the chief steward. "Tell that feckle to cast off. We won't reach the duchess before her dinner at this rate."

"I think you should step out for a moment," Turley said.

There was a snort of derision, but the boat began to rock as first Turley withdrew and then Graycen clambered out onto the dockside.

"You are a lazy, timewasting—" Graycen stopped dead as his eyes fell on Prentice standing not three paces from him. "Wh... what are you doing here? You can't be here!" His eyes slid past Prentice to Cutter, waiting a pace behind. "You? You lying slut! I knew you were lying! I hope they beat you bad."

"Shut up!" said Prentice, his voice carrying so that folk from several boats around turned to watch. At his shoulder, Cutter gave Graycen a wicked grin. "You're done, Graycen. The duchess wants nothing more to do with you. You're not going with her, and you're not going back to the castle."

"You can't tell me what to do, convict!"

"Yes, I can." Prentice held up his hand and showed the ducal signet. Graycen's eyes went wide when he caught sight of the ring. "There's no crossing for you. That's her orders."

The poleman glanced to Turley, who nodded.

"It's true," Prentice explained. "Dockmaster's seen the order. He's not to cross."

The poleman also nodded and looked to Graycen, then began to use the end of his pole as a goad to push him away from the boat.

"You can't do this!"

"It's already done, Graycen," Prentice insisted. "You sided against the duchess with her enemies. A dog shouldn't bite the hand that feeds it."

"A dog? You dare call me a dog? You're a convict! You're a wanted man under a sentence of death. I'll get the bailiffs! There's a bounty on your head."

Graycen's voice was getting louder, and his expression was growing wild. Prentice stepped up quickly and punched the former chief steward in the stomach. The man folded and sank to his knees, groaning.

Prentice leaned in and seized him by his collar. "You want to try to collect?" he hissed. "Malden's dead, executed by me, on Her Grace's order. His ratters are all seized, going to the magistrates tomorrow."

"He had the prince's warrant," Graycen said as he gasped, likely as much in shock at Malden's reversal of fortune and death as from the pain.

"It's been revoked on her order. The duchess is the only law in Dweltford again, as it was always going to be. Now bugger off."

"Baron Liam is still castellan."

"Only until Her Grace returns. He cannot save you. Don't be in the castle when she gets back."

"I need to see her," Graycen whimpered. "I can explain this. I can make it right."

"No," Prentice said flatly.

"She's got no time for you anymore," Cutter sniped, still smiling like a happy child with a sweet.

Prentice looked over his shoulder, holding up his hand to shush her, but she just shrugged and pouted cheerfully.

Her undisguised joy made Graycen sneer. He shrugged off Prentice's hand and forced himself to his feet, groaning as he did it. He glared and looked up at Prentice, hate in his eyes. "She's just a milkmaid's get," he said, repeating Daven Marcus's term for the duchess. "She wasn't worthy of the duke. She's not worthy of the Reach. And she's not worthy of the title of duchess."

"And yet the title is hers, and there's nothing you can do about it," Prentice said.

The short ex-steward sniffed, but to his credit he did not cry, even though he looked like he wanted to. He began to shuffle off the dock, holding one hand against his sore stomach.

"Almost feel sorry for him," said Turley, as the pathetic figure disappeared into the crowd.

"Not me," Cutter chirped, her smile not failing for a moment. "Should have seen how happy he was at the prospect of the ratters getting your heads. And he watched while that other bastard felt me up. He wanted to do it himself, you could see it in his eyes."

"I said I almost feel sorry."

Sir Gant pushed his way through the crowd. He had his sheathed sword in his hands again and a harried look on his face. "There you are," he said. "This is pandemonium. It would have made more sense, by far, to take the boats down the shore and pick them up from afield."

"We didn't make the plan," said Prentice. "We're just commandeering it."

"The prince's people are fools."

"No arguments here," Cutter said.

"Well, at least the dockmaster's men seem to have it under control."

As they looked around, it was clear that the apparent chaos was resolving itself into order as skilled dockers competently judged the capacity of each lighter, skiff, riverboat, and barge, then herded the right number of convict chain gangs aboard. They took care to make sure at least one mercenary or overseer was on even the smallest boat, staff or whip in hand to keep order. There was little chance of trouble, however, since a convict overboard would sink under the weight of the chain, as well as drag their fellows over too. Each convict was chained to six to ten others, forming gangs. The fetters would make it all but impossible for one to swim. If there was any real trouble on a boat, the ones at greatest risk were the convicts themselves. Slowly, with lamps being hung against the darkening sky, the boats of Dweltford began to wend their way north across the lake.

Prentice took Turley's hand and shook it. He wanted to wish his friend good luck, but at the last moment said, "God bless." The two men looked at each other, both surprised by the unexpected expression of faith.

"Watch yourself getting off on the other side," Prentice warned, to cover his own surprise. "Someone might have noted the convicts not coming and ask questions."

"I know how to be slippery when I need," Turley answered, and no one standing around doubted it for a moment. Sir Gant shook his hand and then Cutter. Turley offered her an embrace, but she gave him only a handshake.

"You'll have to figure out if you're a girl or a boy soon enough," said Turley, and then he hopped on the skiff and waved the poleman to push off. Cutter blew him a raspberry.

Turley's skiff was long out of sight in the crowd of boats before Prentice clambered onto one of the larger craft, which held nearly two hundred convicts, along with a half dozen mercenaries and overseers. Cutter joined him, while Sir Gant went aboard another large craft that soon was full and set off. Prentice's lighter had a simple wooden cabin at one end, and he climbed up onto the cabin roof to watch the progress of the loading. It went even faster than he had hoped. The end of the column could be seen in the lamplight.

Out on the lake, the boat lamps were dimming swiftly as a mist began to rise. That was good. It would add to any confusion on the far bank. He looked from the water to the town again and was surprised to see Cutter standing next to him. She had joined him so quietly that he hadn't even noticed.

"So, we're headed north?" she asked.

He nodded.

"What's up there?"

"A dead town called Fallenhill," he answered. "The one the invaders sacked in the summer."

"The one with all the folks chained together and burned?"

Prentice nodded again. In his mind's eye, he could see them—the corpses, little more than charred skeletons, twisted by the fire that had consumed them. To make a point, the invaders had formed a mound of every piece of precious metal in the town, every bit of gold and silver they could find, and chained the baron of Fallenhill to the top of it in his ceremonial armor. Then they torched the walled settlement. They had not come to loot. They were not thieves. They had come to destroy, and they left the precious metals all melted together to prove it.

Prentice looked west and wondered what the prince and Duchess Amelia would find there. No one even knew the invaders' names or nationality. Daven Marcus was sure they were from the Vec princedoms, soldiers of an ancient enemy, but Prentice agreed with the duchess; that just didn't make sense.

But where, then, did they come from, and what motivated such hatred?

He was certain they would come again. And they would be stronger, with more men and more of their beast-men who could change their form by magic, or else be melded between the shapes of beasts and men, like the Horned Man. No matter what power they returned with, and in what force, Prentice was resolved to be ready for them. He had led a pack of rats to capture the duchess's town back for her, but rats weren't enough to face another barbarous force from the west.

The Reach needed soldiers of its own, courageous lions who would stand fearless and fight. The duchess needed them too, and Prentice planned to give them to her. The lighter shifted suddenly as the pole team pushed off from the dock. A change in the wind blew a strong whiff of the convict smell at him, a filthy combination of sweat, dirt, and waste from ragged bodies that almost never got to wash.

These are the raw materials I have to work with, he mused as he looked down at them. They'd have to be cleaned, fed, and trained; refined and forged, like iron into steel. He wondered how many had what it would take.

Next to him, Cutter hawked and spat. "Never thought I'd forget that smell," she said bitterly. "It's only been a season, and already it makes me sick to my stomach."

"You're changing," he told her.

She looked surprised by the idea. "I guess I am."

"To that end, we need to talk about your name."

"My name? First, it's my clothes, now it's my name?"

Prentice shook his head but smiled. "Sal's your name, you said."

"That's right. Sally, but I've been Sal to most folk since I can remember."

"Cutter Sal."

"They called me that in the pits. First time I fought, I got called that."

"And now you're just Cutter?" he said.

"Can't pass as a boy and call yourself Sally."

Prentice nodded and looked out at the other fading lamplights strung ahead on the lake. "The thing is," he said, "Cutter's a name for a thug or a convict. And you aren't either of those. Not anymore."

"So, I got to change my name? What are you going to call me? Just Sally?" She shook her head vehemently. "You try that on, and we're going to have to have some words. Steel-edged words."

Prentice smiled again. "No, you need a new name. Just like the rats needed to be respected, you need to have a name that can be respected."

That also caught her by surprise. "I never... I mean... wh-what did you have in mind?"

He paused a moment, thinking about what he wanted to say. He liked Cutter. She was loyal and fierce, and her tale reached a compassionate part of himself that he hadn't known still existed, not really. She had fought so hard to overcome the burdens that life had thrown on her, and he wanted to show

how much he respected that, just as he respected Turley and Gant and their strength.

As he respected Duchess Amelia.

"Righteous," he said to her, looking her straight in the eyes, only just able to make out her expression in the lamplight. From the look of her, he wondered if she would scoff. Instead, she seemed quiet, serious in herself.

"You think that's what I should be called?" she asked.

"You've proven it to me over and over. Righteous Sal, or just Righteous."

"Righteous," she repeated. "I think I like it."

"Then that's what it is. Cutter no longer. Righteous."

In the dimness, he thought she looked like she was smiling, but it was hard to tell. With Dweltford receding behind them, he gazed into the distance, as if he could see the future in the mist. There were so many challenges ahead. The rats had won a place in the Reach. They had gone from convicts to righteous men and women, serving the duchess. Now he had to forge a pride of lions. A year ago, he had been a convicted heretic, eking out a life on a chain gang. Where would he be in another year? Would he even be alive? Would the duchess?

Would the Reach?

GLOSSARY

The Grand Kingdom's social structure is broken into three basic levels which are then subdivided into separate ranks: the nobility, the free folk, and the low born.

The Nobility

King/Queen – There is one King, and one Queen, his wife. The king is always the head of the royal family and rules from the Denay Court, in the capital city of Denay.

Prince/Princess – Any direct children of the king and queen.

Prince of Rhales – This title signifies the prince who is next in line of succession. This prince maintains a separate, secondary court of lesser nobles in the western capital or Rhales.

Duke/Duchess – Hereditary nobles with close ties by blood or marriage to the royal family, either Denay or Rhales.

Earl; Count/Countess; Viscount; Baron/Baroness – These are the other hereditary ranks of the two courts, in order of rank. One is born into this rank, as son or daughter of an existing noble of the same rank, or else created a noble by the king.

Baronet – This is the lowest of the hereditary ranks and does not require a landed domain to be attached.

Knight/Lady – The lowest rank of the nobility and almost always attached to military service to the Grand Kingdom as a man-at-arms. Ladies obtain their title through marriage.

Knights are signified by their right to carry the longsword, as a signature weapon.

Squire – This is, for all intents and purposes, an apprentice knight. He must be the son of another knight (or higher noble) who is currently training, or a student of the academy.

The Free Folk

Patrician – A man or woman who has a family name and owns property inside a major town or city. Patricians always fill the ranks of any administration of the town in which they live, such as aldermen, guild conclave members, militia captains etc.

Guildsmen/townsfolk – Those who dwell in large towns as free craftsmen and women tend to be members of guilds who act to protect their members' livelihoods and also to run much of the city, day to day.

Yeoman – The yeomanry are free farmers that possess their own farms.

The Low Born

Peasants – These are serfs who owe feudal duty to their liege lord. They do not own the land they farm and must obtain permission to move home or leave their land.

Convicts – Criminals who are found guilty of crimes not deserving of the death penalty.

Military Order

Knight Captain, Knight Commander & Knight Marshall – Every peer (King, Prince or Duke) has a right to raise an army and command his lesser nobles to provide men-at-arms. They then appoint a second-in-command, often the most experienced or skilled soldier under them. A duke his Knight Captain; a prince his Knight Commander; and the King his Knight Marshal.

Knights – These are the professional soldiers of the Grand Kingdom. All nobles are expected to join these ranks when their lands are at war, and they universally fight from horseback.

Men-at-Arms –A catch all term for any man with professional training who has some right or reason to be in this group, including squires and second and third sons of nobles.

Bannermen – This is a special form of man-at-arms. These are soldiers who are sworn directly to a ranking noble.

Free Militia – The free towns of the Grand Kingdom have an obligation to raise free militias in defence of the realm.

Rogues Foot – A rogue is a low born or criminal man and so when convicts are pressed into military service, they are the rogues afoot (or "on foot") which is shortened to rogues foot.

Other Titles and Terms

Apothecary – A trader and manufacturer of herbs, medical treatments and potions of various sorts.

Chirurgeon – A medical practitioner, akin to a doctor or surgeon, especially related to injuries (as opposed to sickness, which is handled by an apothecary).

Estate – A person's estate can be their actual lands, but can also include their social position, their current condition (physical, social or financial), or any combination of these things.

Fiefed – A noble who is fiefed possesses a parcel of land over which they have total legal authority, the right to levy taxes and draft rogues or militia.

King's Law – This is the overarching, national law, set for the Grand Kingdom by the king, but does not always apply in the Western Reach.

Magistrate – Civil legal matters of the Free Folk and Peasantry are typically handled by magistrates, who render judgements according to the local laws.

Marshals/Wardens – Appointed men who manage the movement of large groups, especially of nobles and noble courts when in motion. They appoint the order of the march and resolve disputes.

Physick – A term for a person trained in the treatment of medical conditions, but without strict definition.

Proselytize– Attempt to convert someone from one religion, belief, or opinion to another.

Republicanists – Rare political radicals, outlawed in the Grand Kingdom and the Vec who seek to create elected forms of government, curtailing or overturning monarchical rule.

Seneschal – The administrative head of any large household or organisation, especially a noble house of a baron or higher.

Surcoat – The outer garment worn by a man-at-arms over their armor. Typically dyed in the knight's colours (or their liege lord's colours in the case of a bannerman) and embroidered with their heraldry.

Te tree – A tree, known for its medicinal properties.

The Rampart – A celestial phenomenon that glows in the night across the sky from east to west in the northern half of the sky.

ABOUT AUTHOR

Matt Barron grew up loving to read and to watch movies. He always knew he enjoyed science fiction and fantasy, but in 1979 his uncle took him to see a new movie called Star Wars and he was hooked for life. Then Dungeons and Dragons came along and there was no looking back. He went to university hoping to find a girlfriend. Instead, the Lord found him, and he spent most of his time from then on in the coffee shop, witnessing and serving his God. Along the way, he managed to acquire a Doctorate in History and met the love of his life, Rachel. Now married to Rachel for more than twenty years, Matt has two adult children and a burning desire to combine the genre he loves with the faith that saved him.

Learn more at:

*https://www.bladeoftruthpublishing.com/
mattbarron*

ALSO BY MATT BARRON

Rage of Lions

Prentice Ash
Rats of Dweltford
Lions of the Reach
Eagles of the Grand Kingdom

More from Publisher

Be sure to check out our other great science fiction and fantasy stories at:

bladeoftruthpublishing.com/books

Made in United States
Troutdale, OR
02/13/2025

28922662R00235